The Sleepy Hollow Incident

Book Three

PD Alleva

Chamber Door Publishing, LLC

Chamber Door Publishing
Delray Beach, Fl

ISBN:
Paperback: 979-8-9938039-3-7
Hardback: 979-8-9938039-4-4

Cover: Cherie Foxley
Editor: Chamber Door Publishing
Interior design: Chamber Door Publishing

Printed in the USA

"But soon the world
Had its evil way
My heart was blinded
Love went astray
I'm going through changes."
~ Black Sabbath (*Changes*)

Part V

Lori sat by the window looking over the gray winter morning. The trees swayed in the subtle wind. She could feel the cold. The window was icy to the touch. A parking lot sat beneath her window. Lori watched people entering and leaving the hospital while waiting for her mother to arrive.

Lori attended a meeting with Dr. Reese this morning to assess her current mental state. She'd played this game before and knew exactly what to say. She never denied the suicide attempt, which would have made her seem crazier than they already believed she was. Just admit to it, she told herself. Give reasons-namely that she stopped taking her medications and the suicide was an accumulation of the months spent in the throes of a manic episode-and convince them that with their new medication regimen she felt all prime and better than ever. It's always good to stroke their ego, just a little, enough to make them feel it but not too much to create suspicion. All those doctors know is medication. You'd think they'd look into alternative therapies instead of pumping their patients with pills that have side effects no human being should have to endure.

But her little ruse was a success. Lori had to accept weekly case management appointments including home visits, weekly therapy sessions and monthly psychiatric appointments before Dr. Reese approved of her discharge. Now she was waiting for Elena to pick her up. Or at least Gerard. Either will do, but she hoped for Gerard. Lori wanted nothing to do with her mother. Despite what these doctors thought Lori knew there was no way she took those pills. Not a chance, which meant one thing. Elena had poisoned her and the reason she did was to stop Lori from returning to the Hollow.

Talk about being misguided. Lori knew her mother was evil, but the fact that she almost murdered her own daughter spoke volumes to just how insane the woman was. Lori made up her mind. She's going to leave her mother and everything she knows about her family and walk away. She thought about California. Thought about Europe too. She couldn't care if she ever saw her mother again. The bitch deserved it and it's not like it would matter anyway. Elena will more than likely live the rest of her days in the same manner she went through her entire life, always reserved to putting up a façade so the rest of the world would never know how miserable and meek she truly was.

But what she couldn't shake was the dream or the memory of Marc's demon. She could see him now as if the demon was watching her in this very room. A reflection in the window. The shadow in the corner. Always watching. Always listening. Is he just a part of Marc's imagination or is the demon real? As real as you and I. She thought about Marc, wondering where he was at this very moment. Wondering if she's playing the pawn in a game of catch me if you can while Marc sits back and pulls her strings, turning her mind into madness. Is she just reaching? Trying to rectify the past with an indulgence in fantasy, bending reality to meet her needs, wants, and desires. More than likely, Marc was doing just fine and had moved on with his life. More than likely, he'd already forgotten about Lori Francon.

There was a knock on her door. Lori turned to the nurse who stepped into the room.

"Ms. Francon?" said the nurse-Sharon was her name, Lori remembered from when she met with Dr. Reese. Sharon had stood by the door during the meeting watching Lori with intense focus. "Your discharge paperwork is ready. You can leave now."

Lori said nothing. She turned to the window. No limo. No Elena. No Gerard.

"Lori?"

Lori cleared her throat. "Is there someone that can give me a ride home?"

Sharon shook her head. "Hospital policy, we aren't allowed to transport patients. Is there no one who can pick you up?"

"I left a message for my mother. Not sure if she got it yet." She paused, thinking of something to say. "She rarely checks her answering machine."

Sharon nodded. "We can give you a bus ticket. Or call a cab."

Lori stood up. "A cab will be fine, thank you." She looked around the room. Barren. Considering how she arrived at the hospital there wasn't one item she brought with her. She didn't even have a coat, and it was damn cold outside. "You wouldn't happen to have a coat, would you?"

"You can look through the donations while I call a cab." She gestured for Lori to follow her. "Come on. I have a few papers for you to sign."

Lori walked to the door. "Whatever I need to do to get out of here I'm good with."

The Warner Library overlooks the Hudson River and the Tappan Zee Bridge. Carver always found the view spectacular. He wasn't someone to hang out in libraries, but he came here frequently when his children required resources for school and all he could remember about the library was the view. It was inspiring.

Carver had woken up with a jolt this morning. Woke up struggling to breathe as if whatever dream he'd been having drove him into a panic and his hyperventilating snapped him awake. He didn't remember the dream but the tightness in his chest and the suffocating sensation sure did the job of waking him up. It was as if something daunting and dire had happened in the wee hours of the early morning darkness that filtered into his dreaming state of subconscious thought.

He woke up and he could feel it. A change in the tide. Something was different. It felt like gravity pulling down on his bones with the strength of a thousand men. He had a dull headache, too. Pressure between his temples, creating confusion wrapped in a blanket of indecision. He felt it all morning but chalked it up to too many drinks last night. And a lack of sleep. He'd only been able to sleep for five hours and after such a long trip, he figured he was just worn out.

But when he went outside, he could still feel it. Something was in the air. Everything appeared the same but seemed different. Strangers passed each other on the street with skeptical and paranoid stares. Untrusting. Suspicious. Not that it wasn't there before, but now it seemed to take center stage. A default mode for all the citizens in Sleepy Hollow. Even when he arrived at the library, he could feel it, like a dark cloud hovering over his city sending waves of paranoia filled with fear into the minds of his citizens.

He asked for books on the history of Sleepy Hollow and was directed to the basement floor of the library. He noticed the librarian looked at him as if he were going to rob the damn library. Carver didn't appreciate the stare or the chip the librarian had on his shoulder. As if he was annoyed with Carver's inquiry. But Carver tossed it off to a bad morning and took the stairs to the basement. He found the books-exactly where the librarian had said they would be-and selected six that he brought to a table to read and thumb through old pictures.

He wasn't exactly sure what he was looking for. Any mention of the house would be good. Although he had an inclination that there was something more happening in the Hollow that would not be found in a book. Some dire secret unfolding between the lines.

The devil is in the details, Carver thought.

Keep your mind open.

Estella Ramirez had her job like everyone else. Mostly, she loathed her duties. Her employers were difficult to deal with. They were condescending, treating her like she was some meek nobody without an understanding for the finer things in life. Nevertheless, it all took a back seat when she saw the smile on little Edward's face when she strolled him into Patriots Park. It was their daily ritual and despite the cold weather, Estella knew it was healthy to be outside. Good for the lungs and good for the blood. Unless it was raining, of course. On those days, she'd bring Edward to the Warner Library for their afternoon story time, although she knew he would rather be outside in the park.

But today there was no rain, just the cold overcast sky. And a nagging sensation that Estella couldn't shake. She seemed off today and couldn't put her finger on what the cause was. Edward was a bit off himself. More whining and defiant than usual, especially for a four-year-old. Estella's patience had worn thin quickly this morning, so she brought Edward to the park a little earlier than usual hoping to ease some of the tension.

She couldn't believe she yelled at him; she'd never done so before. But she wanted to do more. She wanted to spank his bottom blue. Estella didn't know what came over her. She chalked it up to a sleepless night. Her sleep was plagued by nightmares, and she'd awakened in the wee hours of the early morning darkness angry and anxious. Even now as she pushed his stroller into Patriots Park, she could feel the anger boiling beneath the surface like a dark thought she couldn't control. She was hoping they could run out the anxiety and return home for a quiet lunch.

She tried to maintain. Tried to squelch the anger rising in her chest, but the moment she unstrapped Edward he took off racing down the incline towards the stream in the center of the park that was flanked by a cobblestone bridge and two stone staircases on the opposite side from the bridge that led down to the stream and the cavern beneath the park. She didn't want him to go there. He could have at least used the stone staircase instead of climbing down the incline.

"Edward, come back here now," she ordered, with one hand on the stroller. The chilly breeze numbed her skin, and she noticed how quiet it was. How still and quiet. No one else was in the park. No cars on the street. Edward laughed and when she searched for him, he was gone. "Edward, no!" She went to the bridge and there he was, climbing down into the stream.

"Edward, I'm not going down there to get you. Come up here right now."

But all Edward did was laugh like some demonic child, smile, and climb further down.

"Dammit Edward," Estella huffed, then stomped across the bridge to the stone steps that led down to the stream. He laughed again and when she looked for him, he was staring into the cavern on the opposite side of the bridge where the water was coming from, trickling down into the stream. "Edward now!"

He stepped into the cavern, and it seemed like the darkness reached out and swallowed him whole. "Goddammit Edward." She rushed down the steps and when she looked for him again, he wasn't there. Now that anger boiled into her brain. "Fuckin Edward," she hollered, trolling down the steps when she heard that laugh again and she slipped, landing on her back with a thud and an ache, curling her spine in pain. Her feet slid into the stream.

Another laugh from Edward, followed by a series of caws, grating coos, rattles, and clicks. She went to get up, and her spine twisted her face into a pinch. Another laugh and more coos and caws. "Pretty bird," she heard Edward say. "Hungry birds."

"Edward, get out of that cavern immediately." She pushed herself to her feet, feeling the ache in her back. She searched across the cavern's entrance but all she could see was darkness. No Edward, although she was certain he was inside.

"Hungry birds. Hungry birds."

She stomped through the stream, freezing water sloshing across her jeans.

"Hungry birds. Hungry birds."

She came to the entrance and looked inside when an icy chill tightened her spine. "Edward?" She looked in, but seeing nothing she stepped across the threshold while gritting her teeth. "Edward, I said come here n..." Her words died in her throat from the nauseating stink that lifted to her nostrils. Foul and putrid, Estella covered her nose.

She groaned. "What is that? Edward?" Her voice echoed inside the small enclosure.

Another laugh. It seemed miles away. She stepped further, her eyes adjusting when she saw Edward on the ground with his knees in the mud.

"Hungry bird. Hungry bird."

At first, Estella wasn't certain what she was looking at. Little Edward's hands were covered in blood, pulling and tugging what looked like a rope with no end covered in red and slick with what looked like skin. A murder of crows flitted around Edward, dipping their beaks into the body sprawled across the ground, nipping little pieces of flesh across their tongues when Estella realized Edward was yanking the intestines from the corpse's stomach.

"My god," she whispered. Her hand moved to her mouth and all she could see was little Edward yanking and pulling and tugging, hand over bloody hand.

"EDWARD STOP!"

He giggled something awful and it turned her blood on fire. Estella stomped over to Edward and yanked him by the arm with such force she heard his bone snap followed by the most wretched cry she'd ever heard.

He immediately dropped the intestine he'd been yanking from the body. The sound that came from that child was disturbing beyond belief and Estella was certain everyone in Sleepy Hollow heard him. The crows did too. They started flapping and flying, nipping at her skin with their beaks and claws. She gripped the screaming, flailing Edward tight against her chest and ran out of the cavern. The crows relentlessly nibbled on her skin. Ripping the hair from her skull. The two of them were screaming but the crows refused to relent, swarming around them as if they were a fresh meal.

"Get em off, get em off," she screamed while thrashing and hopping when she dropped little Edward. All she heard was a wet splash and a smack, followed by silence.

The crows lifted off her, flying into the overcast sky above. There was blood on her face and lips and chin. Thick beaded gobs of blood. Gashes burned across her scalp and face as she watched the crows fly away. When she looked down little Edward was lying face first in the stream, his head resting against a rock as his blood turned the water red.

"My god," she heard someone scream. Heard commotion on the bridge too, but all she could see was little Edward, lying dead in the stream.

She couldn't have been more relieved.

Lori was looking at the property after the cab turned onto her street, searching for a sign that someone was home and hoping no one was. It would be so much easier if no one were home. She could slip in, grab her belongings and make a beeline to the train station. She'll have to go into the city first, to Penn Station then take the subway to Grand Central where she can catch another train to Sleepy Hollow.

From that point on she'll figure it out. Grab a motel room and start searching for Marc. But for now, she needed to get and go. The cab pulled up to the locked gate and stopped. Lori looked up at the long, winding driveway where the family car waited outside the front door. She gritted her teeth while staring at the car.

They're home.

She breathed in deeply while shaking her head. She'll have to sneak in and be as quiet as possible and maybe, just maybe, they won't be any wiser to her presence than they are about any human being they deem unworthy.

Lori turned to the cabbie-an older gentleman she placed at around forty years old. "Would you mind waiting ten minutes? I just need to pack a quick bag then go to the train station."

The cabbie eyeballed the house, obviously contemplating Lori's request. He seemed like he didn't want to stay, as if he wanted to get as far away as possible and as quickly as possible. The silence was thick with tension. She thought he was going to refuse, which would put Lori in a bind because then she'd have to call another cab and wait for it to arrive. Either that or she walks and that would take a lifetime.

"Sir?" She swallowed her breath.

"Okay, but please be quick." He paused while staring at the house. "This place gives me the creeps."

Lori cocked her head. "You have no idea." She opened the door and climbed out of the car into the icy chill; grateful she found a dark beanie at the hospital. She scanned across the property, hoping to see someone. Some sign that would tell her what part of the house they were in, but there was nothing to tell her where they were. She couldn't see much of anything through the windows other than the snow-covered grounds they reflected. A slight breeze drifted across her, the icy chill nipping at her nose. It was so quiet, Lori could hear the ocean behind the house. She closed the cab door.

The house stood like a symbol of foreboding. It seemed to carry a life of its own, staring at Lori, anticipating her arrival and the opportunity to swallow her whole. She approached the gate. Of course, she wasn't going to use the intercom to call the house. Nope, not at all. Instead, Lori squeezed her tiny frame through the bars, stepping up and over the horizontal bar while ducking her head beneath the bar above.

She wondered what the cabbie was thinking as she made the trek up the driveway. She wouldn't have been surprised if she heard the cab putter back down the road. Lori looked up at the second-floor windows. Again, she could see nothing beyond the windows although she couldn't shake the sensation that she was being watched

"Ok, Lori. Let's do this." She pulled the beanie over her ears and pushed through the cold, trekking across the long driveway to the front door. All the while, hoping no one saw her drive up to the house. And hoping, praying, she'll get out of the house without a hitch.

126

Carver sat back, gnawing on his toothpick and thinking. Thinking he was on the wrong path. Not one book mentions the house in the western woods. It wasn't even listed in the archives of the Historical Society. It seemed as if the house was the victim of a brief memory.

Sure, he found multiple stories about Sleepy Hollow, but most were associated with Washington Irving and the myths that ultimately inspired his classic story, conjuring the legend of the Headless Horseman from stories about the Revolutionary War where a hessian was known for cutting off the heads of his opponents. And then there were the Dutch settlers from centuries ago, but nothing with any substance regarding the house. Nothing he could use to shed some light on the house or its history. It's as if the house was always there and always abandoned. Forgotten. A ghost. The house was as mysterious as a serial killer without an M.O.

"I think I need to change direction," he said out loud and to no one in particular. He shook his head in disappointment, leaning back in his chair when someone burst through the side door of the library. The door that led to the adjoining Patriots Park.

The woman was huffing when she said, "Call the police. There's been a murder."

Carver shot up from his chair like he was sitting on a spring. "I'm a police officer," he announced, and everyone in the library turned to look at him as he took his coat off the back of the chair, squeezing his arms through the sleeves as he walked over. The lady, Carver put her at around forty, looked at him with suspicion. He understood why. What is a police officer doing in the library? What were the chances that he would be here at this exact moment? Carver wondered himself. He flashed his badge to put everyone at ease.

"What's going on?" he asked.

The lady swallowed her breath before she answered. "There's a dead body below the bridge and some woman dropped a child." Her voice stifled when she said child. "He's dead."

Carver looked at the librarian. "Call the police," he ordered, then addressed the woman. "Show me," he said, and she did just that. Carver followed her outside through the side entrance where he could see the entire park. In the center of the park was a bridge with stone steps that led down to a small stream. A small group of people surrounded the bridge. There was a woman sitting on the steps with her arms wrapped around her waist, rocking back and forth while someone attempted to console her. He saw the child too, lying half in and half out of the stream. A tall woman hovered over him, checking for a pulse.

"No one had a phone," he heard the woman say. "So, I came up here to call the police."

Carver didn't pay her too much mind while on his way down the steps. "Stay here," he ordered. "I'll need to take your statement, so don't go too far." He raced through the small parking lot then beelined down the hill into the park. A murder of crows jumped off the grass as he approached.

Carver went into detective mode seamlessly, flashing his badge and ordering everyone to step aside. He took the stone steps down to the stream, his eyes on the child when he noticed the blood in the water and the bloodstain on the rock. The boy's face was littered with small nips across his skin, and his hands were slick with blood.

"Let me see," he told the tall woman hovering over the child when she stepped away from the boy. Carver took a knee and immediately assessed for a pulse. There was none. The boy was cold to the touch and not the bitter cold of winter weather, but the cold of the dead. He dropped his head, then turned to the woman with her arms wrapped around her stomach, rocking back and forth. Her face was covered in blood. Carver looked at the tall woman while removing his jacket. "I need you to remove yourself from the crime scene." But she never responded. She couldn't take her eyes off the boy. Carver draped his coat over the child then stood up and put his hand on her shoulder. "Mam?" She shot her stare at him, startled. "Return to the bridge, please. I'll question you when I'm done." She nodded and wiped the tears from her eyes.

Carver scanned across the scene. He was certain the first woman said there was a murder in addition to the boy who cracked his skull. He saw no such thing. He stepped over to the woman rocking back and forth. Blood was dripping in thick streams from multiple gashes in her forehead, face and across her scalp. Her eyes were lost, staring at nothing. "Mam, I'm detective Carver. Can you tell me what happened?"

She didn't answer at first. "The crows," she said. "There were so many of them." She paused again and he could see she was reliving what had happened, her eyes lost in thought. "They kept biting me. They were everywhere and I... I dropped him."

"Why would the crows attack?"

Her head snapped in his direction, and her face contorted as if some driving pain was kneading its way up her spine. "They were eating the body."

Carver's head snapped back. He scanned across the park. "What body?"

The woman, sniffling and guffawing, stretched her arm as if it weighed a thousand pounds and pointed to the cavern across from the bridge. "In there," she said through a wail of tears, her voice a whining cry. "He's in there!"

Carver turned to the cavern. It was so dark he couldn't see more than a few inches inside. He turned to the woman. "Stay here, please. The ambulance is on its way." All she did was nod frantically before resting her chin on her knees. Carver heard the call then. The Tarrytown Fire Department had a distinct alarm that sounded like a dying cow. He approached the cavern, unclipping his flashlight from his belt, and cautiously approached, his head tilting from one side to the other attempting to get a better look inside. He stepped up to the entrance.

Now he could hear police sirens approaching as he swept the flashlight across the cavern, revealing the dead body lying within. He stepped inside, his shoes buried in the thin stream of water coming from both sides of the cavern where they converged, exiting into the stream outside. The cavern was short; he had to duck down to get inside. The foul odor then invaded his nostrils. He'd experienced the stench before, and it reminded him of Zoe Hardwood.

His flashlight shook in his hand, the beam bouncing across the body, revealing the carnage in front of him. It was a male, and Carver could see the kid had been tortured. His fingers and toes had been cut off and there were patches of skin that had been removed from his head to his toes. His innards had been pulled from his stomach and were draped across the body and the cavern floor. The chest was cracked open and the bone separated, creating a cavern in the chest. Carver shined his flashlight into the hole.

"No heart," he whispered, shifting his toothpick from one corner of his mouth to the other with a roll of his tongue. The sirens were growing louder now, and Carver heard tires screeching on the asphalt. He swept the flashlight across the cavern and paused when he saw it. His heart seemed to stop beating, staring at the pentagram written in blood on the cavern wall.

The words **Initium Novum** were written beneath it.

And Carver said, "Well, I'll be damned."

It looked like Jerry's calling card belonged to someone other than Jerry.

127

Lori slipped through the front door into a cold, dead house. She stood by the door, listening. Her eyes roamed around the house. She was hoping she'd hear them first. Knowing their location would allow her to do what was necessary to sneak into her room and pack a bag before they knew she was home. Any time she could give herself would be beneficial. She wanted to avoid her mother at all costs.

The mother who tried to murder her own daughter.

Lori was convinced Elena had poisoned her. She knew the woman was sadistic, but she would never have believed she could commit filicide. This was all too surreal. Like living in a waking nightmare. As if one of her night terrors had taken a permanent space in her brain and had become reality. A reality Lori refused to accept. The time had finally arrived. Lori will walk away from this house and never look back. She was certain of it.

Now she heard a creak on the second floor, and she arched her neck to look up the staircase. Nothing. Could have been the wind outside the house. She heard no sounds. Saw no people and hoped they were outside. Maybe on the beach. There was no way to tell where they were.

Best to get moving, she told herself. Cabbie's waiting and it would be a complete shit storm if she had to call another cab then wait for it to arrive.

Lori looked up the stairs and made her move. She cautiously walked to the staircase, listening for any subtle creak or voice.

Nothing.

She took the first step up, holding the banister on the way, being sure to place each step as softly as possible.

When she reached the top, she looked through the window overlooking the ocean. Looking for them. No one was on the beach.

So, where the hell are they?

She turned right, scanning down the hall. All the doors were closed. A thin veil of dark gripped the hallway. She looked to her left towards her mother's room where she could see light beaming into the hall. The door was open, but she couldn't see inside the room. Not yet. Not from her vantage point.

Lori took two soft steps away from the staircase and craned her head to look inside her mother's room. Her heart stopped when she saw Elena. Her spine tightened at its base, staring at her mother sitting on the edge of the bed, hunched over with her mouth open. Mesmerized. She seemed like she was in the throes of hypnosis.

"Come, Elena. Time to take your medicine."

Lori's eyelids fluttered. Confused. She was certain that was Gerard's voice. Sounded like him, that gruff voice. She craned her head further and she could see them. Could see Gerard standing in front of Elena, his back to Lori. He was holding something. Lori heard a subtle tap of metal. Then Gerard reached towards Elena's open mouth and placed a spoon on her tongue. Elena's mouth closed over that spoon, followed by a gulp with Elena's throat bobbing up and down. She swallowed with a gasp.

What the fuck is this?

Elena just sat there, unmoving as Gerard pushed her shoulders and Elena flopped on her back to the mattress.

Gerard said, "Now for some true medicine," as he unbuckled his jeans and dropped them to his ankles then shuffled closer to Elena, pulling off her pants then tossing them over his shoulder. He then climbed on top of Elena. The sudden movement caused Elena's head to flop to the left.

Lori cringed when she saw her mother's eyes. All black like the thick dark inside a cavern where no light can penetrate. Gerard started pounding, moving his hips and rocking the mattress. Elena bobbed back and forth on the bed. Grunts in Gerard's throat, he put his hand over Elena's windpipe and squeezed. His hand was so large he dipped his finger over Elena's lips, and she opened her mouth wide to nibble on his finger.

Lori whipped her head away.

This is something I wish I'd never seen.

She looked around the hall before padding down the hall to her room where she opened the door as softly as she could manage and slipped inside, closing the door behind her.

She stepped away from the door; her heartbeat stuck in her throat. Lori had a fleeting thought that they would come charging into the room at any moment. She paused, watching the door and listening to the sound of her own breathing. Listening to Gerard's heavy grunts and then he howled. Howled like a wolf at the full moon.

"Sick fucks," she whispered. "Literally."

She shook her head and turned around. The window was open, floating the white drape into the room. She could see the cab was still outside. She scanned the room, but things were different. Nothing she owned was here. The room was empty. Cleaned out and prepared for some uninvited guest that will never arrive.

Other than the bed and furniture there was nothing. Nothing on her desk. No papers or notebooks or notepads she'd written in over the last few months. Barren. As if she never lived here. Even the posters she had on the walls were gone. She went to the chest of drawers and opened the top drawer. Nothing. None of her clothes were there. She checked all of them. Every drawer. Empty. All were empty. She went to the walk-in closet and pulled the string to turn the light on. None of her clothes were there. No coats. No shoes or sneakers and all the shelves were empty.

She went into the bathroom. No toothbrush. No hairbrush. No makeup, face cream or foundation. Everything she owned was gone. She walked back into the room. There was nothing for her. But where did they put it? Lori knew she didn't have time to search the entire house. She'll have to cut her losses, lick her wounds and go. She can go to the bank and empty her account to pay for what she needs.

Starting over from scratch.

Now she heard yipping and yawping. Flesh slapping against flesh along with reciprocal moans filled with pleasure.

Meaning Gerard was about to climax, and she needed to get the hell out of here before that climax.

Talk about a failed mission.

Lori went to the door and slipped back into the hall, cautiously padding to the steps as Gerard continued to yip and yawp. She took the steps down.

There was one item she wanted above all. Marc's notebook. She felt she would need it. For what reason she wasn't certain, but she was reserved to find it.

128

A uniformed officer stretched yellow tape around the park. Carver was scanning the spectators with the understanding that the murdering son of a bitch who cut up that young man may be in attendance, watching the police marvel over his work.

The street next to the park was littered with people all cramped on the sidewalk by the church. Carver scanned every one of them, looking for a unique set of eyes. Eyes that held dire secrets. Not one of them fit the profile, although he could see they were all angry. Their pinched faces and tight jaws were a telltale sign of anger.

He understood why. He was angry too. Angry that a child lost his life and angry over the cut-up victim lying dead in the cavern. But even more, Carver was steaming like a hot cup of coffee over the fact that he was right the whole time. The situation from six months ago was just the beginning and he was correct in his previous assessment that Jerry did not act alone. Not only did he not act alone, but there was also a unique possibility he was acting at the behest of someone else. Someone who pulled the strings and had yet to reveal themself.

Marc Saduj.

He shook his head, rolling his toothpick to the corner of his mouth when his gut went into overdrive. He was staring at Father

McKenzie standing on the bottom step to the church. His eyes were narrow while watching the scene unfold, a scarf around his neck blowing gently in the subtle wind. He looked frightened, as if some dire secret had just seen the light of day.

He looked like a man defeated.

"Detective?"

Carver turned to the flatfoot approaching him. Carver placed him in his late twenties. He carried the same defeated stare as Father McKenzie. His name badge identified him as Lieutenant Weaver. Carver took one look at him and said, "Where are my lights?" Carver had requested spotlights capable of turning the cavern into a bright summer's day. He needed to investigate the cavern.

Weaver carried a stare that told Carver the man had seen better days and, considering this one just started, he knew he was in for a long haul.

"They're on the way," said Weaver, but Carver knew that wasn't all Weaver had to say. He swallowed his breath. "Captain Flannery is on his way, too. He wants an update."

Carver nodded. "Typical. He probably wants to point out all the mistakes I'm making." He looked at Weaver, whose expression never changed or faltered. "Something else, officer?"

Weaver looked around as if to assess whether they were out of earshot. His voice was low and gruff when he said, "They found another body, sir."

Carver bit down on his toothpick. "Another body?" Weaver nodded. "Where?"

"Down by the river. It was discovered an hour ago."

"Found by who?"

"Another officer. Patrolman Bellinger discovered the body and immediately cordoned off the area. No citizens are aware of the discovery. Not yet anyway."

Carver assessed Weaver. He seemed like he had more to say. "Go on."

"Captain Flannery said to keep it under wraps. He doesn't want everyone thinking there's a serial killer in the Hollow."

"I take it the murder is similar to what we have here?"

Weaver nodded. "The same pentagram and inscription were beside the body, although the means of death were quite different."

"Tell me."

"She..." he started, his voice trailing off until Weaver regained his composure. "There was no blood in the body. Apparently, there are lacerations that cut through her upper torso and her back and her chest was cut open."

Carver gnawed on his toothpick. "Let me guess, there was no heart in the body?"

"Exactly."

Carver shook his head and turned his gaze to the other officers, then to the pedestrians on the sidewalk. "Captain Flannery wants the second victim to remain under wraps for as long as possible. He sent me here ahead of him to inform you of his order. He doesn't want mass hysteria."

At that moment, Carver heard a commotion coming from the church steps. When he turned, he could see the angry stares. Two dead bodies and a very unfortunate accident and his day had just turned south and now it seemed like there was an uprising about to stir the pot.

"What do you need me to do?" asked Weaver.

Carver looked at Weaver, then returned his gaze to the park, the police and firemen, then to the pedestrians who now surrounded the entire park. The police had successfully taped off the park, but there were pedestrians looking from every angle. Every one of them with that angry, nasty stare. He turned to Weaver.

"It's probably best to prepare yourself, officer."

"Prepare, sir?"

Carver nodded. "If everything you're saying is true then this is just the beginning. Prepare yourself for more bodies and prepare yourself for them." Carver gestured to the pedestrians. "Because if we don't catch the son of a bitch who did this… and catch him soon… we may have that mass hysteria on our hands."

"Yes, sir."

Carver stepped forward, gnawing on his toothpick when he saw a truck drive into the park with his requested spotlights. He scanned across the grounds to Father McKenzie the moment the priest turned and made his way up the stairs, opening the door to the church and stepped inside.

That gut instinct started nagging at Carver's brain. Something about the priest seemed off, as if he's aware of information Carver will need. He made a mental note to speak with the priest soon. Considering the body was dumped not more than fifty yards from his church perhaps Father McKenzie saw something he shouldn't have, which gave Carver every reason to question the priest.

He turned to the truck carrying his spotlights, then to the cavern where the body was waiting for his investigation. He then addressed Weaver.

"Make sure no one touch's the other body," he ordered. "I'll be there soon."

129

At the same moment Carver was ordering where he wanted his spotlights set up, Marc Saduj was standing at the edge of his property and staring into the woods. The morning was frosty and overcast, but every so often the sun would break through to cast its golden glow across his body. The sun's heat was a welcome reprieve from the bitter morning air rippling goosebumps up his bare arms. He wore a T-shirt and shorts as if it were a summer day.

Marc awakened this morning in a fever. His stomach burned something awful, and he felt depleted as if there was poison in his blood tainting his insides and rotting his organs. Felt like he was dying a slow, painful death, as if every bit of strength had been drained from his veins like a spigot releases fluid. His stomach boiled with acid. The itch from his scar crawled across his forehead as he stared into the western woods. The cold dead of the woods with the trees and their bare branches standing like a defeated army.

Marc felt drawn to the western woods as if the ghosts from the past called on him for refuge. He understood the cemetery wasn't far from where he was standing. He could feel it, like a dark thought germinating in the center of his brain. Felt the essence of death and suffering in his bones. Felt pain in his chest, right there in a special spot in his chest bone directly over his heart, like a finger kneading into his bone, turning his skin on fire.

Mind your thoughts. Keep your wits in check.

But most of all he could feel the change in the tide, in the essence and energy all around him. It felt sick and twisted. An angry vibration filled with fear that twisted his jaw and gritted his teeth. A thick energy descending on Sleepy Hollow. He turned to the house, gazing over his dilapidated mansion that stood like a demon watching its prey. He could feel the energy slithering into the grass from beneath the ground, swelling into his bare feet through the snow. As if his house were the source of the dark, venomous energy. He noticed the house seemed to sway from the breeze as if it could topple over at any second, holding strong because of the foundation.

The foundation.

Marc ran his tongue across his lips, his stare roaming up to his bedroom window. So dark, he couldn't see past the window to the inside. Seemed like a dark veil he couldn't penetrate from out here in the field.

Everything about his house screamed evil, turning his thoughts into a confused state of anxiety. Angry. Marc felt anger rifling up his bones to his brain when Wren walked into the clearing from the front of the house, pushing a wheelbarrow filled with firewood through the snow.

He stopped cold when he saw Marc. Stretched his back and stood tall.

"My master, it is so cold outside. Shouldn't you be dressed?"

Marc laughed and looked down at himself, then looked back at Wren. "Feels good on the skin."

Wren held his gaze a while longer. "Would you like your morning drink?"

Marc's liver cringed as a nasty flavor invaded his mouth. Tasted like toxins on the back of his tongue.

"Not today, Wren." He gazed into the western woods, feeling the breeze against his scar before turning back to Wren. "Today, I think I'll take a stroll through Sleepy Hollow."

He noticed Wren's startled expression. As if some internal catastrophe had taken a turn into overdrive.

130

Lori searched every place she could think of. But still no notebook. Nothing in her bedroom. Nothing in the living room other than some candles burning on the coffee table with a copper goblet between them. She didn't find the notebook in the dining room or the sitting room either. Sure, she could search every room in the house but that would take more time than Lori had to spare.

She was standing in the sitting room looking through the bay window at the cab on the street, thinking. Her arms crossed, listening to the yipping, yawping Gerard. The noise was disturbing to say the least. The only other places she could think of were the basement or the garbage and considering what happened the last time she was in the basement she would rather not have to go down into that dark cavern.

But she was running out of time.

"Fuck it."

Lori stomped into the kitchen to the basement door. Gerard's yipping, yawping and howling fading in the distance. She gripped the doorknob and opened the door to the thick darkness existing below. Lori gazed into the basement, staring into the darkness as if it were staring at her too. She could see the steps. Could feel the dark energy inviting her in. Lori pursed her lips and swallowed the tension down her throat when she remembered the lightbulb had shattered when she was last down there and the thought hit her.

Flashlight.

She turned into the kitchen and opened a drawer by the sink. The one overstuffed with notepads, papers and knickknacks that had probably been in the drawer for decades but that also housed a flashlight. She took it out and flipped the switch. Yes, it was working. She turned to the basement, shining the light down the steps. She could see the basement floor and how the darkness receded from the light. Lori took the first step down and all the blood drained from her face. She instantly felt weak and depleted. There was an energy coming from the basement. Dark energy that invaded her cells. She took the second step down and stopped. Hard to breathe. She pursed her lips and swallowed her breath when the sensation arrived that she was being watched. That someone was in the basement, waiting for her to step into the darkness while licking their chops in anticipation.

She noticed the heat, too. *Why is it so hot in the basement?* It should be cold, bitter cold, considering the weather outside. Lori wondered if someone left the heater on. The basement felt stuffy and suffocating. Felt like fire close to her skin, rippling heat waves across her flesh.

She scanned the flashlight around the basement. The spotlight revealed an empty floor where there had been boxes when she came down her a few days ago. She craned her head for a better look and swept the flashlight around, scanning across the basement.

Lori took another step down, then another when something glimpsed in the corner of her eye. She saw movement as if some creature darted away from the light. She swept the flashlight towards it, her heart now thudding in her chest. But there was nothing. No other subtle movement. Perhaps it was a rat or mouse or the scuttling of cockroaches scurrying away from the light? Lori shook her head, reminding herself of the time and took the last step down when she was immediately enveloped in heat as if it wrapped around her and squeezed. She swept the flashlight across the basement and noticed it was different.

The basement looked clean, no longer congested but open. Recently used, too. Someone had prepared the basement for some sort of gathering. The boxes that had been in the center of the basement were now stacked against the far wall to make room for the furniture. The old furniture was set up like some demonic sitting room. So odd and peculiar and out of place. The furniture was strategically placed around the marble slab she'd seen a few days ago. Lori swept the flashlight across the pedestal by the wall behind the furniture and the pentagram on the wall above the pedestal. Drips of red paint crawled down the wall from the pentagram. Someone had recently added a fresh coat of paint to it.

Oddly, she could feel heat swelling from the pentagram.

She kept the flashlight trained on the pentagram, her hand shaking with the light bouncing over the concrete. Lori swallowed her breath with a gulp, staring at the paint and how it seemed like it was moving. Her jaw tight, gnashing her teeth, attempting to get a grip on what she was seeing when she stepped closer, nudging against another set of stacked boxes.

She turned to them. They were new boxes; she was certain of it. She opened the top box and saw her belongings.

Son of a bitch.

Her toiletries were in the first box. She heard a groan and snapped around to the sound, sweeping the flashlight across the basement. The beam roamed over the marble slab where she saw something on top of it.

Candles.

And…

She stepped closer for a better view. Her heart swelled into her throat when she saw Marc's notebook and a pair of her underwear beside it. The sight was so peculiar.

What the fuck, people?

Anger boiled in her blood; her face pinched in a scowl. She moved closer to the slab. The candles were halfway melted with thick streams of cooled wax pooled on the bottom. Marc's blue notebook sat on the slab next to Lori's underwear between the two candles. Her underwear was stained with blood. Dirty underwear taken from Lori's laundry basket.

Lori stuffed her underwear into her pocket-she'll be damned before leaving it here for them to conduct some sadistic ceremony-then grabbed Marc's notebook when a rattling moan lifted through the basement as if some creature groaned when she removed it.

Startled, she dropped the flashlight. Heard it crack against the floor before the light went out, casting a dark veil across her eyes.

She immediately turned to the stairs and the light that washed across the steps from the kitchen when a wave of heat breathed across the nape of her neck. She gnashed her teeth as the hair on her neck stood erect.

There were legs on the stairs.

And they were coming down the steps.

131

Marc was staring at his painting-the one with the heart in the tree trunk-while buttoning his red flannel shirt with shaky hands as he gritted his teeth, his scar itching like mad prickly heat. He misjudged a button, and one side of his shirt was higher than the other. He wore his classic black shirt beneath the flannel. He'd squeezed his legs into his jeans and noticed they were too big-he'd lost a considerable amount of weight over the last six months. Considerable wasn't the word. He looked like a skeleton with skin. He curled the belt buckle over to make the jeans tighter around his small waist.

His movements were shaky. Marc sat down on his mattress, staring at his construction boots. Old and tattered, they'd seen better days.

Marc wasn't certain why he wanted to go to Sleepy Hollow, although he believed there was something he needed to see or witness or become a part of. A feeling that kept kneading into his brain. Or maybe he just needed human contact. Marc had been alone for the past six months and it wasn't like Wren paid him any attention other than feeding him with drinks on the go.

He'd been sick for what felt like eternity but this morning after his fever broke, he felt slightly better as if his cells had regenerated, providing renewed vigor coupled with a need for human activity. He wanted to stroll down Broadway. Wanted to visit the local establishments and tour the nostalgia.

And he wanted to be among the people of Sleepy Hollow. His people. His brethren, but why the need to do so was so nagging and preferential he wasn't certain. Just that he needed to go there. He's been having nightmares about the Hollow.

Marc squeezed his feet into his boots, tied them then pushed himself to his feet when he was hit with a wave of nausea, his head spinning, his eyes rolling in his head. He took a step forward to steady his legs. His insides were empty, like a dark void in outer space between one galaxy and the next. He understood why. His liver was begging for a drink. He breathed through his nose to ease the dizzy spell. His scar itched, and he pushed on it, his skull flitting with a burn from the push.

He took another slow and steady breath while closing his eyes, hoping to steady his rapid heart. Pursed his lips and swallowed with a gasp. He felt like a cavern had been opened in his soul, the hollow space filled with hurt. After a long pause when he stared through his window at the cold woods outside, he stepped out of his room to the stairs, the dark and creaking staircase with walls that were clearly in anguish, falling apart around him. He held the banister on the way down.

Rounded the corner to see Wren holding his morning red eye. Marc froze when he saw the drink. He started grinding his teeth. Felt his liver cringe. It took him a moment to see the three people surrounding Wren.

Wren held the drink out for him. "Your escorts, Master Marc. Seems they all wish to venture into the Hollow today."

Marc looked at each one of them, all with the same determined stare, looking at him as if he were a fresh meal. He wondered where they came from.

"The children of forever night," said Wren and Marc noticed the female stepped forward. "With such a big house, I thought you'd be more than willing to offer refuge to the unfortunate."

Marc said nothing, just stood there with his mouth hanging open.

"Come," said Wren, pushing the drink further towards Marc. "You should leave soon if you plan to return before nightfall."

Something was off about the Wren threesome. They seemed rather anxious.

"Master Marc?" Wren's voice was abrupt and loud. He craned his head, staring into Marc's soul.

Marc swallowed his breath, staring at the drink in Wren's hand. His stomach roiled like a beast. "Yes, Wren," he said. "I think I will have that drink after all."

And Wren grinned. Marc noticed the other three stared at him like wolves locked in on their prey. Their skin carried a hint of yellow with veins that looked like spiderwebs within the deep recesses of their flesh. Their eyes seemed to sink into their skull.

He could swear he'd seen them before. He just couldn't put a finger on where.

132

Perhaps it was the heat already baked into her skin that turned up the intensity in the basement. Or maybe, just maybe, that pentagram over her shoulder had suddenly awakened and breathed into the basement from a fire born in hell. Lori felt the heat erupt across her skin like fire. Bullet-sized drops of sweat dripped across her temples from her forehead as she watched with bated breath the legs moving down the steps.

Then again, perhaps it was Gerard who amplified the heat as he walked down into the basement. All he wore were boxer shorts. His skin was covered in sweat. He took each step down with a slow precision. His hands were on the banisters as he craned his head to investigate the basement. His lips parted into a demonic grin. She could have sworn there was evil in his eyes. Those dark black eyes.

"Why Lori, how nice to see you've returned." And he laughed, a slight chuckle, then ran his tongue across his bottom lip as he stepped into the basement.

Lori looked at the door to the kitchen, then back to Gerard as he craned his head, glaring into her eyes. She could have sworn she'd seen a flicker gleam across his irises.

"Do you have nothing to say?"

Lori looked up the stairs again, then to Gerard. He followed her gaze to the stairs, then turned back to Lori. She swallowed her breath under the veil of his cold scowl.

"Lori? Are you ok?" He shook his head. "We wouldn't want you to go off the deep end again. Perhaps you need some family love and support." And he grinned again. "Yes, that's what it is, isn't it? Some family love before you return to the Hollow in search of your beloved."

Lori pursed her lips and swallowed. "Where is my mother?"

Now Gerard cocked his head, his eyes narrowed in suspicion as if the question was asked for the simple reason to provide distraction. Or nothing else to say.

"Oh, she is quite subdued at the moment." He cocked his brow. "Worn out for the time being."

Lori gripped the notebook closer to her chest as if it were a shield for her soul. "I'm not surprised. Whatever you sick fucks are doing should be criminal."

Gerard shot his head back. "Oh, please Lori. Stop being such a prude. Your mother is a vibrant woman, and she has her needs." He stretched his arm out and curled his fingers into a fist. "Why not provide the indulgence with a little extra sensation?" His nose curled into a snicker and the stare in his eyes turned Lori's blood cold. "Why not try some, Lori? You may find it… *rapturous*."

He took a step closer, and Lori jumped, startled as a whine escaped her throat.

"Oh, my my Lori. You seem so frightened. How marvelous." And he stepped again with a hiss from his open mouth that turned Lori's blood on fire. And then he laughed. Laughed out loud and shook his head. "Oh, Lori. You've always been the sweet one. Since you were a child, I have taken care of you. Nurtured you and provided safety. To both you and your mother. Do you think she could have done anything after your father's passing without me?" He stood erect, raising his chin. "She owes me everything she has. As do you Lori."

"You're a sick fuck whose drugging my mother." She shook her head. "Did you think I wouldn't find out?"

"Please, Lori. Your mother is an adventurous woman. Her indulgences are her own. As I said before, you should try it yourself."

"Get away from the stairs, Gerard. I'm leaving and you and my sick mother can do whatever the fuck you want."

"Oh…" He gestured to the stairs. "Ok, then. Please, feel free to leave."

Lori paused, assessing Gerard. "Back away from the stairs. I don't trust you."

He clucked his tongue while shaking his head. "Such a pity, Lori. Decades of service and we come down to this. This finality filled with ridicule and suspicion." His eyes narrowed. "It's rather daunting."

"I could give a shit what it is. Move away from the stairs."

"Always the Francon," he said as he stepped to Lori's right, disappearing into the darkness. "Always treating others like we don't matter."

Lori braced herself. She could see his silhouette in the thick dark of the basement. She swallowed her breath and stepped forward, watching him through the corner of her eye as she padded across the basement to the steps.

"Your father was always treating me like that, too."

Lori took the first step up, holding the notebook close to her chest while maintaining a watchful eye on Gerard. His silhouette seemed to melt into the darkness.

"It must be a Francon trait."

She took the next step up when Gerard stepped away from the darkness and into the light.

"That's why I had to kill your father, Lori."

Lori's heart stopped on the last step up, pausing her climb. It took a moment for his comment to register, completely horrified by the revelation. "What did you just say?"

Gerard nodded. "That's right, Lori." He craned his head. "I bashed his fucking brains in and then sodomized your mother on that same night."

Lori's jaw hung open.

"But that's nothing compared to what I'm about to do to you." And he rushed up the stairs when Lori darted into the kitchen and slammed the door shut, listening to the stairs groan under

Gerard's feet. She locked the door the moment she saw the doorknob turn.

She stepped back, further into the kitchen, keeping her gaze fixed on the door. She expected him to be pounding on it, but no such sound arrived other than Gerard's heavy breathing. She wasn't sure what to do other than run but her feet refused to obey her thought. All she could do was stand and listen as a tightness crept across her skin like some invisible hand wrapped around her and squeezed. Her breath caught in her throat.

The doorknob started to move. Lori's eyes narrowed as she craned her head, staring at the doorknob as it turned and the door popped open with a whining creak.

Move. Fucking move already.

Gerard stood in the doorway, half in the light and half in the dark. His eyes carried a red glint that widened Loris' eyes, her jaw hanging open, unbelieving what she was witnessing. She felt paralyzed, too, as if the ability to move was taken by the fear that gripped her spine. She wasn't certain, but she could have sworn she'd seen a deathly pale face with a host of veins staring at her. His mouth opened in a demonic grin as he stepped into the kitchen. No more veins or red eyes, but she knew she saw them. Perhaps it was a trick of the light.

"I see you're still here, Lori. What happened? Are you having trouble moving?" And he laughed. Laughed out loud. "How… marvelous. It's as if he wants me to fuck you ragged. A gift from Baphomet for services well done."

She could feel it then, the beginning of a rat race.

"Run, Lori," whispered Gerard.

"Ruuuuuuuuunnnnnnnnnnnn!"

His ear-splitting scream broke Lori from her frozen state and she darted to the front door. Had her hand on the doorknob when Gerard snatched a handful of her hair then slammed her skull against the door. She saw stars followed by darkness. Felt blood on her forehead before she was flung backward. She hit the ground hard, sliding across the marble floor into the sitting room.

The last she saw was Gerard walking stealth and satisfied towards her. Then the darkness arrived and escorted Lori into oblivion.

133

Now Carver, having strategically set up his spotlights, crossed the threshold into the cavern where the body was waiting for his inspection. The cavern floor was covered in mud. He made a mental note on his own footprints. The boys too, which were obvious to the eye, then calculated he'll need to know the nanny's shoe size if he's going to assess which footprints belonged to who. He was looking for a fourth set from whoever dumped the body.

The body had been laid to rest with the arms by the sides. The eyes were open, and that fact alone sent shivers racing down Carver's spine. A thick piece of skull, flesh and hair had been carved off the forehead. All fingers and toes were missing. He'd been castrated too, and his skin was a bloodied mess that looked like a jigsaw puzzle of cuts and gashes and slices across his entire body. His chest was sawed open and of course the heart was missing. Staring at the intestines that had been pulled from the stomach and draped across the body, Carver wasn't certain if that's how the body was before the child came to play or if the crows had nipped into the dead skin, dislodging the intestines when the boy arrived. He could see where the crows had feasted on the dead, swallowing tiny pieces across their beaks. Carver squatted down, gnawing on his toothpick while scanning the body then assessing the cavern.

There wasn't much room at all. The cavern was no bigger than a six-by-six hole with a round circumference. The ceiling was no higher than six feet and made from stone, the same as the walls and the ceiling. The ground was a mix of mud with sporadic rocks and pebbles. Carver looked at the footprints in the cold mud on the opposite side of the body from the cavern entrance. There were two sets of footprints, neither of which looked like his or the boys and he would take a gamble that they didn't belong to the nanny either. He noticed the footprints were scattered around the body, but none were close to the exit.

He took the toothpick from his lips, assessing the footprints again, wondering if they covered up their footprints on the way out.

How else could they have gotten out?

Carver stood up while staring at the pentagram and inscription, popping his toothpick back between his lips. He'll need forensics to match the blood on the wall to the body lying next to his feet. He was certain it was the same, but you could never be certain until certainty became reality. The blood had trickled down the cavern wall in thick streams frozen in time. He saw footprints in front of the inscription, pointing towards the wall, then assessed those footprints following them back to the body and noticed they were pointed towards the body, towards the opening, but the only footprints between the cavern opening and the body were his, the unfortunate child's, and another set of footprints he believed were from the nanny but no others. The two additional sets of footprints were reserved to the opposite side of the body, away from the opening and were scattered closer to the back wall where the pentagram and inscription were.

Carver's gut instinct went into overdrive. It made no sense unless they covered up their footprints on the way out, but why bother? *If you're going to cover up your footprints, why not cover all your footprints?*

Something wasn't adding up. And then the question arrived as to why. Why was the body dumped here? What's the significance? The first body-Zoe Hardwood-was discovered behind The Sleepy Hollow Tavern. The second here, in a park between the library and the church, and the third by the river.

Carver wondered if there was a pattern to the locations. In his experience, there had to be a reason the three locations were selected. Some significance only the murderer is aware of. Strategically placed to send a message. But a message to who? His first thought was that the message was for him-or law enforcement in general-but that reasoning didn't sit well with Carver. It seemed too trivial, too clean.

I need hearts for the master.

He looked down at the body and the empty chest.

Looks like the master got what he wanted.

He looked outside the cavern, assessing the murderer's view, attempting to make sense of the location. Perhaps the killer wants him to see something? The view was a direct line to the stream and the bridge but not much else. It didn't make sense. *Why here?* It didn't make sense at all.

"Detective," a flatfoot was walking hurriedly down the steps towards the cavern. He waited until he was in the cavern with Carver before he continued. "Forensics wants to case the cavern. The photographer is here, and the city morgue is ready to transport the body." The man paused before saying, "Captain Flannery is here, too."

"Thank you, officer. Tell him I'll be there in a minute."

"Yes, sir."

The officer went to step away when Carver called him back.

"Yes, sir," he said again.

Carver took the toothpick from his lips. "Do you feel something strange in this cavern?"

"Strange? Like what, sir?"

Carver looked around the cavern. "It's hard to explain. It's like... energy." His eyes narrowed. "Like a hum of electricity but not like electric shock, more like... depleting. Like gravity pulling down on the bones." He looked at the officer. "Do you feel it?"

The officer raised his eyebrows then gazed around the cavern, his eyes narrowing the longer he looked. "Yeah," he said. "I can feel it. It's subtle but... profound." He looked at Carver. "Honestly, detective, I thought that was just the somber mood outside the park. There's a lot of people out there." He looked over his shoulder, then back to Carver with a shake of his head. "They're not happy. But then again..." He gestured to the body. "I can understand why."

Carver breathed deeply, looking around the cavern. "Me too," he whispered.

The officer stepped away, leaving Carver alone. He couldn't put a finger on it, but there was something beneath the folds that was nagging at his instincts. Something he couldn't see, taste, or touch. But it was there, feeding silently off fear.

Carver stepped out of the cavern and froze.

He could feel it, that same energy, like prickly heat across his back. Carver turned around, staring deep into the cavern.

He was certain of it. Whatever this dark energy was, he could feel it. And it was coming from the cavern.

134

Lori's eyes fluttered open. Daylight washed through her vision in a blur. A faint sound of a continuous click behind the light, along with a crackling dull roar. Her neck groaned when she turned to her side. Staring at the fireplace and the fire burning effortlessly, devouring the wood, eating it raw. Her eyes rolled into her skull, and she shook her head to wipe away the cobwebs clinging to her brain.

"Glad you're up."

She shot her head towards the voice. Gerard was sitting on the couch, hunched over and continuously flicking a *Zippo* lighter. His dark, piercing eyes unrelentingly staring, roaming over her body with a noxious expression across his face, still in his boxer shorts, his skin glistening with sweat. He looked over his shoulder through the bay window.

"Your cab is gone." He laughed with a chuckle in his throat. "Guess they couldn't wait any longer." And he turned to her, his beady eyes like tiny marbles in his head. "No worries, Lori." He shook his head. "I'll drive you to Sleepy Hollow if that's what you want to do."

Her head seemed to weigh a thousand pounds when she sat up, her temples tight, turning her stomach into a knot. She was surprised she wasn't tied up. Surprised he hadn't restrained her. Lori looked around the room for a weapon. Something. Anything she could use to fend him off, but all she found was a medicine bottle with no label and a spoon beside it sitting on the coffee table in front of Gerard.

He saw her staring at it. Said, "To relieve inhibition and enhance pleasure." And he grinned. "Got to take your medicine like your mother does. It's all for the best."

Lori looked around the room. "Where is she? Where's Elena?"

Gerard paused flicking the lighter. Sat there unmoving and staring. Staring as if Lori's question were futile and insulting. He craned his head, glaring at her. Seemed like his stare lasted a lifetime. Then he started flicking the lighter again when he said, "Upstairs. Sleeping." He ran his tongue across his teeth. "You should check on her. Make sure she's still living." And he grinned again when he flicked his lighter.

Lori stared at Gerard. The person who had been a constant in her life since she was a pre-teen. She couldn't believe her own eyes. All this time, right beneath her nose, there was Gerard pulling the strings. And he murdered her father. Her heart groaned with a hurtful sting.

"Why did you kill my father?" she asked, and Gerard paused his lighter flicking, staring at Lori.

"Baphomet required it." He craned his head. "As evil as your father was, Lori, he was too ambitious. So many people believe they're evil when all they are is a pawn for the devil." Now he shook his head, slowly back and forth. "He needed to know his place. He would have caused more grief than he was worth. No, we already had you and your mother. His existence at that point was insignificant. Should he have discovered it was you we were after, he may have caused an uproar. No, it was his bloodline that was required. The long history of the Francon blood lives on…" He pointed at her. "With you Lori. And we have that now, don't we?"

Lori turned her head, thinking. Everything he said seemed cryptic and incomplete. "We? Who are you talking about?"

He paused, staring at her. "Baphomet," he said, leaning back on the couch. "And his many devils across the world." He looked around the house. "This house may belong to the Francon name, but it is tied to the master, Mr. West. Even since his move to California, he still has his demonic hold on the home. You've been in the basement. Did you not see his transformative throne?" He closed his eyes when he said, "His presence is felt everywhere. In every room and every piece of furniture. His essence exists inside the atoms in the air between us. He is the foundation that keeps the home tethered to Xibalba."

"Shwhat?"

He glared at Lori like he was going to scold her for her ignorance. He continued without answering her question. "Then there is the demon Holer, who rounds out the *we* part of your question. You've met him before, Lori. Don't you remember? He is your night terror. He's been with you for a very long time. Always watching. Pulling the strings to bring you to Sleepy Hollow where his ghost demons have found refuge in the ether. And you, a gift to

Baphomet for allowing his services to continue uninterrupted. Your union will be glorious. You'll be a queen, Lori. A queen with all the power of hell at your fingertips." He returned his attention to the lighter, and started flicking it open then closed once again.

So many thoughts spiraled through Lori's brain at that moment. So many questions. So many insurgencies and revelations. She thought about the demon Holer from Marc's story. It was obvious that's where Gerard had gotten the information from. Obviously, he read the story. She looked at Gerard with his sickly grin as he flicked that fucking lighter time and time again. He was obviously insane. Probably has been since the very beginning. Lori knew there were no demons running amok. It's just sick and evil human beings needing an excuse for their hateful tirades.

He read the notebook. He knows Lori suffers from night terrors. All else was made-up, shook-up, bullshit. An excuse to get his rocks off on her mother. Which only means one thing: Gerard is as crazy as a fuckin loon. Completely out of his mind, and this was not going to end peacefully. She required a reprieve, time to think to find a way out.

"Can I see my mother now?"

He ceased his flicking, devouring Lori with his eyes. "Indeed. She waits for you, but I hope you're not squeamish. She's had some trouble as of late."

She didn't know what that meant, but she knew she wasn't about to have a conversation with fucking Gerard about the current state of Elena's health as if they were two concerned family members.

"Go on. She's waiting for you."

Lori sat there, paused and unmoving. She knew this was a trap. Knew she needed to keep her wits in check and understood that what she finds in her mother's bedroom may be something she does not want to see. She looked at the front door. Saw the deadbolt was locked, assessing how long it will take to open the door if she needs to run at lightning speed to get out. Lori knew there was no way he was going to allow her to walk out the front door. She's going to have to play this through to the end but if she could just find something. A weapon. Something. Anything to bash Gerard over the head with and run out the front door into safety.

"Well…" Gerard raised his voice. "We're all waiting."

"I just want to go," she said, her voice soft with a cry beneath it.

"Oh Lori. Stop your whining. You and your mother have been at odds for so long. Don't you think it's best for you to be with her in her time of need?"

Lori started crying. Her tears falling effortlessly, rolling down her cheeks.

Gerard stood up and Lori jumped in her seated position. He looked at her. "Oh please, Lori. Stop your fearful antics. I already told you you'll be a queen. Start acting like one."

Her bottom lip quivered. All she wanted to do was run.

"How about this, go and see your mother Lori and then I'll allow you to leave?" He gestured to the door. "You can walk right out the door. Is that a satisfactory outcome, Lori?"

She nodded.

"Very well then." He gestured to the second floor. "Go then. She waits for you."

Lori nodded again but didn't move. She felt frozen to the ground. Frozen with fear.

"Go Lori," he hollered, and Lori whined in her throat as she pushed herself to her feet. "Go on. Go now, Lori."

Lori walked to the staircase, sensing how Gerard took a step closer. She saw the notebook on the floor by the stairs. Felt Gerard's eyes on her, and she braced herself for an attack, her hands shaking as she gripped the banister. She took the first step up, listening for a sudden movement from Gerard while scanning the house, searching for a weapon.

She was certain she needed it. For Gerard, yes, but also for whatever was waiting in Elena's room. Lori rounded the corner to her mother's room and glanced down the stairs.

Gerard walked into view and stopped before the stairs, his stare burrowing into her soul. Elena's door was closed.

"Go on," he said, gesturing for her to go inside.

She gripped the doorknob and turned.

135

Marc was enjoying the cold winter day that filled his lungs with clean, crisp air while clearing his head. His red eye swam in his stomach, offering a state of heightened awareness coupled with a relaxed guard where everything seemed natural and acceptable.

Accepting his escorts, no matter how odd they seemed. They had an air about them, like innocence married with nefarious intent. They traversed the woods as if they were exploring for the first time in their lives. Exploring in a state of childlike wonder, but no matter how much they explored or ran or puzzled over a tree or direction, Marc could feel their eyes on him. He could feel them like walls closing in around him, and all he wanted to do was remove himself from their presence. Take off exploring on his own.

He was drawn to the cemetery. Some nagging sensation impulse in his brain kept turning his thoughts back to the cemetery. Kept seeing a crypt in the darkness. The door was open and inside was an inky black that buzzed as if it were alive. He could feel it in his bones, vibrating, raging his cells into overdrive like steam from a pot of boiling water. Felt it in his gut. Felt it in his chest, tuning his heart into a fluttering beat filled with trepidation. Turning the itch across his scar into a mad fever. He pushed on it relentlessly.

A few more steps forward and Marc found himself on top of a hill overlooking Sleepy Hollow. He could see the Hudson River in the distance across the small town he'd always called home. A wave of nostalgia lifted in his bones.

Six months, he thought. Six months locked up in that house- with the exception of the alcohol-fueled bar fights and one-night stands that he could never remember. Always so close to home yet a million miles away as if he'd been living on a distant planet and now, here he was, returning to his home. It seemed like it was forever since he was last here. Since he opened the door after a terrible night filled with anguish to find Wren waiting for him. He went without question. Like a dense fool, broken and lost. Wren had talked to him. Whispered in his ear and Marc followed him like a puppy needing a home. It was the first time Wren had offered the absinthe. He could see the bottle now, the green liquid shimmering in the candlelight. Wren's voice behind it, incoherent, like he was talking underwater.

He wondered what had become of his apartment. Until now he never thought about it. He'd left everything he ever owned. Walked out as if it all meant nothing. Walked out and left the past behind. But this new life seemed malicious and riddled with fear. And as he gazed upon his hometown, he could feel the same vibration existing like a dark stain on the wind, filtering into the cells of his neighbors and infecting their minds with internal catastrophe.

The snap of a branch followed by the crunching of dead leaves in the icy winter morning turned Marc's eyes to their corners. Beside him were his three escorts. Hal on his left. Andrew and Sarah were on his right. They weren't there a moment ago, as if they materialized out of thin air to stand beside him. His stomach twisted while sensing their presence barreling down on his shoulders. They made him feel like a captive. Even here, in the wide expanse of earth and sky he felt as if he were in a prison. Inside the crypt with no place to go, no retreat nor safety.

Marc knew they wished him harm, but there was another side to the coin. He also understood that no matter what happened they would provide protection. Even if that protection protected him from himself, as if they required Marc to live and breathe and would do anything to guarantee his survival. So odd and confusing. Like they were three voices in his head. Three characters in his story who followed him wherever he went. Always in his thoughts, knowing his ambitions, intentions and dreams. He questioned if they were even real. He wondered if Wren was real too or if he'd completely lost his mind and everything he witnessed was a manifestation of a delusion brought on by extreme heartache and trauma.

Marc scanned across Sleepy Hollow to the cemetery a mile away on his right. It looked so drab and cold. A thin fog hung above the tombstones and crypts, casting a gray gloom across the bare trees. The fog looked like a canopy of smoke floating over the cemetery. He pursed his lips and swallowed when Andrew stepped forward. Marc stole a glance at Hal and Sarah. Saw how their eyes devoured Sleepy Hollow like a wolf devours its prey. Their stares sent a shiver down his spine.

They didn't talk, these three escorts. Haven't said one word since Wren introduced them. They seemed like specters in the wind, driving fear into the mind from the wings of a subtle breeze. Marc didn't notice it at first, but he was gnashing his teeth, his jaw tight as his scar burned mad across his forehead. He watched as the three escorts stepped forward, walking down the hill ahead of Marc.

Marc looked over Sleepy Hollow, then to his escorts descending into the heart of the Hollow. He felt like he opened a door and unleashed hell upon his hometown.

As if he were the shepherd who brought the wolves to the sheep.

136

Lori slowly opened the door. Daylight washed across the plush carpet from the windows on the opposite side of the room. Elena's armoire was against the wall on her left beside the door to the walk-in closet. The room was hot and stuffy, the heat flowing in waves across her skin. It felt suffocating. She heard a creak behind her and craned her head to look downstairs. Gerard was no longer there.

Shit!

She looked over both shoulders, thinking he'd come barreling out of the darkness to push her into the room. But nothing was there, just the calm quiet of the early afternoon with a subtle backdrop of ocean waves behind the house. Lori bowed her head, thinking.

Where is he?

Certain Gerard would show his face soon, she thought about racing to the bedroom window and climbing down the ivy to safety. It was an option, yes. If she needs to, she will.

Still, she thought, let's find something to defend ourselves.

Lori stepped through the door, closing it quickly and locking it the moment the door closed, then back-stepped away from the door as if Gerard was about to push through at any moment.

Nothing came. Lori pursed her lips and swallowed, then scanned across the bedroom. Her head snapped back when she saw her mother lying on the bed with her arms extended and her wrists tied to the headboard. Her head leaned to her left against the headboard. Her feet were crossed at the ankles and tied to the bedposts. Lori's jaw dropped when she saw her eyes, all black like dark mirrors with a metallic glint. Elena's mouth hung open. She never moved or stirred. Lori scanned across the scene to the pentagram written in blood above the headboard with the words Initium Novum beneath it.

Marc's story.

She swallowed her breath down her gullet and scanned the room again. There were candles burning on the side tables and across the top of the furniture, the chest of drawers, and the desk by the window. A bottle-or a second bottle because Lori was certain Gerard had the same downstairs-sat on the side table next to the bed. A spoon beside it.

She snapped back to the door when she heard a smooth click. The doorknob was creeping back and forth. Gerard was behind the door; she could see his shadow in the crack on the bottom. Lori looked around the room and her eyes stopped at the desk.

There's a letter opener in there.

She darted to the desk, threw open the drawer and rifled through it, finding the letter opener on the bottom. Lori looked at the bedroom door. The knob didn't move. No more shadow beneath the door. She turned to the window, then back to her mother.

She couldn't leave her like that. No matter what has happened between them, she didn't have the heart to leave Elena all tied up the way she was. Plus, Lori had a gut feeling that perhaps it wasn't Elena who poisoned her. Considering current circumstances, she had to concede that perhaps it was Gerard all along. And even more, maybe Elena was as innocent as Lori. Maybe Gerard was playing his game of sadism, murder, and debauchery like a master chess player, always three steps ahead and using her mother as a pawn.

What she knew without a doubt was that Gerard would come through that door and she was running out of time. She felt trapped, battling with the decision to toss up the window and climb down to safety or release her mother, who may or may not have tried to murder her own daughter.

"Fuck."

Lori stomped over to the bed, assessing the tied ropes around the ankles then immediately went to work untying those knots, dropping the letter opener on the bed. But they were pulled so tight she couldn't get her fingers through to untie one end or the other. She took the letter opener and started sawing the rope. Lori noticed that with enough pressure, the rope splintered. She kept her eyes on the doorknob as she sawed across the rope. Her heart thundered like a rabbit in her chest as the rope gave in and released Elena's first ankle. Lori did the same to Elena's wrist restraint, then hurried to the other side of the bed and went to work on the right ankle when a wet gurgling groan escaped Elena's throat. Lori snapped her head to it. There was green vomit gurgling and foaming across Elena's lips, the stank putrid and vile, invading her nostrils like noxious gas.

Her anxiety went into overdrive.

Lori sawed on the second ankle rope that gave in quickly, wondering if her mother was overdosing on whatever Gerard had given her. She eyeballed the medicine bottle on the nightstand as she went to work on the second wrist restraint. The word oxycodone was printed on the label.

The rope splintered and cut. Elena's arm dropped to the mattress. Her eyes were disturbing, as was the vomit that seemed to burn into the bedcover. Lori checked for a pulse. Still beating, although weak and irregular. She needed to get her up. No matter what she'd done, Lori couldn't live with herself if she didn't try to help her. She looked through the window and couldn't believe she wasn't running for her life.

Which is exactly what Gerard wanted, knowing she wouldn't leave after seeing Elena. Keeping her here. *But… why?* If he wanted to take advantage of Lori, he had the chance and could have had his way without a problem. But he wanted her up here. Why? Certainly, it wasn't to save Elena. That much was true.

Fuck.

Lori squeezed her arm beneath Elena's head, attempting not to touch the green vomit. She pushed her up to a sitting position. Elena's eyes never wavered, remaining wide open and black as if she were in a trance.

"*Come on,*" Lori ordered, her anxiety getting the better of her.

Lori forced Elena's legs over the side of the bed then draped Elena's arm across her neck before she lifted her to her feet.

Heard a sound like something was being dragged across the carpet. She looked around the room. The bedroom door was closed. Elena groaned, her head leaning against Lori's shoulder. The light in the closet went on and then off with a sudden pop and fizzle, as if the light exploded. A scream hitched in Lori's throat. Her heart tightened in her chest. Elena's head lifted off her shoulder. Felt her weight soften as that groan evolved into a rickety growl.

Heard feet padding across the carpet in the closet.

"He is here." Elena's voice was guttural and gruff, a huff across her lips.

Elena stepped forward, mesmerized. She stepped away from Lori towards the closet. Lori went to grab her arm but with no luck. Elena kept walking as if she was commanded to do so.

Lori kept waiting for Gerard to reveal himself. Kept thinking she should have gone through the fucking window.

"Mother," Lori whispered. "Come back…"

Lori didn't know what she was looking at. What was standing in the dark of the closet, staring directly at her. Its skin was molded into the darkness, revealing only the face, the deathly pale face with violet-colored veins that looked like spiderwebs stretching from its jaw to its forehead and surrounding the eyes. His red glaring eyes.

Elena kneeled before it, bowing to whatever this thing was.

It stepped out from the closet and into the light, and Lori did a double take. Her eyes squinted, confused. It was Gerard. In the light, it was Gerard. His skin glistening with sweat.

"My sweet Lori." Gerard closed his eyes, craning his head back. Lori swallowed the breath that caught in her throat when Gerard opened his eyes, marveling over the room. "This is where it began," he said. "Where the master claimed his throne." His eyes found Lori. His pupils were so dark, Lori believed that if she continued to stare into the dark depths of his eyes, she would lose her grip on reality. Would fall into Gerard's mesmerizing trance. "In this room, Lori, where I murdered your father. It's the energy. The stain left by the master's rise." He was nodding now, nodding and glaring at Lori. "Let us consummate the moment, Lori. Can you feel it? The energy begs to devour every fiber of your being. *Innocence…*" he hissed, "*…is evils addiction.* We devour it like hungry wolves." And he grinned. This thing, this demon or devil or Gerard or whatever the fuck he is, gestured behind her. "Drink," he said. Lori forced herself to turn.

The spoon beside the medicine bottle filled with the liquid she assumed came from the bottle. Lori's eyes widened with every drop added to the spoon. Her brow pinched, staring confused at the spoon, certain it was a trick. Some magical bullshit illusion.

"To make our time together more pleasurable. To drop the inhibitions and mask the fear."

She turned to Gerard and the sickly grin plastered across his face. Looked at Elena, kneeling in front of him, unmoving. Gerard noticed Lori's stare and turned to Elena. He cupped her jaw, lifting her eyes to him. "Take your seat," he commanded and without a moment's pause Elena rose to her feet then shifted over to the red leather high-back chair in the corner where she sat and stared, looking like a demonic queen on her throne, her arms on the armrests, her fingers like spiderwebs across them.

"Your mother welcomed the demon long ago, Lori. But like all humans with power, the moment they discover they are no longer the top feed they snap their jaws and destroy all in their path." Lori couldn't take her eyes off Elena, sitting and watching, lost and mesmerized. Her breath was shallow, her jaw hung open, her head resting against the chair. Noticed how pale she looked, how pasty her skin was and how sunken her eyes were, as if they retreated into her skull.

Possessed. She looked possessed.

"She gave chase once she learned the truth. Lori, with her feeble existence. Lori with the naïve heart, always seeing the best in others, but once Baphomet has married with your heart, you will think differently. You will see them for what they are, pitiful and disgusting vermin. Your mother thought it would be her who was owed that honor. You must forgive her transgressions. For her attempt to dissuade you from the Hollow."

Lori gripped the letter opener in her palm, holding the blade up against her forearm, hidden from Gerard's view. Gerard ran his tongue across his lips.

She swallowed her breath. "Are you gonna keep talking, or are we going to get this over with?" She looked from Gerard to her mother, then back to Gerard.

His eyes lit up with elation. "She comes willingly," he whispered and stepped towards her.

"She carries a weapon."

Gerard stopped in his tracks and Lori's eyes closed. The warning was spoken from her mother's lips, but the voice did not belong to her. It seemed guttural compared to Elena's high-pitched whine. Lori opened her eyes to her mother, sitting with that blank stare as if she stared at nothing. Gerard stepped cautiously towards Lori, his head tilted, staring at Lori's right hand where she held the letter opener. She was squeezing the weapon so tight she couldn't feel her hand any longer. Now Gerard was in front of her. She could feel his breath across her skin. Felt paralyzed, as Gerard reached around and gripped her right arm, turning the arm in his direction then pried the letter opener from her hand.

She couldn't move. Her jaw trembling and her lips the same. Gerard dropped the letter opener when Lori locked eyes with him. He snatched her hair and yanked her head to the side as a squeal escaped Lori's throat. She couldn't move. Couldn't speak. He gripped her throat and squeezed, and Lori's eyes bulged from their sockets. His grip was like iron and now he used both hands and the air was pulled from her lungs with immediate abandon.

She slapped and punched him, but his grip never wavered. She wrenched her nails across his face and all he did was laugh. He raised her off her feet, gnashing his teeth behind a wide-open grin as she kicked and flailed and then he tossed her onto the bed where she bounced then dropped back down and the air rushed into her lungs, gasping and choking and coughing.

Her eyes wavered, rolling across the room. Gerard picked up the letter opener. "Thank you, Elena," he said. "I can always count on you."

Lori coughed some more.

Gerard was staring at the letter opener when he lifted his eyes to Lori. He stepped to the bed and gripped Lori's ankle, pulling her towards him then punched her thighs, holding the letter opener in his tight fist. His punches sent waves of agony rattling through her bones, his shoulders swaying as he punched left, then right. Left, then right. With each punch, her legs weakened as Lori wailed then rocked Gerard over the skull with a punch of her own. All he did was grin, then returned the favor, hammering Lori across the temple. She dropped like an anvil to the mattress.

Her eyes rolled behind her eyelids when the bed shifted, and Gerard climbed on top of her. She tasted blood in her mouth, her head throbbing, pain rattling between her temples.

"It's that fight we love, Lori."

He ran his tongue across her face.

"Please, feel free to continue."

He bit into her jaw, and Lori screamed into the heavens. The pain was too much. Felt her skin being torn between his teeth when all Lori could see was the candle on the side table. She gripped that candle tight, then smashed it into Gerard's face with every ounce of strength she had, driving the candle into his skin and garnering an immediate scream from Gerard. Sparks and little fires burned across Lori's face as candle wax seared across her jaw. Gerard gripped his eye socket. His mouth gaped open with a wailing eternal scream. Lori battered him with the thick candle with as much force as she could garner. Gerard lost his balance and fell off the bed with a thud, landing on the carpet and screaming bloody hell.

Lori took advantage of the moment and scurried off the bed while Gerard wailed in agony. The thick drone from his wail, constant and maddening. She backed up against the wall beside the desk, assessing her way out. Saw Elena gazing at her with some sickly grin across her mouth.

She went to run but Gerard lifted off the ground. His skin seared across the left side of his face. His left eye socket melted into his skull.

"Bitch," he hollered.

She looked at the bedroom door, assessing her immediate path, but Gerard was blocking her exit. She'll have to run right through him if she wants to get out of the room. She looked around. Elena had that same possessed stare, watching the scene play out.

"I'm gonna make you pay for that, Lori."

She kept looking. Her eyes flitting from one corner of the room to the other, hoping to find something, anything to defend herself. Gerard took a step closer.

Lori felt defeated. What else could she do? There was no place to go. She backed up against the wall. She had no weapon. No way to defend herself. Gerard crept closer to the bed.

"We're going to try this again, Lori. Let's not repeat our mistakes."

She saw the candles on the desk then turned to Gerard. She gripped the nearest candle. Gerard stopped in his tracks.

"This room… you said it was sacred, right?"

Gerard nodded, his eyes burrowing into Lori's soul as he ran his tongue across his lips.

"Evil lives here," she said. "Then evil should be eradicated so that it can cause no more harm."

Gerard's eyes narrowed, confused.

Lori tossed the candle onto the bed.

"What are you doing?"

She gripped a second candle then tossed it across the bed to the plush carpet. Then another that she threw across the room. It crashed into the far wall. Little fires started burning across the bed and the carpet.

"No," said Gerard when the strangest thing Lori had ever witnessed took her by surprise. It was as if Gerard's spine twisted, his shoulders rising then twisting as he stepped back, receding away from the bed. His lips pressed tight as a whining moan escaped his throat.

"Not this place," he whined. "Not his place."

She took a fourth candle then dipped the flame to the curtain. Fire crawled up the drape to the ceiling.

"Damn this place to hell."

Lori gripped the candle tight in her palm, waiting to bash it into Gerard's face if she had to. But when she looked up, Gerard was receding towards the closet, his head moving left and right. The fire was gaining ground, eating and devouring the carpet, the drapes, ceiling and the bed. The heat rising and the smoke turning thicker by the second.

"The master will be so angry with me. Can't do this. Can't." He stepped back now, fully into the closet where the darkness wrapped around him and Lori could see the devil return in the darkness. "His most sacred room."

Lori stepped forward, holding the candle tight. "Get back," she ordered. "Get back or I'll burn it all to hell."

And just like that Gerard was gone, vanished into the darkness, but she could still hear him, his voice commanding, whining and guttural. "Protect our sacred space, Elena. Protect us from… the liiiiiiiiightt."

Lori was halfway to the door when Elena howled, jumping off the chair with the speed of a cat. Lori swung the candle around and hammered Elena over the head with it. She dropped to the floor with a thud, spinning Lori around when she felt arms wrap around her.

"Gotcha," said Gerard. He lifted her off her feet then body slammed her onto the plush carpet. Lori's head bounced off the floor as pain raced down her head, neck, and spine.

Her vision wavered. For a second she saw black before her vision returned. Elena was lying next to her. The fire was dancing across the walls, the flames devouring the carpet. Paint melted off the walls.

"There's only one thing I want from you before Baphomet has claimed your heart."

She looked up. Gerard was standing over her. There were flames crawling across the ceiling above him, crackling and burning, licking and slithering.

"I want to taste that innocence." He dropped to his knees and gripped her throat, squeezing the air from her lungs as he lifted her head and shoulders off the floor and started shaking her throat violently.

Lori's eyes bulged from her skull, gasping for air that was no longer there, her head rocking back and forth. Her arms were flailing, searching across the carpet when she found it. She knew what it was the moment her hand touched it. The letter opener.

"Just a taste," he said, wrapping his lips around Lori's mouth, sucking on her lips. Lori screamed into his mouth then tossed that letter opener into his neck with a wet pop. His grip slipped off her throat. Her head dropped to the carpet, gagging and sucking air into her lungs.

Gerard sat on his knees, holding his neck where the letter opener was wedged into his throat. Blood rained across his neck and shoulders as he gagged and gurgled on his own blood and breath. Lori kicked him dead in the face, and he dropped onto his back into the flames, grunting his last. The fire crawled across him like he was a fresh meal, devouring his flesh and bones.

The fire was everywhere now, creeping towards Lori's legs. She scurried to her feet and looked at her mother, the evil bitch who'd been under Gerard's spell. She wanted to leave her, a victim to her own evil deeds, but she couldn't. Couldn't bring herself to allow her mother to die in such a way.

That would make me you.

Lori gripped Elena's arm and forced her up, draping her arm across her shoulder, immediately hoping this would not be a moment filled with regret. Sweat dripped off Lori's skin in thick bullet sized droplets. She tasted blood in her mouth. Her skin felt like it was melting off the bone. She eyeballed the door, now covered in fire gnawing on the wood, then turned to the closet and the thick inky black that seemed to call to her. The armoire was burning, and the fire danced across the carpet, eating and roaring and crackling and devouring.

She thought about dropping Elena through the window, but when she looked over her shoulder the flames were dancing across the window frame. She turned back to the closet. Gerard had gotten into the room through the closet, which means there had to be a way out. Some door Lori never knew existed. Maybe it went through the entire house?

Hopefully, it led outside.

But if she's wrong, they'll be trapped in the closet and will certainly burn into the afterlife in a fiery blaze of anguish. Still, it was her only hope. Elena slumped into her embrace. Gerard was dead on the floor.

It's now or never.

Lori dragged Elena through the flames, through the smoke that gagged her throat and burned her eyes. She forced her arm further into the crook of Elena's armpit, guiding her to the closet where she pushed Elena in first, then shuffled in herself, joining Elena in the darkness when she heard a roar as if Satan growled at the intrusion. She looked over her shoulder. The pentagram was engulfed in flames. The bed collapsed in front of it like a demonic altar to hell and damnation. Lori returned her focus to the closet.

The smoke was suffocating, coating and strangling her throat. She could feel the heat from the fire on her back, but the flames provided enough light to see the end of the closet and how the wall was propped open.

A hidden door.

She didn't know where it led, but knew it was her only chance.

"Come on, mother. It's time to go."

She shuffled to the door then threw it open. More darkness existed beyond the entrance. Lori felt heat inside the walls in the dark secret room. Felt breath on the nape of her neck. She looked over her shoulder. The fire was crawling across the ceiling like a snake slithering towards its prey. She hitched Elena's arm across her neck and stepped into the darkness.

The first she heard was breathing. The first she saw were eyes.

137

The bus's wheels squealed across the icy pavement. John felt the sudden jerk and his body hitched forward. His arms instinctively reached out, bracing himself with the seat in front of him.

When he woke up this morning, he could sense something was different. As if the world had changed while he slept. He felt angry and paranoid as if evil invaded his cells and ramped his vibration into overdrive. He felt the same when he got to school.

Everyone seemed on edge today. John had noticed the unsavory long stares from students and from faculty as if collective paranoia had become the norm. And John felt it too.

Nagging at his gut as if some phantom confusion had boiled in his stomach, turning a knot in his gut that added fuel to the anger. He noticed there was less talking, not just on the bus but during school too. As if everyone were battling with personal demons and were too lost in their own thoughts to speak out loud.

He rested his head against the seat while staring through the window when the bus door slapped open and a few students walked off the bus towards their houses.

"John?"

His attention was taken by Logan when he sat next to him.

"Are we still on for our covert operation?" asked Logan.

After what happened yesterday, Logan and John made plans to travel to the abandoned house after school. They agreed to go before sunset. Not only will Grandpa Claude not be suspicious, but in case John was right, they figured daylight was their best defense.

John nodded. "Yes, definitely. Let's drop our stuff at home and meet at the end of the cul-de-sac. There's a straight line from there directly to the house and Grandpa Claude won't see us going in."

The bus turned onto their street.

"Sounds like a plan."

John stood up, slinging his backpack across his shoulders. He saw Michael and Chad at the back of the bus do the same. They looked at him, and Michael nodded.

"Hopefully we can avoid some people." He looked at Logan, who returned his gaze then looked over his shoulder at Michael and Chad.

Logan got up from his seat as the bus stopped. The doors were flung open, and Michael and Chad strolled down the aisle past John's seat.

"Don't worry about them. I talked to them and its cool."

John cocked an eyebrow. "What does that mean?"

"Well, I extended an olive branch, and they won't cause you any more trouble. They're interested in what's going on." Logan gestured to leave. "Come on."

John followed him to the front of the bus. "I still don't know what that means." As he passed, he noticed the other students were all staring at nothing, looking mesmerized by their own thoughts.

Logan stopped by the door and looked at John. "I promise you don't have to worry about them." He turned and took the steps to the street then looked back at John still standing on the top step.

"What did you do?"

Logan shrugged. "I invited them."

John's jaw dropped.

Bus driver said, "Time to go, kid."

Logan gestured for John to join him. "Come on. It'll be okay. I promise."

And reluctantly, John stepped off the bus.

138

When Lori stepped through the hidden door she stepped onto the top of a staircase. Some mechanical hum existed in the darkness, constant and unwavering. It sounded like a revved-up engine that quickly died only to begin again a moment later.

The staircase was drenched in inky black. She couldn't see past the first six steps, but she estimated there was another hidden door at the bottom that would bring them to the first floor.

There were eyes staring at her from the darkness at the bottom of the staircase when she first stepped onto the landing. Red beaming eyes that stopped Lori in her tracks. She'd seen them before. So hauntingly familiar. The same red eyes that have visited her dreams since childhood. They were watching her. Lori's heart seemed to have stopped beating, standing frozen on top of the stairs with the fire burning in the closet. The smoke drifted into the staircase.

And then the eyes were gone as if whatever demon they belonged to was engaged in some demonic game of catch me if you can. Lori coughed something awful, the smoke burning in her lungs. She hitched Elena up for a better grip.

She shook her. "Elena," she screamed, "Mom. Get up!"

Elena grew heavier by the second. Lori was surprised she could carry her this far. She assumed it was the adrenaline pumping through her veins that brought the strength to do so, but now the weight was becoming unbearable.

"Moooommmmm!" But no such luck. Maybe Lori hit her a bit too hard with that candle?

Lori licked her dry lips then wiped her sweaty forehead across her arm, her eyes stinging from the smoke. She investigated the closet and the approaching fire, listening to the roaring flames devouring the bedroom. She turned to the stairs and the darkness then took the first step down, dragging her mother with her.

Kept moving, hobbling down the steps, feeling the heat on her back and the smoke billowing like a cloud around her and Elena, stinging the eyes and burning the throat and lungs. Lori's arms were burning from the pressure of her mother's weight. She took another step and heard a crack. Felt herself slipping, her breath hitched in her throat. The stairs fractured and the two of them fell through the staircase into the inky darkness below.

Lori landed with a thud; her mother dropped beside her. Pain raced across her neck and back. Every bone and muscle in her body ached something awful. She coughed and hacked. The air down here had yet to be tainted with smoke, and the fresh air felt soothing in her lungs. Lori achingly turned to her side, hacking up smoky phlegm and bile. Her eyes burning and filled with tears.

She heard a roar and snapped her head toward the sound. Looking above into the hidden staircase, she could see the fire was making its way down the stairs like some demonic phantom chasing her down. Lori started looking around, assessing where she was, her arms and hands were trembling. Her breath stuttered in her throat.

Everywhere she looked was darkness. The inky black stretching its vile hand to wrap around Lori and squeeze the fear from her cells. She climbed to her knees, listening to the fire overhead. There was only one place she could be.

The basement.

Which means she could use the cellar door to escape. Lori turned to her mother, her silhouette like a pasty glow in the dark. Elena rose slowly. Her eyelids fluttered-her eyes filled with confusion but no longer a metallic black-when something exploded somewhere in the house.

She turned to Lori and said, "This isn't how it was supposed to happen." She looked so pale and sickly, her nerves shot to all bloody hell, trembling from head to toe. The fire raged overhead. Elena looked up to the flames when a profound sadness passed through her eyes. Lori could see the tears forming.

Pathetic, was Lori's first thought but she didn't have time for thoughts other than trying to get out of wherever the hell they were. They fell through the stairs inside hidden pathways that stretched like a maze through the house. They could be anywhere in the basement. Lori looked around, sensing the heat descending upon them. With the house on fire it was only a matter of time until the top floors came crashing down on top of them. She needed to get out and get out now.

Lori searched for a door, feeling across the wall for a doorknob or hidden crevice. Elena just sat and watched the fire, mumbling under her breath. Words and phrases like, *Initium Novum,* and *Humanity's end as a new beginning, follow the red eyes,* mixed in with *Now she'll return,* and the one that stung like a bee, *My poor, poor Gerard.*

Anxiety hitched into Lori's throat. She couldn't find the door and with the fire crawling down the stairs, closer with every passing second, she was certain they were about to meet death in a hellish blaze. Now the smoke billowed into their little room. The heat on its heels.

Lori turned to her mother and screamed, "Where the fuck is the goddamn door?" Fear dripped off her tongue, her heart thundering in her chest.

"No worries, Lori, the eyes will find you." She looked like a child, hugging her knees to her chest, her head down in some mask of shame and guilt. "They have always found you." She looked up at the fire. "The eyes need you. You Lori, and not me. It was always about you."

Thick smoke billowed into the room, choking the air from their lungs. Lori felt tears in her eyes, threatening to unleash. She shook her mother. "Where's the damn door so we can get out of here?" Elena's eyes grew wide, staring at Lori as if she were mad. "We are going to fucking die in here if we can't find the door. Do you understand what the hell is going on?"

Elena pursed her lips and swallowed, then ground her teeth. "Behind you Lori."

Lori snapped her head around and those red, beaming eyes were there. That freezing sensation clasped Lori in an iron grip. Even the smoke stinging her eyes didn't matter. She felt nothing at that moment, couldn't even hear the roar from the fire nor feel the heat from the flames as they danced into their little room. But the red eyes disappeared. Disappeared through the door that then popped open. Lori's eyes narrowed. Her jaw trembling, her hands shaking.

"They need you, Lori," said Elena. "It's always been about you. Darkness is always attracted to the light it seeks to destroy."

Elena's voice, floating in the distance, seemed like she was talking underwater or a million miles away as Lori stood staring at the open door.

"Don't be afraid, Lori. Welcome them to your embrace."

Lori spun around to her mother. "Stop your nonsense." She gripped Elena's arm and pulled her to her feet. "I've had just about enough of it." Lori snatched Elena's wrist, pulling her towards the open door into the basement. The far side of the basement, where the darkness bled across their eyes.

Heard a creaking, crackling groan as the ceiling twenty feet ahead of them collapsed into the basement in a fiery blaze. She could see the first floor above was engulfed in flames. Soon the entire house will collapse. Collapse on top of them.

Lori looked at Elena. "Follow me," she said. "We need to get out now. The house is going to collapse."

All Elena did was nod. Lori scanned across the basement to find proper footing and a clear path to the cellar door when she realized she was standing on a pile of bones. Human skulls and bones were littered across the basement. There was one body that was fresh, although dead. The woman's eyes were black to the core with death and fear.

"What the fuck?" hollered Lori.

"Gerard," Elena said. "He's been a very busy boy."

Lori snapped her head to her mother when disappointment washed over her. "Oh mother," she whispered, seeing the tears in Elena's eyes. She gritted her teeth then stepped forward with Elena on her heels, through the smoke and around the fire, the collapsed floor burning like some demonic bonfire in the center of the basement. Heard bones being crushed beneath her feet. She used the fire to illuminate her trek to the opposite side of the basement.

She saw the red eyes in the distance, as if whatever phantom they belonged to was standing at attention by the stone slab Lori had seen previously as if paying homage to the demons that were conjured there. Heard a roar behind her and Lori looked over her shoulder. The fire was crawling across the secret room they had come from, racing towards them as if it knew this was its last chance to devour them. Lori turned and hurried around the collapsed floor, the basement filling with smoke that choked the lungs.

Walking furiously to the other side of the basement when Lori stopped in her tracks. Marc's notebook was propped up on the slab. She stared at it, confused. Lori was certain it had been in the living room when she first walked up to Elena's bedroom. She remembered seeing it sliding across the floor when Gerard tossed her across the living room.

Elena whispered, "The demon."

Lori looked at her, then returned to the notebook. She gripped the notebook, then beelined to the end of the basement and hurried up the steps to the cellar door where she pushed with all her strength. A few inches open were all she could manage. She tried again, then scanned across the basement, frustrated and fearful. The fire was slithering towards them, gaining ground. Smoke consumed the basement like a specter of darkness. The house shifted with a droning roar, and she knew it was about to collapse. She heard sirens too, growing louder with every second.

But they will be too late. She couldn't wait and hope. She had to open the door. Lori braced herself and pushed with all her strength and fear until that door broke open into the freezing cold of winter. She climbed outside and turned to her mother, offering her hand then pulled Elena up the stairs.

"Move away from the house," ordered Lori when she heard that groaning creak from the house again, the house shifting under the weight of the fire. The entire house was engulfed in flames. She looked back down into the basement the moment black smoke washed over the red eyes, billowing out of the door. Lori took a few steps back when glass exploded from somewhere in the house and she turned to Elena. She was already walking to the front of the house to greet the fire trucks with their blaring horns racing up the driveway.

Lori swallowed her breath through a chalky burning throat then followed her mother when the kitchen windows exploded behind her and she hurried to the front of the house into the long winding driveway to greet the firemen and watch the world burn.

All the while clutching the notebook close to her chest.

139

The second body was discovered by the river in a vacant lot that used to serve as a GM plant until mid-June of ninety-six. Carver knew several developers had submitted plans to turn the lot into housing for well-to-do citizens, although no formal plans had yet to be announced, which kept the lot vacant and dismal. An eyesore to say the least. He scanned across the large and empty lot to the Hudson River not more than fifty yards from where he was standing. The icy air drifted off the river to chill his bones.

He was staring at ninety acres of nothing. When GM shut down the plant they took everything all the way down to the last screw they could find. All that remained was a ninety-acre slab of concrete-the floor for the multiple warehouses that had once occupied the lot-and sparse foundations of metal and steel that stuck out of the ground in various locations.

Perfect place to dump a body.

But why the two locations? Why was one in the middle of a residential community while the other was down here where no one ever came except teenagers to party in secret?

Zoe Hardwood was found behind The Sleepy Hollow Tavern. That's three bodies, all in different locations. All with the same calling card. Carver looked over to the dead body sprawled across the concrete. Above her head and written in blood was the pentagram and inscription. The girl was naked, stripped down to her bare bones, and there was no blood in the body. Considering the sizes of the gashes to the girls' front and back, he wasn't surprised. They tortured the poor girl, but what instrument was used to do so he couldn't tell. It was as if there were two murderers standing on opposite sides of the victim as they wrenched their knives into her.

Marc Saduj and his faithful servant Wren came to mind.

He could hear her screams as if they were stuck inside the body, having been squelched by a tragic death but still wanted to be released. Of course, there was no heart in the body. Someone had cut her chest open and removed the heart. This case was becoming more surreal with every passing second. Carver looked away from the body, listening to her screams yelp across the vacant lot, echoing pain and fear to his ears as he watched the forensics team gather evidence. The photographer's hands were shaking, taking pictures of the body.

Carver was grateful Captain Flannery allowed him to continue as the lead detective in the investigation, although that gratitude only stretched so far. He was certain that if Flannery had another detective more suitable to take the case he would have handed it over in a heartbeat. But considering Carver was the lead detective in the Hardwood case, Flannery thought it was best for Stephen to become reacquainted with the calling card.

Stephen had yet to tell Flannery about his visit with Jerry. He'll leave that one out until tomorrow, at least. The way he saw it, the current situation was proof positive that Jerry did not act alone. There was someone else pulling the strings. Jerry's master.

Marc Saduj.

Carver popped a toothpick between his lips. He needs to find a link between the victims and Marc Saduj. Needs to find a reason to investigate the basement.

"Pick your team." That's what Flannery said, and Carver knew he'd need help with his investigation. Multiple bodies always meant there's a serial killer on the loose and he will need a team to help with the investigation. There's only a matter of time until the public finds out about the second body and considering the Hollow was still reeling from Jerry's day of murder and mayhem, they will demand answers.

Flannery planned on calling a press conference later today, but until then, he ordered Carver to keep the second away from the public eye. He wanted to gather as much evidence as possible prior to the flood of calls he was certain would arrive by the truckload after the press conference-most of them with dead end leads to nowhere. He was also hoping to get IDs on the victims prior to the press conference, which means he'll have to search through recent missing persons reports.

Carver set up a meeting with his fellow detectives and had a few flatfoots combing through missing persons reports at this very moment. Things were off and running, but that nagging sensation was tearing his stomach apart, knowing more people were going to lose their lives if he didn't find the link to Marc Saduj as fast as possible. A part of him wanted to storm the house right at this very moment, but with no evidence, any arrest would never see the light of day in a courtroom.

Sometimes this job is frustrating to the max.

He already ordered a stakeout on the house. There will be a patrol car following Marc's every move from here on out. Hopefully, something gives and breaks the case wide open. Hopefully, some lives will be spared.

"Detective." Carver's attention was taken by the forensics specialist, Cage Greenbriar. "I think I got something. It may be a minor detail, but then again, the detail can at least shed some light on the type of person we're looking for."

Cage was a short little man with glasses that made his green eyes seem larger than they were. Carver rolled his toothpick across his lips to the corner of his mouth. "What did you find?"

"Well," he said, removing his glasses then using a rag he pulled from his coat pocket to wipe them clean. "I can't be one hundred percent certain, but it seems to me the method of death can be attributed to a very specific device."

"And what would that be?"

He raised his glasses above his head, looking through them for clarity before placing them back on. "Well," Cage huffed. "Do you know anything about medieval torture?"

140

Marc was standing on the corner of Broadway and Beekman Street, staring at the Sleepy Hollow Millenium Clock that stood on a small island in the center of Beekman. His escorts were standing on the island. He allowed them to cross ahead of him, but Marc never took his foot off the sidewalk. He wanted to go to the cemetery, but every time he moved in that direction one of the three would deter him towards the river.

They barely talked. Barely isn't even the best word to describe them. They never said more than a sentence and every time they talked all they did was deter Marc's travels towards the river. Their eyes glued to him with every moment that passed.

There were two specific places Marc wanted to visit today. The first was his old home, the apartment building where he grew up. A check-in with Mrs. Leiter would do him good. Plus, he had a few questions about his mother he hoped she could answer. The second was the cemetery. He felt drawn to it, as if there was something in the cemetery that would settle his recent confusion. It seemed like the entire world had been smeared across his brain and he couldn't latch on to a single thought to fruition. As if there was someone else in his head feeding him thoughts and visions he wasn't entirely certain were real.

The last six months had gone by in a blur. He realized he'd been drunk for the better part of it, but even then, he'd spent most of the last decade juiced to the max so that shouldn't be anything new. But this was different. He was constantly battling with the dark recesses of his mind and thoughts. Plus, such strange occurrences have taken place during that time. The house for one, and of course Wren. And now these three escorts. He could feel their eyes on him, staring, assessing. Even when he wasn't looking, he could feel those eyes as if they followed him, clinging to him as if they'd taken a permanent space in his brain. So strange and peculiar. They turned his nerves into overdrive. He could feel it in his gut, roiling and bubbling as if he'd breathed noxious gas. And he was trembling.

That was the other side of the coin. He felt sick. But not just sick, he felt as if he were dying, being depleted from within as if his organs were failing him, rotting. His liver being the main offender. He could feel it now, as if the organ were being wrung dry. The pain arrived in rolling waves of anguish that rushed to every part of his body. He was unsteady, shaking and confused. A nervous wreck, sick and twisted.

"Where to, Mr. Saduj?" The one Wren introduced as Hal hollered from across the street. He seemed angry, his jaw clenched, staring at Marc with beady, nefarious eyes.

When they arrived at the corner, Marc let them cross ahead of him as he remained standing, hoping he could put some distance between them. Hoping they would leave and go on with their day on their own. He was beginning to think he'd have no such luck.

"Visit an old friend," Marc hollered through the wind and passing cars.

It was Sarah who answered. "Lead the way," she said. "We'll follow you."

Marc had no reply. He simply just turned around and walked towards Tarrytown. He figured he'd pass through the park for a minute of nostalgia. Patriots Park had been a mainstay throughout his life. He'd been going there since he was born. It was right across from the church where he was baptized.

The same church where his father lost his life.

141

The noise and commotion were loud and sometimes unbearable. Lori sat with a blanket wrapped around her shoulders, watching the firemen douse the house from the hose on top of one of the four fire trucks in her driveway. The notebook clutched against her chest.

When the firemen first arrived, the hellish blaze consumed the entire house. Windows were blown out, and the flames were licking the air like a caged animal flickers its tongue. The rage was all-consuming. She watched as the roof collapsed under the weight of fire and heat. It seemed like a bonfire from hell. Lori and Elena were rushed out of harm's way to the firetruck Lori was sitting on now. She was given oxygen and medical attention while watching the battle between man and nature unfold.

She noticed the paramedic never asked about the bite marks on her face. Lori was thankful for that, at the moment at least. She didn't want to say anything about what happened. Not yet. Now, all she wanted to do was go.

It had taken all four trucks and every fireman on patrol to get the fire under control, as it was now. Smoke smoldered from the ashes, drifting into the heavens from hell and damnation. Lori was certain all sixty-two bedrooms were in ashes, or, at the very least, burnt to a crisp. The firemen were still working on the back of the house, dousing the remaining flames.

She had yet to be questioned, but she knew the interview was coming.

Wait until they search the house and find all the bodies in the basement. Now that'll certainly spark an investigation.

She searched the crowd for Elena, finding her talking to a fireman. She was wrapped in a similar blanket, the two of them talking, staring at the house.

Explain that one Elena.

She wondered where and when they'd find Gerard's body. Wondered if the letter opener was still wedged in his neck or if the fire had claimed that too. Lori thought about how charred all those bodies in the basement had to be.

Will they be able to identify who those people are? Or were?

Considering the number of skulls and bones she trampled over, Gerard was certainly a busy boy as her mother had so eloquently described.

Lori's stomach turned from the thought. All her young life, Gerard had been a mainstay. Now she knew why. Like a typical murdering son of a bitch, he required a façade. A mild-mannered position that held him in high regard with plenty of witnesses. A necessary commodity in the life of a serial killer. A needed pawn to come to the rescue with a claim of innocence and a clean judgment of character.

Not this time. I know who you are, Gerard.

The thought burned her gut, fueling her anger over his deeds.

You got what you deserved, she thought, but then thought about the bodies in the basement and reconsidered. *Actually, you got off easy you son of a bitch.*

Lori scanned across the house and felt nothing. She was glad it was destroyed. Eventually, everything comes to an end.

Now Elena turned in her direction. A subtle grin across her lips that was disturbing in every way possible. Lori gritted her teeth, watching her mother stroll towards her as if she didn't have a care in the world.

"Everything's going to be fine," she said. "We have nothing to worry about."

Lori's jaw dropped. "You're not serious, are you?" She gestured to the house. "Wait until they find all the bodies in the basement." She locked eyes with Elena, witnessing her mother's narrow gaze that she'd grown accustomed to. It meant death for the recipient of that stare. "What? Did you really believe we were just going to sweep this under the rug and forget about it? There's a basement filled with dead bodies and the murdering bastard who did it is lying dead with a letter opener in his neck." She shook her head. "You don't think there's going to be an investigation?"

"I know the Fire Chief, Lori. None of this is on us. It was Gerard who murdered all those women, not me and not you. Why should we be dragged through the mud for his deeds?" She looked like she was about to cry, but Lori knew Elena would never cry. Not in public. Not ever. It's a weakness she couldn't afford. Instead, she'll lash out with a sharp tongue.

Lori shook her head again. "It's always about your reputation. There are people in there who met their death under your roof, Elena. Their families deserve to know what happened to them. To give them some peace of mind and closure. You can't just toss them aside like they were nothing." She gritted her teeth, anger swelling in her throat. "And who's to say you didn't know what was happening?"

Now Elena was gritting her teeth, glaring at Lori. "Watch your tongue, young lady. I had no idea what he was doing."

"I find that very hard to believe. And here's another question, mother. How do you know they're all women unless you had a hand in it?"

Elena stepped forward and slapped Lori across the face. Hard. The slap stung like a bee, turning Lori's head, her cheekbone burning.

"Don't you talk that nonsense to me," scolded Elena, pointing her bony, trembling finger at Lori. Her face flushed with anger. Or is that shame? "I've had just about enough of you. Blaming me for what everyone else does. I'm tired of it."

Lori rubbed her cheek, glaring at Elena. She nodded. "I've had enough of you too, mother." She was on the brink of tears but refused to allow them to fall. She gritted her teeth and breathed forcefully through her nose with a grunt in her throat. "Consider this goodbye." She dropped the blanket off her shoulders, holding the notebook, looking for a way to get away from Elena.

"What're you doing?"

Lori snapped her attention to Elena. "Getting the hell out of here. Even if I have to walk. I don't care. I just can't be around you any longer." She stepped around Elena, looking for someone to help her with a ride out of town or at least to the train station.

"Where are you going?"

"You know where I'm going. The sooner I get there the better off I'll be." She walked towards the street. Elena on her heels.

"You can't go to the Hollow, Lori."

Lori could feel her mother's breath, the heat against her back.

"I can go wherever the hell I want."

"Don't you see what's going on? Didn't you see what happened? For Christ's sake Lori, you're playing right into their hands." Elena must have stopped because Lori no longer felt the heat. "You need to be done with Marc Saduj!" Elena hollered, her voice gruff and salty. Lori spun around, and Elena gestured to the notebook. "And burn that book. Its only purpose is to bring you back to Sleepy Hollow. To him, and to them." She was shaking her head. "This won't end well for you, Lori. Don't return to the Hollow. Everything I've done, I've done to protect you. You must understand that."

Lori craned her head. She thought she saw something. Some internal shame in Elena's eyes. A revelation of deeds and confessions covered up with rage. "You wrote the letter, didn't you? The one I thought was from Marc." Elena's jaw dropped. Lori looked at the notebook. "I compared Marc's writing in the book to the letter, and the handwriting is different. It's a very slight difference, but the difference is there. It was you, wasn't it?"

Elena looked at the notebook, then gritted her teeth and stood tall. "I did nothing of the sort. This must all end, Lori. If you don't go to the Hollow they can never win."

But Lori didn't hear what Elena said. She tuned out after the denial. Leave it to Elena to never admit her transgressions. "Stay out of my life, Elena. I'm done with you. All you've done is cause pain and heartache." She backed up. "Enjoy your life, mother. Not even your money can save you from what's coming." And she walked away. Walked onto the street where several patrol cars and an ambulance were waiting. Empty. They were all empty.

"You're not understanding me," Elena hollered after her. Lori scanned the street, hoping to see a car. "Did you not just witness the same thing I did? There're forces we're dealing with. Nefarious forces and they've got their eyes on you."

Lori looked at the house, her head shaking. "What I see is a murdering rapist who finally got what he deserved." She turned to Elena and the paramedic walking towards them. "And his demonic drug addicted whore who's trying to cover it up." Elena's jaw dropped. "Goodbye, mother." She flagged the paramedic and asked to be taken to the hospital. From there, she can get a cab to the train station. She'll be in Sleepy Hollow by midnight.

All she wanted to do was get away from her mother.

142

Marc was staring into Patriot's Park, his stomach churning, twisting. His stomach felt like there was a scolding hot rock sitting in his innards that kept twisting its serrated edges into his intestines. Felt like he was going to throw up while watching the police brigade move back and forth across the cordoned off park. Bystanders stood idly by. So many of them-too many to count-looked on as if whatever was contained in the park held the answers to life and death. And then there was the essence that weighed him down, pulling on his bones and turning the pain in his gut into overdrive.

He was sweating, despite the chilly winter afternoon and in spite of the fact that the sun was nowhere to be seen, covered in an icy gray overcast that ushered in a wave of bitter cold with a subtle, icy wind that chilled the bones. He noticed everyone around him seemed angry. All those bystanders had blood in their eyes as if whatever catastrophe had weaved its way into the Hollow boiled their blood. Marc had felt the same on his way here but now that he was closer to the park the sensation was more prominent as if the park itself pumped that noxious, rage-filled energy into the Hollow.

He was standing on the corner by the church, staring into the park. His three escorts surrounded him. Marc scanned their faces. Their eyes were filled with demonic delight. Sarah turned to him as if she knew he was staring at her. A sickly grin across her lips as if she was well aware of what was happening in the park.

"How marvelous isn't it?" she said. "Chaos always brings the finest people."

Marc's brow furrowed, staring at Sarah, crooked and suspicious. He noticed Hal and Andrew both carried the same grin. Marc turned to the person closest to him, an older lady wearing a long black overcoat. "What happened?"

She never looked at him, her hands buried in her coat pockets. "They found a dead body in the park. There are similarities to the murder from last summer."

Murder last summer?

He had no memory of a murder last summer. No memory at all.

"We should go." This was Sarah. She wrapped her arm around Marc's then led him through the standing crowd. "We can stand here all day and not see anything. No sense in wasting time."

Marc obeyed, weaving through the crowd with Sarah on his arm. He followed dutifully, as if he had no other option other than to obey her command. They were moving through the crowd when Father McKenzie walked through the church door to the outside. He looked worse for the wear. As if he'd seen hell arrive on his doorstep and could do nothing about it. He noticed Marc too, and his eyes widened as if he'd seen a ghost.

"Marc Saduj?" His voice was like a whisper that met Marc's ears.

Sarah pulled on his arm, but Marc let hers slip, stopping in his tracks to talk to Father McKenzie. Marc hadn't been to church since his father's passing. He had a difficult time standing in the same place where his father's heart attacked him one sunny Sunday morning. His father had gone to church every Sunday since before Marc was born. Sometimes his family was with him. Often, he came alone.

"Father McKenzie, did you see what happened?" Marc's question brought more than a few inquisitive stares as if the priest held the answers they were all looking for. Father McKenzie shook his head to the disappointment of all in attendance.

"No, nothing at all. It seems the police are as baffled as we are."

Marc noticed Father McKenzie's gaze drifted to his three escorts. It seemed like he tightened up. His mouth hung open. He looked like he saw a ghost. He locked eyes with Marc.

"I would love for you to attend services again, Marc. Seems like you could use God in your life."

It was Sarah who answered. "Seems like God didn't help the dead body in the park, Father. Why give in to control when you can ride the tide towards freedom?"

Marc wanted to respond, but no words arrived. He stood, stunned and reeling, watching Father McKenzie's startled stare. He felt irritable, as if some nagging sensation rifled into his brain. The priest's presence was irritating.

"Dark is the path of the righteous who walks without God."

"Darkness is nothing more than light turned inward. We are all the subjects of chaos. It is through chaos that change is born."

Father McKenzie's head shot back. Marc suspected he witnessed something he shouldn't have. Something that was odd with Sarah. Marc turned to her and her hateful gaze directed at the priest. He looked at Hal and Andrew and saw they carried the same. Father McKenzie addressed Marc directly.

"Perhaps you should take confession? I always have time for those in need." He gripped the door handle and opened the door. Marc's gaze drifted to the church when his stomach lurched. "Please, come in."

His eyes widened, staring into the church, witnessing the pews and stained-glass windows depicting Christ amid sacrifice. He gazed over the statue of the mother Mary when his blood turned hot in his veins, ramping up the heat in his already boiling skin. His hands were trembling, his lips too. All he wanted to do was walk into the church as if some invitation had been offered that he'd waited for an eternity to receive. He gripped the handrail to take the three steps to the church doors when his confusion returned tenfold. Every thought was drained from his mind. He had to think about where he was for a brief second. He felt mesmerized, as if some internal monster had awakened, draining his thoughts and his strength. He looked at Father McKenzie, standing with the door open and waiting for Marc.

His feet refused to move, standing with his hand on the cold handrail, paralyzed as if some dark hand had wrapped around his core and held him at bay. His every movement was a struggle against the bitter cold that nipped at his skin. He looked at the priest, and he wanted to speak. To agree to the invitation but no words arrived off his trembling lips. He pressed those lips together and swallowed his breath with a gasp.

"Come Marc," said the priest. "I believe it is all for the best."

Marc felt Sarah's fingers wrap around the crook of his arm. "We haven't time," she whispered. Then to Father McKenzie, "Some other time, *Father*." And she pulled Marc away, weaving through the crowd with Hal and Andrew on their heels. Marc looked over his shoulder at Father McKenzie. The priest crossed himself while staring at Sarah. He seemed nervous, his jaw trembling. Marc turned back to Sarah.

"Why did you do that? I wanted to talk to him."

Sarah turned abruptly as they stopped at the end of the street. "To confession?" She laughed, a slight chuckle in her throat. Marc could feel Hal and Andrew standing behind him. He could feel their breath on the nape of his neck. "Trust me," she said. "We aren't allowed in."

And she winked with a small, hidden grin tucked in the corner of her mouth.

"Not yet." Her voice was a faint whisper beneath her breath.

143

John kept the house in his line of sight as they walked through the woods. The further he walked, the heavier his legs seemed. Every step was a struggle. It felt like gravity pulling down on his core. John wondered if the others felt it, too. Not that he would ask them. John was completely aware he might have been set up. Maybe Logan isn't the nice kid across the street like John had hoped. Maybe they wanted to come to the abandoned house to dole out some much-needed punishment. John being the recipient of that punishment, although he came ready. If any of them try anything physical against him they'll be met with the end of the blackjack he had stored in his pocket. Better safe than sorry was John's excuse for taking the weapon.

On the way over, they saw a police cruiser in the woods. They weren't certain why the officer was in the middle of the woods, although John assumed he was supposed to be watching the house. Ironically, all the officer was doing was catching up on his sleep. They walked right by.

Now they were coming closer to the house. John looked at Michael and his heart jumped in his chest. Michael looked like a wolf waiting on his prey. Waiting for John to catch up with him. He felt surrounded, as if his personal escorts were the very people he should hide from. Logan and Chad were behind him. He could hear their footsteps crunching across the frozen ground.

"We're almost there," said Michael. John noticed he tossed a small rock into the air and caught it a second later. John stepped up onto a small incline, and the house came into full view. The clearing where the house was located was not more than twenty yards from where he and Michael were standing. "Looks as abandoned as it has been for years." John looked at Michael as he tossed his rock up again, catching it and eyeballing John through the corner of his eye. "You still sure about what you saw? Doesn't look like anyone's there."

John looked at the clearing, located the remains of the bonfire and pointed at it. "That's the bonfire from a few days ago." He turned to Michael. "If it's so abandoned, who started the fire?"

Michael shrugged. "My brother comes out here with his friends. Maybe it was them who started the fire. Doesn't mean there's a vampire in there."

Logan and Chad joined them on the incline. Chad was obviously out of breath, hunched over with his hands on his knees and breathing heavy. Logan stood, eyeballing the house.

"Asthma?" said Michael to Chad, who nodded feverishly. "Did you bring your inhaler?"

Chad labored through his breathing. He looked like he was coaching himself to take steady breaths. "Forgot it." He looked pale and sickly. John noticed he was sweating.

"Sit down and try to breathe easy." This was Logan. He looked visibly concerned, and before anyone could second Logan's instruction, Chad sat down.

Michael tossed the rock up again and caught it. "Okay, heart eater, what's the plan?"

John noticed Logan's stare darted in his direction. John hated that damn phrase, but what he wasn't going to do was start a fight with Michael. It was best to let it go.

John looked at the house and swallowed his breath. "Well, we're here, so let's start with the bonfire then make our way to the house." He turned to Logan. "See if we can find someone. Or something. Some proof of the murder."

"Like we're some sort of children's detective agency," said Michael. He rolled his tongue inside his mouth. "Yeah, I can deal with that." He stepped forward, moving tree branches away from his path while walking down the incline towards the clearing.

John turned to Chad and Logan. Chad with his hunched over labored breathing and Logan with an expression that revealed he may not want to go any further. He addressed Chad. "Why don't you stay here and be a lookout. If you see anyone coming, pick up that branch and hit that tree three times. Three times and then repeat. If you don't see us, start screaming."

Chad nodded. "Got it," he said between breaths. "Three times, then repeat. Start screaming if I have to."

"Perfect." John then looked at Logan. "You ready?"

Logan looked at the house, then turned to John and gave a quick head nod.

"Okay. Let's go."

John walked down the incline to the edge of the woods where he stopped to join Michael. Michael's gaze was fixed on the clearing and the house. Logan stepped behind them.

"You feel that?" Michael said. John looked at him. His eyes were open wide as if he was staring at a prize he'd always wanted, anticipating the moment when it was in his hands. He turned to John. "Feels like… excitement."

He walked into the clearing. John watched him go as Logan stepped beside him. They locked eyes. Logan was obviously nervous, his stare confirmed it. John provided a reassuring smile before joining Michael.

Although the moment he stepped into the clearing every bone in his body screamed for him to run.

To run and never look back.

144

"What should I take from you now, Ian?" Wren stood in front of his beloved. Ian stared through a narrow slit in his one good eye. Lost and weary, his eye rolled to the back of his skull. "Not your other eye, of course. It's best for you to see what is coming." Wren's eyes glinted when he cocked his brows. "Helplessness is a tool best paired with truth."

Ian no longer attempted to remove his restraints. No longer cried or hollered or wailed through his gag. His skin was ghostly pale, his bones prominent beneath his emaciated skin. Eye sunken into his skull and looked bruised and battered because of the dark rings around his eye sockets. Wren knew he was dying, dying of starvation and dehydration. Wren refused for his prize to die from a loss of blood, but he knew there was no way for the human body to outlast starvation or dehydration. After five days with no water, the human mind turns monstrous and primitive. But eventually, without food, the human mind becomes ravenous. Wren grinned at the thought of Ian turning cannibal on his friends, devouring their flesh raw. Such a pleasant sight that would be. Ian is like a pet. Wren could see him by his side, crouched down on all fours as Wren stroked his ginger hair like a dog.

He craned his head, assessing Ian when the thought hit him. Wren clucked his tongue, studying Ian's face before turning to the fire where he had placed an iron rod. He glanced around at his victims, standing shackled and helpless with that same emaciated presence. Cheryl and Nikita were slumped in their shackles, their knees buckled, hanging from their restraints. Briefly, he wondered if they had perished, but only briefly. He could still feel their hearts beating with a thick intermittent drum.

Wren gripped the knife off the stone slab then turned to Ian. "For today, your nose, Ian. Tomorrow…" He stepped closer, snatching Ian's forehead with an iron grip. "Either your teeth or your toes, I'm not certain which. Not yet anyway."

Ian's body jerked inward as if he could disappear through the wall behind him. His body twitched, attempting to move his head away from Wren's knife. Wren gripped Ian's gingered hair tight in his palm, then carved into Ian's nose from the nostril up to the bridge. Ian's hands trembled in their shackles, his lips closed tight, his head shuddering in Wren's palm as blood flowed from his nose across Wren's hand and down across the gag, dripping to the stone floor. Wren twisted the knife around to the other nostril and, with a quick flick of his wrist, dragged the scalpel around then squeezed the nose off his face, pinching it between his fingers, sliding it off the skull. It came off with a wet suctioned squish. Blood ejected from the severed appendage, raining across Ian's mouth and gag. His head jerked back and forth. It sounded like he was suffocating, gagging on his own blood. Wren removed his stare from the nose pinched between his fingers to look at Ian. He was choking on the blood that was pouring from his severed nose.

"Just swallow it, Ian. Get drunk on your own blood." He thrust his open palm into Ian's chest. The sudden jolt widened Ian's mouth beneath the gag, and he swallowed with a gasp. "There you have it." Wren eyeballed the substantial blood flow, then turned and walked over to the firepit. He dropped the nose in the fire, and the portal glowed a dark violet. Wren grinned at the scene, gazing at the light over his head before he took the iron rod from the fire, turned around and approached Ian. "Wouldn't want you to die from blood loss, Ian." He pressed the rod to Ian's severed nose, cauterizing the wound as a deathly wail escaped Ian's throat. The wound hissed. The blood bubbled and boiled. The walls shook from his scream. The ground rumbled beneath their feet. He kept the rod pressed against Ian's face, inhaling the scent of burning skin and blood like an aphrodisiac.

When he was finished, he stepped back to admire his work. "Now that is a work of art." And he laughed, laughed that conniving blood curdling evil from his throat. "I cannot wait, Ian… to eat your heart."

Wren turned and returned the iron rod to the firepit, then gripped the gallon sized water jug with an attached tube and pump from off the floor.

"Going to need you all clean and pristine for the master," he said. "Can't have you all dying before your sacrifice."

He went to Ian first. "Here's your daily dose of water."

145

John stopped cold in his tracks when a scream echoed into the woods. "Did you hear that?" There was a unique possibility that the scream originated from the house.

Michael stood beside him, with Logan on their heels. They all froze, the echo from the scream reverberating in their chests.

"Maybe this isn't such a good idea." This was Michael, his voice cracked and weary. John looked at him, his breath pluming over his lips like vapor.

Logan replied, "It's probably just a bird or something. Or some old lady fell and can't get up and she's screaming her head off."

The moment was thick with tension and John noticed how quiet it became, how eerily quiet.

"I don't think so," said Michael, and John could see how frightened he was. How petrified and stuck, as if his feet were frozen to the ground.

"Why don't you stay with Chad?" John gestured to the woods. "It's better to have two lookouts, anyway."

"I don't think you should go either. I mean, what's the point? To prove there's someone in the house?" Michael backed up a step. "I think we just found out that you're spot on right about that one." He looked at the house when John witnessed Michael shiver from his neck to his toes. "Maybe we should call the police?"

Now Logan turned to Michael, a surprised stare across his face. Neither of them expected Michael would wimp out. "You're lame, my man. Police don't do shit, and you know it. Besides…" He gestured to John. "You already called the police, didn't you?"

"Yes."

"See, and they did nothing." He shook his head. "The police come to investigate after the crime is done, not before. They need evidence, and that's what we're here to find."

Michael backed up again. "I'm sorry guys, but this just doesn't seem right to me." He looked at John. "I'll be with Chad."

John gave an acknowledging head nod. "Okay. Same thing. Hit that tree three times if you see someone coming."

And with that Michael nodded and turned around, trooping across the snow to the woods.

"I will say this, kid, you've got balls." Logan turned to John. "Didn't think it was possible, but here we are." And he grinned with a cock of his brow. "What's next?"

"Well, Detective Carver already checked the bonfire."

"Yeah, no dead bodies though. Maybe they buried it somewhere." He turned to the house. "Could be anywhere. Where do you want to start?"

John turned to the house, too. "Honestly…" He looked at Logan. "I have no idea."

Logan stepped forward, assessing the house. After a moment, he turned to John. "Well, when all else fails.

"Try the front door."

146

He could feel a rumble in his stomach as if some internal catastrophe had just taken hold. Marc rounded the corner and stopped in his tracks. His old apartment building hovered over him. He looked up to the roof where a dark cloud stretched across the building and wrapped its demonic hand around it. It seemed out of place, as if the building were the lone recipient of the dark cloud. Meant just for his building.

Standing and staring at his old home, Marc licked his dry cracked lips and tasted dried blood on his tongue. He could feel the cracks across his lips, like a sting across his mouth, the stiff wind like a squeeze to summon pain. Felt a twinge in his hand and when he looked down, he could see his hands were chapped and red. His fingertips were gnawed down to nothing. He had cracks in his skin across his thumbs. Looked like a cavern had been torn open, his skin burning cold and bleeding. Noticed his knuckles had tiny cuts across them. Marc was certain that in the days to come, they, too, will be bleeding. His scar itched like a madman out for revenge.

"Are we going in or just standing out here in the cold?" This was Hal and Marc noticed his three escorts all laughed at the comment.

He paid them no mind and walked across the street to the front door that he swung open then stepped into the small foyer by the mailboxes and intercom and the locked door that led inside. He pushed the buzzer for Mrs. Leiter's apartment. He wished he had his key, but that thought never manifested and now that he was thinking about it, he wondered exactly where his key was. Marc pressed his head against the cold glass door. The hall was empty, devoid of life. He pushed the bell again. Three times.

Nothing.

"Maybe they went to watch all the commotion like the rest of this godforsaken town." Hal again. Marc could see him reflected in the door's glass. He was holding the front door open, standing behind Marc as if ready to pounce at a moment's notice.

Marc stood tall, pushing the doorbell with a fever. "C'mon Mrs. Leiter… open the damn door."

But no one came. All he could see was an empty hall and the stairs he'd taken his entire life. Barren and cold.

"No one's coming." Marc turned to Hal and his cold eyes. "We should cut our losses." Hal looked up at the overcast sky. "Sun won't be up for much longer. This time of year, night comes a lot faster."

Marc had no reply. He just stood there, eyeballing Hal and his devilish grin. Turned to Sarah and Andrew standing behind Hal on the sidewalk, talking in hushed tones and watching Marc through the corners of their eyes.

Andrew said, "So, where to captain?" And Sarah laughed.

If he could, he'd ditch them, but Marc was beginning to understand that no matter where he roamed his escorts would be by his side as if their purpose was to stay his hand and drive him towards a finality he was unaware of. His stomach lurched and roiled and contracted, his liver was in dire straits. He needed a drink, that much was certain. He could see the green liquid now-the absinthe-and he licked his dry cracked lips.

Hal craned his head, staring at him. "Well, captain?" A big grin across Hal's lips. "The man asked where to?"

Marc looked through the glass door to the stairs as his jaw rumbled, gnashing his teeth. "Wait here," he said, pushing past Hal. He walked hurriedly to the end of the building.

"Where are you going?"

This was Andrew. Marc eyeballed him before disappearing around the building. He knew they were following him, hot on his heels. He rounded the building to the back where a small alley was flanked by a green fence and his apartment building. There was a wooden crate next to the fence. He took it and propped it beneath the fire escape. Marc stood on it and gripped the cold steel ladder, pulling it down then ascended, the steel's bitter cold numbing his hands as he climbed. Saw Hal standing on the sidewalk, watching him. Turned around on the fire escape and climbed to the next floor. Saw Sarah standing next to Hal, the same demonic glare stained in her eyes. Marc swallowed the breath he didn't realize he was holding. Kept climbing, two more floors up when he saw Andrew was now in attendance. All three of his escorts were watching his every move as he climbed to the top floor and paused, returning their stares. Heavy breath, he swallowed with a gasp. His heart thundered in his chest. The wind nipped at his skin, his hands like ice, and he felt a rumble in his stomach and pain wrench across his liver. Marc turned and craned his head to see inside his apartment. He tried the window, and it slid open with relative ease.

As he climbed in, he noticed his escorts were standing beneath the fire escape, staring up at him. He slammed the window shut, his hands trembling cold and aching, and locked it in place. Looked down and they were looking up with those sickly grins.

Marc stepped away from the window and breathed a sigh of relief before he took a good look around, realizing it was the first time he'd been alone in months. He felt empty, like a giant hole had erupted in his chest.

The front door creaked open with a soft ache. The door looked heavy but opened like it was hollow. John swallowed his breath, looking in. Logan was standing just off the front porch, watching him.

"What do you see?" asked Logan, craning his head to look inside the door.

John shook his head. "Not much," he whispered, then looked up to the top floor windows. He had a feeling he was being watched. Unfortunately, in the daylight, he couldn't see inside the windows or if anyone was standing by the window.

"What do you want to do?"

John gazed through the open doorway. From what he could see, there wasn't much to see. The room looked barren except for a red leather high-back chair with a small side table next to it set up in front of a fireplace that he was certain hadn't seen a fire in over a century.

"Let's just go in. Take it one room at a time."

John noticed an anxious crack in Logan's voice. Noticed how quiet it was, as if that scream from earlier had frightened off every wild animal in the area. He couldn't hear anything other than the slow-moving subtle wind breathing against his ear. Logan gestured for him to walk inside, and John turned to the open door and did just that, taking a step in. Then another. And another, and he was in what he assumed was a living room. There was a dilapidated kitchen on his left and a long hallway on his right with a staircase at the beginning of the hall. The room he was in was large and open. The floorboards were uneven and crude. Blown out windows on the far wall looked out to the bonfire and snow covered clearing with the western woods behind the clearing.

It was dark in the house, a result of the overcast sky. Shadows crept across the walls.

Can vampires come out if there's no sun showing?

"Doesn't look bad at all."

John turned to see Logan standing in the open doorway, scanning across the room. He looked at John, who pressed his finger to his lips.

"So, what's next?" Logan whispered.

John looked at him and shrugged. "Search the house."

Logan nodded his head, thinking. "Do we have a plan on where to start?"

John rolled his tongue inside his mouth. "I didn't think that far ahead."

Logan stepped forward. "Well, we're looking for a vampire, right?" He turned to John, who nodded. "And its daytime right now, so what do vampires do when it's daytime?"

"They sleep."

"Exactly. So, let's look around for a coffin." He looked over the house. "I wonder if there's a basement." He studied the floorboards. "Usually there's a basement in houses like this. Or at least a crawl space. Right?"

"Makes sense."

Logan turned towards the hall. "You ready? We don't have a lot of time until the sun goes down." He turned to John. "Wouldn't want to give the vampire a chance to catch us after nightfall. That probably wouldn't be good at all."

"Agreed."

"You search down here. I'll take the stairs and see if I can find proof that there are people living here." He looked at John. "Let's meet back down here in ten. If we don't find anything, I'd say this was a failed mission."

John nodded his agreement.

"See you soon." And with that, Logan took the stairs up leaving John alone.

He wasn't certain, but he felt like he couldn't move. Hadn't moved since he walked inside. Standing in the barren dilapidated house with the wind creaking the foundation, he forced himself to take a step towards the hall.

All the while, he was certain he could feel his mother's presence telling him to run and never look back.

Wren was staring at the ceiling while standing in front of a weak and weary Savannah as she coughed, gagging on the water he just pumped into the corner of her mouth. He was gritting his teeth, assessing who on earth was in his house.

Couldn't be his host with his three escorts. He would have felt their arrival. No, there was someone in his house who had no right to be here. Savannah gasped, and he looked at her. Her eyes rolled in her skull. Her wrists were bleeding. Bleeding from the restraints that cut into her skin. Bleeding because she couldn't stand any longer and her weight was pulling down on her wrists; her legs buckled at the knees. Her eyes were sunken into her skull; her short curly hair matted across her face.

"No worries, Savannah." Wren stepped away, maintaining his focus on the ceiling, listening to footsteps traverse the floor above.

Police?

Nah, they would have stormed into the house loud and obnoxious like. There would have been a horde of them rushing through the front door but from what Wren could hear there were two, maybe three people above him, their footsteps soft and light.

Children!

Wren licked his lips and turned to Savannah, spraying her down as she turned her head against the wall. He was aware she was freezing, perhaps freezing to death. He noticed earlier she was running a fever. Best to ramp it up. Sometimes a fever will bring hallucinations, which excited him to no end. Fear escalates when the tortured recipient is hallucinating. He grinned, thinking about it. Thinking about tonight's festivities, especially with the ghost demons in attendance.

He wondered if the master would unleash more of them tonight. He hoped so. The three so far have proved their worth. They were calm and calculated and didn't miss a beat. He couldn't wait to unleash all the master's ghost demons into the Hollow. Couldn't wait for the day when they are released across the world, turning the minds of humanity into a frenzied state of confusion where fear, evil, and hate washes across the planet, drenching humanity in utter darkness with the master and Wren at the helm.

Plus, he was excited to see who the ghost demons brought into the fold tonight. More sacrifices were needed to break open the portal. The days were running down to the ultimate finality.

Another step from above. They were moving to the stairs now. Wren looked at Savannah, wet and tired and weary and depleted. He placed the water jug on the floor then looked around. He took the knife off the slab then went to greet his guests.

Marc hadn't been in his apartment in months, but everything looked the same. There was a glass on the small side table next to his recliner with a stain of dried scotch on the bottom that apparently was growing fungus. The glass was stained with a white web of mold.

He had wanted to talk to Mrs. Leiter and ask a few questions about his mother, but when she never answered all he wanted to do was get away from his escorts. Now that he's done that, he didn't know what to do. And they were still standing outside, waiting for him. He was certain they were there, but he refused to look to confirm his suspicions. They were creepy, those three, sending shivers down his spine every time he looked into their eyes. As if they knew information Marc had yet to discover.

Marc looked around his apartment. He felt nothing, no sense of nostalgia, no coming home sensation. Everything looked dead and ancient as if they belonged to someone else or were from another life, or from a movie he had once watched. He felt no connection to anything, but still that depressive feeling washed over him. He could feel it like a painful wrenching through his chest, a dark abyss where hurt and pain squeezed its dark hand around his heart.

Shadows crept across the walls; the apartment was growing darker by the second. Heard a creaking like metal being crushed into oblivion as if the shadows were groaning from their ethereal plane of existence, creeping along the walls towards the hall. Marc scanned across the walls to the hall where his father was standing in the doorway to the master bedroom.

"Dad?" Marc stepped towards the hall and craned his head. The shadows rolled across the walls towards his father.

"It's in the drink, son." His father's voice faded as the shadows washed over him and he vanished.

Marc remained standing, staring into what had been his parents' bedroom. The room then glowed with a red beam of burning light. He knew what was waiting for him in the bedroom. More of his mother. More ridicule and shame.

You were right to do what you did.

The voice in his head. He knew who it belonged to. The man in black.

She would never have stopped. Think of all the years of suffering you saved yourself from.

"Get out of my head!" Marc screamed.

A laugh then, goading and manipulative, echoing between his ears.

Why are you here, Marc? What brings you back to your home?

He looked down, his eyes lost. "I don't know. I just wanted to get away."

So, you came here? Another laugh. *How vile. You came back to me.*

"I don't have any other place to go." His voice was a childish whine. He pushed on his scar, rubbing it back and forth.

Seems the Hollow has turned its back on you, Marc. You felt it, didn't you? The change in the tide. It's only a matter of time until they fold into my embrace.

"I can't do anything about it."

That laugh again. He could hear it booming inside the walls. *How right you are.*

Marc didn't notice it at first, but he was rolling the threads from the rope around his wrist.

"I just want to be alone."

We are one now, Marc. I am always with you.

He looked at the rope around his wrist and stopped twirling the threads, staring blank faced and lost at the rope.

The bond is forever, Marc. The consequence of desperation.

"You tricked me," he said. "And now people are suffering because of it."

You got what you wanted.

"I'm a prisoner. You turned me into a prisoner in my home. I can't get rid of you."

And yet all is for the best, knowing your precious Lori lives and only because of my *power. The rest is simply the aftermath of good intentions.*

Marc ran his hand across his face, gripping his jaw and squeezing.

I know every thought you have. All that you see, I too see. All that you feel I feel. Just like I know your stomach is burning. How your insides feel depleted and dry.

Marc felt how his head moved on its own accord. How his body moved with it. Staring at the fungus crusted glass.

Drink, Marc.

Magically, the glass became filled to the brim with absinthe; the fungus dried up instantly, leaving nothing more than a clean drink. The green glow shimmered in the glass with sparkles from the fae dancing in the liquid.

Settle your nerves a bit. Clear your head for a while.

He pursed his lips as his stomach twisted. His liver begged for the drink, burning in his solar plexus.

A toast to Lori. A toast to a better life. And a toast for better days.

Marc stepped to the table, staring down at the glass, numb to his core. Numb but shaking. Trembling in fact, shaky and nervous, he couldn't think of anything other than the drink in front of him.

His hand reached for the glass and picked it up. The sweet scent of absinthe burned in his nostrils. He gasped out a breath, his lips trembling, his jaw quivering.

Drink my beloved and all the confusion will wash away. Allow me in, my precious host. Let me take the helm and relieve you of your conscience. Just for a little while. I'll take away all the fear and confusion.

All the pain and hurt. Wash it away like magic. Let you feel vibrant once again. Without a care for the world. Without having to say you're sorry. Just enough, let me be beneath the surface, washing away the past. Let's paint the town red tonight, my precious Marc. No more fear or hurt or pain. Allow the drink to wash away all your fears and kill off loneliness with an iron fist. Let us give the Hollow something to think about in the morning. This town is yours Marc Saduj and I... I am always with you.

Marc whispered, "And I with you," before he took a gulp from the glass. The sensation was immediate. Marc was already drunk the moment the faeries touched his lips.

No more hiding, Marc. No more locking yourself in a dark cauldron of fear.

He already felt different. As if he could tackle the entire world in one fell swoop. Marc gasped across his lips, holding the glass like his last lifeline. His eyes were wet and burning. His throat was dry and chalky. He could feel the warmth in his stomach. It felt like coming home.

That's a good boy, Mr. Saduj. Tonight, let me show you something new. It is time for you to begin to see!

Marc stared into the glass, following the green liquid that swirled within. He finished it with one large gulp.

Wake up this town with a push. Tonight, we begin our calculated desolation of hope.

His eyes were closed, his mind was swimming, his thoughts drifting. Gone.

Let's play a game.

A knock on his door. Marc knew who it was. He didn't even have to think about it.

We'll call it… catch me if you can.

Marc opened the door to his three escorts standing in the doorway. He grinned at their presence.

I can't wait for you to see what we have in store for them.

He didn't find much. After John walked to the end of the hall he went through the door on the left, which brought him into a hallway with six empty rooms. There was nothing in them but dust, dirt, and mold. The floorboards seemed like they could buckle under the lightest possible weight. He then walked back into the main hall and crossed the hall, opening the opposite door and when he stepped into the large open room, he thought he'd been swallowed. Considering it was daytime outside, the fact that the room was bathed in darkness turned John's blood cold. Even with the overcast sky hovering over the house there should be some light in the room, considering there were windows scattered across the walls.

He didn't do too much searching, either. Just walked in and stopped cold with a sensation of familiarity as if he'd been in the room before when a bright yellow light washed over his vision. John snapped his eyes shut, took a deep breath, and then opened his eyes, confused over what he was witnessing. There were three stately gentlemen talking and drinking, donning clothes he assumed had to be from a long time ago. A woman sat on a couch on the far side of the room. Her white gown soaked in blood. Her eyes were black and dead. The stately gentlemen were talking as if she didn't exist, the content of their conversation faded in the backdrop and difficult to decipher. Their skin was pale, with veins that looked like spiderwebs across their cheeks. The room was immaculate in his vision. Golden, the furniture was pristine as if it were new. The walls beamed with light from the many candelabras scattered across the walls.

John snapped out of his haze with a shake of his head, erasing the vision like an etch-a-sketch, returning to the dark drab of current reality. Confused, he hoped Logan was having better luck. He could hear his footsteps creaking across the floor above. John stepped into the hallway, his lips pressed tight as the cold air nipped at his skin. His nose was wet and nasally.

He expected to find more. Or at least something that would indicate there was a vampire living in the house. But there was nothing. No furniture. No clothes. The only items on the entire first floor were the red leather chair and the table next to it.

But vampires sleep during the day. If he was looking for a coffin, it had to be hidden somewhere in the house. He looked down at the floor. *Maybe there's a basement?*

If there was, he hadn't seen a door or any sign of a crawl space beneath the floorboards.

Think, John. Think. It's got to be here somewhere. I know what I saw. I'm not...

He swallowed his breath.

Crazy!

The thought of his father passed through his mind. He hadn't thought about him in a day's age. After all that happened, John had simply let it pass. Swallowed it down and forgot about it, but now the door to the past was open and that reality was washing over him, pulling him down into oblivion. He closed his eyes and tried to think of his mother.

I wish you were here.

Footsteps then rushed down the steps, and his heartbeat caught in his chest. His breath hitched back into his lungs. Waiting to see who was coming down the steps when Logan stepped onto the first floor. He turned to John.

"You've got to see this." His eyes were wide as if he'd just found Pandora's box. "There's definitely someone living here."

Wren slipped onto the ground floor through the front door. He'd come up through the hidden cellar to the outside. At first, he wasn't certain who was in his house, but after careful inspection what he knew most was that whoever it was they were not the police. More than likely, a few teenagers were making use of the abandoned house in the middle of the woods.

And that fact heated Wren's blood into a boil. How dare they set foot on his property? He had the right mind to cut them into tiny little pieces. His mouth salivated from the thought. Young hearts always tasted better. There were fewer pollutants coursing through the veins of the young. Their blood had yet to be tainted from decades of processed foods, medications and poor air quality that stain the blood over the years with disease. But Wren knew not to rock the boat. Choosing wayward adults was one thing, but cutting up a child was a completely different story. Not that he wouldn't indulge if he could, but a local child gone missing may bring the heat a little too close for comfort and with the master's plan on the verge of manifestation, Wren knew it was best to ignore his appetite.

But what should he do? Scare the living shit out of them? Or choose to stand as a law-abiding citizen protecting his property from strangers? Either way, he hoped he could soothe his anger considering he was already gnashing his teeth just thinking about the intrusion. Sometimes Wren's anger got the better of him. And when that happens, he goes off the rails. It's how he got caught so many years ago. You've got to keep your emotions in check. That much was true. And if you can't respond appropriately to the anger, you're a slave to it.

He closed his eyes, seeing himself bathing in the blood of whoever was in his house. The thought brought ecstasy to his hot, pumping blood, sending flutters of pleasure rippling across his skin. That anger was barreling down now. He could feel it like a pressure cooker on the verge of a catastrophe. He knew they were upstairs. Wren had seen them when he was watching through the front door. He saw their legs move up the steps. His hands now clenched into fists, Wren opened his eyes. He could hear their hearts beating with a thunderous boom. He could taste those hearts on his palate as he ran his tongue over his teeth then stepped to the staircase.

His anger fueled his walk.

Everyone's got something to work on.

The hospital was alive with commotion, chaos, and mayhem. Apparently, there was a ten-car pileup on the freeway and ambulances were bringing in patients two at a time.

Lori sat inside the emergency room hallway. When she first arrived, they gave her a bed but asked her to move after the accident was announced over the intercom. They needed the bed for those who were on their way and considering Lori's injuries weren't life threatening, the nurse asked if she was okay with taking a seat in the hall. Of course, Lori obliged. She couldn't care less about her burns or scars or the fact that her jaw was throbbing from Gerard's bite. All she wanted to do was leave. A task she would have jumped at if she wasn't told there was a police officer requesting to speak to her about the fire.

A conversation Lori wasn't looking forward to. Considering when it was all said and done, it was Lori who started the fire, and it was Lori who drove a letter opener through Gerard's throat. She wondered if she'd be able to leave the hospital at all. She also wondered what Elena had told them. Her mother was so bent on Lori never returning to the Hollow she wouldn't be surprised if Elena told the police about Lori's arson and murder. At least, she wouldn't be surprised if that's how Elena explained it to the police. Elena could even use the fact that Lori was just released from the hospital after an apparent suicide attempt to her advantage, using the incident to explain Lori's dire state of mind. The end goal would be for Lori to spend her time behind bars and not somewhere in the Hollow looking for Marc. Now that would be a true show of power if there ever was one. Power over her own daughter. No, Lori wouldn't be surprised at all.

She crossed her arms, feeling the burns across her arms, then uncrossed them and kept her hands on her legs. Her arms were draped in gauze and an ace bandage that stretched from her wrists past her elbows. A burn cream beneath the gauze, watching nurses and doctors provide medical attention to the wounded. Marc's notebook was on the table next to her. She wouldn't allow it out of her sight.

"Ms. Francon?"

Lori looked up at the nurse standing beside the nurse's station. An older woman she placed at about her mother's age. Lori cleared her throat before she answered. "Yes."

The nurse cocked her head. "The police are here. They're waiting for you in exam room one-eleven." And she smiled as she slid a folder off the counter and hugged it. "Whenever you're ready."

Lori nodded her head before the nurse went on with her work and Lori scanned across the emergency room. There was so much commotion. She heard doctors giving CPR to one of the victims from the accident. Listened to the steady and unrelenting beep signaling the end of the person's life. Lori pulled the beanie over her ears, then stood up and slid the notebook off the table, holding it close to her chest. She eyeballed the numbers for the exam rooms. One-eleven was close to the door to the emergency entrance. She looked around. Saw a winter jacket hanging off a chair in the nurse's station and raised her head, scanning across the emergency room again. She knew no one was watching. Most of the staff were busy trying to save the man's life; others were tending to more victims. Everyone was distracted. Lori took the jacket then padded to the exit, hurried yet inconspicuous, slipping the jacket on as she walked past room one-eleven where she glimpsed the two policemen waiting.

And Lori Francon walked out of the emergency room. Walked into the waiting area-also packed to the max-then through the front door. As luck would have it there was a cab outside the main entrance. Lori stopped when she saw a couple emerge from the cab. The husband or boyfriend or whoever he was helped a pregnant woman out. Lori dipped her head down to see the cabbie and gestured for a ride. He responded with a wink.

She stepped to the door and held it open. "Best of luck to you," she told the woman whose stare revealed she was not ready for the pain she was going through. Lori forced a reassuring smile before taking her seat in the cab.

"Where to?" asked the cabbie.

Lori eyeballed the front door, waiting to see if the police came walking out looking for her.

"Mam?"

No one was coming. No one was there. Lori turned to the cabbie. "Train station," she said, sitting back and cradling Marc's notebook, keeping it close to her heart.

The cabbie cocked his head and clucked his tongue, clicked on the meter and put the car in drive. "And here we go."

Lori closed her eyes as the cab moved away from the hospital. She felt like she climbed to the top of Mt. Everest and now that it was over she could breathe a sigh of relief, leaving the past behind for good while walking into the future.

John was staring at a painting of a heart inside a tree trunk. He thought his own heart had stopped the moment he laid eyes on it. Felt paralyzed, standing there with his jaw hanging open. All he could see was the heart.

"What do you think it means?" Logan's voice was calm, compassionate.

John had to admit he found current circumstances ironic. His father ate hearts and for the briefest moment an image passed through John's mind of his father gnawing on the bloodied organ. He closed his mouth and swallowed, pressing his lips together.

He was wrong to want to come here. John stood in the middle of the room, mesmerized by the painting. Couldn't think. Couldn't catch a single thought. Paralyzed. As if he'd been hit over the head and all he could do was stand there, stunned and frozen.

"Hey, are you okay?"

Logan's voice called to him from the far depths of consciousness. As if he were calling John through a long tunnel, his voice echoing across the tunnel walls to John's ears.

It seemed like reality was crashing down around him. This house. This room and that damn painting clawed at the past and brought it center stage. After his sister was murdered. After his father was arrested. And after his mother put a bullet between her eyes, Grandpa Claude was all he had left, but he never talked about what had happened. Most of what John knew he had discovered by watching the news, and only when he could sneak in a few minutes behind Grandpa Claude's back because he was told not to watch. That he'd hear things that simply were not true.

"Can't trust the news anymore," Grandpa Claude had told him. "Ever since the news became about ratings, everything they toss on the screen is meant to keep you wanting more. They can take an entire speech and highlight one simple half sentence to prove their narrative. It's all mind control."

But that didn't give John the complete story and Claude was always tightlipped about it. Maybe he just wanted to put the past behind him? Maybe he didn't want his grandson growing up knowing his father was a murdering son of a bitch. Or perhaps he couldn't face the truth, living to forget what had happened by forcing it into the dark recesses of his mind so he could move on with life with his head in the sand?

John didn't know and all he did know was that he regretted coming to the house. The vision he had downstairs was one thing, but this, this heart in the tree trunk, was completely different. As if he was meant to see it. Some cosmic force across the universe, a natural intelligence existing in the folds between time and space, brought him here to face the truth.

Logan put his hand on John's shoulder. "It's okay," he said. "Let's check the third floor."

John was blinking rapidly, staring at Logan.

"There's nothing else on this floor, anyway." He walked to the door and John watched him, wide eyed and stunned. Logan turned around. "Come on."

A peculiar thing happened at that moment. A flash of white light jumped out of the dark hall and wrapped around Logan.

"What are you doing, little boys?"

He heard the voice but saw no one. All he could see was Logan wrapped in white light, struggling to free himself. He noticed Logan was staring at him, wide-eyed and fearful.

"I said, what are you doing in my home?"

It took him a second to realize the person was talking to him. His vision came into focus. Behind the white light was John's vampire and he had his arms around Logan. The vampire that was staring into his soul. He slammed Logan against the wall and John's heart jumped. His entire body jumped.

"Get off of me," Logan whined from the back of his throat when the vampire gripped his throat then lifted him off his feet. Logan was struggling to breathe, his feet kicking empty air.

Before he knew it, John had the blackjack out of his pocket. He raced over to the vampire and slapped him across the head. His hands immediately went to his head, releasing his grip on Logan's throat. John hit him again and saw blood fly across the room when the vampire's arm crashed against his chest. He hit the ground hard. His head rocked against the floor, but his nervousness and fear retreated, and he shuffled to his feet despite the pain in his back and neck.

He gripped Logan and hauled him out of the room. How, he wasn't certain, but his strength was immense. John looked over his shoulder as they raced through the door. Saw the vampire with blood across his skull leering at him and John's heart jumped in his chest.

Logan stumbled down the steps, crashing into the floor below.

"*Come on*," John hollered, picking him up by the shoulders. The vampire was on the top step, racing toward them.

They scuttled out of the hall into the living room then bolted through the front door. Logan stumbled through the snow. John slammed into his back, gripped his waist then pushed him forward and they both took off running like a bat out of hell. His breath hitched in his throat, but he saw the woods and picked up his pace.

He didn't want to look over his shoulder any longer.

He knew his vampire was watching.

Kept moving. Kept watching the trees as if they were moving towards him and not the other way around. They raced into the woods and kept going until Logan stopped to catch his breath. John ran a few more feet but stopped too. Looking around while catching his breath he could see they were safe in the woods. He looked back at the house and saw the vampire in the front door, watching them.

John turned to Logan, and Logan looked at him.

"That was crazy," said Logan. "I guess we just met your vampire."

John stepped forward, nodding, his breathing heavy. His heart was racing. Logan seemed to have calmed down, although his hands were visibly shaking.

"Thank you." Logan was staring at John. "I thought he was going to kill me."

John cocked his head, staring at Logan who seemed like he was on the verge of a panic attack. John looked at his hands. Empty. Looked back at the house and noticed the vampire was no longer in the door. John looked all around, assessing.

"What is it?" Logan said, confused.

"I left the blackjack."

Logan shrugged. "So what?"

John looked at the house again. "It's got my father's name on it."

His head was bleeding. Wren kept pressure on the wound, ceasing the blood flow while gnashing his teeth. His anger raged like a demon out for vengeance.

He never expected such a result. He wondered what that little son of a bitch hit him with. His head felt like a cracked eggshell throbbing across his skull.

The master will not be pleased. Not pleased at all.

His headache was in full bloom. Wren scuttled back up the steps, gripping the banister all the way up.

What were they doing in Marc's room? Why had they come? It was apparent to Wren that those two little shits didn't come here because they thought the house was abandoned. People don't bring weapons when they know a house is abandoned. No, this was a planned event. But planned for what? And why? They knew someone was in the house and had come prepared for battle.

He stepped onto the second floor and stopped. Pulling his hand away from his head, he saw blood on his palm. The sight of his own blood turned that anger into a full-on rage. Wren had the right mind to race into the woods and rip out their hearts. He'd watched them from the front door until they disappeared into the woods. Would they come back was his question, although, after such an incident, a recurrence was more than unlikely. He was certain he scared them off.

But the little one was weighing on him. When Wren first stepped into the room it seemed as if the smaller of the two was mesmerized. In the throes of some inter-dimensional consciousness. As if he couldn't see Wren but knew he was there. Plus, Wren felt something else in the room with them. Some specter that was protecting the child. He could feel the presence of something unworldly wrap around him as if shielding the boy from catastrophe.

He closed his eyes and pinched the bridge of his nose. His head was pounding between his temples and his skull burned around the wound. Wren took a deep breath then stepped into Marc's room. The scene of the crime.

They were searching the house. Judging by the footsteps and stealth manner in which they arrived, he was certain of it. Searching for something or someone. Maybe just to see who was in the house? Perhaps they were locals who had seen the bonfire and came to investigate. Little kids are always thinking they're something bigger than they are. It's a forced reality meant to distract from the fact that they were just kids.

Wren scanned across the room, looking for anything off. Or anything of consequence when his stare landed on the weapon of choice. He stared at it for a while, knowing exactly what it was. Wren had used a blackjack to abduct his first victim.

"And I'll use it to bash his skull into oblivion."

He picked it up and examined it, his eyes narrowed when he saw the handwriting. Written in purple permanent marker was the name: J. Hardwood.

His laugh caught in his throat. He curled his fingers around the weapon.

"How splendid," said Wren, gripping the blackjack close to his chest. "The boy has begun."

Carver trudged through a group of reporters towards his office. He'd just given a press conference about the two dead bodies. He felt like he issued a state of the union address, standing at the podium for longer than he felt comfortable, although it was only a few minutes. Carver never enjoyed being center stage with cameras flashing and reporters hurtling questions by the dozen.

The press conference was a direct order from Captain Flannery. After Carver's conversation with the forensics specialist revealed the method of torture was closely associated with a medieval device referred to as the iron maiden, the GM plant was suddenly swarmed with reporters. Flannery then ordered Carver to conduct the press conference, although they agreed to keep the iron maiden possibility to themselves.

He refused to answer questions during the press conference. Even now, as he made his way to his office, he was tightlipped. One thing about reporters that Carver could never stomach was how they spin narratives in their favor. They can take a story with zero validity, even if the story was completely nonsensical, and hype it up so their viewers' blood would boil and all they can do is keep watching to discover more. And when there is nothing more to tell they'll dangle a new carrot in front of the viewers' eyes. The next shiny object theory. Like cattle. People are like cattle, willing to be herded into whatever line their favorite newscast wanted them in. Society was becoming pathetic, according to Carver. And he couldn't see it getting any better.

Walking back to his office seemed like walking through knee-deep mud. The reporters were relentless. He'd given them all the information the police were willing to share. Namely, that the Hollow had a potential serial killer walking among them. How else could he spin the fact that there were two dead bodies with similar means of torture and the same calling card? The nannie who discovered the first body had already done an interview. Carver scoffed over the interview. Considering the woman seemed to be in a state of shock when Carver first discovered her in the park she came to rather quickly. And then someone in his own precinct leaked the information about the second victim and the pentagram and inscription were all over the news. He thought about John and the toll that such a discovery may have on the young boy. The police also issued a curfew. Everyone had to be off the street by ten o'clock. No ifs, ands, or buts about it.

Carver didn't feel safe until he opened the door to his office. He shut the door and shut out the reporters who were being redirected by a uniformed officer. Carver stood in his office. Ran his hands over his face, then shook off the anxiety with a shake of his head. Carver didn't turn the light on. He needed some darkness, time to think. The front of his office was all windows and the light from the precinct was enough to keep him completely out of the dark. He scanned across the outside parking lot from his second story window. The reporters were setting up to record their next report. Carver popped a toothpick between his lips then strolled over to his desk and took a seat.

A file folder sat on his desk. The coroner's report for the first body. On top of the folder sat a piece of paper with a scribbled message that was obviously taken by the receptionist.

The message was simple: Father McKenzie called to speak to him about the murders. Carver remembered seeing Father McKenzie at the crime scene.

Maybe he saw something?

Carver rolled that toothpick to the corner of his mouth and sat back, staring at the message. Father McKenzie was on his list of people to interview. He looked through his office window, then over his shoulder to the reporters. He needed to get out of the precinct. As far away from the reporters as possible. He had a meeting with his team scheduled for tonight at eleven. They were all given specific tasks to complete before the meeting. Investigative work, but Carver knew something they all didn't. Whoever did this is something more than human.

A master manipulator with a knack for driving insanity into the minds of the weak and vulnerable. Look at Jerry Hardwood, who, at this very moment Carver could only conclude had been coached and driven to murder by whomever was still among the people of Sleepy Hollow, continuing a tirade that Carver was certain would go on forever. Go on until the son of a bitch is caught.

He put the message off to the side then slid the coroner's report closer. He opened the file when there was a knock on his door. The moment he looked up, he saw Detective Montgomery opening the door. Montgomery was on his investigative team. He had a knack for fitting the pieces together, connecting dots that most investigators couldn't see. He was young-as was most of Carver's team-but not wet behind the ears. Montgomery joined the police force directly out of high school. Now in his mid-thirties, he had a passion for investigative work that was still fresh and untainted. Carver hoped the current investigation wouldn't take too much of a toll on the young detective. Certain cases could do that to an officer-set their passion on fire then douse it with an accelerant before smoldering the passion and extinguishing the flame. He hoped Montgomery could roll with the punches. Carver was certain his will was about to be tested with the current investigation.

Carver had tasked Montgomery with overseeing the uniformed officers assessing missing persons calls. Recent missing persons calls. He hoped Montgomery had good news.

"Got some potentially bad news."

Carver's shoulders slouched, disappointed.

Montgomery paused after witnessing Carver's reaction.

"Go on with it," said Carver, leaning back in his chair.

"Press conference went well. You look good on camera."

Carver cocked an eyebrow, waiting for a punch line. Obviously, Montgomery was stalling. "Well, if this detective thing doesn't work out, I'm glad I'll be able to take up acting." He shook his head. "Now quit stalling and tell me what it is."

Montgomery gave a quick nod. "Flannery wants to see you."

Carver rolled his eyes and shook his head. "About what?"

Montgomery shrugged. "No clue." He looked through the office window. "Probably to point out all the mistakes we're making."

"I don't have time for that. He'll be updated during our meeting at eleven." Carver had a certain disdain for Flannery. He was old-school Sleepy Hollow, which meant he didn't like strangers in his town, and he definitely didn't like out-of-town city dwellers on his police force. He fought Carver tooth and nail during most of his time in Sleepy Hollow. Good thing for Carver, he was the best investigator on the force, a fact that Flannery seemed to grapple with from time to time.

"Trust me, I got you on that one. If he keeps micromanaging every step we take, we'll never break the damn case."

Carver fell silent, cracking his knuckles while staring through the window at the reporters. It looked like they were taking a break from newscasting after having recorded their most recent update. He thought about Flannery. The last thing he needs right now is another inquisition. Carver swiveled around in his chair when he glanced over the paper with Father McKenzie's message. Carver picked it up then stood up and took his jacket off the back of the chair.

"Looks like I've got a potential lead on my hands," he said, squeezing his arms through the sleeves. He eyeballed Montgomery. "Tell him I went to follow it up and I'll update him when I return."

"No problem."

"Any luck with missing persons?"

"Nothing yet, but we'll keep looking."

Carver zipped up his jacket. "If you find anything, let me know a-sap."

"Of course."

Carver met Montgomery at the door. "Something else?"

Montgomery paused, his lips pressed tightly together.

"What is it?"

"It's just that this all seems surreal, doesn't it? I don't know what it is, but when I woke up this morning, I knew something bad was gonna go down." He looked through the window. "It's like the entire town was on edge even before the bodies were found." He turned to Carver. "Seems almost unnatural. Like there's something beneath the folds we're unaware of."

Carver gnashed on his toothpick, assessing his fellow officer. Sheila Hardwood passed through his thoughts. The Hardwood Realty office, too. Then Jerry.

Detective!

Jerry's voice boomed between his ears.

I need hearts for the master.

Pentagrams written in blood.

Initium Novum.

Carver nodded. Pulled that toothpick out. "Honestly, I know exactly what you mean."

John and his newfound friends walked back home through the woods. He could see his street now, and he breathed a sigh of relief.

After he and Logan escaped the wrath of the vampire, they found Michael and Chad waiting where they left them. They said they saw no one outside. Never heard a sound from inside the house either, which seemed strange to John. How could they not hear them screaming and hollering? As if the house was soundproof, swallowing every scream down its gullet with nefarious satisfaction. His second thought was that they were lying. Lying to cover up the fact that they dropped the ball and were too frightened to warn them about the vampire.

No one said a word on the way home. The silence was golden. It allowed John to think about his next move. He couldn't believe he left the blackjack in the house. Everything had happened so quickly. The weapon must have dropped from his hand when the vampire slammed his arm into John-he could still feel the arm across his chest. Even more, he couldn't believe he had written his dad's name on the blackjack. It was all he could think of, and he wanted to go back to retrieve it. That was his first thought, at least, but more than likely the vampire had searched the room and found the weapon that split his head open. Which meant there was a unique possibility that the vampire not only had the weapon but also knew the owner of the weapon.

He was concerned, to say the least. Concerned for himself and Grandpa Claude. John was already thinking about his plans for the night and what he'll need to do to protect the house and Grandpa Claude when he stepped out of the woods onto his street. They stopped in front of John's house. Stopped and shared a moment of silence.

"Are you gonna be, okay?" Logan asked John.

John didn't have an answer. He looked at his house, seeing Grandpa Claude through the window sitting in the living room watching television.

After there was no answer, Michael stepped up and patted John on the shoulder. "He'll be fine. This guy's got balls of steel."

John grunted in his throat. He didn't feel like he had balls of steel. He was petrified over what was lurking in the woods. He wished he'd never seen that damn bonfire and wished he'd never gone to the house. He looked at his friends, one by one, their stares confirming their own concern. "Yeah," he huffed. "I'll be fine. Lock the doors and pray for dawn, right?"

"Exactly." Logan patted him on the shoulder, too. "Remember, it's not a vampire, just a tired old man who can't take a hit over the head. I think we're good. That son of a bitch probably has a headache right now. I'm sure he'll be nursing it until tomorrow."

John didn't share Logan's optimism.

"I'll be fine," was all John could say.

"Cool beans," said Michael, walking backwards. "See you in the morning." He smiled before turning around when Chad joined him and John watched as they walked down the street to their homes.

"Don't worry about it," Logan said. John locked eyes with him. "I'm good with computers. I'll do some research on the house and try to find out who this vampire guy is."

John nodded. "Okay. Let's talk tomorrow."

Logan took a few steps back. "Without a doubt, my man."

"Thank you."

Logan shook his head. "No, thank you." He turned and hurried towards his house.

John turned back to his house. Grandpa Claude sat motionless, staring at the television as if whatever he was watching had caught his full attention and refused to let go. He turned back to the woods, then looked up to the crescent moon hovering above the trees. The wind howled from the woods. The chilly wind nipped at his nose.

Turned back to his house and started walking up the driveway to the front door. There were whispers in the wind. He knew it was true. Subtle whispers telling him the worst was yet to come.

It is best to be ready.

157

Turn all the pain inward, squeeze it into a ball of energy that feeds off the beating of your heart, squeezing the organ to the point that all the pain turns into hate and unleashes a tidal wave of suffering that spews from your red beaming eyes into the surrounding world. Without remorse or disgrace. Without a care for the world.

That's how Marc felt on that fateful day after he drank the absinthe. As if the man in black removed all the heartache and fear. He didn't even mind his three escorts any longer. He paid them no mind, feeling capital, large and otherworldly. As if he could engage in any depraved evil act without guilt or conscience. And he was angry. His pain evaporated inside a dark cauldron and forgotten. Forgotten because hate is all he felt and it provided power he could never imagine. His focus was like tunnel vision, framing desire with an appetite to devour all that came in his path.

"Freedom..." The words flew off his lips, hearing his voice as if it belonged to someone else. As if he were a voyeur, hiding and listening secretly to all the surrounding activity. He turned to the woman beside him. "Is never having to say you're sorry."

The jazz club off Main Street in Tarrytown-just a stone's throw away from Sleepy Hollow-was a hive of activity. It looked like it belonged in the 1920s with its ambiance and classy stylized tables and booths. The bar where Marc stood was polished to a fine shine, made of redwood that gleamed under the light. Beveled mirrors lined the wall behind the bar. The band-drummer, sax player, and guitar player-filled the bar with a rendition of Louie Armstrong's *What a wonderful world*. The guitar player's thick baritone filled the bar with wonder and trees of green. Marc wavered when he tipped his head back to down his scotch.

He snapped his head forward with a gleam in his eye and a small smile curled in the corner of his mouth. The burn from the alcohol, enough to fuel his pain into rage. He turned to the lady beside him. Her name was Jessica-Jess for short. She wore a dark purple flannel shirt over a black *Nirvana* T-shirt, blue jeans and a pair of black boots to match. Her hair pulled back in a bun with long wavy tendrils that cascaded down her temples to her jaw. Her eyes were sparkling blue, and she smelled like buttercream. Her skin was milky white. Marc thought about sinking his teeth into her flesh. A thought that curled that smile into both corners of his mouth. Jess sat on a barstool, her elbow on the bar, her head resting in her palm. She sipped her drink-gin and tonic with a splash of lime-then shook her head before leaning back.

"Wouldn't that make you a psychopath or something like that?"

Marc stared into her eyes, those crystal shimmering blues. Her stare proved innocence lived within her soul. He laughed at the statement, a high-pitched cackle, and despite how loud it was in the bar several patrons turned to him. To see who was belting out that evil laugh.

"My lady," he huffed with a shake of his head. "Evil is defined in context. What one calls psychopathic, another refers to as the true essence of free will."

Jess shook her head and turned away, looking straight ahead. Marc followed her gaze to the beveled mirror behind the bar where the man in black was staring at him with his gray and purple blotched skin, dark eyes with the faintest hint of red and long dark hair. He looked like a walking corpse. Marc smiled at the man in black and he smiled back before Marc turned to the bartender and gestured for another round. He turned to Jess who was talking to the friends she'd come to the bar with-two females dressed in similar grunge attire. He stared at the back of her head and noticed her friends looked at him from over her shoulder, their eyes narrowing the longer they stared.

The bartender placed their drinks on the bar. "Last call," he said. "Bar's closing early tonight." Disappointment hung from the patron's lips in shallow huffs and whining groans. "Sorry, police issued a curfew, which means we need to close early and get home before ten." The band finished their set with a fading *Oh yeah* from the singer.

Marc took the moment to locate his escorts. Sarah sat in a booth with an older gentleman dressed to the nines in a dark Armani suit. Hal was on the other side of the bar talking with a group of ladies who seemed as if they couldn't take their eyes off him. And Andrew, the largest in Marc's little group, sat at a table alone. They were all staring at Marc. He grinned at them, sensing how their blood just turned hot in their veins.

Marc turned to the barkeep and closed his eyes. His head twitched, his brain squirmed as if something was crawling across his brain, slithering into his consciousness. Pain twitched in his chest. Gritting his teeth he opened his eyes to the barkeep and the scene was different. More dulled than before as if the color was drained from the bar. He addressed his question in a loud, booming voice. "May I ask a simple question?"

The bartender-wiping down a glass with a dish towel-stopped cold, staring at Marc.

"Does that mean you are also closing the back room? Or are the people in there immune to the very laws they bestow upon us meek and feeble citizens? Considering they are the ones who make the laws, perhaps they feel they are immune to its consultation."

It seemed like everyone in the bar turned and stared at the bartender. Not one person moved, the bar was as quiet as the furthest existence in the universe. "Well barkeep? *Does it?*" Marc didn't know where he was going with his inquiry. It seemed to come out of nowhere and he was distracted. Distracted by the rise building in his chest. The rise of fear and pain and suffering that was slithering into his brain. Losing control again, confused but still here. Although he felt like he was center stage too and loved every second happening in front of him. Loving their stares and how they were looking at him. Like he was a god among mortals.

Heard Jess ask, "What back room?"

The bartender cleared his throat while shaking his head. "Get outta my bar, mister." He gestured to the front door. "You're no longer welcome."

Marc considered the bartender's statement. He looked from one patron to the next. "No," he said. "Perhaps it is everyone else who should leave. More than likely, that is a splendid idea for all involved."

The bartender's mouth hung open in a classic O. He shook his head. "You're a twisted sonofabitch and you're drunk. Get out and go home."

Marc raised his hands. "Well, I gave you all the chance to leave. Humans," he scoffed. "Always so impractical. Your egos give you rise to entitlement."

"Just go."

Marc noticed Jess's spine stiffened in her seat. He felt rage build in his chest, suffocating his throat, forcing its way into his brain.

"I said leave."

Marc cleared his throat, then grinned that devilish grin. "Of course," he said with a cock of his brow, then turned to the door, aware that everyone in the bar was looking at him, watching him tuck tail to the front door. He gripped the doorknob and looked outside. The street was barren, dark and empty like a ghost town. He smiled at the man in black in the glass reflection and locked the door, twisting the dead bolt before pulling the doorknob, splintering the wood in the doorframe to lock that door in even more.

"What the fuck are you doing? Unlock the *goddamn* door right now!"

Marc turned around, sliding on his heels. "I gave you all a moment's pause. A brief interlude to remove yourself from this hellish place." He looked up at the ceiling. "I can hear them in the back room. Talking." He eyeballed the bartender. "Talking about meeeeeeee." Every patron seemed to stiffen in their seats. "But their foolish ancestry has done nothing to keep them safe. In fact, quite the opposite. Their victory has brought suffering upon their coddled generations. Tonight, we escalate our toil." He inhaled slowly into his nose. "I can smell the ether begging for blood." He looked at his escorts. Their eyes beamed with a red glow and their veins swelled across their cheeks. "Let us feed it properly."

The first screams came from the ladies Hal was talking to. Not because he slashed at them or bit into their necks, but because his fist tore through the barkeep's back. He pulled out the man's heart, holding it still beating in his hand then looked at the surrounding ladies while the barkeep dropped to the floor. "We need hearts for the master." And in one fell swoop, he cut the throats of the three women around him. Cutting off their screams, their eyes bulging from their skulls wide with disbelief as blood fell like a waterfall from their throats. Hal laughed, giddy with excitement.

The man in the Armani suit stood up abruptly. "My god," he hollered before Sarah plunged her sharp nails into his stomach then rose to her feet toppling the table over, dragging her nails up to the man's chest as he wiggled and trembled, blood cascading in sheets from his stomach. She bit into his neck with a ferocious snap of her jaw, guiding him back down into his seat. Her fingers inched up beneath his chest bone while swallowing his blood when she squeezed his heart and tore it from his chest.

There was a mad dash to the front door and another to the back door. People were screaming and crying and whimpering and whining. But Andrew had already locked the back door. He shared a stare with the master as Hal and Sarah tore through the patrons closest to them. Jess attempted to run past Marc, but he gripped her hair and tossed her to the ground. She landed with a stumble, skidding across the wooden floor. Her forehead rocked against it, but she anxiously shuffled to her knees, huffing and attempting to flee.

"And just where do you think you're going?" He looked around. Looked at his hands. *Wish I had my cane*, he thought, shaking his head. He gripped a beer bottle off the table closest to him. Jess was scuttling to her knees when he smashed the bottle across the back of her head and Jess flopped to the ground, gripping the wound. Blood raced out of her head, her hands red and slick with blood. Seeing her like that-so feeble-brought rage to the forefront of his brain.

He stabbed down with the smashed bottle and Jess hollered something awful. He continued driving his arm down, stabbing into her flesh. Her skull. Her back. Her spine. Kept stabbing. And with every stab blood followed his arm, raining into the air, his eyes wide and mad and frenzied over the sight of blood. His mouth was wide open and peppered with drops of blood across his tongue and lips. She was dead already, but the man in black refused to relent. He brought that broken glass down across her back and spine until his rage was satisfied then assessed his work and the bloodied mess he made of the fair lady, Jessica. Cocked his head and licked the blood off his lips. "Well, that was satisfying. Now let that be your lesson in the true essence of free will." He dropped the glass then stepped over her lifeless body. "Remember that in your next life."

Hal and Sarah emitted fog from their mouths that slithered and coiled around unsuspecting citizens, clawing into their orifices and invading their internal systems. Blood and chunks of organs, bile, and innards oozed from their eyes and mouths, their ears too. Hot boiling blood and disintegrating innards released like a waterfall when their bodies dropped dead to the floor, their skin melting off the bone. The entire bar was covered in fog, snaking and slithering and hissing like feral animals.

Andrew plunged his first into the back of one of the patrons who scurried to the back door. The man dropped to the ground with a thud. For the next in line, he twisted her head completely around, snapping the neck. Andrew smiled for the dead black eyes, loving the fact that he was the last the woman had ever seen, then plunged his fingers into the neck of the nearest frantic patron. The tips of those fingers tore through the man's throat, severing his spine and he dropped to the ground like a sack of bricks. Andrew spun around, his elbow crashing into the jaw of the woman screaming by the back door, snapping her neck too. Her screams were cut off instantly, tossed into oblivion. The last by the back door, a woman dressed in more flannel, hollered something awful, sliding against the door to the floor.

"Please don't hurt me," she cried, holding her arms up to defend herself.

Andrew snatched her throat and raised her to eye level. "No worries, my lady. It's just a little bite, then all the pain will be over." He clamped his jaw around her neck, puncturing the vein, then swallowed a gulp of ecstasy.

Sarah continued her blood lust. Hal the same. And the man in black walked across the wooden floor.

He addressed his ghost demons. "Be sure to save three for the dungeon. And bring the hearts with us. They'll do well to strengthen the portal." He was walking towards the back. To the secret room the man in black knew was there.

And, more importantly, who was in there.

"As they say ladies and gentlemen," the man in black grunted as he came to the hidden door. "Revenge is a dish best served cold." And with a click of his thoughts, the door opened. Opened to the sound of whimpering, fearful men. The spawn of the master's demise. The shadow government of Sleepy Hollow. He stepped into the dark room; their dreadful, fearful stares highlighted by the light from the bar. "Well, gentlemen, let us talk. And in talking, perhaps you can tell me where I can find the book your ancestors wrote about me."

158

Carver parked outside the rectory and killed the headlights. The rectory was small; the exterior constructed from stone and connected directly to the church. He saw there was a light on behind the closed blinds. The light dimmed when someone stepped in front of the window, pushing the blinds open. He saw Father McKenzie in the window. Carver stared at McKenzie and the priest stared directly at him. He killed the engine and opened the door, then stepped out into the icy sting.

Quiet. Cold and quiet. The stillness of that quiet contracted his bones and perked up his ears. There were whispers in the wind, subtle whispers, the words tumbling on top of each other as if all the dead in Sleepy Hollow were talking all at once. He could feel a rumbling beneath the street as if the bowels of hell had opened far below the city and were clawing to the surface, tainting the oxygen he breathed with venom. He could feel it in his blood, a certain curdle in his veins that turned his blood hot with rage. He noticed he was gnashing his teeth, his jaw tight.

He looked over the parking lot and noticed the rectory did not face the park. He had been hoping the priest had seen something or someone, maybe from the rectory window, but unless there's a window overlooking the park he knew he set himself up for disappointment. Carver turned back to the window and noticed the priest was no longer there, the blind waving gently. He closed the car door then popped a toothpick between his lips before walking to the front door.

Father McKenzie opened the door before he knocked.

"Good evening, Detective. I'm grateful to see you." McKenzie looked around the parking lot. Carver noticed his hands were shaking. His face was stoic. His eyes, tired and dry. He looked like he hadn't slept in a day's age. He seemed jumpy too, as if he was waiting for a threat to jump out of the dark and claim his soul.

"Of course, Father. I got your message, but I already planned to speak with you."

McKenzie's stare settled on Carver; his expression filled with fear. He studied Carver as if assessing his intentions. Maybe even deciding if he should invite him in or not. The priest was staring directly into his eyes as if he could tell by Carver's stare if he was trustworthy or not. Then the priest assessed his skin, his cheeks mostly.

"May I come in, or would you like to talk outside?"

The priest swallowed his breath. Carver could see the man was paranoid. What had befallen the weary priest to cause such internal strife? What had he seen?

Father McKenzie stretched his arm, pointing to the church. "I'll meet you in the church," he said. Carver followed his arm to a back door to the church. "The door is open. Please go in and light a candle. I'll be there momentarily."

Carver went to say something, turning back to the priest, but the door closed in the same moment with a soft thud. The deadbolt then clicked into place.

Carver had seen his share of paranoid witnesses before. It was always best to make them feel comfortable. What he knew about the paranoid was that they're either as tightlipped as a priest who had taken confession, or they sing like a hummingbird hums. There was no in-between. So, Carver did as he was told and went into the church and lit a candle. He said a silent prayer, asking the almighty for help with his investigation then took a seat on the front pew and waited, staring at the cross hanging high above the altar.

Hoping the priest could shed some light on the murders. And hoping he can catch the person responsible before any more blood is spilled.

159

It won't be long now. Lori sat up in her seat, wiping the sleep from her eyes. Her train was arriving at Grand Central Station. From there, she'll need to take a Metro North train to Tarrytown.

She'd fallen asleep on the train, her exhaustion finally taking full effect the moment she sat down. She dreamed of Gerard and her mother. Dreamed of Marc Saduj and the demon he wrote about in his book. She looked at the notebook on the seat next to her. Ran her fingers across the cover when the train dove into the dark tunnel that would take her to the final stop in Grand Central. Sudden darkness swept across the train when the overhead lights flickered on and off as if the darkness sought to destroy the light within. Lori gripped the notebook and held it close to her chest, turning her gaze to the darkness outside the train.

A million thoughts passed through her mind in that moment, an attempt to grasp some sort of logic behind what she'd seen. The red eyes that followed her as if they wanted her to get out of the house. Wanted her to live and breathe and escape the fiery breath of death. But why would evil show mercy? It made no sense. No logical sense whatsoever.

There're forces we're dealing with. Nefarious forces and they've got their eyes on you.

Elena's words were on her mind. *Got their eyes on you.* She saw those red, beaming eyes again. Remembered seeing the demon in the closet, the demon who was Gerard and when he stepped into the light, the demon was gone as if the light destroyed the reality in front of her.

He's just a man. A sick, twisted, murdering bastard. She could still feel the heat from the fire burning in her mother's room. How hot it was in that room even before she tossed the candles. Remembered Gerard's bite across her mouth. Lori looked at her reflection in the window. Gerard's bite marks were prominent across her mouth. Lori could still feel his teeth biting into her flesh and bone. She looked twisted and sick. A spot of red stained her right eyeball. The broken blood vessels would take time to heal.

Heard the wet gurgling pop from when she stabbed Gerard with the letter opener. He instinctively grabbed his throat, his jaw grinding, moving back and forth like a typewriter as he fought to draw air into his lungs. Blood burst from the wound in a thick geyser that leapt into the room and rained over her. His breath whistled through the hole in his neck.

Tears in her eyes now. Lori looked up and over the train. A bulky man was watching her. Watching her cry. He turned away a moment later. Perhaps to provide a moment of peace after he was caught intruding on her private moment of desperation and heartache. Perhaps to provide a sense of pity to the battered woman he was staring at. Lori wiped the tears from her eyes with her sleeve as the train barreled out of the tunnel into the brightly lit terminal.

"Grand Central Station," the conductor announced over the intercom.

The train eased to a stop then settled into position before the doors slid open. She exited the train, stepping onto the platform towards Grand Central, surprised how barren the station was. Sure, it was getting late, but not late enough for the city that never sleeps. She walked straight to the ticket booth, but the woman behind the glass told her she couldn't go to Sleepy Hollow. The police had issued a curfew, a revelation that caused Lori to cringe.

"Don't you watch television?" the woman asked. "It's been all over the news. Local channels mostly."

Lori shook her head. "I haven't today, no."

The teller rolled her eyes while shaking her head. She sighed before she answered. "You can take the train to the next town over. I'm sure you can grab a cab to Sleepy Hollow. At least you'll get there tonight. If not, you'll have to wait until morning."

Lori paused, thinking. "When does the train leave?"

The teller scanned her computer. "One hour."

"I'll take it, thank you." The last thing she needed was sleeping on the floor in Grand Central Station. Yes, she could get a hotel room, but in the city any hotel worth staying in was astronomical in price and at the moment she had little money. And all she wanted to do was get to Sleepy Hollow. She was convinced that once she set foot in the Hollow everything would feel right. At the very least she'll be on the right path.

She paid for the ticket. An hour's wait wasn't too bad. She took the notebook and ticket then strolled to one of the bodegas where she purchased a granola bar, banana, and four small bottles of wine. She needed a drink to settle her nerves. Her anxiety was in full effect for multiple reasons and the sympathetic stares she received from everyone she laid eyes on was nothing more than a reminder of that stress. Lori knew how battered she appeared. How broken and lost too. She took a seat on the floor in a hallway and leaned against the wall. She wanted to be alone. Lori couldn't stand to be in anyone's presence. She felt safer alone.

Across from where she sat a row of televisions were showing the local newscast when a breaking news report gleamed across the screens. The sound was muted, but she recognized the park immediately. Patriots Park was filled with police. The headline on the bottom of the screen read: **Two Dead in Sleepy Hollow. Curfew in place for Ten PM.**

The scene then shifted to an interview with a Spanish lady-whatever she was reporting was lost to Lori's ears-then panned across an empty parking lot.

The GM plant.

Lori remembered it. She'd strolled past the lot with Marc on multiple occasions.

Then the view crept closer, zooming in on the lot. Lori's head tilted as she looked as if she could see better.

Her jaw dropped when she saw it.

The blood rushed from her face.

She flipped the notebook over. Saw the words written in Marc's hand.

Initium Novum.

They were the same she was staring at on the television.

160

At the same time Lori discovered the connection between Marc's story and the murders in Sleepy Hollow, Father McKenzie opened the door to the church.

Carver's bones turned tense the moment the priest opened the door. He came in from the rectory behind the altar, shuffling with a hurried step towards Carver. He knelt by the altar, crossing himself, his head bowed to Christ. Carver noticed he remained in position a little longer than expected. Carver raised his eyes to the cross, scanning across the face of Christ when McKenzie pushed himself to his feet. The church was quiet. He could hear the subtle wind outside howling like whistled whispers seeking entrance into the house of God.

Father McKenzie eyeballed Carver as he took a chair from the side of the altar and brought it over to face him. Carver noticed the priest's hands were trembling. He appeared nervous and when he sat down he looked like he was about to say something, but no words arrived off his lips.

Carver raised his hand to stop Father McKenzie from being the first to speak. "Thank you for talking with me, Father. As I mentioned earlier, you were on my list of people to interview." Father McKenzie nodded, his hands on his lap, fingers interlaced. He seemed like he was attempting to be calm. What was obvious to

Carver was that the priest had information he wanted to share but seemed to be at odds with providing the information. Could be a confessional, Carver thought. It was possible that someone had confessed to the murders and the confession was weighing on his conscience. Conflicted over his sacrament and his duties as a human being and a citizen of Sleepy Hollow. "I can see you have something to share…" Carver considered his next words carefully. "For now, we are on the record." Carver took out his notepad and pencil from his shirt pocket, then looked at the priest. "For now," he reiterated, concluding that at least part of their conversation may need to take place off the record. "Would you like for me to start, or do you want to talk first?"

"Let us move past the preliminaries first. I'm sure you have questions. Let us have at it and move on."

Carver nodded while chewing on his toothpick. "Very well then. First question: did you see anything? Anything at all pertaining to the body in the park."

Father McKenzie moved his head left to right. "Nothing at all. I found out about the murders like everyone else that was out there today watching the scene unfold."

Carver nodded, writing the priest's denial in his notebook. "Have you seen any odd occurrences lately? Anyone strange hanging around the church or the park? Anything at all?"

Again, he shook his head. "No. No new parishioners. No strange occurrences."

Their conversation continued in the same manner. Carver asking questions and the priest offering denials, leaving Carver chomping at the bit to learn what information Father McKenzie did have.

"One last question," said Carver. "Why did you want to talk in the church and not in the rectory?"

"Bit odd, isn't it?"

Carver nodded, staring at the priest through narrow eyes. "And why are you so nervous? Seems like you saw something that's got you all… paranoid."

Father McKenzie paused, staring at Carver's notepad. "Are we off the record, Detective?"

Carver put the notepad and pencil down on the pew. "We are now."

Father McKenzie nodded, his lips pressed tight together and looked at Carver with a stare filled with desperation. He then sat back, assessing Carver. "Detectives are normally reserved to simple logic, which meets their needs just fine. In normal circumstances, at least. In times when dealing with the evils that are born from the human heart." He shook his head. "But are you ready, Detective? Are you willing to suspend logic? Because that is the only way you're going to stop the tidal wave of suffering that has been set loose on the Hollow. There are forces at play in our town, Detective. Forces that basic logic can never account for. Are you able to see with larger eyes the things that exist beneath the folds? Like those whispers you keep hearing in the wind."

Carver's eyes narrowed.

"I know you hear them too. And I know you've been witnessing events you can't explain. It is in these things that the answers you seek exist. Things that are not of this earth. Things you can't touch, but you can feel them. Can't you, Detective? Like the energy we all felt out there today hovering over the park like a dark veil, waiting for the precise moment to strike down on the Hollow."

Carver couldn't deny what the priest said. His words were the truth Carver felt in his heart. Something nefarious was at play in Sleepy Hollow and it was born from the folds of dark energy. There are things you don't admit to in the open because, in doing so, the world would deem the believer insane. Just look at Jerry Hardwood. But the priest needed to know, needed to know Carver felt it too. The priest stared at him, anticipation prominent in his eyes.

Carver nodded. "Yes, Father. I understand what you're referring to."

The priest closed his eyes, nodding. He lifted his head with a sigh as his eyes opened. "Thank you," he said, but Carver knew the priest wasn't talking to him. Father McKenzie looked at Carver dead in his eyes. "In order to fully grasp what is happening in the Hollow I will need to tell you a story. A bit of a history lesson on Sleepy Hollow."

Carver shifted in the pew. "Please, Father. Continue."

Father McKenzie paused before he continued. Carver could see the cogs in the man's brain working, possibly attempting to pinpoint where to start. He leaned back in his chair, his hands on his lap again, fingers interlaced. "The western woods are haunted, Detective. But haunted by what is the question. For longer than we know, perhaps even before humans ran free in the Hollow, the woods were haunted. The Weckquaesgeek tribe knew about it. The tribes that littered this land for centuries knew it to be true too. They passed down stories and warnings about the western woods, and they knew not to travel there."

Carver pulled the toothpick from his mouth, staring at the priest with dire concern. "If it's not haunted by the ghosts of Sleepy Hollow's past, then what is the cause of the haunting?"

Father McKenzie paused, his bottom lip tucked under his top teeth. "It's difficult to ascertain. The Weckquaesgeek talked about a cave in the woods, a place where darkness exists like a portal to hell."

"Hell?" Carver raised his eyebrows. "Father, that's a bit..."

McKenzie cut him off with a wave of his hand, cleared his throat then continued. "The Weckquaesgeek referred to it as Xibalba. The cave held the power of transcendence. Tales were told about people who never returned after they entered." He paused again, as if to contemplate his next statement. "They also told stories about how... sometimes, the person would come back, although completely changed. More nefarious than they had been. More evil. And sometimes, *he* would come."

"He?"

Father McKenzie nodded. "The demon," he said.

"The demon? Father, excuse me, but this is…"

"Unbelievable," McKenzie offered Carver his conclusion.

"Correct."

McKenzie nodded. "Agreed, Detective, but that does not mean it's not true." Carver cocked his head, staring at the priest who rose from his seat. Carver watched him as he stepped to the wall, staring at a stained-glass depiction of the crucifixion. "Allow me to divert the story then to our more recent history." He looked over his shoulder at Carver and Carver gave a slight nod, as if to say, *continue.* "The history of Sleepy Hollow that we all read about is not accurate. Well, some of it is. The more basic elements are, but the substance, and what exists in the foundation has never seen the light of day. Not over the past two hundred years. There's a history that has been kept undercover. Events that very few are privy to and those that are aware have attained their knowledge through secret study, from one generation to the next. Always operating beneath the shadows. In doing so, they took control of the Hollow, strategically positioning themselves in the event of a resurgence."

"Resurgence?" Carver rolled his toothpick from one corner of his mouth to the other.

The priest nodded his head. "Correct. A resurgence of the demon and the events that took place in the Hollow over a century ago."

Carver shook his head. "Father, this is a bit… over the top."

McKenzie walked back to his chair. Taking his seat, he said, "Which is why I asked you to suspend disbelief." He sat back, folding his hands over his lap again. "I will admit that I didn't believe it myself." He looked up. "God only knows what mysteries exist across the universe. Who am I to question that knowledge? But I did. Mostly scoffing at the notion as a simple ghost story with depictions and elements that were born from the ravings of a diseased mind. In short, I always thought that those who kept the secret did so to pursue their own favor. But I was wrong, Detective. After Zoe Hardwood was murdered and the events that transpired with Jerry, I thought differently, and my suspicions were confirmed today with the most recently deceased." He reached into his pocket. The paper he presented was folded in half and old, the edges frayed and yellow. "May I ask, have you seen something similar to what is on this paper?"

Carver stared at McKenzie for longer than necessary. It seemed to him that should he look at the paper it was an admission to the priest's story, a kind of submission to accept all that he said. He had a feeling he knew what was on that page. He looked into McKenzie's eyes, his stare stoic as if to tell Carver that it was okay to see what was written on the paper. Okay to take it. Okay to accept the truth, even if that truth was outlandish in its nature. Carver gnawed on his toothpick when he took the paper, so thin and old he thought it would crumble between his fingers. He opened it and his spine stiffened.

"Have you seen this symbol and inscription, Detective?"

Carver was staring at a black and white drawing of an upside-down pentagram with the words Initium Novum written beneath it. In the corner was the year 1856. The pentagram had been written on a stone wall. His first thought was that the priest had drawn this exact picture after learning about the pentagram and inscription on the news. He didn't want to believe it was true, but the paper was clearly old.

"No need to answer, detective. I can tell by the look on your face that you have." After a pause, the priest continued. "The story goes that a coven brought the demon to the Hollow. By reciting chants in the western woods, they conjured a protector for their way of life. But in doing so they unleashed the devil and his minions on the Hollow. From what I've read his minions are vile creatures like parasites that feed off a living host. Those who were immune sought refuge here." He gestured to the park and the church. "Not the actual church because there was no church here at that time, but the ground had been cast in a protective spell. This area was also the staging point for a ceremony that concluded with the demon's demise. Several citizens were a part of the battle, and the coven cast a spell on the demon and on the house that had been constructed over the cave where the demon dwelled. Those brave souls who fought the demon and his ghosts passed the information to their kin with knowledge on how to disperse the demon should he come again to wreak havoc on the Hollow."

"Who are these people? And why haven't they shown their faces over the last six months? If they're aware of what is going on, why haven't they come forward to the proper authority?"

The priest laughed. A guffaw that escaped his throat that he immediately squelched. Carver's eyes narrowed over the odd reaction. A smile spread across the priest's face. "Because they *are* the authority. They own most of Sleepy Hollow and our adjoining Tarrytown. Remember, Detective, that until recently Tarrytown was Sleepy Hollow. They take turns in political positions, always maintaining an arm's length to power. After the events with Zoe and Jerry Hardwood they mobilized their efforts."

"Is Jerry a part of this… this secret group?"

McKenzie shook his head. "The Hardwoods have history in Sleepy Hollow. History that runs deep in the Hollow. A Hardwood ancestor played a pivotal role in the demon's destruction. This knowledge and charge have been passed down to the Hardwoods, however, considering Jerry's…" He cleared his throat. "Condition, he himself had no knowledge, but before his passing Jerry's father provided the information to another to hand down to Jerry's son."

"John?"

The priest nodded. "Correct, Detective."

"He's just a child."

"Even a child can garner strength few adults can."

Carver paused, thinking. "Sheila?" he said, and the priest closed his eyes with a subtle nod. "Jerry's father passed the information to Sheila."

"Correct. But something has changed, detective. We are uncertain what it is, but something has definitely changed. We assume the demon has found a hole from which he may crawl from.

A fly in the ointment, so to speak. A crack in the spell. We are no longer confident in our ability to dismantle the demon."

"Which is why you're providing this information to me?"

The priest cleared his throat then nodded. "We require a fresh set of eyes. Someone who can set aside personal beliefs and discover the crack in the spell."

Carver gazed at the priest long and hard, studying every inch of him. His demeanor and body language. "Who is involved in this secret group?"

The priest stood up. "You'll meet with them tonight. They are waiting for our conversation to conclude."

"So, are you a part of this organization?"

"Correct once again." He looked around his church. "As I said before, a protection spell was cast on this location. It is a saving grace, a place where the demon may not enter. And it is here that we have placed a prized possession."

Carver's eyes lit up. "Prized possession," he repeated.

"Yes, a written account of Sleepy Hollow's history that details the battle with the demon." Now the priest studied Carver as if second-guessing himself. "Remain here, please. I will bring it to you."

161

John Hardwood sat by his window, staring into the western woods. He'd locked every window and door, then double-checked every lock. Just to be certain. He even made the trek into the basement and locked all the windows down there too. His heart thumping in his ears the entire time.

He took three kitchen knives to the room with him. John wasn't certain if he could actually stab another human being, but he took them anyway. He believed it was better to have them and not need them than need them and not have them. Especially in a moment of crisis. He kept the knives close and took the largest with him every time he went to check on Grandpa Claude. He was glued to the television.

When John first entered the house, Grandpa Claude switched the television off in a hurried panic as he shot up from his seat.

"John," he said, startled and attempting to regain his composure. "Where were you?"

Now it was John who had to regain his composure. "Out with friends," he'd said, which was true, of course, although he left out the whole breaking and entering and assault with a deadly weapon part.

Grandpa Claude gave him a good look over and John did all he could to stop his hands from shaking.

"You hear anything today?"

Such an odd question. John didn't know what to make of it. He shook his head. "No."

Grandpa Claude, tightlipped, nodded. He seemed relieved. "Suppers on the table. What are your plans for the night?" Now it seemed like he wanted to get rid of him.

"I'm not hungry," John replied, walking past Grandpa Claude to the steps. "I'll be in my room." He stopped at the first step when he thought about the knives. "Actually, I am a little hungry." He looked at Grandpa Claude. "Can I eat in my room?" Then, after a pause, "Got some homework to finish."

"Of course," Claude blurted. He never let John eat in his room. It was a house rule. Dinner was always about eating together. He guessed that whatever Grandpa Claude was watching he wanted to get back to it. And do it without John in attendance.

He went into the kitchen, grabbed a bowl of beef stew and the three knives that he hid in his jacket, then raced up the stairs to his room, but not before locking the back door. Grandpa Claude never moved. He stood there, waiting, eyeballing John until he climbed back up the stairs. John heard the television click on the moment he hit the top step. He wondered what was on the television. Probably some adult movie Grandpa Claude didn't want John to see.

He then prepared. Locking all the windows upstairs first, then raced back downstairs-noticed Grandpa Claude turned off the television the moment his feet hit the stairs-and used the excuse that he had to find something for his homework. He locked all the windows on the first floor, then went to the basement and locked those windows too before heading back to his room. Satisfied he'd done everything possible to secure the house, he hunkered down for the long night ahead.

He couldn't believe he dropped the blackjack. That was stupid, but what could he do? Everything happened so fast and he was so scared he hadn't a chance to think. Seeing Logan being strangled like that brought out a rage inside of him he couldn't stop, as if it came boiling over without a sign that it had ever been there to begin with.

In the heat of the conflict, everything seemed to slow down. He could see himself with the blackjack, slapping the vampire across the head. Saw blood and the next thing he knew, he hit the ground hard. That's when the blackjack must have dropped out of his hand. Also, when time hopped back on track and sped up like wildfire.

He'd grabbed Logan and hurried down the steps. Hurried outside and saw the vampire at the door, watching them. John was certain the vampire did not chase after them because of the sun. But how was he awake during the day? John rationalized it was because the sky was overcast. Maybe that's why John was able to hurt him.

A vampire's power is weaker during the day. He was sure he heard that somewhere.

What his thoughts kept looping back to was the light. The blinding white light he had seen around Logan when the vampire attacked. It was as if the light took his fear away, providing the strength necessary to hit that vampire over the head.

The light was comfortable.

The light provided strength of mind and heart.

The light reminded him of his mother.

162

Father McKenzie dropped a book on the pew next to Carver. It landed with a thud. The brown leather-bound book was thick, wide, and long and reminded Carver of an encyclopedia. Imprinted in the leather cover were the words: The Demon and Sleepy Hollow. Beneath the title was an imprint of the Sleepy Hollow Cemetery. Carver looked at Father McKenzie.

"There's a title?" He didn't know why, but he found that odd, as if it was a work of fiction and not some prized possession detailing facts.

"A means to ensure that if the book was ever lost, whoever found it would think it *was* fiction."

Carver nodded, gnawing on his toothpick that he was certain was on the verge of splintering. He ran his fingers over the cover, still smooth after all these years. He opened the book to the first page. The page was yellowed and frayed around the edges. He read what was written.

"The Demon and Sleepy Hollow. A true account of the last half century written by the Original Knickerbocker." There was a date beneath: 1856.

Carver turned to Father McKenzie. "The Original Knickerbocker?"

McKenzie nodded, taking his seat. "Washington Irving coined the phrase knickerbocker. It is he who wrote the book and it is he who had a vital role in dismantling the demon."

Carver's eyes narrowed. "Looks like it didn't work. Considering current circumstances."

The priest closed his eyes, shaking his head before opening them to Carver. "Considering current circumstances, I would have to agree with you. But this is not legend, detective. The book is an authentic account of the demon and his rise in Sleepy Hollow. It is the same story that was passed from generation to generation by the authority after the rest of our Sleepy Hollow compatriots were willed to forget the demon and his tirade. Although how that occurred, we still do not know but we hear of it often. Whispered on the wind from the western woods. Beneath the slip of a tongue or an enigma that we just can't put our finger on. It's always been there, feeding off the citizens of the Hollow."

Carver stared at the book. "Are you certain this book isn't just fiction, Father?"

"Considering all that is going on in the Hollow, I'd say this book is our saving grace."

Carver nodded, rolling that half splintered toothpick across his lips. He looked at the book. "What do you want me to do with it?"

"The answers you seek are in the book. Take it with you. Discover what is required to send the demon back to the hell it came from before we pass the point of no return." He gestured around the church. "There's venom in the air, detective. Venom that is infecting the minds and hearts of everyone in Sleepy Hollow. If the demon is not confronted, he'll unleash an army across the globe. Think of all he can do with his ghost demons running rampant to every corner of the earth." He paused before he said, "Initium Novum's translation is *a new beginning*. Humanity's end as a new beginning. What do you think that actually means?"

Carver had no response. This was all a bit much to take in. Even more to accept. The fact that the priest was telling him he will need to confront a demon-a real true to life demon-seemed astronomically insane. And yet, he couldn't deny the things he'd seen. The ghost of Sheila Hardwood guiding his hand. The energy in Sleepy Hollow that the priest had talked about and that he himself also felt. The murders. The methods of torture, and the consistency between the murders and a book that was written close to two centuries ago. Too many coincidences make for one alarming truth: there is no coincidence.

Carver cleared his throat. "If it's such a prized possession and a spell protects the church…" He shook his head. "Why are you allowing me to take it?"

Father McKenzie closed his eyes, his lips pressed tight as he moved his head from left to right. "Because I fear the spell will not last. I fear it can be broken, and the demon will return." He pointed to the book. "Within its pages is the method to dismantle the demon and when such a thing exists, the devil will return to claim it."

"Why me? Why not you or the authority?"

"Read the book. I have added bookmarks to the most important pages. They will tell you why."

Carver looked at the book then flipped through the pages. There were many pages with bookmarks. "Excuse me, Father, but it'll take some time to read through all of this." He turned to Father McKenzie. "Perhaps you can enlighten me for a minute."

The priest thought for a moment before he answered. "Because you are an outsider much like Mr. Irving was when he came to the Hollow with no ties to the land or the ground. No ancestors to speak of. In short, your ancestry does not take root in the Hollow and therefore the energy has not infected your blood. It allows for clarity of mind. You think differently and without such ties there is no hesitation to total obliteration."

Carver cocked his head.

"But don't take my word for it." The priest stood up. "Let the authority put your mind at ease. They wait for us. Are you willing to meet them?"

"Father, I wouldn't miss it for the world."

163

"Poor Marc. It appears he fled during our moment of triumph."

The fire was raging inside the firepit, roaring as if it was aware a feast was on the way. The dungeon was hot despite the bitter cold outside. It seemed like the stone structure was sweating, beating red and breathing as if it could swallow the victims chained to it. Its ragged breath like that of a sleeping giant in the throes of a nightmare and absolutely loving it. A dark purple hue beamed into the dungeon from the fissures. The man in black stood center stage, glaring into the center fissure while leaning on his trusted cane.

"He's weak in heart and mind. His constitution is feeble and unstable," said Wren, standing beside his master. "His will is pitiful, how he takes to the drink the way he does." Wren clucked his tongue. "But how did your little ruse develop? How did you manage with only half of your strength at your disposal? Were you successful in your endeavor?"

"Indeeeeeeeed," hissed the master as he turned to Wren. "The authority is no more, and the location of the book has been discovered. Not even my reduced strength was a deterrent for our purpose. The astral plane has grown strong, Wren, quickening my full manifestation and willing more power to my cells than I have felt in centuries. Our host came dutifully, as I expected. The ghost demons played the boy like a fiddle, returning him to my embrace.

But just as he was beginning to see, he ran like a frightened child. It appears, Wren, that we will need to force the situation upon him. Some humans simply refuse to accept the truth of their deeds. Marc is one of them."

A high-pitched scream, bloodcurdling and endless, interrupted them, echoing across the dungeon and disturbing the master's victims, their eyes rolling awake. They continued their conversation without skipping a beat.

Wren cocked his head, eyeballing the master. "He cannot hide for much longer, my master. We shall force the truth upon him even if we must claw his eyes out to do so." He paused when another scream sliced through the dungeon. "Where is the location of the book?"

Wren could see excitement clawing through the master's stare. "It's with the priest. I should have known they'd keep it there. In the place where I cannot travel."

More cries and screams and hollers. Shuffling feet, coming closer.

"Understood, my master, but how shall we retrieve it? Can the ghost demons cross the church's threshold?"

"In time, Wren. Once the dark energy from Xibalba has consumed the minds of the Hollow the spell will be broken." He turned to the staircase; his hands folded over the top of his cane. "That's when I'll personally pay a visit to the priest."

The ghost demons walked into the chamber. In tow were three more victims. Replacements for the ghost demons. They tossed them to the ground. Two were bound and gagged, one woman and one man with a second woman who was not bound nor gagged. Wren deduced she was the one screaming. She fell on her hands and knees after Andrew tossed her to the ground. She was shaking, trembling like a leaf and clearly traumatized. The other two did nothing and said nothing other than stare and whimper.

The master crouched down beside the woman with dark curly hair on all fours. His cane draped across his lap. She sat on her legs then, continuing to investigate the dungeon. The ghost demons stood like dutiful students waiting for their instructor's praise. The woman's face was blotched red with tears that streaked down her cheeks. Her eyes were wide, flitting from one corner of the dungeon to the other. Her breath stuttered across her lips, petrified, when her stare settled on the master's gaze. He pressed his finger to his lips.

"Let us do something special tonight." He ran his tongue inside his cheek. "It's time to ramp things up. Unleash a pack of ghost demons across the Hollow to quicken our resolve." The woman was looking over the dungeon; her breath hitched in her throat with a subtle whine beneath the breath. "Let us begin with this one." She turned to the master. Her stare was pitiful, her bottom lip quivering. "She's already ripe with fear. Let us pluck this low hanging fruit and toss it into hell." A single, thick tear dripped from her eye then rolled down her cheek. The master cocked his head, his lips pressed tight into a tiny grin. His stare was stoic, unfeeling. "My love," the master addressed her, but her head was swiveling now, panicked, eyeballing each victim chained to the wall. "Do you know what brings unrelenting fear to those who choose to be brave?"

She kept looking around the dungeon. Attempting to find a way out, Wren was certain. Her voice caught in her throat, her breath stuttering across her lips. The master reached his hand to her chin, guiding her head around to meet his gaze.

"It's simple, really." His head moved from left to right. "Total destruction of the innocent with no recourse to salvation." He gestured to the two people gagged by her side. "Once they see my power, do you think they will still search for hope? Or will they give in to hopelessness and resolve to give in… accepting a fate they never knew was possible?" He paused, glaring at the woman, waiting for an answer. "Well, which one is it going to be?"

"Please," she cried, closing her eyes and bowing her head. "I just want to go home."

The master closed his eyes when he proclaimed, "There's no place like home."

Wren could feel a tremble in his bones, a shifting power of immense magnitude, intense in its purpose, rise in his veins.

"This..." the master said, "is the part of our little story where the supernatural takes form. Let me show you a death you never knew was possible."

Her body tensed, her eyelids stretched wide when the master took her face in his hands. His jaw opened wide when crimson smoke hushed over his lips and he breathed that smoke into her mouth. She immediately began trembling, suffocating. The master held her head in place, but the rest of her body was flailing, convulsing. Her stomach stretched and then compacted. Then compressed some more, her bones were caving in. White foam garbled hot and smoking off her lips. Her skin turned wrinkled as smoke lifted off her shoulders. That same skin turned gray then dark like burnt charcoal. Shriveled, a skeleton with a thin layer of rotting flesh. Dead! The crimson smoke filtered back into the master's throat, then he plunged the cane's knife into her brittle chest. The bone broke away like porcelain. There was no more blood in the veins. The master released her body, and she dropped to the floor like a withered doll. He slipped the knife back into the cane then punched the chest bone, caving it in. The bone fell away like smashed glass, emitting a foul noxious odor.

Muddled whimpers escaped from the remaining victims as the master pulled the woman's heart from her chest, the organ dried and shriveled. It looked like an old rotten apple. He handed the heart to Wren.

"For the fire," he said, then glared at the remaining two on the floor.

"Yes, my master," said Wren, offering the heart to the fire.

"Soon, my beloved," the master never took his eyes off his victims. "Soon your hearts will join the fire too."

They tried wriggling free, but Wren knew they would go nowhere tonight. The master stood, holding his cane and staring down at his victims.

"Let us have our way tonight and bathe in their blood." He looked around the dungeon. To Wren and his ghost demons.

He pointed at the man with his cane. "Toss his body on the slab and let the torture begin."

Carver wasn't certain what he was looking at. The door was caved in, and all the lights were off in the jazz club.

"Perhaps we should go around back?" Father McKenzie stood behind Carver, closer to the street on the sidewalk.

When they first pulled up, Carver had a gut feeling that something was off. At first, he'd thought it was because the street was barren. Not a soul in sight. The curfew he'd put in place was in full effect, but he'd never seen the street so obsolete, so devoid of life. It turned his instincts on high alert and kept his thoughts clear, but he couldn't help the sinking feeling in his gut. Some nagging sensation signaling that all was not right in the world. He told Father McKenzie to wait by the car while he strolled up to the jazz club. Even out here in the dark the club looked like a shadow had fallen over it, casting the club in a veil of death. Carver's only light came from the streetlamp casting a dull yellow glow over the sidewalk. The building looked centuries old but not the polished and restored centuries old. The club looked like it had been abandoned years ago and neglected. A dark stain in the middle of the street.

Carver pressed his face to the glass but couldn't see more than an inch beyond the door. Seemed like the darkness draped itself inside the club like black ink where no light could penetrate.

Felt like he was staring into a black hole, unable to see anything beyond the event horizon.

The wind howled across the street, blowing fierce and foreboding. Carver turned to the street and Father McKenzie. The cold enveloped him like an icy hand that curled into his bones and squeezed. Father McKenzie seemed paranoid, looking up and down the street as if he were waiting for the devil to come out of the darkness to claim his soul.

"What're you thinking?"

Carver didn't know what to think. According to McKenzie, the authority was here and waiting for him to arrive. Apparently, the club had a private room where they held their meetings. The elite discussing the will of the people.

Well, if that's true then why is the club completely dark and locked up?

Carver went to his car and keyed into the trunk. Father McKenzie was watching his every move. Carver gripped his flashlight, clicked it on to be certain it was still working, then closed the trunk.

"If they're supposed to be waiting for us, Father, then why is no one here?"

McKenzie stuffed his hands into the crook of his arms. "I'm not certain. Maybe they're following your orders on the curfew?"

"I doubt it," he said. "Stay here Father." He walked back to the door.

"Do you suspect something sinister?"

"Something like that." Carver beamed his flashlight through the door. It didn't take more than a second to see the first body lying on the floor three feet from the door. She was covered in blood. He shook his head and swept the light across the club. There were bodies everywhere.

Fuck!

Carver gnawed on his bottom lip-no toothpick at the moment-while scanning across the club when he saw it. On the opposite side of the club, directly across from the door where Carver was shining his flashlight was the pentagram and all too familiar inscription.

"What do you see?"

Carver held the flashlight down, his brow knitted in dire thought. He turned to Father McKenzie, staring wild-eyed and confused, his breath pluming off his lips like vapor.

"Detective Carver?" McKenzie paused. "What is it?"

A million thoughts raced through Carver's head at that moment. Apparently, his long day was stretching into an even longer night. He locked eyes with Father McKenzie.

Said, "I don't believe your meeting is happening tonight, Father.

"Not tonight and not ever."

The train hobbled across the tracks, slowing to a stop. Lori swallowed the lump in her throat as she held the handrail above the seat she'd been sitting on. Her hands were trembling.

The image of Marc's inscription was burned into her thoughts. Lori didn't know what to think. She was gnawing on her bottom lip, her thoughts racing like a conveyor belt turned on lightning speed. She knew Marc did not hurt those people. Lori knew his heart. Knew his mind too and yes it was warped and often disturbed, but not so much that he'd go on a rampage. That thought was so far out of left field it made no sense. No sense at all.

There had to be another explanation. Some cosmic makeup packed with coincidence. Maybe he'd become tangled in a web of premonitions. A clairvoyant of sorts, able to predict the future but believing that future was spawned from a dream and the dream's essence spilled over into creativity. A simple misunderstanding or misreading of the signs. Lori couldn't put her finger on it, hoping to find the truth within all the confusion.

What she knew was that she needed to see him. And see him soon.

The train squealed to a stop. The door opened with a ding and a rolling hiss. She stepped onto the platform and was immediately greeted by an icy wind that rattled her bones as she pressed forward toward the stairs that would take her to the waiting cabs and a ride into the Hollow. From there, she'll check into a hotel. Considering the time and the fact that a curfew was in place it was obvious she wouldn't be searching for Marc tonight. It was best to get cleaned up and have a good night's rest then head out in the morning. First stop on the find Marc tour was his apartment.

She couldn't wait to see him. Couldn't wait to discover the answers to every question racing through her head. Couldn't wait to wrap her arms around him.

There's nothing better than coming home.

She hoped the feeling would last forever.

"This one's different," said the witch, her voice echoing from the depths of Marc's memory. "The soul has been tormented for far too long. It causes a shift in energy. A natural occurrence for survival. The heart has been soured by admiration and foolish endeavors. Love is the catalyst to this change. We must elicit recourse back to wretchedness. Through pain!"

Marc stood in the cemetery, watching as a white fog slithered from the western woods across the tombstones towards him. The evil witch from the dark crypt with her malicious coven in the back of his thoughts. What he heard her say brought confusion. *This one's different.* The notion was perplexing.

They tortured him. After the witch draped her hands over Marc's eyes the world went dark. He woke up stretched across a stone slab with the coven nipping their fingers into his skin. Across his chest. Their fingers burning as they inched further into flesh and bone. Needless to say, he wished to avoid all future entanglements with the coven existing in the crypt.

Not that what he witnessed in the jazz club was any less daunting and fearful. After the man in black advised him to drink the absinthe to settle his nerves, Marc had to admit he felt strong, without a care in the world. He felt high, high as a kite. In control, although he knew deep in his subconscious that the control was an illusion. The man in black made certain of it. Marc remembered seeing him in the club although he could never locate him other than in passing, inside windows and mirrors, watching him, wanting Marc to indulge the same as he does. He's always wanted that. He's always wanted Marc to indulge in the flesh and carnage. Only once did he oblige, and that event has haunted him for all his days. He couldn't stop what happened in the club. He had to run. To run far away, which led him to the cemetery. Back to the tombstones and mausoleums. He chose the cemetery over the indulgence, wanting nothing to do with such violence.

"There's got to be a way," he whispered. "Got to be a way for it all to end."

He could still see their faces when the man in black appeared. How scared they all were. How frightened, running for their lives and begging for mercy, knowing mercy would not be provided.

It's a funny thing hope is. Even in the last moments before death people still give in to hope.

Now a red light beamed from the western woods. Inside the light, he could hear the steady rumble of things to come. As if his future belonged to the woods.

"Hope." His voice was desperate and broken. "It's much too late for hope."

A hiss from above. Marc looked up at the horned owl perched on a tree limb high above him. Its mouth gaped open, its wings spread wide. The owl looked down on him, hissing and screeching with its wings extended.

I'm a stranger in its home, Marc thought. *A foreign traveler whose presence is both unwelcome and unnerving. Neither living nor dead, but something in-between.*

He scanned across the cemetery. So barren, empty.

Where are the dead tonight? Seems like even the ghosts are frightened.

He heard whimpers now, choked back tears and cries. He knew who it was. The skinless woman wanting to exact revenge for nefarious deeds. His heart hitched in his chest while listening to her anxious pleas.

"Jennifer," he whispered, rolling his tongue inside his mouth, although he didn't know how he knew her name. A notion that brought guilt to his already bleeding heart.

Marc looked around, locating his trusted mausoleum. He reserved himself to enter the crypt-the only place where he felt safe-but on his way there he could hear Jennifer's whimpering pleas grow prominent across the cemetery.

"Help me, please. There's so much blood. So much blood. So much."

It was obvious she was crying. Marc's heart sank, standing in the cemetery, listening. He looked at the mausoleum, waiting for him to enter.

"Help me, please."

He turned toward her voice.

"There's so much blood."

Marc closed his eyes.

What could he do? She was dead, destined to walk the cemetery for eternity. And why? Because of him. Because he made a deal with the devil and now the devil was loose. And Jennifer was his bounty.

Marc opened his eyes and traveled toward her voice. He found her sitting by an oak tree. Her skin had returned, but there were thick gashes littered across her face and body, bleeding relentlessly. She was covered in blood. Every inch of her stained crimson. He stepped away from the tree into her line of sight. She looked at him with wide, tearful eyes.

"It just keeps bleeding," she whined, staring at him. Her face was slick with blood. She was in obvious pain, as if every drop of blood was born from a slice across her flesh. Her clothes clung to her bloodied skin. "I can't stop the bleeding." She wiped her arms, slicking blood to the ground, but still more blood flowed from those gashes. "I want to go home," she pleaded. "Why can't I just go home?"

Marc, his lips pressed tight while gritting his teeth, swallowed the lump in his throat. Jennifer's eyes, her stare so heart wrenching, her confusion so profound it brought Marc to tears. "I'm sorry," he said. "I wish I could go home too."

She had no response. It was as if he didn't exist. She simply just returned to wiping blood off her arms. "I can't stop the bleeding."

Marc watched as the red glow in the western woods intensified. It looked like the woods were on fire. Another hiss from the owl. Marc snapped his head to it as the owl lifted off the branch and flew into the crimson horizon.

"I just want to go home."

Snapped his attention to Jennifer. He closed his eyes, shaking his head before he sat next to her, leaning against the tree. "I'm so sorry, Jennifer."

She folded into his arms, and Marc wrapped her in his embrace. The crying, fearful, Jennifer wept in his arms. "If I could do something to help you, I would. I just don't know what to do."

Jennifer whimpered and cried. "I'm so tired," she said. "So tired."

"Sleep then," he told her. "I promise nothing will hurt you tonight." But before his words were finished, Jennifer had fallen asleep. Marc sat there with the sleeping Jennifer for a long while before he gathered her in his arms and walked with her to the peaceful mausoleum. He hoped its energy would have the same effect as it did for him, regenerating his cells and hopefully Jennifer's skin. At the very least, she'll be safe from the devils in the cemetery. He kicked the door that opened with ease, stepped in and laid her down with a gentle hand. He brushed the hair from her eyes, watching as the blood seeped from her skin and he hung his head in shame.

"Got to be a way," he said, his hand on Jennifer's head as if in prayer. Heard deathly hollers rage outside the mausoleum as if the ghosts were angry with his isolation. He looked at the coffin in the center. He could feel the energy coming from it. It was relieving, calm, and compassionate. Marc looked over his shoulder to the darkness existing in the crypt. He could hear whispers in the darkness. Incoherent whispers toppling one on top of the other. He looked at Jennifer.

What if they come for her? Whatever exists beyond this crypt may not be kind. Even though this was the blonde woman's crypt he still didn't know what existed beyond the darkness and considering his crypt experience so far, he couldn't risk it. She'll be safer if he stays by her side.

Marc looked through the open door to the cemetery and the thin fog lifting off the ground. He reached for the door and pulled it closed, leaving it ajar to be safe. The last thing he wanted was to be trapped inside. He sat down with his back against the wall.

He leaned his head back. "Got to be a way for it all to end."

Marc sat and waited, listening to the wind and the echoes from the darkness when his mind went blank-devoid of thought-and he heard the squealing sound of a train hissing in the distance, unsure if he was sleeping or awake. Dreaming or playing with the thoughts in his head.

Footsteps now. Someone was walking across a platform, shivering in the cold. He could see the person in the distance as if he were racing down the train tracks towards them.

She stopped abruptly; her last footstep echoed across the platform. He was studying the back of her head when he noticed the sign for the train station read Irvington, which was two towns over from Sleepy Hollow and one from Tarrytown. She slowly craned her head over her shoulder and turned around as if she knew he was there. Her body stiff, her eyes narrow, confused, staring at something she couldn't see.

"Lori?" He reached for her. His hand disappeared through her skin. He noticed she was holding his notebook.

She looked left then right, then straight at him. She was gnawing on her bottom lip as she stepped back before turning around. Marc watched her take the stairs. Watched as she hailed a cab.

"But I told you not to come," Marc whispered.

The cab pulled away from the station and his heart sank.

"Now, things have gotten worse.

"Worse isn't even the right word. Tragic, that's what this is. An absolute tragedy!"

The cab disappeared down the darkened street on its way to the Hollow.

"But I told you not to come."

Part VI

When daylight broke the next morning Sleepy Hollow woke up to what could best be described as a forever night. Dark frozen clouds hovered above the town, draping the Hollow in a dark veil.

As above, so below, John thought as he gazed through his window. Grandpa Claude found him this morning huddled under blankets on the floor of his bedroom. He'd fallen asleep at some point during the night although he couldn't remember what time it had been. It seemed like he waited by his window for an eternity before succumbing to sleep, which seemed to go by in a blink. His eyes were dry and tired when he looked through his window, at first thinking Grandpa Claude had woken him too early. John had thought it was still nighttime, but after a quick glance at his alarm clock he understood this was not true.

The clouds disturbed him. Like a premonition of what was to come, and even when the sun drifted higher the powerful ball of gas and fire did little to shed sunlight across the town. Instead, a dark gray glow was cast across the landscape bathing the Hollow in a surreal manifestation of a black and white film. And then there was the rumble beneath the earth as if Hades was clawing from the depths of hell towards Sleepy Hollow bringing death and suffering on his heels.

John's stomach held a constant rumbling. A sickly sensation twisting his insides into a knot as tight as a tourniquet. He felt unsteady. His hands had the slightest bit of a tremble as if his bones knew something sinister was on its way. His thoughts were caught in a web of confusion, difficult to think, process and evaluate. He chalked it up to being tired.

He brushed his teeth then ate pancakes at the breakfast table. He noticed the television was off. Grandpa Claude always watched the morning news. Every morning without fail. The same Grandpa Claude who took a seat at the kitchen table, his stare fixed on John as he ate.

"I've got something to tell you before you got to school today," Claude said and then looked through the kitchen window. John could tell he was having trouble finding the right words to describe whatever it was he needed to say. John's first thought was the blackjack. Perhaps the police arrived last night while he was asleep. But that's not what Grandpa Claude said. What came out of Grandpa Claude's mouth was something else, something more dreadful than John could fathom.

Murder. Two murders from the day before and just this morning, more grim news. A jazz club had become a cesspool for blood and carnage. And then there was the kicker. The murders carried the same M.O. as a certain family member.

The information was difficult to process. John sat there with his jaw hanging open, not knowing what to say. His appetite completely gone.

"Do you have any questions?" Grandpa Claude, his arms folded over the table.

Questions? Sure, he had a ton of questions, but he couldn't latch on to any of them. Shock! He felt numb. All he could do was shake his head before looking Grandpa Claude dead in the eye and asking if he could be excused. He wanted to get to the bus stop. Wanted to talk with his newfound friends to discover if anything had happened on their end throughout the night.

Grandpa asked if he wanted to stay home from school and normally, he would have jumped at the offer but today was different. Everything was different. He respectively declined, grabbed his backpack and walked out the door into the dark gray hue, lost in his thoughts. He didn't even hear the bus until it was almost too late. When he looked up, the last student was climbing onto the bus. He raced to it after calling for the driver to "Wait," then huffed up the stairs and stopped cold. Everyone was looking at him, staring as if he'd done something wrong. Even the bus driver's eyes seemed off. Somehow, they seemed off, and that tourniquet tightened in his gut.

John held onto each seat as he made his way towards the back of the moving bus to the empty seat next to Michael. Chad was standing up, leaning against the back of the bus while glaring at John. Logan was in the seat next to Chad. He mouthed, "I need to talk to you," to which John gave a quick nod before looking back at Chad. His eyes seemed different, his skin too. And that sickly stare was unnerving. He seemed like he could devour John with his stare.

The bus was quiet. Too quiet, everyone looking straight ahead in silence. Maybe they were all in shock. Or perhaps they were beaming with anger over the current murders. Maybe they secretly blamed him?

He flopped down in the seat next to Michael, who was staring out the window.

"Some weird stuff is going on this morning," John whispered. He had a feeling that everyone was listening to him. His eyes darted from one seat to the next, then he looked over his shoulder. Chad was still in the same position, glaring at him and seething as if he was on the verge of lashing out. John's eyes narrowed, and he turned around. Shook his head then turned to Michael, staring at the back of his head. "You, okay?"

Michael turned and John's eyes widened when he saw his eyes. There was a red tint to his irises that John was certain was not there yesterday and his skin was different. More pale than usual, but also, his veins seemed to have risen to the surface of his skin. They looked like purple and pink spiderwebs. Michael grinned at John's reaction, craning his head while pursing his lips. John's jaw hung open, mesmerized by Michael's stare.

"So," said Michael. "I think we should go back to the house after school. See if we can find your *blackjack*." John noticed he stressed the word blackjack. The sudden change in tempo rippled through John's chest. His heart constricted, afraid to continue beating.

Noticed the smile on Michael's lips, conniving and treacherous.

"Why John, you're trembling. Is everything okay?"

John's lips flapped open and closed like a fish out of water trying to drum up his voice. He cleared his throat. "Perfectly fine," he said, then broke the connection with Michael by turning away. "I think I should have stayed home."

He didn't mean to say that last statement out loud. He was thinking it, and the words just flew off his lips.

Michael laughed and turned to the window. "It's going to be a great day," he whispered under his breath.

John scanned across the bus. He felt trapped.

Like a sheep among wolves.

Another news conference concluded. Carver was already tired of the pop and snap from the cameras, the unrelenting questions from reporters and the never blinking eyeball from video cameras recording his every move, twitch, and bumble. He couldn't imagine living a life in front of the camera.

The Native Americans were right; those things deplete the soul. Always concerned about the way you look. It's a superficial life. And by the time you've grown old, your soul is so thin it's close to nonexistent.

He was in his office again, sitting at his desk and staring through the window while pondering the news conference and the last twenty-four hours. Thoughts that made his head spin a million miles an hour. His toothpick firmly planted between his lips and teeth.

His meeting with his team never happened last night. Instead, everyone was called to the jazz club, provided specific tasks and were scheduled to report their findings this morning at eleven, a full twelve hours after the initial meeting was supposed to happen. He hoped his team had found something. Anything to give him a reason to go back to the house and Marc Saduj.

He eyeballed the book on his desk.

"Don't let anyone know you have it," Father McKenzie had warned before he returned home to the rectory. "The evil that has come to the Hollow will be looking for it. It's the reason they came here tonight." He'd gestured to the club. "They hope to destroy the book. Destroy our only hope to send him back to hell."

Carver didn't believe in the supernatural. The way he saw it, there was always someone human pulling the strings-Marc Saduj in this case-but after all he's seen over the last six months he'd be a fool not to heed the priest's warning. Were the answers he was so desperately seeking contained in a book? He wasn't so sure, but his hope was high, especially after the bloodbath he'd witnessed in the club. Bloodbath wasn't the best word to describe it either. Some victims died from methods that have yet to be identified. Carver couldn't be certain but to him it looked like the victims were instantly mummified. He couldn't explain it any other way.

And the people in the back room-the authority as Father McKenzie referred to them-had received the worst punishment. Their heads were severed and their hearts torn from their necks. Each head sat on the table in front of the decapitated body they belonged to, and each member of the authority had been strategically sat down with their hands on the severed heads in front of them. It was a disturbing scene to say the least.

The hearts were never found.

Taken, Carver thought, by the devil himself. *Taken back to hell.* He gnawed on his toothpick.

I need hearts for the master!

What do they need the hearts for?

He eyeballed the book again. He didn't know why but every time he looked at it his heart jumped as if some part of him was too afraid to read. Ironically, this was the exact book he was searching for in the library. How strange was it that the very book he wanted was across the street from the park in the hands of a priest and kept within the confines of the church? The same park where a body was discovered.

Carver looked at the clock above his office door. 9:40 AM. There was so much to do before his eleven o'clock meeting he didn't have time to sit and read. What the hell would everyone say? Multiple dead bodies, but you took time to read a book?

Carver understood he was dealing with the unknown. Even if it isn't supernatural, whoever is involved apparently believes what is written on those pages.

Knowing their minds is the key to capture! Understand how they think and what they believe, and it becomes easier to anticipate their next move.

He'd be a fool not to read it.

I need hearts for the master!

Jerry. This all started with Jerry.

My son. Bang!

Carver's entire body twitched. Hearing the gunshot that tore through Sheila's skull.

Maybe it ends with John.

He turned to the book then ran his fingers across the brown leather cover before flipping the cover to the title page. He then looked through his office window to the bustling precinct and flicked that toothpick from one corner of his mouth to the other before returning his attention to the book.

Carver flipped the page and started to read.

FBI Agent Henry Clavell never expected that his doorbell would ring so early in the morning. Even more, he would never have expected in a million years who that bell ringer was, ringing frantically as if the world was about to explode.

Elena Francon was that bell ringer. She rushed in the moment he opened the door as if she owned the place. She was frantic, shaking and pacing across his house like a trapped animal, talking so fast Henry couldn't understand a word she said, although he heard Lori's name mentioned several times. Something about a fire and Lori being committed for a suicide attempt. Henry didn't know what to say, the nighttime cobwebs were still clinging to his brain. He needed coffee, that was certain, and took a seat on the stairs, wiping his hands across his face to hide his yawn then stretched his eyelids to the cold morning air.

"Mrs. Francon, please try to relax. I can't understand a word you're saying. What happened to Lori?"

Elena stopped pacing, staring at Henry with a dumbfound expression as if she were thinking Henry was the insane one.

"Look," said Henry. "Let me make some coffee and then you can tell me everything. Okay?"

Elena nodded. "Just make it quick. This matter is time sensitive."

Henry's head shot back. "What is time sensitive?"

Elena tucked her bottom lip into her mouth, glowering at Henry. "Lori's in trouble. Haven't you heard a word I said?"

Now Henry's eyes narrowed. "Mrs. Francon, I just woke up and you're talking a million miles an hour. Mostly sounding like gibberish, so just slow down and tell me what you need me to do?"

Her voice was stern, spoken through a tight jaw and gritted teeth.   "I-need-you-to-go-to-Sleepy-Hollow-to-find-my-daughter-and-bring-her-back-to-me. And I'll pay you one million dollars to do it."

Now he woke up. Perked up is more like it.

"Do you hear me now, Mr. Clavell?"

Lori was standing across from Marc's old apartment building. Standing in the cold overcast morning wondering what will happen when she sees Marc. What will his first reaction be?

Surprised, she was certain, but will he welcome her with open arms or curse the day she was born?

In her head, Lori had pictured the reunion as welcoming. A burst of tears and a homecoming embrace and then they'd be together forever and never look back but now that she was here, she felt something different. Lori felt a rumble from her stomach to her chest that squeezed her heart, staring at the building and the icy gray clouds hovering over the rooftop like an omen for death and suffering.

She could feel the energy beneath her feet as if something were clawing its way to the surface with blood in its mouth and death on its breath and eyes blazing a fire red. Coming to claim its prize. Wind whipped across her skin, tightening her flesh and narrowing her eyes. She turned to the front door. The glass reflected the overcast sky.

Lori swallowed her breath. "It's now or never," she whispered, pulling the black beanie over her ears then scuttled across the street to the front door. Felt a growl erupt beneath her feet with a rumble that tore through her bones. She opened the door and stepped into the small foyer, the door closing behind her with a soft thud. Her hand shook when she pressed the intercom for Marc's apartment.

She waited.

Nothing.

Pressed the button again then stepped back and stuffed her hands beneath the crook of her arms while staring at the intercom as if it held the answers to Lori's future.

Again, nothing.

Maybe he's not home? Went to the store or something like that. Marc had always been an early riser, so maybe he went out already having completed his morning ritual writing and reviewing. She pictured him at his desk doing just that. He could be home but had his headphones on and didn't hear the ring from the intercom. That made sense too and truly speaking, it made the most sense because he rarely left the house before noon.

She wished she still had the key to his apartment. Now that she was here, she couldn't remember where it was. She had no recollection of seeing the key since the accident.

What to do?

She ran her tongue inside her mouth then pressed her lips tight together, staring through the foyer's second door that led to the hallway on the first floor. She eyeballed Mrs. Leiter's apartment.

Did she dare? Mrs. Leiter always gave Lori the creeps. Her voice was witchy, creaky and drawn, and she always had a look in her eyes like she was devouring Lori and could eat her up like a fine meal. She'd probably feed her flesh to her husband too. That poor man, having to live under the thumb of that woman. It had to be a feeble existence.

She tried Marc's intercom one last time and waited, her head pressed to the glass hoping someone would come, possibly leaving for work or going to the store who would allow her entrance. Nothing. The hallway was devoid of life. She looked up the stairs. Also, barren. Looked at Mrs. Leiter's door again and shook her head.

"Well, Lori. You came here to find him. Don't stop now." She pressed the button for Mrs. Leiter's apartment. Pressed it twice just in case the old lady had trouble hearing.

A moment later, she heard the raspy sound of static coming from the intercom. But there was no voice, no one speaking. Just static.

"Hello," Lori said into the intercom. "Mrs. Leiter… it's Lori Francon. Marc's…" She cleared her throat then pressed the intercom again. "Marc's girlfriend. I forgot my key. Can you let me in, please?"

Again, more static, like ripples from outer space. Lori wasn't certain, but she could have sworn she heard garbling like someone choking, the air being squeezed from their gullet.

"Mrs. Leiter? Are you okay?"

More static. More garbling and choking.

"Mrs.…"

The door buzzed unlocked and Lori jumped, startled by the sudden buzz. But then relief. Thank God, she thought and pulled the door open stepping inside the hall when she heard a groan from Mrs. Leiter's apartment that sounded like the old man was writhing in pain.

Lori stopped by their door.

"Don't you move," she heard Mrs. Leiter say from behind the door. "I've had just about enough of you today." Heard slaps and groans filled with pain and fear. "Now stay there and don't say a word. I don't need to listen to your groaning today." Now a thud. More like a kick, and Lori's stomach squealed. Then two more slaps followed by a loud painful groan. "Tired of your antics." Mrs. Leiter's voice was rickety and drawn. Lori always hated her voice. It was melodramatic and she always highlighted certain words with a whine that Lori found rather annoying.

She was about to leave, to head up the stairs to Marc's apartment when Mrs. Leiter's door creaked open. Mrs. Leiter stood in the doorway. She was a short woman no more than five feet tall, with bluish-gray hair so thin it was almost nonexistent. Her beady black eyes sat behind a pair of oversized spectacles attached to a chain around her neck.

"My Lori dear. My my... haven't seen you in a day's age." She shuffled over to Lori and came in for a hug that Lori allowed. She felt slimy in that embrace, like noxious gas emitted from Mrs. Leiter's skin, oily and foul.

"Good to see you, Mrs. Leiter." She didn't know what else to say. "Have you seen Marc recently?"

Mrs. Leiter held that hug a little longer than she needed to, her arms sliding off Lori as if she meant to soil Lori's skin in her stank and grime.

Mrs. Leiter gazed at Lori from over her glasses. "Can't say that I have."

Lori looked up the stairs. "Does he still live here?"

"Pays his rent on time but I haven't seen him."

Now another groan came from within the apartment and Mrs. Leiter snapped her head to the sound. Her snarl was unremarkable. Her nose curled in a sneer.

"Wretched fiend," she growled and stepped over to the door and closed it with a creak, softening Mr. Leiter's continuous groans.

"Maybe you should check on him," she said, then cleared her throat once Mrs. Leiter's stare stabbed at her heart. "Sounds like he needs help."

Mrs. Leiter shuffled over to Lori. "Gas pains today," she said. "Such a vile result, really. I can wait for it, believe me." And she smiled. Grinned something awful and Lori couldn't help but twitch. Her teeth were rotten, black and yellow like she just gulped sewage that stained her pearly whites. The stank rifled off her lips, souring Lori's expression. "Come," she said, pulling a key from her pocket. "Let's welcome you home to Mr. Saduj.

"I'm well aware he will be more than ecstatic to see you."

171

Excerpt from *The Demon and Sleepy Hollow* by the Original Knickerbocker Dated 1856.

The Witches of Sleepy Hollow

Some will say that all witches are evil, which is certainly not true for there is good and bad in everything that walks the earth, so why would this simple fact not extend to witches, too? Unfortunately, there are few walking the earth today who would agree with me, for witches have received the all too familiar label of witchery and witchcraft for far too long, and it is perhaps this judgmental characteristic that has helped the evil witch manifest a cult following.

But I implore you to look with wider eyes so that you may wash away such idiocy. Because when it comes to the witches in this story, yes we can certainly say that it was a coven who summoned the demon to Sleepy Hollow-a circumstance that as my days continue seems to have been inevitable, witch or no witch-but it is equally true that it was a witch's spell that was ultimately responsible for the dismantling of said demon.

Her name was Olga Von Brom, and she had become a good friend and confidant.

This is her story, a summary of how the demon came to the Hollow.

It all began in the autumn of 1849. We all felt it. One morning when the Hollow greeted the sunrise we could feel it in our bones. Something was different. Some nefarious ripple of energy that everyone could feel but said nothing about. It seemed that everything changed in an instant, as if reality had shifted taking with it all the grand smiles, laughter, and joy. In their place were melancholy, anger, and a simple sensation of constant exhaustion. Weak, as if the earth were tapping the lifeforce from our very veins, pulling down on our energy.

At first, we all believed a sickness had arrived in the Hollow. Citizens stayed inside believing it was best to wait it out, rest up and nurse ourselves back to health. Unfortunately, as time went on, the opposite was true. It seemed as if we would never be able to shake the sickness, destined to live depleted for the rest of our days. We gave chase, inquiring in the nearby villages if they were experiencing the same. However, our inquiries received negatives from all the surrounding areas, and it was then that we looked internally for an answer. Perhaps it was the water or maybe the soil our crops had grown from had become tainted. Perhaps the ground was sour. We discovered no such issues or concerns, but still the sickness continued.

And then the first body was discovered on the morn of All Hallows Eve. There had been an early winter that year and although no snow had yet fallen, a frost settled over the fields along with a fog that lifted off the Hudson that devoured our sky, draping the Hollow in a grey veil. We should have known then that there was a demon among us.

The first body was found by local farmer, Stephen Van Demeer, while he was on his way to the market for the day, his rolling cart filled with pumpkins and squash. I can only speculate how his jaw must have dropped, his eyes wide, more than likely not understanding what he was first looking at, with an edge of creepiness and an air of foreboding barreling down on his shoulders the closer he came to the body.

She must have looked so strange propped up against the bridge with her heart cut out.

———

Carver slammed the book shut just in time before Captain Flannery stormed into his office. He quickly placed today's paper over the book as he stood up. He felt like a kid who just got caught with his hand in the cookie jar. The two officers stood in silence, glowering at each other.

Carver had respect for Flannery's position, but that's where the respect started and ended. They'd been at odds with each other ever since Carver transferred to Sleepy Hollow from Manhattan decades earlier. Over a decade ago they were both up for the same position-Captain of the Sleepy Hollow Police Department-which ultimately went to Flannery, but not because he was the better cop or investigator. No, not at all. Carver was clearly the better cop among the two, but Flannery's roots in the Hollow went back centuries and, in turn, the position was given to Flannery. But their so-called coopetition-as Carver so elegantly thought of it-continued from that point on. Considering Carver's knack for investigative work, Flannery would have been a fool if he didn't provide his best investigator with the time of day. In turn, the two giants on the force learned to coexist, and that's where the relationship ended.

Now they were just staring at each other, both men sizing the other up. Carver took the toothpick from his lips and Flannery gnashed his teeth. Carver thought the captain looked sick. His skin was a whiter shade of pale, and he looked frail with his veins prominently displayed across his cheeks.

"Tell me we have a lead." Flannery, his shoulders went slack. He had this look in his eyes, some state of paranoia that Carver chalked up to the most recent bloodbath in the jazz club. Carver knew some of Flannery's friends were in the club. Plus, his city was under siege, so yeah, Carver understood where the man was coming from.

Carver shook his head. "Unfortunately, no." He popped his toothpick back between his lips.

"The murders are similar to Jerry Hardwood. Are we looking into the family?"

Carver tilted his head. "The only surviving member of Jerry Hardwood is his son, and the boy is a child... considering the extent of these murders that's a far reach for a child to pull off."

"Some connection then? Maybe a follower of Jerry?"

"Not likely. At least none we've discovered. What is apparent is that Jerry did not act alone. I have a suspicion Jerry was coached by whoever is doing this."

"And what about this Marc Saduj?" Carver's heart stopped. *There's a portal to hell in the basement.*

"I hear you have him under surveillance. Is he a person of interest?"

Carver nodded. "He is, but there's not much to go on. He is the person who purchased the house Jerry had been showing on the day of his murders, but so far, our investigation has not yielded results. Plus, his record is clean."

"Do you plan on following up? See where he was last night?"

"I do. I plan to question him after our eleven o'clock meeting. But at the moment, there's nothing I can use to start a more in-depth search of his property."

"People are dying!" Flannery's voice raised. Again, he started gnashing his teeth.

"I'm aware of that, but if we bring in the cavalry and find nothing, we're worse off. He's under twenty-four-hour surveillance… believe me, he's incapable of coming and going without being seen. All indications reveal he hasn't left his home since yesterday morning."

"Maybe he has another way out?"

Carver tipped his head left, then right. "I thought about that, but how? Where? It's not like he can disappear."

Flannery shook his head. His jaw clenched as he looked out the window at the reporters outside the precinct.

"Captain, you know how investigations work. They're never easy and it takes time to build a case. We're starting with nothing here… all we know is that we've got some sadistic cult on our hands and they're uniquely organized. Probably been planning this for years. They're light years ahead of us but we'll catch them. Without a doubt, we'll catch them."

Flannery looked at Carver. "So, you think it's multiple people?"

"How can it not be? Considering the murders in the club and the multiple bodies scattered across the Hollow it makes sense that there's more than one."

"Like the Manson Family?"

Carver nodded. "Like the Manson Family."

Now Flannery shook his head. He stepped towards the window. "The entire world's gone to shit. It's like we're broadcasting the end of the world and all anyone can do is sit on the edge of their seat and watch it crumble."

Humanity's end as a new beginning!

Carver said nothing in return. He looked at the newspaper covering the book. *The answers are in the book.*

Flannery walked to the office door. "Whatever you need to solve this is yours, Detective." His hand on the doorknob, he turned to Carver. "Anything at all. I'm giving you full control. Just find the sonofabitch. And find him soon." He looked through the window again. "I have a feeling this is just the beginning."

Henry Clavell climbed into Elena's blacked out SUV. She shuffled over for him to take a seat. The black leather cushions were comfy and warm from the heater blasting through the vents. The driver-introduced as Jeremy Wiles-waited for him to close the door before pulling out of the driveway. They had a long drive ahead-plenty of time for Elena to catch Henry up on all the needed tidbits about Lori Francon.

According to Elena, Lori had been wrestling with the loss of her relationship with a man named Marc Saduj that occurred after a terrible car accident that almost claimed Lori's life. Henry remembered his night with Lori, the two of them grieving over the past, but she seemed-at the time at least-to want to move on, making the current circumstance a bit more suspect. There had to be a reason that caused Lori to change her mind.

"It's that damn notebook," Elena said. "His notebook. Marc's a writer and Lori found one of his unpublished stories and took it upon herself to read the damn thing. Against my wishes, of course. And now she won't get him out of her head."

Elena was also forthcoming with a few additional details, namely that Lori fell into a deep depression after reading the notebook which prompted a suicide attempt that she was properly committed for. She'd tried the same before, many years ago, and

Elena knew her daughter. Knew her enough to know she was acting out of psychosis, hoping to rekindle the relationship and blaming her mother for the breakup.

"As if I had something to do with it." She scoffed at the notion. "That boy's a disturbed individual and he needs to stay away from my daughter."

Henry had some questions. More than a few. "What happens if she refuses to come home? I can't force someone to do something they don't want to do. Last I checked, it's still a free country."

To which Elena looked through the window to the rolling street and fields surrounding them. Henry noticed her hands were clenched over her lap. "My daughter's not well, Mr. Clavell. She needs to be far away from Marc Saduj. I have a rehab scheduled to take care of her mental health issues. Once she's stable, she'll be able to see this for what it is. Our goal is to escort her to the plane that'll take her to rehab."

"And that's it?" he asked with a shrug. "Just get her on the plane?"

She turned to Henry and looked at him dead in his eyes. "Correct, Mr. Clavell. Get her on the plane and you get your money."

"And when is this plane scheduled for?"

"Two days," Elena said. "We have two days."

Henry nodded, turned to the window and whispered, "Two days."

"Correct," said Elena.

Henry looked at the driver, then turned to Elena. She was staring through the window. The car hummed across the highway in quiet solitude. He knew something was off. Something Elena wasn't telling him. She was withholding information; he was certain of it. This seemed too easy. And the story that Lori dove into a deep depression seemed distant, if not troubling. He was with Lori a few days ago and she showed no signs of depression. Not that it couldn't happen. Henry had his battles with depression over the last year and understood it could come at any minute. Sometimes you just wake up with it.

Still, there was more to the story. But a million dollars? Henry can set himself up big time with a million in cold hard cash, and it was all to help a friend. Someone who was suffering. Yeah, he could do that. Perhaps this was the beginning of a new career. Henry Clavell: Bounty Hunter for the Well to Do. Nevertheless, he had a sinking feeling in the pit of his stomach. A nagging sensation telling him to return home and forget Elena's offer.

173

Lori was waiting on the top step, mere inches from Marc's apartment waiting for Mrs. Leiter to come strolling up to meet her. When she shuffled over to the banister on the last flight of steps, Lori shot her head back. The look in Mrs. Leiter's eyes was sinister, staring at Lori as if she could devour her flesh. The old lady cracked a smile.

"So, kind of you to wait for an old lady." Lori stood up, stepping out of Mrs. Leiter's way as she gripped the banister and pulled herself up another step.

"It's no problem, Mrs. Leiter. I'm grateful you're letting me in."

Mrs. Leiter climbed that last step, paused a second, then stepped over to Marc's door, reaching into her pocket and retrieving a set of keys. Lori stood behind her as she slid the key into the lock when something scurried beneath Mrs. Leiter's grayish-blue hair that sent a cringe racing down Lori's spine.

Mrs. Leiter was mumbling something under her breath. Or- Lori turned to the other apartments on the floor-maybe someone left a television on. It sounded like fast-talking gibbered whispers.

"Young love… *young love…*" whined Mrs. Leiter, but still Lori could hear those muffled whispers. She twisted the key, unlocking the door. "Always so complicated when life is so simple.

Keep it simple and…" She turned around with the key in her hand. "Everything falls into place, my dear." That foul sewage gasped across her lips. Lips that moved in unison with those whispers. Mrs. Leiter twisted the doorknob and the door opened with a slight creak. Leiter's beady eyes glared at Lori. "After you, my dear." She ran her tongue across her bottom lip.

Lori looked through the open door, then craned her head to see further.

"No need to wait, dear. The apartment is safe."

Mrs. Leiter gestured for her to walk inside. She even pushed the door open further, the apartment unfolding in front of Lori's eyes.

"Come, my dear. All is for the best. All is safe. *All is safe.*"

Lori felt her breath hitch in her throat. "Marc!" she called, coddling her arms close to her chest. It seemed wrong to enter his apartment without warning. What if he had another girl in there? What if he's nursing a hangover and doesn't want people breaking into his apartment? Because what would she say? Hey, I broke your heart, so I got your landlord to let me in to apologize. Yeah, that wouldn't go over too well.

"Maybe he's sleeping?" Mrs. Leiter again, Lori looked at her and that beady, anticipatory stare. "Come, my dear. Perhaps we shall sit and wait." She shuffled inside.

The apartment was draped in darkness from the overcast sky outside Marc's windows. Thunder cracked above the building with a sonic boom. Lori flinched, shuddering from head to toe before she stepped into the apartment and those muffled whispers ceased the moment her foot landed inside. Mrs. Leiter waited by the window, watching Lori's every move.

Her stare was disturbing, sending waves of displeasure shuddering through Lori's bones.

174

The school cafeteria was somber. Most of the students ate their lunch in quiet solitude. Occasionally, someone said something out loud to the receipt of laughter that lasted no longer than a brief chuckle. Even the lunch ladies with their hairnets and gloves and plastic aprons had little to say. Their eyes were bloodshot and tired, scooping helpings of hamburger and pasta in a zombie-like trance.

The scene was disturbing. Every student with their eyes staring straight ahead, moving in the lunch line single file as if they were soldiers in a zombie war at the command of some phantom pulling their strings from the netherworld. All but John. He seemed immune to whatever evil his fellow students had succumbed to.

Maybe they're in shock with all the murders.

Which seemed like the most logical reason for the somber mood, but John wasn't sold on the idea. He felt a nudge against his arm and turned to Susan Chambers-a girl he'd known since kindergarten. She gestured for him to move forward.

John pursed his lips and swallowed. "Sorry," he said then moved to the hot lunch section where he eyeballed Mrs. Hallowell and his head shot back. She was glaring at him. Her eyes carried the same red tint as Michael's and her skin was the same too-those spiderwebbed veins prominent across her cheeks.

"Good morning," she said with a tilt of her head. "So nice to see you, John."

John had no reply, standing with his jaw hanging open eyeballing Mrs. Hallowell's stare and the subtle smile that curled in the corner of her mouth. After a pause, she gripped the serving spoon then scooped hamburger and pasta onto his plate. He noticed she put a little extra on top. There was a sparkle in her eyes, some gleaming glint in the corner of her pupil that highlighted his fear with a twinkle. "A little extra," she said. "A young man needs his strength." She paused, holding the serving spoon as a smile crept into the corner of her mouth. "Seems like you'll need all the strength you can get."

John put his head down, took his tray and walked into the cafeteria. He paused at the entrance, scanning across the quiet tables packed with students. Some with their heads down, not eating. Not talking, sitting quietly and stunned. A few nibbled on their food and others were staring directly at him. John pursed his lips and swallowed the lump in his throat. He saw Chad, Michael, and Logan sitting across the cafeteria, staring at him. Chad and Michael had hate in their eyes while Logan was looking at him with a dire stare as if to say, *Don't sit over here.*

He discovered a table on the opposite side of the cafeteria with only a handful of students. He took his tray to the table and sat down while feeling eyes on him. Eyes from the lunch line, and eyes from the tables surrounding him. He scanned across the other students at the table. John knew who they were-the misfit geeks of

Sleepy Hollow Middle School. They said nothing and just sat at the table either staring straight ahead or with their heads bowed when he heard a loud smack from across the cafeteria and everyone at the table jumped in their seat. Startled and unnerved, John turned to the sound. Chad was standing up, glowering at him, his backpack on the ground in front of him. A second later, he bent over and picked it up then Chad, Logan and Michael got up from their tables and walked towards him.

John looked straight ahead, his spine tightening with every step they took in his direction. He gripped his chocolate milk and opened it. His hands were trembling. John watched them from the corner of his eye when Chad's arm and hip pushed against him as he walked by sending shivers filled with cringes racing up John's spine. A crumbled piece of paper was dropped over his shoulder onto his plate. John eyeballed the ball of loose-leaf paper then reluctantly watched his new friends exit the cafeteria.

And like a flick of a switch the cafeteria turned loud and excited. John's brow furrowed when he scanned across the cafeteria. They were all talking as if the world had hit the play button and now those conversations were extra loud to make up for the intrusive pause. John investigated the hall.

Was it them?

Looked back into the cafeteria and the normalcy made him feel a little less on edge. The sudden laughter, chatter, and occasional spill brought him back from his dire sensation. He eyeballed the crumbled paper then looked back outside the cafeteria. Empty. No one was watching. He took the paper and opened it.

Logan's handwriting.

Things aren't safe. Come to my house after school. I have to show you something.

He stared at that paper for longer than he was aware before crumbling it up and stuffing the paper into his coat pocket. His stomach grumbled hungrily, but when he looked at his food something scurried underneath. He used his plastic fork to move some of the pasta and beef around, revealing maggots on the bottom of his food when his stomach lurched. Head shaking to ward off the sensation to puke, he looked at the students sitting with him. Their eyes were all black and they were jamming their mouths with heaping spoonfuls of beef and pasta, filling their cheeks like squirrels gathering food. He watched as they chomped down on the food. The maggots were gnawed into smashed mush across their tongues. Their mouths filled with pus like thick white paste then swallowed down their gullets. John scanned across the cafeteria and noticed every student had the same black eyeballs.

Mrs. Hallowell stood at the entrance to the lunch line leaning against the entry, arms crossed and glaring at John. John snapped his head away. Eyes front, his breath hitched in his throat, staring at the students across the table chomping on their food. Pus and bile dripped off their lips and chins. John saw it drop onto the boy's plate and one of those maggots scurried into the pus.

He couldn't help it. John puked all over the table and immediately the cafeteria turned into a rumble of catastrophe.

"I think I'm sick," he said, his skin hot and moist. His nerves were unsteady; his hands were trembling. When he looked up, he noticed all their eyes had returned to normal.

175

A layer of dust covered every corner of Marc's apartment. It looked like he hadn't returned since the accident. It seemed completely devoid of life and whatever had happened happened in a hurry. A glass sat on the table next to Marc's recliner, stained with a green glow and white mold. The beds were unkempt, still with the sheets crumpled over the mattress and there was dried mud all over the master bedroom, the bed included. His toothbrush was still in a cup by the sink and his clothes hung in the closet with more clothes in the armoire. Untouched, but that didn't mean he hadn't been in the apartment. Maybe he just didn't care how he lived. The scene was perplexing and then there was the added sensation that clung to the apartment. Something was off other than the apartment's presentation. She could feel it in her stomach, jarring and unnerving. The apartment was stuffy too and warm as if fresh air hadn't graced the apartment in a long while.

"Best to open a window," said Mrs. Leiter. She was in the living room while Lori searched the master bedroom. "*So, drab... drab and lifeless.*"

Lori heard Mrs. Leiter open the window when an icy wind tore through the apartment like a python slithering hungry towards its prey. She stood in the center of the room. The same room where she and Marc had spent so many days and nights. Looking it over, wondering what to do next. Judging by the mold in the glass and the dust, apparently Marc hadn't been in the apartment in a long while. It seemed like he took off and left in a hurry.

Lori gazed through the window at the Tappan Zee Bridge in the distance. Marc's favorite view. He wouldn't give it up for anything. She stepped to the window; her arms crossed over her stomach. The Hudson River reflected the dark clouds that turned the bridge's lights into little twinkles of fire.

Where can you be? What happened?

Lori ran her tongue inside her mouth as her arms wrinkled with gooseflesh-the cold was bitter even through her clothes. What she knew was that either Marc had become so enamored with current circumstances he gave up on cleaning and chose to live in filth, which, she knew, was not his M.O. Marc had always been a clean freak. He had a persistent need to feel clean as if that cleanliness could wipe away the trauma from the past. Or he no longer lived in the apartment, which was possible but came with a host of new questions. She thought about the murders and the connection to Marc's book. Maybe he discovered something and that something reared its ugly head and snatched him out of thin air.

Maybe he's in trouble.

Without a doubt the scene was disturbing, creating more questions than offering answers. If he left, he took off without a concern for the apartment but if that was true then why pay the monthly rent? Considering Marc's annual salary, he'd have difficulty affording two apartments. *Then where did he go?* He doesn't have any family he could stay with. For all intents and purposes, Marc was alone. He had no one. No one but Lori. This made no sense. No sense at all.

Lori walked to the door. "Mrs. Leit…" Her voice trailed off. The apartment was empty. She could have sworn Mrs. Leiter was standing by the living room window. The front door was open, gently waving in the subtle wind. She could see the open window in the living room and the curtain that drifted into the apartment.

"Mrs. Leiter?" she called but received no answer. She cautiously stepped into the hall when the sky turned darker outside Marc's windows casting shadows across the wall. Shadows that crept across the framed pictures hanging in the hallway. Lori looked at the pictures and her heart raced into overdrive. Every picture was different than she remembered. These were family pictures. Pictures of Marc as a child with his mother and father. In a park by the river. At Playland Amusement Park. Trips to the city. Lori had seen the pictures before, but these were different. In every picture his parents' heads were flopped to the side as if their necks had been cut and their heads were hanging on their shoulders by a string of bloodied flesh. Their eyes were all black. Black as the darkest night. And the young Marc was glaring at the camera in every picture.

But readily apparent was the intrusion on the family picture. In between both parents and directly behind Marc was a man dressed in all black with long dark hair that fell to his shoulders in wavy tendrils. His skin was pale gray and ghostly with eyes beaming red. Lori noticed he held a red cane. She knew she'd seen him before but where or when she couldn't put her finger on as if his memory drifted from conscious thought in a game of catch me if you can.

Her mouth hung open, staring at the pictures, assessing every one of them. The man in black was in every picture as if he'd always been there. Now she heard sniffing. Ragged sniffing like a dog on a hot trail. Her brow furrowed. She turned to the second bedroom where she heard movement like someone shuffling across the floor behind the closed door.

"Mrs. Leiter?"

Lori pushed the door open and froze. Mrs. Leiter had her head buried in a pile of Marc's dirty clothes. Lori was certain she was sniffing through them. She picked up a pair of boxer shorts and ran her tongue across it, drawing the scent into her nostrils as her head flopped back as if in ecstasy. Lori heard a groan erupt in Mrs. Leiter's throat. The scene was disturbing to say the least.

Lori didn't know what to make of it. She took a step back, closing the door. That was probably the strangest scene she'd ever witnessed. She looked back to the master bedroom, then to the living room and walked towards it, believing it was time to leave when she heard a door creak open followed by a clickity click on the ceiling and she immediately picked up her pace, feeling a cringe tear up her spine. More scuttles now, like a ticking clicking above her head as if someone were crawling across the ceiling. The front door swayed open as she stepped into the foyer by the kitchen when something glinted in the corner of her eye.

The kitchen was tiny, with enough room for a stove, sink, and refrigerator and a small nook where Marc had a small table in the corner. There was enough room for two seats. An envelope sat on the table. Lori didn't know why, but the envelope caught her eye with a freeze of her heart. She stood by the front door, staring at the envelope then looked back into the hall to locate Mrs. Leiter. She was nowhere to be seen. There were no more sniffing or grunting sounds either. She wondered what Mrs. Leiter had gotten into now. Lori pursed her lips, then swallowed a breath down her gullet as she turned to the envelope. Her hands trembling, she stepped to the table and grabbed the envelope recognizing the handwriting immediately. It was a spot on forgery of her own.

Elena!

She paused, smoothing her fingers across Marc's handwritten name on the envelope before she looked up and around the apartment. Everything was quiet. Conflicted, she was afraid of what she would read, certain that the message was the same she received herself. Gritting her teeth, she opened the envelope and took out the letter. Her eyes roamed across the words on the paper as a sour taste erupted in the back of her throat. The more she read the worse she felt. Tears pricked in her eyes, threatening to unleash.

Now she understood Elena's play. Forge competing letters ending the relationship based on catastrophe. Her thoughts swam through her mind, desperate and filled with rage. Looking at the paper but no longer reading, Lori gripped it tight between her trembling palms when a single tear fell to the ink. She wiped her tears on her sleeve then folded the paper, returning it to the envelope that she stuffed into her coat pocket. Heard a crash like glass shattering and skittering across the floor. She immediately looked up, startled and unnerved. Her heart beat like a drum between her ears.

She pursed her lips and swallowed. "Mrs. Leiter?" Her voice was weak. Lori cleared her throat, craning her head into the apartment. "Mrs. Leiter," she called, a little louder this time. She stepped into the living room where she saw the glass-the one with the green liquid and string of mold-was shattered across the floor. Lori looked at the open window and the wind flapping the curtain into the room. Soft and gentle. *Was it enough to push the glass off the table?*

No word from Mrs. Leiter. Maybe she wasn't finished sniffing and licking. Lori shuddered at the thought.

She called out again, hoping for an answer. "Mrs. Leiter?"

Nothing. No noise. No answer. Just the whispering wind whirling off the Hudson. When she looked down at the shattered glass she saw blood. Spots of blood were scattered across the floor. Her heart hitched in her chest like a hand snatched the organ in a vise grip, stealing the breath from her lungs.

Suffocating. She felt like she was suffocating, struggling to bring air into her lungs as the room shifted and seemed to bend around her. Sweat slicked across her forehead, nauseas and sick. She heard fire crackling, and those voices filled with gibberish and laughter between her ears.

Mrs. Leiter stood in front of her, wavering like the room, bending and crooked. Lori was more than certain Mrs. Leiter peeled herself off the ceiling to stand directly in front of her.

"My dear," she said. "So sick. *Sooo sick.*" She took Lori's hands and Lori shuddered. Her hands were as cold as ice. And her eyes. Her eyes were as cold as stone, beady and steadfast. Lori couldn't remove her stare from those eyes. Mrs. Leiter's breath invaded Lori's nostrils, the foul stench hushed across her face, hot and putrid.

"I think I'm gonna throw up," said Lori, standing on weakening legs.

"Just a taste. Just a taste." Mrs. Leiter grinned at Lori, bashful yet nefarious as she pulled Lori's hands closer. Pulled her head down too. Mrs. Leiter's mouth opened. "*Juuust a taaaaste.*" Her tongue, a blackened stick of putrid disgust jutted between her lips. Her nail nipped into the meat on Lori's wrist with a stab filled with pain.

The sudden ache tore Lori awake as if she'd been in a trance. She shook her head and stepped away from Mrs. Leiter then jerked her hands away from Mrs. Leiter's grip. The room was normal. The shattered glass contained no blood. "What're you doing?"

Mrs. Leiter scoffed. "Forgive me," she whined. "I'm an old lady. Sometimes the moment gets to me, and *I rant and I rave.* Pay it no mind, my dearest." She reached for Lori's hands again, but Lori pulled away.

"Don't touch me." Lori's voice was abrupt, staring at Mrs. Leiter through narrow eyes.

Mrs. Leiter seemed to not care about Lori's sudden boundary, smoothing that thick black tongue across her bottom lip. "Just *a taste*," she whispered with a crinkle of her nose.

Lori stepped away from Mrs. Leiter, shaking her head but never taking her eyes off her. "No, thank you."

Mrs. Leiter reached for her hand and again Lori stepped back with a jolt. "I said don't touch me." Mrs. Leiter stepped closer, and Lori took another step back, inching closer to the front door. Heard the glass crunch beneath her feet. She looked down and the blood was back, but not just spots of blood. There was a puddle of blood on the floor. Lori snapped her attention back to Mrs. Leiter.

She was moving. Not walking, but moving, as if floating. Her shoes were scraping the floorboards as she moved closer. "I must admit, I had you pegged wrong from the beginning."

What? Lori kept backing up. Mrs. Leiter's movements were slow but continuous, her small frame barreling down on Lori with a dark, fearful energy. The scrape from her toes across the floorboards shuddered through Lori's bones.

"But I see that innocence now. He was right to choose you."

"What the hell are you talking about?"

"Did you really think you'd come back and all would be right?" She laughed, holding her hands out like talons ready to strike. "Foolish girl. *Fooooolish girl.*"

"What did you do to Marc?" Her question was received with immediate laughter when Lori tripped over the chair and dropped onto her ass.

"Nothing he didn't do to himself. Just a taste, my dear. *Just a taaaste.*"

Lori snapped her focus to Mrs. Leiter. She was coming closer, holding her hands out, clawing towards Lori. Mrs. Leiter's tongue wiggled between her lips, her eyes wide and black to the core. Lori heard footsteps outside the apartment. Someone was coming up the steps.

"Help," Lori screamed, and Mrs. Leiter's head snapped to the front door that closed with a heavy thud that made Lori's heart jump.

"No need for them to intrude on our private moment."

Lori shuffled to her feet in a hurried panic then raced to the front door. She gripped the doorknob and pulled but the door never moved. The deadbolt was locked. Mrs. Leiter's fingers crawled across her shoulders. Her voice in Lori's ear.

"Just a taste, my dear. Then I'll allow you to leave to search for your beloved."

Lori's thoughts stopped. Her fear and anxiety ceased. She felt like she was floating.

"Come, my dear. Let me have a taste of forbidden fruit."

Mrs. Leiter was escorting her towards the bedroom when she felt a sting in her palm followed by the warm flow of liquid. Blood dripped across her palm from where Mrs. Leiter's nail sank into her flesh. The bedroom was coming closer and no matter what, Lori knew she did not want to go into that room. The doorway bent and shifted, and Lori's eyes rolled in their sockets.

"A taste for you, too." Mrs. Leiter looked at Lori from over her shoulder and grinned. Lori's stomach twisted. "Just a taste." That tongue again, wiggling across her lips.

Lori felt another pinch in her palm that snapped her awake. She snatched her hand away.

"I said don't touch me!" Whatever trance she had been in was gone. Now the anger arrived, but Mrs. Leiter started laughing. Laughing a high-pitched cackle. Lori shook her head. "You're insane."

"Come my dear. Just a taste." She started walking forward with her hands in front of her as if she meant to snatch Lori again. *"Just a taste."*

Lori kept backing up. "Not a chance you sick twisted bitch." She turned on her heels sprinting to the front door, her heart pounding against her chest as she twisted the deadbolt then threw the door open, frantic and panicked, racing down the steps at a lightning pace. Hurrying as fast as she could, rounding staircase after staircase when she heard that tick tick clickity click above her head. She jumped a few steps to the first floor and hit the ground running, barreling through the door like she was shot out of a cannon.

When she turned to the foyer, Mrs. Leiter was standing on the bottom step watching her.

"What the fuck?" Lori whined, then backed away from the building while rubbing the wound on her palm. It stung something awful.

Lori didn't know what to think, but she knew she wasn't going back to the apartment ever again.

176

Excerpt from *The Demon and Sleepy Hollow* by the Original Knickerbocker Dated 1856.

The Witches of Sleepy Hollow

The same night the first body was found-a transient we could never identify-the second body was discovered along the river. The murdered was none other than local seventeen-year-old Katrina Van Brunt. Her body had been severed in half and her heart pulled from her decapitated torso.

We were never able to find the hearts of either victim.

Now, at the risk of sounding cold I do admit that the discovery of the first body did not create the same outrage that Ms. Van Brunt's dismembered corpse had caused. The reason being that the first victim was an unknown transient while Ms. Van Brunt was one of us, escalating our rage over the situation. The townspeople were in shock and-rightfully so-demanded retribution. It had become quickly apparent that a murderer was among us, although during that time we did not see the connection between our own sickness and the recent murders. How could we? Such things have never been known to occur prior to our misfortune.

As a result of our rage, we created a team of twenty men to investigate the murders and hunt the sadistic fiend. Some of us desired to contact the constables in New York City to provide aid in our endeavor, although the idea was denied. It was believed that justice would best be served from within our own community. For whom, other than those most explicitly affected, could serve the best interest in discovering the wretched fiend who'd inflicted such terrible heartache upon our town?

It was during our first council meeting that Olga made herself known to us. My compatriots mocked the poor girl with religious fervor filled with hate and misunderstanding. But her story intrigued me, and I requested to speak with her in further detail about her claims.

Olga reported that the coven known among the witches as The Coven of Baphomet was responsible for conjuring the demon. Olga, being a witch herself, had come forth under great scrutiny after her own coven refused her desire to speak with us. In turn, she may have betrayed those she cared for most. A consequence she had informed me she was willing to accept if it would mean the demon would be sent back to the hell he came from. I was immediately intrigued, for no reason other than her sincerity regarding her claims. As a result of our meeting, she earned my favor and I came to believe every word she said, even the most outlandish and surreal. In my lifelong studies I've heard of such nefarious events, although I had never witnessed one unfolding firsthand. Unfortunately, that claim would not last.

The Coven of Baphomet had occupied for centuries the woods on the outskirts of the Hudson River in what you will now see has been coined Storm Street and Wiley Road, merely a stone's throw away from where the first body was found. Olga further indicated that the Baphomet witches had been drawn to the western woods after one of their own disappeared and had yet to return, prompting the coven to investigate.

They came back changed. *Different* was how Olga referred to them, but different in the most nefarious and sinister way imaginable. They ate the hearts of the young and referred to themselves as ghost demons capable of supernatural feats. It was only a matter of time before one of the Baphomet witches sought refuge in Olga's coven. In turn, a sickness had come over Olga's coven the same in which we all felt on the morning of All Hallows Eve. It was then that the leaders of Olga's coven made the trek into the western woods. Only one member returned, the most powerful witch among them-Catarina Milese-who perished within hours of her return.

She said she fought for her life and soul to return and had endured the worst torture imaginable. Catarina returned without her eyesight. Her eyes had been plucked from her skull after entering an underground passage that she described as a portal to the underworld where the vilest demons, devils, and fiends exist. And it was there that she saw the demon in control of the ghost demons. She described him in full detail despite having lost her eyes. He was tall and wearing a dark cloak. His skin was gray with dark plump veins that spiderwebbed prominently across his face. His frame was thin, emaciated thin, but his strength was immeasurable. More powerful than a hundred men. His hair was a dark black that hung in tendrils down the side of his face.

He was the embodiment of evil.

And he had come to the Hollow to destroy all of humanity. To enslave us and feed on our hearts and souls.

Catarina's story detailed a house in the western woods. She described a mansion, although there had never been a record of such a house nor did any residents claim to know of its existence. It was this claim of a phantom house that provided Olga's naysayers with a reason to dismiss her story. Although, as we later discovered, such a house does exist. I shall provide details on the house in upcoming chapters but know this, the very house we discovered in the western woods is evil. It breathes the fires of hell and damnation and turns sane minds mad.

Catarina's story also detailed how they had found the original witch who had been deemed lost living in the house. It was this witch who provided aid to the house's owner and had taken occupancy with him. Olga referred to her as Selena Vonder Dutch. Selena admitted to hearing a great calling coming from the house. A calling that prompted her to stand at the right hand of the owner.

He had been used as a conduit for the demon to enter our world. His history continues to be shrouded in mystery, but from what we've learned he came from the mountainous region known as Transylvania in Eastern Europe, constructing the house shortly after the Revolutionary War.

His name was Sam J. Curad.

———

Carver opened the door to the conference room where his team waited. They were talking about the case when he entered but shut up the moment he opened the door. All eyes were on Carver. They were staring at him with what he assumed was either pity or sympathy.

Considering the current situation not one officer in the room had ever come head-to-head with the same. Sure, there were murders in Sleepy Hollow just like every city and town in America, but this was something different. Multiple murders from what Carver was certain were multiple murderers and a rising body count. It wasn't a matter of if but when the next body would be discovered.

The question Carver had been contemplating for the past few hours was what the endgame was for the team of murderers. Any typical serial killer had an endgame, and that endgame was either getting caught or dying. But this was different. A team of serial killers posed a multitude of concerns. Namely, if a lone killer's endgame was to keep killing or die, does the same ring true for a team of serial killers? Was their plan to murder the entire town and then move on to the world at large?

Humanity's end as a new beginning.

Carver shook his head to rid himself of the thought then addressed his team. "We have a lot to discuss so let's start with updates."

His team comprised six detectives ranging in ages from the late twenties to the early forties. Four men and two women. Detective Montgomery sat at the far end of the table, Joan Whitfield on his right along with Andy Sheffield and Tom McCoy. On Montgomery's left were Theo McMaster and Cindy Morgan. The table was littered with folders, papers and photographs. It was Cindy who talked first.

"Coroner's report came back this morning on the burn victims from the jazz club." She reached into the pile of papers and folders, took one of those files then looked it over to make sure it was the right one before handing it to Carver as he took his seat.

"What was the conclusion?" Carver asked.

"You'll never believe it."

"Try me." It's not like the case could get any stranger.

Cindy addressed the team. "Spontaneous combustion."

"What?" Carver drew his head back.

"That was my exact reaction. The coroner said he'd never seen anything like it. It's as if their internal organs were suddenly lit on fire and burned from the inside out. When he opened them up, everything inside the body was more charred than outside. He couldn't explain it other than spontaneous combustion."

"There were bodies all over the club," said Carver. "But these victims just suddenly burst into flames at the same time everyone else is being murdered and decapitated? That seems like a stretch. Is there anyway someone could have caused the fire?"

"I asked the same question and received a resounding no. The doctor said that if someone had caused the fire there would be an entrance point on the outside of the body, but he couldn't find any marks that were used as an entry point. His only conclusion was either spontaneous combustion or…" She looked over the team as if assessing their level of scrutiny. "Something supernatural."

Carver raised his eyebrows then shifted in his seat. He dropped the file on the table and rolled his toothpick to the corner of his mouth.

"What are your thoughts?" Montgomery shifted closer to the table.

"I think we need to start at the beginning. Considering the calling card is the same as Jerry Hardwood's there's obviously a link to his murders and the current situation."

"Maybe we can speak with Jerry? See if he knows anything?" This was Tom, the youngest on the team.

Carver shook his head. "I talked with Jerry a few days ago. He's as crazy as he's ever been." Carver looked at the whiteboard on the wall behind them. "Let's start jotting down all the players in this little game and go from there." He turned to Tom and gestured to the board. "That means you're up. Take the marker and let's figure out how to catch the son of a bitch who's doing this."

Tom jumped off his seat like he was sitting on a spring, grabbed a black marker and waited for the first instruction.

"First name I want you to write is Marc Saduj."

177

The shower was cold, freezing cold, but Marc knew that bathing was a requirement for the day. His hair was thick from the cold water. He brushed it back, wincing when the brush scraped across his scar. There were beads of blood littered across the scar that itched and burned across his scalp.

He looked at himself in the mirror, the cracked and grimy mirror, and barely recognized the person in the reflection. His eyes were lost and sunken with dark circles around his dry and tired eyes that carried a dull yellow sheen across his cracked eyeballs. He was gritting his teeth and noticed the slightest tremble in his jaw as if the nerves had been broken with no recourse to regenerate.

His shoulders were like knobs on top of an emaciated torso. He'd never been so thin before. His ribs were prominently displayed, and his belly was small and flat and sunken. His legs were like toothpicks. He looked like a skeleton with a thin layer of skin. His swollen liver sat prominently in the center of his torso. He was waiting for the pain to arrive. For his liver to attack, sending rolling waves filled with gut wrenching pain to every corner of his body and mind. The organ required alcohol, the only substance capable of stopping the pain. The pain that was about to escalate into overdrive. He could feel it, a hollow rumble in his solar plexus squeezing the organ and rolling his eyes to the back of his head.

Sweat dripped off his forehead. His dried, cracked and bloodied hands were trembling when he deposited his finger between his gritted teeth, biting his close to nonexistent nail. He wanted to shave but his hands were too shaky, incapable of holding a razor. Standing. Staring. Lost in confusion with still-framed images flitting through his thoughts.

Put em in the crypt.

Marc closed his eyes and inhaled slow, steady and deep into his nose and down into his belly. His nose crinkled from the liver pain when his breath brushed across the organ. Felt dizzy, Marc gripped the sink to steady his gait, grunting in his throat before he exhaled across his lips. His eyelids were heavy when he opened his eyes, stretching those eyelids to gaze at his reflection. His nose was running, and he sniffled the wet snot.

He understood the man in black was always listening. Listening and watching his every move and thought. But it was when he was inside the crypt that he found refuge. The crypt where he stayed with Jennifer last night. He discovered that when he stayed in the crypt the next day he felt better. A little more like himself as if the crypt held magical regenerative powers and he could think clearly. He hoped the same would happen for Jennifer.

But the crypt provided another idea.

Put your thoughts inside a crypt in your mind. A place where the man in black cannot find them. Like playing mind games with a voice in your head. It's where he put Lori, the reason he wanted to shower. Marc knew Lori had returned to the Hollow. A fact he wished to keep to himself. So, in the crypt Lori went. Forgotten, but always close.

I told you not to come.

He shook his head violently, forcing Lori from his thoughts and back into the crypt. His plan is to search for her today. To tell her to leave no matter what he must do. She shouldn't be here. Can't be here. He didn't know why, but he had an inclination that the man in black wanted Lori. For what reason he wasn't certain but the blonde woman's crypt not only regenerated his strength, but his confusion was funneling into clarity, and he was beginning to piece things together. There was more going on than he knew, and, in his heart, he understood Lori was the key.

Marc turned to the door and opened it. He stared into the hall, so subtle and quiet.

Where are they?

He was hoping to leave without an escort. He had to leave without an escort. He had to find Lori without their knowledge. Should they discover that she's here her life was in danger and that *cannot* happen. Marc pursed his lips and swallowed, his skin still moist from the shower. He felt sick, on the verge of vomiting, his liver squeezing acid into the back of his throat while sending waves of shaking trembles across his bones and joints. Waves filled with aching, living pain.

The house was quiet. Not a soul stirred. Marc plodded across the hallway to his bedroom, keeping his ears open, listening for a sign that would tell him where Wren was. He has to be somewhere in the house. In all his time with Wren the man never left the house. At least, not when Marc was awake although he disappeared occasionally, and yet, even then, he was somewhere in the house or outside tending to the bonfire, adding new wood if necessary.

Marc dressed quickly, his clothes loose, cascading from his shoulders like a tent. He tied his boots tight before he stood up and paused, thinking.

How can I leave without being noticed?

He couldn't tell if there were people downstairs. His escorts could be anywhere and the last thing he needed was to walk downstairs and find them waiting for him. They'll be on him like white on rice. He turned to the window.

Do I dare? How else am I going to get out?

The view through the window was ominous. He could see the dark clouds above the Hollow, unmoving as if they discovered the perfect place to stake their claim and refused to leave. Marc went to the window and investigated his property. The ground was covered in ankle deep snow; the bonfire stood crumpled and defeated in the center of the property. But no Wren. No escorts. He traced a path to the woods from the window then stretched his neck and looked directly below. The snow stopped a yard away from the house, the ground there covered in mud. Marc swallowed his breath then forced the window open when the bitter cold rippled into the room and the house groaned as if inhaling a fresh breath.

He scanned across the grounds, watching the snow swirl in the wind.

It's now or never.

Marc looked over his shoulder at the desolate hall and listened carefully. When he was certain no one was coming he sat on the windowsill and draped one leg through it followed by the other. He extended his body and dropped down. His feet hit the mud, and he fell back with a thud, staring up at the window while freezing in the snow.

A sudden sense of relief washed over him, but he didn't allow it to freeze his progress knowing he still wasn't safe. Marc clambered to his feet when his liver wrenched in his solar plexus with a pain that came close to toppling him over. A rolling pain that contracted every muscle and bone and when he stood tall his face winced, gritting his teeth and shuddering.

And with the pain rifling through his bones, his hands shaking while clutching his liver he scuttled across the grounds to the woods. Marc looked over his shoulder at the house and swallowed his breath with a gasp, his head swimming and his thoughts nonexistent. The house-his house-stood at attention, its windows like the eyes of darkness. Marc had a strange feeling that the house was watching him.

He turned to the woods and took the first step towards finding Lori.

John was watching through his telescope. Watching while a man he'd never seen before fell from the window.

One of their victims, John was certain. The man looked like he'd been held captive for a lifetime. His frame was frail as if he hadn't eaten in forever, his face so thin John could see his cheekbones, and he had a nasty scar across his forehead that disappeared beneath his hairline.

Has to be one of their victims. If it wasn't, he would have used the front door.

The fact that John watched him climb through the window then drop to the ground confirmed his suspicions. John watched him as he trekked into the woods, hoping he was headed to the police because if he was this would all be over very soon. Carver will bring in the cavalry, and they'll tear that home apart and find all the victims they have stashed inside the house.

They'll find my blackjack too. But that was secondary to Carver putting a stop to all the murder and mayhem that was turning the Hollow into a madhouse, everyone on edge, paranoid, and angry. John clucked his tongue after removing his eye from the telescope when he heard footsteps in the hall and John padded over to his bed and slipped beneath the covers.

After he puked all over the lunchroom the school nurse called Grandpa Claude who raced to the school to pick him up.

Can't have a student puking everywhere and not be sent home. Any kid that sick shouldn't have been in school in the first place. So, Grandpa Claude came running, brought John home and sent him to his room while he made chicken noodle soup to help settle his stomach.

Grandpa Claude knew John wasn't sick, more like nervous, his anxiety in overdrive and when the nurse attempted to scold Grandpa Claude for sending a sick student to school he stopped the nurse in her tracks, giving her a piece of his mind that John was certain-judging by the look on her face-she was not expecting.

Maybe you should go back to school because obviously you can't tell the difference between sickness and anxiety, which is probably why you're a school nurse and not a real nurse. Can't hack it in the real world.

John privately cheered for Grandpa. Now he pulled his covers up to his neck when Grandpa Claude opened his bedroom door, balancing a tray with his bowl of soup as he walked in and brought the tray to the bedside table, placing the tray on top of it.

"You should eat something," he said. "It'll settle your stomach." He stood tall, staring at John then touched the back of his hand to John's forehead. "You're not running a temp, so I think it was just nerves." He paused, his lips pressed tight in a concerned smile. "You okay, my man?"

John nodded and cleared his throat. "I'll be fine. I don't feel sick anymore."

Another pause, thick with tension. John looked at Grandpa Claude. He looked older as if he'd aged a decade since this morning. There were wrinkles around his eyes.

"It's just the two of us," he said, and John found the statement rather strange. Grandpa Claude was looking through the window. "Whatever you need to talk about, I'm here. You can tell me anything," he said and turned to John. "I got your back, little man. I understand things must be difficult, but… just know that no matter what I'm here for you."

"I know," John said, his voice cracked in his throat. It's not like he could tell Grandpa everything that had been going on and he definitely couldn't tell him about breaking into the house and he sure as shit wasn't going to fess up to slapping that vampire with his blackjack. Best to keep that tidbit of information to himself. And let's not forget that his dead mother-Claude's own daughter-was sending him signals from the afterlife and that he's having visions of another life.

He'd more than likely have John committed.

Grandpa Claude tightened that concerned smile and nodded. "Eat your soup," he said. "I'll check on you in an hour." He leaned in and kissed John's forehead. "Get some rest too." Claude went to the door but stopped abruptly, turning back to John with tears in his eyes. John had never thought about how difficult this all must be for him. His wife had been dead for ten years, his daughter gone, his granddaughter too. An old man taking care of a young one. "You're all I got," he said with a shake of his head. "I'll never allow anything to happen to you."

"I know."

"We're a team, right?"

A smile spread across John's lips and he nodded. "Definitely."

"Okay." He looked around the room before turning to John then gestured to the soup. "Don't forget to eat before it gets cold."

"I will."

He was about to close the door when the doorbell rang. Claude's eyes narrowed.

"Now who the hell can that be?"

Carver noticed the commotion outside the conference room. Like a buzz that started soft then continued to rise by the second.

Carver and his team had been providing updates on the investigation. The whiteboard was littered with names and possibilities, explanations, consistencies and inaccuracies, and the link to it all circled in red marker in the center was Marc Saduj. The police received a missing person's report on a group of local students attending Fordham University's Tarrytown campus. They had gone out for a drink and never returned. The missing students shared similarities with the two victims discovered yesterday. Carver tasked Montgomery with interviewing the bartender working at The Sleepy Hollow Tavern on the night in question.

The tavern, Carver thought. *Same place where Zoe Hardwood's body was found.*

Now he saw Captain Flannery walking towards the conference room.

"What is going on out there?" This was Joan, obviously annoyed with the commotion when Captain Flannery burst through the door, the blind disturbed and rattling against the door's window.

Carver stood up.

"They just found two more bodies," said Flannery. He looked at Carver and gestured to the board. "And your boy just left the house."

Carver felt an immediate twinge in his chest as his clenched teeth bit into his toothpick. He shook his head, taking his jacket from the back of his chair. "Where were the bodies found?"

"Which parts?"

Carver stuffed his arms into the jacket's sleeves. "Come again?"

Flannery paused. Clearly, he was gritting his teeth. He cleared his throat. "The head was found on the gates into Sleepy Hollow Cemetery. Other parts were scattered across the cemetery on the surrounding wall. The second body was discovered on the grave of Washington Irving. The groundskeeper discovered the body while doing his morning rounds and while he was walking down to call in his report he saw the body parts around the cemetery. He's waiting for you to meet him there."

Carver took his badge off the conference table. "Tom, get a black and white to cordon off the cemetery. I don't want anyone going in or out." He looked at Montgomery. "When he's done, take him with you to Sleepy Hollow Tavern to question the bartender. Joan and Andrew, I want you to find out everything about the cemetery. Every in and out and see if it has cameras that may have recorded the cemetery last night. Theo and Cindy, follow me to the cemetery. And someone contact the black and white watching the

Saduj house. Make sure they follow Marc everywhere he goes. I want a full report on his whereabouts for the day."

"I got it," said Montgomery as he slid his chair away from the table.

Carver looked at his team, everyone getting ready in hurried anticipation, jumping off their seats and grabbing jackets and badges. "Good luck everyone." He looked at Theo and Cindy. "I'll see you there." He received head nods and yes sirs. Carver looked at the whiteboard and the name Marc Saduj circled in the center before walking to the door where Flannery was.

"You still think he has something to do with it?" Flannery gestured to the whiteboard.

Carver rolled his toothpick to the opposite side of his mouth. "Whatever is going on in the Hollow begins with Marc Saduj."

John crept out of his bedroom, padding across the carpet as quietly as possible. He could hear Grandpa Claude at the front door talking to whoever rang the doorbell. Their voices were difficult to interpret when he was in his bedroom and he wanted to hear what was being said.

When the doorbell rang something stirred inside John. He referred to it as intuition, instinct, his wits on high alert. Something was off about the person at the front door. He knew it was true, his head buzzing with fear. Afraid for Grandpa Claude. John shuffled close to the wall by the stairs, out of sight but not out of earshot. Grandpa Claude had just told the man at the front door a resounding, "No. We're not interested."

"Just an interview," the man said. "A chance for him to tell his story."

"My story!" John whispered. He crept his head around the corner, wanting to get a look at the man at the front door.

"Let us in," the man said. "This won't take long at all." The voice was monotone, mechanical, as if he needed to stop and think before speaking.

"He's not even home," said Grandpa. "He's at school."

Now he paused and John could see the crooked stare plastered across the man's face. Or at least part of his face because Grandpa Claude was in the way.

The man shifted his head from left to right. "We know he's home. The school said he came home early." A pause then, and the man cocked his eyebrows. "Seems he tossed his cookies all over the lunchroom." And he started laughing. Laughing some high-pitched cackle that cringed John's bones. A second later the laugh dwindled into silence. "Come on, let us in. If you think I'm the only reporter you'll have to kick off your doorstep with all that's going on you'd be dead wrong." His voice changed, his tone now sinister and goading. "Quite obvious there's a link between Jerry Hardwood, his son and the recent murders…"

There was more the reporter was saying but his voice drifted from John's ears as a cringe shuddered down his spine from the nape of his neck as if a hand had brushed across his neck and squeezed. Like drifting inside of silence, the world around him muted. All he could hear were footsteps. Footsteps in the snow. Multiple footsteps. Directly opposite him was the third bedroom on the second floor. The door had been closed-the door was always closed-John was certain of it, but now it drifted open with a subtle creak.

John investigated the room. The bedroom was clean and well kept. A queen bed in the center. A chest of drawers sat opposite the bed with a rocking chair in the corner. The rocking chair that was rocking gently back and forth as if someone was sitting in the chair, rocking calm and slow.

"Mom?"

More footsteps in the snow. John moved to the window and his heart stopped. A group of people were in the backyard, staring up at the window beneath the overcast sky that now sprayed a mist across the snow. He scanned their faces. They all had the same spiderwebbed veins and their eyes carried the slightest hint of red in the irises.

The rocking chair creaked to a stop. John's mouth hung open as he stepped back from the window, his head rotating to the chair. His mother was in the chair, her head bleeding from where that bullet tore through her skull.

"This is the moment they take you," she said then moved her head to the left and right. "Don't be afraid, John," she whispered before she vanished.

"Well, at least allow me to call the station. Let them know it's a no go."

He felt paralyzed, as if some phantom had taken his ability to form words. His mouth gaped open and closed like a fish out of water as he turned to the door where Grandpa Claude was standing tall, his hand on the doorknob. Now John heard more footsteps in the snow coming from the backyard. Heard Grandpa say, "I guess that's fair."

John tried to stop it. In his head he screamed, *Don't let him in*, but the words never jumped off his lips.

"Come in," Grandpa said.

The reporter stepped into the house. John could see him clearly through the open door. The man's eyes beamed in John's direction. A grin spread across his lips.

"Thank you," he said and closed the front door, locking it.

"What're you doing?" This was Grandpa Claude. John heard the fear hitch in his throat.

Heard glass shatter from somewhere in the house. Heard the punch that dropped Grandpa to the ground. John raced out of the room. The man was beating Grandpa Claude; he could see blood flying into the air from the man's fist and Grandpa's face. John went to the master bedroom, to the window. There was another outside, also staring up. He darted back into the hall. Heard footsteps creaking up the stairs and the unrelenting desecration of Grandpa Claude.

"Come out, little one." A new voice, crawling up the stairs. "The master requires your presence."

John looked around. There was no place to go.

"Come out, come out, wherever you are."

He slipped into his bedroom. Went to the window and saw there were more people in the yard staring up at him. He turned around, his heart pounding like a rabbit in his chest, his eyes darting from one corner of the room to the other. To the closet door that he raced over to and slipped inside, hiding in the back of the closet at the moment he heard those footsteps walk into his room.

"Well, let's see," a voice said outside the closet. "Oh, where oh where can my little John be?"

John hugged his knees, staring into the dark when the closet door opened. He recognized the man immediately. His bus driver, Mr. Mitchell, glared at him from his bedroom. He was holding John's blackjack.

"Is this yours?" he asked.

John had no reply.

"It has your name on it. J. Hardwood." He looked at the blackjack, then turned to John and cocked his head. "Come, little one. The master wants to see you."

And with that, he stepped into the closet.

"Where can she be?" Marc was searching, thinking of all the places Lori could be. He hadn't thought it through. Had no plan to find her. Nothing except blind instinct and following his gut, but his gut was twisting nausea into the back of his throat. His liver was wrung out to dry, sending waves filled with pain wrenching his insides into a knot, poisoning his insides. Part of him didn't think he could go on.

He'd gone home first. Considering the circumstances he was certain that would be the first place Lori would look for him. But he arrived too late. According to Mrs. Leiter Lori had already come and gone.

"She looked so sweet, that one. Sooo sweet. Like a frightened little rabbit when she learned you were no longer here." Mrs. Leiter's eyes narrowed. *"Where did he go, Mrs. Leiter? She asked. So feeble. Soooo fragile. She's like porcelain. That face. That face."*

Marc's stomach was twisting while talking to Mrs. Leiter, shaky and unsteady. Felt like he couldn't breathe when he was with her.

"If she comes back, Mrs. Leiter, please tell her to stay here," he'd said. *"I need to speak with her."*

"Of course. Of course," she'd replied as her narrow eyes narrowed even more, staring at Marc over her glasses. *"Best to be*

leaving now Mr. Saduj. Judging by the way you look I'm certain the devil's gotten into you."

Marc had no reply, opting to walk out of the building he'd always called home. Now he was on the street passing Patriots Park, taking the side street across from Broadway. Walking beneath the dark gray clouds and the gentle mist that fell relentlessly. It seemed like the sun was overtaken by the forces of darkness, removing the light from the Hollow and turning day into night. Cars passed with their headlights beaming and the streetlights were on, shedding light across the dark road.

The park was still cordoned off. He stopped and gazed into the cavern where they'd found that boy all cut up and dismembered. Stood for a little longer than he should have, losing himself while staring into the dark depths of the cavern. He could hear whispers coming from the cavern. Incoherent whispers beneath a buzzing energy that tainted his blood with venom. A police cruiser drove slowly past the park.

They're trying to stop me, he thought, driving that thought into the crypt inside his mind. Marc knew the man in black was watching and listening, attempting to stay his hand and lead him back to the house.

Stay the course, he told himself. *To them, it appears as if I'm trying to escape. Either that or looking for time away. Or maybe they already know Lori is here in the Hollow. Maybe I'm just playing right into their game, delivering Lori on a silver platter.*

"Stop thinking!" he hollered, clenching his fists.

He deposited his fingernail between his lips, nipping at what little nail he had left. His chapped, cracked and bleeding lips were swollen with a painful sting across the slit on his bottom lip. He noticed the police cruiser was heading down Wiley then turned onto the same street Marc was on. Marc turned and kept walking, keeping his head straight as he passed the church and watched from the corner of his eye as the cruiser passed him, the tires spraying rain and mist across the sidewalk. Kept walking, observing where the cop was going. Straight into Sleepy Hollow that's where he was headed, close to the tavern he and Lori frequented. The same tavern where his mother used to drink.

His mouth salivated with the thought of a drink. His liver groaned with the need for alcohol. The organ like a cold stone that burned inside his body.

Not now, please.

He couldn't help it. The pain arrived like a freight train, rolling waves filled with anguish to every part of his body. He bent over, clutching his solar plexus then dropped to his knees. His hands were shaking, his breath stuttered and held in his throat as another wave of pain twisted his liver. He dry heaved across the sidewalk.

Just a drink.

"This is all I need. Someone seeing me tossing cookies across the sidewalk." He wiped his mouth.

A drink is what is required.

His arms across his stomach, his lips trembling. Felt like every bone in his body was shaking, his eyes rolling behind lazy eyelids. Body temperature rose to the max. He was sweating. Cold drips of sweat the size of bullets raced down his face. Marc wanted to lie down and die. The pain was immense, unrelenting in its purpose to force him to take a drink.

Get up! He screamed in his head. That cop will be back soon, and he'll have every reason to question him. *Get UP NOW!*

Come for a drink, Marc. This is useless. You escaping the way you have. There's no reason for it. We have your best interest in mind. We are your family, Marc. We take care of each other and here you are, writhing in pain in the middle of the street. What will the neighbors think? That we can't take care of our own. Tsk. Tsk. Tsk.

The drink is what you need. It'll settle your stomach. Give your liver what it needs and then you can go about your day and complete your tasks. Then you can find Lori and warn her off.

Laughing now. That conniving laugh.

We don't need to see to know she is here. We can feel her presence. It is inevitable Marc. It was always inevitable. The crypt in your mind?

Laughter again.

I am in your mind, Marc. Sharing your thoughts. You can't keep secrets from me. This is futile. Drop your efforts and accompany me to the tavern. Let us ease the pain. Wash it away with a drink of absinthe.

Marc pushed himself to his feet, shivering from head to toe. The pain toppled him over, but he refused to relent. Got to his feet again and draped his arms across his stomach. His mouth was dry like desert heat, his eyes wet with tears, but still he pressed on. Teeth clenched and he couldn't stop his right hand from shaking. Felt acid in the back of his throat, washing across his teeth.

Now thunder rolled across the heavens.

At least have enough sense to get out of the rain.

The mist then kicked up a notch into a light rain. He kept walking. Walking into Sleepy Hollow where the police cruiser was waiting, parked across the street from where he stood on the sidewalk. He looked around. So many stores and places to hide. The rain fell harder. His scar was itching. His skin was crawling. He looked up and noticed he was standing in front of the tavern. It looked so warm inside.

He opened the door without thinking about it. Stepped in and walked across the old wooden floor that clapped beneath his steps. The two people sitting at the bar stopped and looked at him as he took a seat in the first empty booth. They were all empty. The only people in the tavern were the bartender and the two patrons.

"What's your poison?"

Marc looked up at the bartender standing over him. His vision was blurred from tears, but he knew the bartender was one of them. How, he couldn't be sure, but he was certain the bartender was one of the escorts from the day before. The prominent veins on his cheeks and the red tint in his eyes gave him away.

Just a drink, he told himself. *To stop the pain and then back to searching for Lori. I need to think clearly to find her. She's here somewhere in the Hollow. Maybe she'll even show up here at the tavern, looking for me like I'm looking for her.*

He pursed his lips and swallowed. The barkeep was staring at him with a tightlipped grin, his eyes gleaming and beaming with a red tint, waiting for a response.

"Sc…" He cleared his throat. "Scotch." Now the barkeep's grin stretched in the corners of his mouth.

"Of course. Anything for you."

Marc watched the barkeep return to the bar. His breath was shallow, attempting to keep the pain at bay. His solar plexus tightened, sending a cringe racing up his spine to his neck. His hands were shaking on his lap while watching the barkeep pour his scotch, losing himself in the caramel liquid. Every sound was like an echo. The patrons conversed with the barkeep, laughed then looked at his table. Looked at him, their laughter reverberating in his bones. Marc clenched his teeth when his liver cringed, anticipating the touch of scotch across his lips. The thought was like bliss to his dying liver.

There's not anything you can do, Marc. You gave yourself to me and in return Lori has lived and breathed.

The barkeep brought his drink over.

"On the house," he said, placing a napkin on the table and the drink on top of it. He looked at Marc and their eyes met. "To assist you in your endeavor." He winked before returning to the bar.

And in turn she belongs to me. It is my power that released her from the grip of certain death. I shall do with her as I please.

Marc couldn't stop his hand from trembling. Couldn't pick up the glass either because it was shaking so much.

"Just one sip." He closed his eyes and dipped his lips to the glass then slurped his first sip. The sensation was immediate, flowing across his liver with a warm embrace, cooling the burning in his veins. Everything came into focus. He breathed deeply; his hand now had a slight tremble. No longer shaking. No longer moving with a mind all its own. Marc gasped out a breath and took up his glass. Feeling normal and in charge, he took another sip that turned into a gulp. And he closed his eyes, feeling the warm thrill of ecstasy in his bones.

When you find her please tell her I said hello.

"Not a chance," he said out loud. "Not if I can help it."

And the voice in his head, the man in black, the master who loves human hearts, began to laugh.

In time, Marc. In time we will see just how strong your resolve truly is. When confronted with your own death, what will you choose?

Marc took up his glass and downed the rest of his drink.

"I'll choose Lori. Every. Single. Time."

More laughter. Laughter followed by a sigh.

We shall see. We most definitely will. Look around you Marc. You're surrounded by my minions. All alone, Marc. All alone. Humanity belongs to me now and you, you are the key that handed them over. No matter what, this is all coming to an end.

The front door opened. Marc could hear the falling rain, the cars on the street and the footsteps across the floor. He felt the icy breeze across the nape of his neck. The patrons and barkeep all turned to see who walked into the bar. Marc looked too, over his shoulder. Looked at the two police officers who just strolled into the tavern.

"Tonight, Ian, we will spill an ocean of blood." Wren was in the dungeon, preparing for the coming of Baphomet. They had done well last night, sacrificing five weary warriors including the three the master brought from the club and Savannah and Philip. The master brought more ghost demons into the fold too. They were now in the Hollow, preparing for the coming of Baphomet and the final act that will deliver humanity into the master's embrace. The astral plane was strengthened too, resulting in a crack in the third door. All three doors now held the same fissure. From those fissures a green light beamed into the dungeon and the heat escalated, the stones burning and sending waves of heat across the dungeon.

And Marc, the host, the one who made it all possible with his perpetual fear of death and his undying love, was on his mission to find Lori. A necessary step in the process of total control. Wren understood that Marc's fear would open the Xibalba doors. An event Wren couldn't wait to witness.

"Your pain in this world will end," said Wren as he glared at the weary, defeated Ian. "And an eternity of insanity will escort you into the heart of Xibalba. For Baphomet and his devils to feed on forever." He looked around the dungeon at the remaining victims. "And all of you with him. We have much to do before tomorrow's constellation opens the pathway. It will require all the blood from your veins and all the fear from your hearts to open the portal." He raised his chin. "I do hope you are all prepared for your sacrifice. You have all been chosen to serve the interests of the master. *Act accordingly.*"

He stepped closer to Ian, taking his head in his hands and lifting Ian's one good eye with his thumb. "And you, my beloved. I'll ask the master to keep you as my pet. I'll take satisfaction in watching you eat your own flesh, feeding me little pieces while we bask by the bonfire of the world." He ran his tongue across his bottom lip. "How about a little kiss?"

Wren snapped his jaw across Ian's cheek, tearing into his flesh, biting down across the cheekbone as Ian squirmed in his embrace, hollering muffled screams from his throat. Blood burst across Wren's tongue. He swallowed it down then tore off a chunk of fleshy meat that he swallowed down his thick gullet. Wren bit into the opposite cheek then, nipping Ian's skin between his teeth and tearing off another fleshy chunk that he gnawed on and squished between his teeth before gulping it down. He licked the blood off his lips then dragged his tongue across his chin, lapping up all the blood from his skin.

Ian's cries echoed in his throat as his eye dripped tears enough for both eyes. If he could fall to the floor Wren knew he would. Lay down and curl into a fetal position, hoping the demon in the darkness would pass him by, but he couldn't. The shackles held him up. Wren noticed Liam, Nikita and Cheryl all looked on with wide, fearful eyes. Their groans and screams dying in their muzzled mouths. Even in their weakened state they still screamed knowing their time for torture was coming soon. The inevitable end always provided the victim with a sense of strength Wren knew all too well, but their bodies were so weak, so frail and dehydrated. Wren understood any fight they could give would be futile. The master had the power of Xibalba at his fingertips, and no human could match his resolve. The master was right about everything. The plan was unfolding in front of Wren's eyes with a subtle air of satisfaction. A satisfaction that intensified when he heard the ghost demons escorting the young Hardwood into the dungeon from the underground tunnels.

"Come on, little one."

Shuffling and pushing.

"The master requires your presence."

Scuttling across the stone steps, footsteps echoing in the dungeon. They tossed the boy to the floor where he fell with a stuttered shuffle, his hands scraped against the hot stone. His chin rocked against the ground, drawing blood. John's hands went to his chin. The boy was in tears. He clawed to a sitting position, wide eyed and petrified while huffing his breath in stutters filled with whines.

Wren stared down at the boy, whose head swiveled in his direction. Wren looked at the ghost demon-John's bus driver-and stretched his arm to him. "Do you have it?"

"Of course." He handed Wren John's blackjack.

"Lower the cage," said Wren as he gazed at the shuddering, terrified John Hardwood. Wren looked at the blackjack and his skull twitched. He then trained his stare on the young boy. "You look more like your mother. I've seen her recently. Watching us from the woods."

John had yet to say anything. His stare was spectacular. The boy was petrified, holding his chin while blood dripped across his hand. Wren crouched down beside him.

"No worries, young man. Your friends will be here soon. They have so much to show you, but that Logan is a bad boy, slipping notes when he has no right to do so." Wren shook his head, clucking his tongue then tilted his head, glowering at John. "He will best serve our needs through blood and pain."

Now Wren could hear chains rattling and the descent of the cage. He held out the blackjack, showing it to John. "This is yours, isn't it?"

John looked at the blackjack then turned to Wren.

"That's what I thought." Wren touched his skull where this young little shit had bloodied him. Rubbed his smooth skull back and forth, then ripped his palm away. Shaking his head, he looked at John as the cage stopped on the floor and the bus driver opened the door. Wren ran his tongue inside his cheek. "The master requires your presence to welcome the conclusion of our little ruse." He gestured to the cage. "You'll spend your remaining days in the confines of the cage. From there, you will watch as we torture all who enter this chamber. You will bear witness to the coming of

Baphomet and the souring of your species." The ghost demons all laughed. "And then, we will keep you in our embrace and deliver generations of revenge upon you until we are satisfied that you have paid the due price for your ancestors. You're simply a spoke on a wheel, a means to execute our revenge and hatred. Your father was weak where you are strong, and it is your strength that we will break. Our resolve cannot be equaled. So, in the cage you will go." He looked up to the rotting Jennifer. "A new ornament for our macabre holiday." He turned to John. "But first… I owe you one."

He thrust the blackjack across John's face, and he immediately dropped to his side. John's cheek and mouth now dripped blood along with his chin. Wren whacked him across the head. Three times he drove that blackjack across his skull, drawing blood and opening gashes across his skin. Wren stood up and then drove that blackjack down again, across the top of John's skull and his eyes closed, welcoming the darkness. Wren then addressed the ghost demons.

"Now, put him in the cage then go about your day. Return to your family. Return to your homes. The master will call on you when the time is right. The host has been put into play. Time quickens to meet our desire."

The ghost demons gathered the unconscious John then placed him in the cage, locking the door once he was inside. Wren tossed the blackjack into the fire and watched it burn. "There. Now he can't cause any more trouble." The cage lifted off the ground, rising to the ceiling, the perfect position to watch the astral plane.

A bird's-eye view to the coming apocalypse.

183

Carver walked in the rain towards the final resting place of the famed Washington Irving. His escort, Sam Locke, led the way, his hands in the pockets of his dark raincoat. Carver's sneakers were getting stuck in the mud. The rain was falling harder now, melting the snow and turning the cemetery into a mud bowl.

When he first arrived, Mr. Locke was waiting for him inside the cemetery beyond the gate. He held a stare filled with shock and awe. Obviously, the old man had seen better days even though his work revolved around the dead. He couldn't take his eyes off the decapitated head on top of the gate to the cemetery. Sam had informed Carver that he normally comes in through a different part of the cemetery every morning to do his rounds and did not see the head until after he located the body across Irving's gravesite.

Of course, Carver asked the necessary questions. Did you see anyone? Does the cemetery have cameras? Any suspicious activity or visitors over the last few days? Questions that received the resounding 'no' from Sam. It was then that Carver instructed the flatfoot cordoning off the cemetery to remove and bag the decapitated head from the cemetery gate. Normally, he would wait for the forensics team before removing evidence, but with all the news vans roaming the Hollow he didn't want to take the chance that the head would be on every news headline across the country by the seven o'clock telecast.

And the fact that it was raining unnerved Carver. All his evidence was being washed away. He needed to salvage as much as possible. Carver called for tarps once again, an order that reminded him of Zoe Hardwood.

Everything's connected.

Even the story, the book the priest gave him was beginning to show favor to current circumstances. Considering the body was left on the gravesite of the very man who wrote the book was proof positive that Carver needed to heed the warnings written on those pages.

Sam stopped cold in his tracks, staring straight ahead at the body lying on the ground in the melting snow. Carver paused, assessing the scene and took a pair of latex gloves from his pocket then stretched them over his hands. The victim was naked and judging by her soft features, young too. Carver put her between eighteen and twenty-two. *The same age as the missing university students.* Whoever dumped the body positioned it too. Her ankles were crossed, and her arms were extended. Her skin was pale, but she was turning a shade of gray. The small incision across her abdomen-bloodied and stiff-was the only method of torture Carver could see.

He didn't need to guess how she was tortured. It was obvious to Carver.

Disemboweled.

Above her head and propped against Irving's headstone like a pile of rotten meat were the victim's intestines. The calling card was written in blood on the headstone. Vapor lifted off the body like the cold plume of breath from a hot mouth.

Still warm?

Even though he knew the girl was dead he checked for a pulse, wanting to feel the warmth of her skin more than checking for a heartbeat. The body was warm but growing colder by the second. He looked at the intestines, smoldering in the rain like a bonfire. The smell was putrid, like rotten meat left out in the hot sun. It turned acid into the back of his throat. He noticed Mr. Locke hadn't moved, staring at the girl while lost in his thoughts. Carver inspected the body, his eyes narrowing the longer he looked. He then pushed on her abdomen with his fingertips, spreading the wound wider. It kept opening, opening wide.

A hand, he thought. *Big enough to fit a hand inside.* His eyes roamed up to meet the victim's stale and wide-open black eyes. *Where he reached in to claim the heart.*

He tilted his head, staring at the face and how her eyes looked sunken into her skull, her cheekbones prominent beneath thin skin. There were dark patches around her eyes.

Lack of sleep?

He could see her ribs too, her stomach flat and sunken.

Carver looked up, thinking, scanning through his memory for when the university students had gone missing. It would make sense that if she was one of the missing students that she was held captive without food and water. Probably incapacitated too, drugged and shackled. He noticed bruises around her neck, wrists and ankles. Her mouth too, and her lips were cracked and split in the corners.

Gagged?

He remembered the bodies that were found yesterday had similar bruising and abrasions.

There's a portal to hell in the basement.

It made sense that the victims were in the basement.

He probably has a frigin torture chamber down there.

Carver breathed deeply, scanning around the body and assessing the grounds. There were footprints leading to and from the body. From what Carver could ascertain, there were at least two additional sets of prints other than his own and Sam's. He stood up, stretching his gloves off that he deposited into his pocket then gripped his box of toothpicks, pinched one between his fingers then popped it between his lips.

The rain was falling harder now. Carver scanned across the cemetery to the fog that lifted off the snow turning the cemetery into a lurid display of ghostly terror. Noticed the fog drifted into the woods beyond the cemetery. The woods that led to Marc Saduj. He turned to Sam.

"How easy is it to get into the cemetery after hours?"

Sam scoffed. "Not hard at all. Most kids just climb over the wall."

"But what about someone carrying a dead body?"

Sam considered the question; his stare fixed on the surrounding barrier. "Difficult but not impossible. Although it would take a very strong person to lift the body over the wall."

Carver nodded, rolling the toothpick to the opposite corner of his mouth when thunder raged across the sky complimented by a spiderweb of pink lightning that speared within the dark clouds. The rain picked up its pace and Carver returned his attention to the footprints. He followed them, wanting to assess where they came from and where they went.

"Are you gonna catch the son of a bitch who did this?" Sam said, but Carver paid him no attention. His focus was on the footprints that were being washed away from the rain melting the snow. "Everyone's on edge," Sam continued, as if his continuance would be met with a response. "There's anger in the air. People teetering in-between insanity."

Sam's voice trailed off as Carver kept walking, nipping on his toothpick, walking between headstones and crypts and leaving Sam behind. He followed the footsteps that continued to melt in the rain. The last few he found-before they completely disappeared-were the curves from the souls of their shoes. Carver looked up to the mausoleum where the footprints stopped. Either melted by the snow or whoever they belonged to had entered the mausoleum. He regarded the cherub on top of the mausoleum, the stone statue staring at Carver with suspicion.

Beside the mausoleum's door was an epitaph that looked like black marbled glass. Carver squinted while looking at it. There was no name on the epitaph. He could feel evil inside the mausoleum, a dark energy infecting his cells. It felt dirty, like poison in his blood.

Now Carver could see the lights trolling across the cemetery. The cavalry had arrived, and the investigation was about to pick up speed. He knew the news vans would arrive soon. Knew his town would not sleep easy tonight. He looked at Sam standing in the rain, his coat slick with rainwater cascading off his coat like a waterfall. Another thunder roll and another complimentary bolt of lightning that revealed ghosts wandering in the cemetery. There were so many of them.

He turned back to the mausoleum when a great horned owl dropped onto the roof and hissed at him. Hissed and gawked and flapped its wings before it lifted off the crypt and flew into the clouds. Carver watched it go. Watched it disappear into the western woods.

His thoughts were wiped clear as if that owl washed away the fear from his heart. Puzzled, he turned to Sam and saw his officers swarming the cemetery. Saw the fire truck pull up too, aware they had his tarps. Heard a whistle like wind funneling in his ear and he turned around.

Sheila Hardwood was standing in the cemetery. She looked like she was glowing, standing with the dark clouds over her shoulders when another bolt of pink lightning spiderwebbed through those dark clouds and the thunder cracked as if God meant to split the earth in half. Carver flinched from the sudden roll. Sheila pointed to the mausoleum and disappeared.

Carver stepped forward and the scene changed as if the world twisted to reveal an alternate reality. He saw his officers stacked high among a mountain of citizens, their bloodied and battered bodies burning. The Hollow was burning too. Fires reached from the cemetery to the Hudson. A perpetual hell on earth.

Initium Novum.

Heard fires burning, flames crackling and roaring devouring the dead between its jaws.

"You okay, officer?"

A hand on his shoulder and Carver jumped out of his spell. Sam Locke was staring at him, suspicious. His hand slipped off Carver's shoulder.

"You look like you saw a ghost."

Carver didn't know what to say other than, "I'm fine." He looked over Sam's shoulder at the officers traversing the cemetery.

"Looks like you had a vision," continued Sam. "Happens around these parts. Damn ghosts love latching on to those who can see." He gave a stiff nod with a gruff grin. "I'll let you get on with it. Gotta catch the son of a bitch. The Hollow won't survive if you don't. Chaos is coming and if he's not caught everyone in the Hollow will turn on each other." He looked up at the rain. "Perhaps they already have."

He turned to Carver, then walked away. Carver's officers were closer now.

"Sam," Carver called. Sam turned on his heels. Carver pursed his lips and swallowed, flipping that toothpick to the corner of his mouth. "Where's the other body?"

Sam's eyes turned dark as if a shadow passed across his irises. As if the thought of that body turned his insides into knots and stained his mind with terror.

"Everywhere," he said. "Fucking everywhere."

184

Lori jumped out of the cab in front of the hotel. She raced inside, shaking off the rain from her coat and hat.

She'd gone to the tavern after her visit with Mrs. Leiter, but Marc wasn't there and the bartender didn't remember seeing him. He didn't even know who Marc was. From there she went back to her old antique store hoping for some odd reason that he would be there. Again, she came up empty, leaving her with little, if anything, to go on. *Where the hell can he be?* She wasn't even certain he was still in the Hollow. Mrs. Leiter said she hadn't seen him in a long while. Maybe he took off and moved to another town in another state? But Lori knew that wasn't true. She could feel him, sensing his presence around every corner and in every shadow she passed. She thought about going to the police to file a missing person's report, but then the murders and that damn pentagram itched their way into her thoughts and she reasoned that may be a bad idea. She wanted to find him, not put him behind bars.

But then what? What can she do? There were only two options she could think of. Staking out Mark's apartment was one, but after the confrontation with Mrs. Leiter she knew that solution wouldn't be in her best interest. She felt different in Mrs. Leiter's presence. As if she weren't in control of her own body and she felt confused as if she were experiencing life from underwater, floating aimlessly and at the whim of the water and where it chose to take her. And that water was Mrs. Leiter. No, staking out Marc's apartment was not in her best interest. But what then? Her only other option was returning to the tavern and waiting for him to show up.

But you don't even know if he still goes there? Her thought screamed inside her head. Marc may have found a new bar to serve his need for alcohol. Perhaps the memory of the Sleepy Hollow Tavern had become too much to bear.

Lori passed the reception desk when she heard her name and froze. She knew exactly whose voice that was. She turned slowly to see her mother.

Lori shook her head. "What're you doing here?" Her eyes narrowed, staring at Elena with contempt.

"You know why," she said, returning Lori's contempt. "You don't belong here. There's nothing but heartache in this town." She gestured around the hotel. "These are not our people." She shifted her gaze to Lori. "Before you cause a catastrophe, it is best for you to come with us."

Lori's head shot back. Her eyes narrowed even more. "Us?" She looked around the hotel. "Who are you referring to?" She crossed her arms, standing tall. Lori wouldn't be surprised if Elena was about to have her committed. Money can buy whatever you want, and she knew Elena would go to great lengths to control everything in Lori's life. Elena had no issue tossing her money around to get what she wanted and most people came running like dogs to a hot lunch the moment she called.

Elena cupped her hands in front of her as she craned her head to look over her shoulder. Lori followed her gaze, watching as Henry Clavell rose from the couch. He eyeballed Lori as he walked over.

"You've got to be kidding me?" Lori shook her head. "She got to you too?"

"She seems to have your best interest in mind." He locked eyes with Lori, and she noticed guilt in his stare as if he were sorry for what he was doing or ashamed of being with Elena. Lori almost felt sorry for him. "Why don't we all get a cup of coffee and talk it out?"

Lori looked at Elena. "What lies did you tell this man to make him agree to come here? How much are you paying him?"

Elena shook her head, eyeballing Lori. "He's here because he cares and doesn't want to see a friend make a huge mistake."

Lori scoffed. She turned to Henry. "You know, I don't blame you. There aren't many people who would turn down one of Elena's generous offers." She looked at Elena. "Go home Henry. My mother likes to tell lies to get what she wants. Whatever she told you is bullshit." Looked back at Henry. "She's wasted your time." Then back at Elena. "So, make sure she still pays you." She took a step back. "I'm done with you Elena. As far as I'm concerned, you're dead to me." She turned around, stomping towards the hall.

"Is she lying about the murders, Lori?"

Lori stopped cold. Noticed the receptionist-a young lady with short curly blonde hair-looked at Lori and then at Henry. Lori shook her head, refusing to turn around then continued walking.

Henry called her name, but she kept going. This was all she needed, her mother poking her nose in her business for what seemed like the millionth time. That bitch was relentless. Lori couldn't wait to get into her room. Get back and shake off Elena's dark energy.

185

"You know," said the barkeep. "I do believe there is an officer waiting for you to leave?"

Marc looked over his shoulder. Looked through glass door at the patrol car waiting across the street. The sky had grown darker since Marc was in the bar, the patrol car's headlights beamed bright through the dark and stormy day. The barkeep stood close to Marc's booth, looking through the window too.

"Lots of cops today. A lot going on in the Hollow." Marc turned to the barkeep. "Lots of nefarious deeds and little nuances of chaos with sinister tongues clucking manipulative lies." He smiled, tilting his head to the side then cocked his eyebrows. "The Hollow will never be the same."

Marc said nothing in response. He simply sat back in the booth and cradled his drink in his hand. Grunted then took a sip, baring his teeth from the burn that crossed his lips and tongue, coating his throat with heat. His head felt like it was swimming. He could feel how wet and glazed his eyes were. How his scar itched and burned across his skull. His cracked and bloodied lips swollen and throbbing with a sting, and how the splits filled with dried blood itched across his cold, chapped hands.

"Do you not care?"

Marc finished off his drink, tossing it down with a snap. "I do not." He swiveled his head to look at the barkeep. His voice was low yet strained when he asked, "What did the others want?"

"Asking questions about Zoe Hardwood and a few missing students from the university." He shrugged. "Nothing I couldn't handle." And he grinned. His eyes carried a glint, a sparkle filled with knowing. "Wild goose chases keep the pigs sniffing in the wrong direction. Little do they know the trough is hidden beneath." He looked down at Marc's empty glass. "Another?"

Marc looked at the glass with puzzled bewilderment. He found what the barkeep said was strange. *The trough is hidden beneath? What did it mean?*

"Are you waiting for someone?" asked the barkeep.

"Hoping for someone is more like it." He turned to the bartender. "You wouldn't have happened to come across a lady by the name of Lori today, did you? About five six with long, silky-black hair, brown eyes and a sprinkle of freckles across her nose and upper cheeks."

"Let me guess, that would make you Marc, right?"

Marc's eyes narrowed. "Maybe."

"Understood. But the answer to your question is a resounding yes. She was here earlier, asking about someone named Marc."

"Did she say she would be back?"

"She did not, but I would admit that if she came here looking for you once what is to stop her from returning? There aren't many places in the Hollow to search, so finding someone isn't that difficult. Especially for someone who wants to be found. In my experience, it is best to just stay where you are, and she will find you."

Marc nodded. The revelation settled his nerves. "I will have another drink then."

"And the cop outside?"

Marc shrugged. "Let him sit until his bones rot. I have no concern for the police."

"As you wish," said the barkeep as he tossed the towel he was holding over his shoulder and walked around the bar. His two patrons were talking and bitching about the newscast blaring on the small television on a shelf above the bar. It was breaking news. Two more bodies had been found in the cemetery.

He saw the officer who came to his house-that Detective Carver-in the cemetery when the barkeep returned with his drink.

"Also on the house," he said, placing the drink on the table. Marc's attention remained with the newscast. The bartender watched with him. "I wouldn't worry about that." He looked at Marc dead in his eyes. "Everything is as it should be," he said. "Everything... is on the right path."

186

Lori heard the footsteps before she heard the knock. She was walking from the bathroom to the desk in her hotel room when she heard them. Then the knock came and she paused, staring at the door and the shadow beneath the door. She noticed it shifted back and forth.

Lori's jaw was tight as she gritted her teeth and shook her head. *I can't believe she followed me to my room.*

"Lori, it's Henry. Can we talk, please? I don't mean any harm."

She couldn't believe Elena brought Henry to the Hollow. Lori wondered how much she was paying him and what Elena expected him to do. Tie her up and drag her back to the Hamptons? Back to what? A burned down house with a cemetery beneath it? There was nothing to go back to, so what was Elena's play?

"Lori please?" Another knock, and Lori shook her head before stomping over to the door, unlocked the dead bolt and slid the chain off then opened the door.

"How much is she paying you?" Lori shot Henry an angry, disappointed stare, then walked back into the room and sat on the bed.

Henry cocked his head with a cluck of his tongue. "A million dollars," he said, closing the door.

"A million dollars? She's insane."

"Well, you may be right about that." He gestured to the chair by the desk. "May I sit?"

Lori shrugged. "It's a free country. But just know I'm not going back." She crossed her arms over her chest. "She needs to stay out of my business. She's caused so much heartache already. None of this would be happening if it wasn't for Elena and her lies."

Henry dragged the chair closer to the bed and took a seat. "What exactly did she do?"

Lori filled him in on current events. The accident and letters Elena had written. The house fire-although she kept Gerard's graveyard to herself-and of course Marc's notebook, which was on the desk. Henry turned to the notebook and Lori was relieved the front cover was showing and not the back cover with the pentagram. She also left out the connection Marc's story had to current events.

Henry listened without saying a word.

"So, where did she go?"

Henry cleared his throat. "I'm not entirely certain. She said she was going to find a motel and camp out for a few days."

Lori's eyes narrowed as she shook her head. "Why? She needs to leave. She's got enough to deal with back home. She shouldn't be here."

Henry shrugged. "Last I heard it was a free country. She can do what she wants."

Lori stiffened from the remark, gritting her teeth. She believed Henry was withholding information. After all, there is a million dollars on the line. It was best to take what he said with a grain of salt.

"So, you can't find him?" Henry asked. "This Marc guy?"

Lori shook her head. "Not at all. I've searched every place he could be. He's not home or anywhere he would normally go." She looked at Henry. "I'm at a loss."

"What's your next move?"

Lori paused before she answered. "I'm not sure. Go back to the apartment or the tavern. He's got to be somewhere in the Hollow."

Henry leaned forward, his elbows on his knees. "But you said the landlady hasn't seen him in months. Maybe he took a trip somewhere. Went down to Costa Rica for some R&R."

Lori was shaking her head. "No, that's not Marc's MO. He's here. I know he is."

Henry leaned back in the chair, his lips pressed tight together, thinking. "Do you want me to put out some feelers for you?"

"What does that mean?"

Henry shrugged. "Well, I am an FBI agent. I can talk to the local police. See if he's been arrested or if there's a missing person's report on him. Kind of pick their brains on the subject." He looked outside the window. "I'm sure they have a lot to do with all the murders, but someone is always willing to help a fellow officer. It's a crapshoot, but it may bear some fruit. Plus, I can use their database to find out more. If he showed up in some other state, I'll be able to locate him."

Lori was staring at him, and Henry put his hands up.

"What do you think?"

She was thinking about it as she crossed her arms again. It's not a bad idea, but if Marc has something to do with the murders won't that put a spotlight on him? She couldn't bear the thought of seeing Marc behind bars and even if he isn't the one murdering these people-and she was certain he wasn't-perhaps he was involved and having the spotlight on him may put him in the crosshairs of the police who are hoping to put a face to the murders and settle the town's nerves. Once the police are locked in on one person, they never look anywhere else. She couldn't do that to Marc.

"What else do you have to go on?"

He was right. There weren't many options available.

"Unless there's something you're not telling me?"

Lori shook her head. "Not at all."

"Okay." He shrugged. "So let me put out some feelers. See what we can come up with. At least it's a start... or the next step in the process of finding him."

Lori tightened her arms around her body. "Okay. But there's no need to ask the officers anything, just search the database and see what you find." She looked at him dead in his eyes. "You can do that, right?"

"I can," he said with a bow before he stood up. "Give me a few hours. I'll meet you back here later tonight."

"Okay."

"Perfect." He put his hand on her shoulder. "Don't worry, we'll find him." Lori nodded and Henry walked to the door.

"Thank you," she said.

"Don't thank me yet. Let's see what we find."

He was about to walk through the door when she said, "I'm sorry I cost you your million dollars."

Henry shrugged with a laugh in his throat. "No worries, Lori. I get the money no matter what happens."

And with that he was gone, closing the door with a thud behind. She breathed deeply, then looked around the room. Her eyes stopped at Marc's notebook and a million thoughts ran through her brain. The story, the demon, the accident, and of course the murders.

I hope you have nothing to do with it, Marc.

She turned away, her eyes downtrodden.

I really hope you have nothing to do with anything going on in the Hollow.

187

Logan checked every window in his house before he left through the back door, all secret and stealth like. His dad, Kyle, was drinking again, screaming at the television and huffing and puffing over the murders while gulping down swigs of whiskey between commercials. Kyle had told Logan this morning he'd be home for the next few days-apparently there was no one to kill in mob land this week-and that fact alone made Logan's life a living hell.

Still, he'd rather be inside than out in the neighborhood with all those demons running around. Kyle may be a blundering, drunken asshole, but Logan knew he was safe in his house. If those demons came looking for him, Kyle would give them the fight of their lives. Where it would go from there he wasn't certain, but at least he had the comfort of knowing someone would help him. If he stayed in the house that is, but now that he was outside, he knew he was exposed. Easy Pickens for any would-be demon.

He stepped out of his house and paused, investigating every corner of his property then scanning the woods behind his house, looking for anything that seemed out of place. Looking for anyone that may be looking for him, watching him from the depths of the woods.

Maybe they can see better in the dark, Logan thought as he looked up at the darkening sky. The rain seemed to be letting up, which was good since he needed to walk. Heard a foot scrunch in the snow and his heart stopped. His breath hitched in his throat. Hairs on the back of his neck stood at attention, on high alert for a threat.

Then silence, followed by a cool wind that breezed across his property as if the woods released a somber breath. Logan looked around the corner of his house, anticipating that someone would be there, standing, waiting to pounce but there was nothing to see. No one was there, but he could see the street now. Could see all the way to Michael's house across the street. Noticed the light in Michael's bedroom was on and Michael was standing by his window, watching Logan's house.

Logan dipped his head back behind his house and shook his head. "I knew they were watching me." He gripped his hands into fists. "FUUUUUUUCK!" he whisper-roared.

What now?

He needed to get to John. There was so much to tell him. So much Logan discovered during his intel operation last night. One thing Logan was good at was computers. He discovered his knack a few years ago when his mother bought him his first computer. He soon learned that he was a whiz with the internet. There was so much out there in the internet cosmos. So much information and Logan could tap into all of it, even the dark web where nefarious desires met with insatiable appetites for greed and sin. Not that Logan used it for such purposes, but he did enjoy indulging in a good conspiracy and discovered information on the dark web that most of the time blew his young mind. Conspiracies and such, provided with evidence that revealed the truth behind what was really going on in Washington.

And last night was no exception. He discovered a little more about the house in the western woods and the link to the Hardwoods. John may not like what he found, but he'll have to accept it if he wants to survive. Logan was also aware there were demons in the Hollow. He read about them last night and after everything that happened at school, he was certain his friends Michael and Chad were compromised. They allowed the demon in. Now Michael was watching him. Maybe they already know that he knows. Maybe they want him to know that they know he knows.

This is insane!

He investigated the woods. Obviously, he wasn't about to walk to John's house in the open. He looked across all the backyards between his house and Johns. All had fences. Someone would see him, and if Michael keeps looking there's a high probability he'll be able to see Logan scaling the fences.

No, his best option was to walk through the woods to remain out of sight then walk up to John's house through the backyard.

"It's now or never."

He heard his dad scream at the television. Something about more bodies. Logan knew his hometown was being turned into a graveyard for demons to roam free. Knew he had the information necessary to send those demons back to the hell they came from.

He gritted his teeth and headed for the woods. His heart thundered in his chest the entire time.

188

Carver sat in the passenger seat while Cindy drove, siren blaring the whole way. They were on their way to Hardwood Realty where a third body had been discovered outside the building. Carver's day was accelerating quickly. Aside from the two bodies in the cemetery and the one at Hardwood Realty, two more victims had been found.

That makes five murders today alone. Bodies were piling up by the minute, and his city was on edge. He feared what would happen when the sun officially retreats from the Hollow. What will happen to his people tonight? How will they respond? Everything depends on his ability to catch the murdering bastards and catch them soon. Naturally, his conversation with Cindy was regarding Marc Saduj. Cindy wasn't completely sold on the idea.

"No priors, no history of violence. Not even a parking ticket. Why would someone wake up one day and start a killing spree? It just doesn't make sense."

"You think I'm wrong?" said Carver, cracking his knuckles and gnawing on his toothpick.

Cindy stole a glance at Carver before returning her eyes to the road. "I think you saw something you couldn't explain and it's messing with your judgment."

Leave it to Cindy to be honest, but from her perspective Carver could understand why she was skeptical, but she didn't see

Marc Saduj. She was never in the house and felt the energy-the sickening depleting energy-that consumed the house, nor was she aware of the book. The house was in the book. Although a Saduj had yet to be named as a part of the conspiracy he was certain the name would make an appearance sometime soon.

"It's more than that, though."

"Like what?" Cindy swerved around a car stopped at a red light, punched the gas pedal and sped through the intersection.

"Gut instinct mostly, but there's more to it. The house's connection to Hardwood Realty and the Hardwoods in general."

"But that could just be a coincidence."

Carver shook his head. "I don't believe in coincidence." He looked out the window at the shops along Broadway. Normally the street was littered with people, but today there were few people out. He'd never seen the street so barren before. Although he was relieved everyone was at home and heeding the police's warning, the empty street still turned his blood cold, creating an empty pit in his stomach.

"But if it is him, who's helping him? All we know about him is that he had little to no friends. Other than his old landlady and the paper he used to write for, no one knows who he is and both of them provided glowing reviews. Are they in on it too? And how is it possible he amassed a cult following overnight?"

"Maybe they came from his partner, that Wren guy he's living with."

"I don't know. We haven't been able to find anything on him." After a pause, she said, "This whole case stinks and it's getting worse by the minute."

Carver looked at her. "We'll get him. I'm confident we will."

They sat quietly while Cindy sped to Hardwood Realty. "At least we know where he is. He can't cause any more trouble if we have him in our sights. If he makes a move, we'll be on him like white on rice. Although I don't know why he left his house today knowing all these bodies are going to be found. Why would he do that?"

"Simple," he said. "He's mocking us. Hanging out in plain sight and probably watching the news from the bar and enjoying the show."

"While we run around like chickens without heads following up on all his dastardly deeds."

"Exactly." Carver looked through the windshield as Cindy brought the car to a stop on the sidewalk outside Hardwood Realty. The flatfoots had already taped off the area, and the medical examiner was kneeling over the body. Several officers stood and watched. Carver looked up to the news helicopter hovering above the building and shook his head.

"And the eye in the sky is watching us all," he said, returning his gaze to Cindy. "Let's act as professional as possible. Wouldn't want us seen on the evening news as incompetent."

Cindy cocked her head, clucking her tongue. "You got that right."

"C'mon."

They walked into the parking lot, ducking under the tape and over to the body. The sudden gasp from Cindy was all Carver could hear. The body was desecrated in the same manner as a few of the jazz bar patrons from last night. Looked like someone sucked the life out of her and all that remained was a gray wrinkled skin wrapped around a skeleton. Her dark hair looked like an electric shock fried her skull. Her mouth hung open in a forever scream and her eyes were wide open, her eyeballs black to the core. Of course, the chest was crushed inward and the heart removed.

I need hearts for the master!

"You see anything like this before?" Carver asked the medical examiner who was crouched in front of the body. He held a pen in his gloved hand.

The specialist never looked at Carver. "Not at all. I can't even begin to explain how such a thing could happen. It's as if she aged a hundred years in a matter of seconds." He stood up, continuing to stare at the body.

Carver looked at the front door and the pentagram and inscription written in blood. "Did you take a sample of the blood from the pentagram?"

"Sure did. But other than that, there's nothing here. Nothing. It's as if she materialized in this spot." He turned to Carver. "It doesn't add up."

Carver nodded and returned his gaze to the body. The chest was disturbing, all crushed and battered as if she were made from clay. "Do you have a time of death?"

To which the examiner cocked his brow. "Yeah, like a hundred years ago. We'll need to do a full examination to find out more." He walked away, peeling off his gloves.

Cindy stepped closer to Carver. "How does someone drain the life from someone's body?" She was shaking her head when she turned around and walked away.

Carver looked through the door. He remembered the last time he was here and how he felt when he was inside. He'd felt a presence then. The same he felt now as if someone was watching him from inside.

"Carver." He heard Cindy call over his shoulder.

Carver turned to Cindy.

"Joan is here," she said, "And a news van."

Carver saw that Joan was approaching him. Saw the news van too and the reporter with her microphone and a cameraman setting up to record. Carver looked at Cindy.

"Get that body out of here as soon as possible." He gestured to the news crew. "Before they get a closeup."

Cindy nodded and said, "I got it," when Joan walked up to Carver.

"Judging by the look on your face, Joan, whatever it is you have to say I don't believe I want to hear it."

"I'm sure you don't but I'm going to tell you anyway."

Carver rolled his toothpick to the corner of his mouth. "Well, don't leave me in suspense."

Joan was holding a file. Carver glanced at it. "First, Captain Flannery wants to speak to you a-sap."

"Of course, the man loves to micromanage."

She paused before she said, "The two other bodies that were discovered today. One was found at Philipsburg Manor by the mill next to the pond. The other by Raven Rock in Rockefeller State Park Preserve."

"This guy loves dumping bodies in historic sites."

"That he does. Same MO too. Both hearts are missing and the manner of death is..." Carver noticed she looked at the dead body. "More in line with the medieval torture devices of our other victims. And one has a head missing."

Something flashed in the corner of Carver's eye. It came from inside the building. He thought he saw movement in the back room and stepped closer to the door. Joan was talking, but he didn't hear a word she said.

"You, okay?"

Carver paused before turning to Joan. "What did you say?"

Joan looked at him like he had ten heads.

"What?"

"Well, it's not like you're not going to find out, but..."

"Go on, spit it out, Joan."

She shook her head, looking away before training her eyes on Carver. "I was conducting research on our primary suspect and discovered a situation that takes him out of the fold in our investigation."

"I don't believe it."

"It's why Flannery wants to speak to you. Marc Saduj was in a hospital in the Adirondack Mountains on the night Zoe Hardwood was murdered. He was discharged and returned home the day she was found so he couldn't have anything to do with this. Or at least he had nothing to do with Zoe or Jerry Hardwood."

"Marc Saduj is the link to all of this."

She paused. "I don't know what to tell you, but Flannery is pissed. He said you're looking in the wrong place and wasting resources."

He studied her, knowing she was withholding information. "What does that mean, Joan?"

"It's not right in my opinion. He should allow you to finish what you started."

"Get to it, Joan."

She looked at him dead in his eyes. "He's taking you off the case and taking over. He's already in Phillipsburg."

"You've got to be kidding me. Now he's doing this?"

"I'm sorry, Stephen, but there's nothing I can do about it."

She turned and left while Carver's blood boiled. He scanned across the scene and all the officers who were staring at him.

One word squeezed off his lips, "Fuuuuuck!"

189

He was waiting in the woods, watching the house. Logan gnawed on his bottom lip, his nose wet with snot, staring. Looking at the house, yes, but also the surrounding neighbors and the sidewalk. From his view he could see the roof of Michael's house although his window was out of sight, obstructed by the house next to Johns.

The lights were on in John's house, including John's bedroom, but Logan had yet to see movement beyond the windows. He wondered if the house had become compromised.

Did they already come to claim John? If they did, what did that mean for Grandpa Claude?

"Shit," Logan muttered with a quick shake of his head then ran his tongue across his top lip. "Well, are you going in or not?"

He scanned across the neighborhood again to the rows of houses standing as quiet as the night with the lights on in the windows. The sky was overcast and now that the sun dipped beneath the horizon a thick blackness descended upon his neighborhood. Seemed like a black hole had opened and was pulling the Hollow into it. Not one star shined in the sky. The cloud cover made certain of it although he could see the slivered moon beyond the clouds, shedding the only light Logan could use to claim his path to the house. The house lights only reached so far into the long backyard.

He looked over his shoulder into the western woods, knowing the mansion was not far from where he stood. He hoped he never had to go back there.

Logan turned back to the house and stepped out of the woods into the backyard as a fierce wind howled across the property, nipping at his skin. He scanned across the property; the snow scrunching beneath his sneakers as he came to the kitchen window, staring at the orange glow from the inside.

He was hoping to see Grandpa Claude or John in the kitchen, but no such luck had occurred, although he could hear the television in the living room, the sound subtle yet prominent. Another howl of wind and Logan looked to both sides of the house, making sure no one was coming. He paused, listening for footsteps in the snow.

When he was confident he was in the clear, he walked up the stairs to the back door then craned his head, looking past the curtain that covered the window. The kitchen was empty, but he could see the television in the living room blaring the news. He knocked on the door.

Went to call out but stopped himself and looked over both shoulders. All was quiet. Then he knocked again, a little louder this time and craned his head, looking through the window and hoping someone would come to the door.

Nothing. No one. No sound. No movement. Nothing.

He knocked again then gripped the doorknob and turned when the door propped open with a suctioned pop. Logan stood, silent and staring. He pushed the door open further and took a step in.

"Hello," he called. "Anyone home?"

No response other than the television. He stepped into the house and closed the door, locked it then looked through the window. He scanned the backyard but couldn't see anything or anyone, so he turned around.

"Hello," he called. He stepped further into the kitchen, walking cautiously while scanning the house. "It's just me, Logan. I need to talk to John." He stepped into the living room and saw the newscast on the television. The reporter was in front of Raven Rock, standing outside an area cordoned off by the police. The headline read: **Five Bodies Found in Sleepy Hollow.**

The volume may have been low, but Logan could hear the newscast. The reporter was talking some nonsense about conspiracies and the end of the world. With the coming of the new millennium, the end of the world was a hot topic, and it was still three years away.

Nothing like getting a head start on the paranoia, Logan's dad had said.

He looked up at the ceiling, daring himself to take the stairs to the second floor.

Either they're here and dead or they went out. Maybe they got out of the Hollow. Took a vacation until everything settled down and maybe they forgot to lock the back door on their way out. Logan couldn't blame them if they did. Considering the murders were all linked to John's father he wouldn't be surprised if Claude decided to grab their stuff and go, especially after what happened at school today.

It seemed like the entire town was compromised.

He walked towards the stairs when he saw Claude on the floor and came close to stepping in the pool of blood that spread like lava from Claude's head. He froze, staring at Claude's face. Or what was left of Claude's face. His bones were crushed in, battered and bloodied. His eyes were swollen shut.

Logan cupped his hand over his nose and mouth. Grandpa Claude was beginning to stink. He wondered how long he'd been lying there.

"Fuck," he muttered, looking up the stairs to the second floor and wondering if John was up there as dead as Grandpa Claude, although he was certain that wasn't true.

According to his research they need John. He plays an important part in their ceremony. Still, he needed to be certain. Logan stepped over the body and the pool of blood, gripped the banister and hauled himself onto the first step then looked up. The stairs and hall were all dark. He paused and looked at Claude, then looked back up the stairs to the hall. He took each step with caution, maintaining silence in case someone was still in the house.

Logan stepped into the hall. The light in John's room was on-he could see the light through the crevices in the closed door-and Logan went to it, turned the knob and opened the door.

John's room had been desecrated. His bed was flipped over with all his toys and belongings littered across the floor. His posters were torn from the walls. In their place, someone had written *Initium Novum Humanity's End As A New Beginning* across the entire room. Inscribed on the closet door was a pentagram. All were written in blood. But no John. No trace of him at all. Logan opened the closet door. Turned on the light and found nothing.

I should call the police. I'm too late, but the police can find him. After I tell them what happened yesterday, they'll have no choice but to go to the house and take everyone down. At least we'll have a chance to end this tirade.

He stepped back into the hall. The room across from John's was open and he could see a cordless phone on the nightstand next to the bed. He picked it up and dialed 911, then put the phone to his ear.

Silence greeted him.

The line's dead. What now? He dropped the phone on the bed. *Go back home and call the police.* He shook his head when something flashed in the corner of his eyes. He looked out the window and his blood curdled in his veins.

Michael and Chad were outside on the sidewalk, staring at him.

Shiiiiiiiiitttt!

Michael walked around the side of the house. Chad walked to the front door.

190

John attempted for the hundredth time to kick the door off his cage. He had already tried picking the lock but that went nowhere. His fingernail splintered, casting a thick stream of blood across his finger. His foot didn't do any better. It seemed like the door was welded shut with no chance to pry it open no matter how much he kicked and pushed.

His heart thundered against his chest the entire time and he was sweating. It was damn hot in the dungeon. He'd read about dungeons before, mostly in history class and mentions in fiction tales and he had to admit his current location was a spot on depiction of what he pictured a dungeon would look like.

After the vampire beat him senseless, he woke up in a cage teetering above the dungeon and staring at the dead girl rotting from the rafters. She was so close that if he could swing the cage a few feet to his left he'd be able to touch her. Not that he wanted to touch her, not by any means necessary. He wanted to get as far away from her dead stank as possible. Her corpse was rotting, and the smell invaded his nostrils. It was everywhere he turned. At least the vampire was no longer in attendance although John was certain he'd be back. Him and his minions.

How many people are they turning?

He looked down from his cage. There were people down there chained to the wall. They looked so thin, so frail and damned and-John knew it was true-they still had hell to look forward to. It was only a matter of time until they were draped across the slab in the center of the room and tortured to death.

He kicked the door again and his hip and knee twisted with pain. His head hurt something awful but at least the bleeding had stopped, the crusted dried blood now turning wet from the sweat on his brow. He wiped it away with his sleeve. Frustrated and with tears in his eyes, he kicked the door again and again pain shot up his leg as he flopped across the cage in the fetal position, holding his hip.

Started crying, thinking about Grandpa Claude. He could hear the punches across Claude's head and John knew he was no longer among the living. Images of Grandpa, bloodied and dead by the front door, flashed behind his eyes.

"I'm so sorry Grandpa," he cried. "So sorrrrrry."

His wails were cut off by the growl that shook the dungeon. John's blood ran cold in his veins. His heart stopped as his body tightened.

Now the growl turned rickety as a bright red glow gleamed through the room. John turned his head, slow and panicked, to the opposite side of the dungeon. To the fissures that he'd thought led into darkness-perhaps another entry to the underground-but now glowed with that beaming dark red.

He rolled over to the iron bars and pulled himself up when he saw eyes in the fissures. Large catlike eyes filled with depths of darkness and rage.

Staring at him as if those eyes could devour him. He didn't realize he hadn't breathed since he saw those eyes. Stiff, every bone in his body had tightened as if some phantom hand wrapped around him and squeezed. All he could see were those eyes.

Then drifting, as if he were floating. Weightless. Watching as a green smoke drifted from the fissures into the dungeon and his heart constricted, mesmerized as the smoke glided towards him. Electric sparks raged within the smoke. Panicked, John backed up as if he could get away. As if he could run and be gone but his back slammed against the bars. The smoke coiled around the cage, then slithered through the bars. His body jolted, then stiffened while the green slithered around him. He could feel it crawling across his skin. His right hand was shaking, trembling with uncontrollable rage.

His throat constricted as if the smoke was choking the life breath from his lungs. Couldn't move, paralyzed with fear. It was everywhere now, blanketing him in a green fever.

More electric sparks raged within the smoke. His eyes wide, struggling to breathe when he saw eyes in the smoke and his heart skipped a few beats, tightening in his chest. The smoke recoiled then darted into his nose and mouth and eyes.

He pushed back against the bars. His head started trembling, whipping violently from side to side.

Blood dripped from his nostrils. He tasted it on his lips the moment everything turned black and cold and empty.

191

"We have to do something."

Marc looked up from his glass and felt his blood boil. The patron sitting at the bar was annoying. He kept talking shit and all Marc wanted to do was bash his brains in.

The anger started after his third drink. Thoughts in his head were cycling fast, running like a conveyor belt at lightning speed. He couldn't stop his thoughts, and that damn patron kept talking nonsense, making declarations and promises Marc knew were nothing more than empty threats. Empty threats that escalated Marc's anger.

Marc noticed the barkeep looked in his direction. Briefly he looked, then returned his attention to the patron-a weathered and worn old man, short and frail with a balding head. Marc placed him in his sixties. The patron occupying the barstool next to the old man wore a thick black winter coat. He looked like a seaman with his coat wrapped around him.

They were talking about the murders and, for some odd reason, that irritated Marc more than he'd been irritated in a long while. The frail one had suggested forming a lynch mob to hunt down the murdering bastard dumping bodies in the Hollow. The barkeep placated them, steering the conversation into new directions. Considering that over the last hour more patrons had entered the bar, Marc was certain the barkeep wanted to keep talk about the murders to a minimum. What good could come from talking about it other than misdirected anger? Such conversations only added fuel to the fire and what would the old man be able to accomplish other than getting his own frail heart ripped from his chest?

Marc turned to his drink. The caramel liquid seemed right at home where it should be, in a glass in front of someone who appreciated what the drink had to offer. Perhaps a little more than most. He stared into the glass, losing himself. Discarding his thoughts. Stared for so long he felt hypnotized.

Where is Lori?

The thought broke through his mesmerized state. The bar was in full bloom, and he wondered just how long he'd been sitting in the damn bar. The booths were occupied, some overstuffed with patrons-mostly college students and locals. It seemed that everyone in the Hollow required a drink tonight. Not an empty stool remained. Marc looked at the small television above the bar and the subtitles scrolling across the screen.

Detective Carver has been removed as the lead detective.

Captain Flannery is in charge.

Five more dead in Sleepy Hollow.

And then the pentagram and inscription took center screen and Marc's scar started itching. Burning. Irritating him to the point that he had to rub and scrape and push, wanting nothing more than to rip his fucking head off. He felt blood on his head, but he kept rubbing, wanting to scrape that scar off his skull. The blood dripped across his eye, cascading down his nose. He wiped it clean with his sleeve. Saw blood streaked across his sleeve, his scar irritated and burning with a sting across his skull.

Marc sat forward, cupping his drink. Saw a picture of Lori in the liquid. Lori as he remembered her on the night he proposed. How she looked under the moonlight when he wrapped his arms around her while they swam in the lake. Making love in the water.

He asked her to be his wife and the smile that lit up his life when she said yes was beaming with gratitude.

Screeching now, tires sliding across wet asphalt when Marc's heart lurched in his chest. Tumbling now, steel crushing against the asphalt. A deadly scream from Lori. Pounding rain, the smell of gasoline, burnt rubber and hot rain. Marc crawled out of the car. Every bone in his body felt broken and bruised but he managed to push himself to his feet. Rain thundered over him, remembering the red eyes that tore through him as he drove.

Cars stopped on the highway. People raced to the car, looking in and calling for help or asking questions. Marc turned and saw himself in the car, pinned to the ground, his head bleeding. Bleeding profusely. So much blood, he watched it as the rain carried the blood to his ghostly feet. Heard the sirens in the distance and when he looked around, he saw the man in black standing in the street. His face was somber yet stoic. Passing cars raced through him, their headlights beaming through the storm.

Marc's breath hitched in his throat. The man in black craned his head and grinned.

"You did this," Marc hollered through the rain. "What is this hold you so desperately need to have over me?"

He looked back to the car and the beautiful people helping Lori, then returned his gaze to the man in black.

"Why can't you just leave us alone?"

The man in black said simply, "It was you who asked for my help. Not the other way around."

Marc jolted in his seat, returning to the bar and all the commotion. He lifted his head slowly, scanning across the bar. The booths, the chatter and music from the jukebox. Saw the frail old man sitting at the bar. Saw the ghost of his mother sitting next to him. They both looked in his direction, their faces contorted and demonic and Marc's heart jumped in his chest.

He turned away quickly.

Lori? Where are you?

192

Logan made it down the stairs before Chad was at the front door. He could see him through the bay window in the living room, although he wasn't certain if Chad had seen him too. Not that it mattered. It was obvious Logan had been seen in the bedroom upstairs.

He stood on the bottom step, thinking. Grandpa Claude's dead body on the floor in front of him. Looked out the window and saw Chad creeping up the walkway to the front door.

Heard shuffling in the backyard.

"Shit," Logan whisper screamed, his head moving left to right, his heart pounding. He could hear the rapid thick beats between his ears as his breath burned shallow in his throat. His eyes darting from one corner of the house to the other when the thought hit him.

The basement.

Every house on the block had a basement and every basement he'd seen in the neighborhood had a door to the outside. He gripped the banister then stepped across Claude's body, past the pool of blood, then shuffled to the hallway where he ducked out of sight from the front door, using the shadows from the dark hallway to cast himself into blackness. Craned his head and looked at the back door where a dark silhouette hovered outside the window.

"Michael," he whispered when the door across from him popped open with a creak that froze Logan's heart and turned his blood into ice as every hair on his arms, neck and legs stood erect. The door swayed open then closed, soft and gentle like, as if it were a part of the wind. His eyes were adjusting to the dark. He could have sworn he saw a wisp of white light go through the door.

Heard footsteps on the back step and his heart jumped in his chest. He immediately went through the open door and froze. Saw the apparition-the ghostly wisp of light-glide down what Logan could now see was a staircase.

The basement.

He gripped the banister and took the first step down when he heard glass breaking. Logan froze on the first step, turned slowly then gently closed the door, finding the lock on the doorknob that he twisted into a locked position before turning around to the stairs.

A thick blackness existed in front of him. He couldn't see where the stairs stopped but he'd be damned before turning the light on.

Again, the wisp led the way down the stairs. Logan followed it down. His soft footsteps brought subtle creaks from the wooden steps. His eyes adjusting to the thick black pitch in the basement.

There were windows in the basement that cast silvery glows from the moon into the room. The wisp disappeared in the moonlight and that was just fine with Logan-he could see the door in the corner. The basement was filled with old boxes and old furniture too. He saw a high bar in the corner when he heard footsteps upstairs followed by Chad's voice.

"Looogaaaannn. We know you're in here."

Then Michael. "Come out, come out wherever you are."

Laughter from Chad. "Can Johnny boy come out to play too?"

More laughter and Logan beelined to the back door. Tried the knob. Locked. With trembling fingers, he unlocked the door as quietly as possible. Put his hand on the door then twisted the knob, easing the door open when an icy wind breezed through the cracked door.

Get and run. The thought jumped into his brain and Logan jumped through the door, up a set of five steps and onto the property. Running for the woods, his feet trudging through the snow when he heard the back door slam open.

"There you are you little conniving shit."

"Fuck." Logan ran as fast as he could into the woods and kept going.

"I'm coming to get you, Logan." Laughter in Chad's throat. Logan could hear his footsteps in the snow.

He kept running further into the woods where the snow dissipated into dead frozen leaves, tree branches, and bushes.

"No, *we* are coming to get you, Logan." This was Michael. Logan was certain he'd come from around the house. Perhaps he went through the front door in case Logan ran around that way instead of into the woods.

He kept going, kept running into the thicket of trees and bushes and small little caverns created from uplifted earth and dead fallen trees. Logan stopped cold in front of one of those wooded caverns. Breathing heavy, he looked around, listening to their footsteps as they entered the woods.

"Where are you, Logan?"

"I think we should bash your brains in. Leave you in the woods for the snakes and wolves to feast on."

Logan snuck a quick look around a tree and saw Chad and Michael walking towards him. He looked around.

Where can I go? Either keep running or try for his house, he wasn't certain, but he knew they would be on him in another second or two if he didn't act now.

Now he could see the wisp again. Logan craned his head, watching as the ghostly tendrils floated into a dark wooded alcove created from an uprooted tree and the cavern it created with the connected brush that led into an unknown blackness where Logan knew he'd find some unsavory bugs and forest creatures.

It was either that or they'd find him and what they had planned for him Logan knew he wanted nothing to do with, so he ducked into the cavern, crawling on his belly across the cold frozen earth. Rocks and roots and branches and leaves all littered the ground as he scuttled to the back and sat, gripping his knees and going quiet and unmoving, listening to their footsteps as both Chad and Michael rounded the tree where he was hiding. He could see them. Although some branches obstructed his view, he could still see them.

He could see their eyes as they stood by the tree, scanning the woods. Their eyes were dark crimson that gleamed in the darkness.

Noticed they both looked at each other when Michael pressed his finger to his lips. Listening. Listening for a sign that he was on the run. Logan's stare darted from Michael to Chad then back to Michael, his heart pounding, his breathing shallow as he did everything in his power to not make a noise when Michael smiled, revealing ivory fangs.

"Perhaps we'll pay a visit to your father," Chad bellowed into the forest, his voice edgy and gnarly. "You'd like that, wouldn't you Logan? Perhaps we'll bash his brains in like good old Claude back there in the foyer. You see how his skull is crushed? Would you like for us to do that to your father too?" He stepped forward, mere inches from Logan, staring into the forest. Logan was certain that if he looked down, he'd see him.

"Where the fuck did he go?" This was Michael, investigating the woods, scanning every branch, limb, and tree. "He didn't just disappear into thin air."

"Not a chance," said Chad and judging by the look on his face he was not pleased. "He's here somewhere. Hiding." He raised his voice as if Logan was somewhere deep in the woods. "We'll find you Logan. No matter where you go, we'll find you. It's not a matter of if... but... *when!*" His holler echoed across the woods.

"Master Wren wants us back," said Michael.

"What about this one?" He gestured to the woods.

"He'll come to us. In time, he'll have no choice but to come to us."

"I don't like leaving loose ends."

Michael stepped closer to Chad. "That's not really a concern," he said, then regarded the woods, screaming, "Is it, Logan?" His voice echoed through the woods. He let the echo die before addressing Chad. "He'll come to us. It's inevitable."

Michael gave another glance into the woods before he walked back to the property. Chad remained, scanning across the woods. Logan could hear his heavy breathing and the gasp that escaped his lips. He stepped forward, so close he blocked Logan's view. All he could see was Chad's winter coat.

Chad grunted before turning and walking away. Logan watched him enter the property. Watched as Chad drifted towards the house before breaking into a run to catch up to Michael. Logan released the breath he'd been holding. Put his hand over his thundering heart and breathed a sigh of relief, every inch of him shaking like a leaf.

He pursed his lips and gasped. Staring, his eyes adjusted to the darkness. He could see the white wisp floating not too far from where he was.

"I guess I should thank you. Whoever you are."

He watched as the wisp floated out of the cavern.

"Wait... where are you going?"

Logan followed the wisp, stepping away from the fallen tree when the wisp floated further into the woods, away from the house and towards the dilapidated mansion where he knew they were holding John.

"Wait a minute," said Logan. "We should call the police. Let them deal with it."

But the wisp kept floating further away. Logan looked back at the house and the street, searching for a sign that would tell him where Chad and Michael had gone. He saw no one. Turned back to the woods and saw the wisp was holding still as if waiting for him.

"I guess you know what you're doing." He paused for a moment, waiting. Wondering what he should do before he followed the wisp. "Just try not to get me killed, okay?"

193

Excerpt from *The Demon and Sleepy Hollow* by the Original Knickerbocker Dated 1856.

The Mansion in the Woods

I do believe an appropriate history must be shared regarding the mansion and the surrounding property. As I mentioned previously, the mansion was built by a Transylvania emigrant we came to know as Sam J. Curad. According to Olga, he had built the mansion-although unknown to the residents of Sleepy Hollow-soon after the revolution and sometime during the late 1780s. Considering I am writing about the house some seventy years after it was constructed one would assume that Mr. Curad was an old man by the time we entered his property. However, this is entirely untrue. Sam J. Curad looked no more than twenty-five at the time, but we shall get to that later. First, allow me to provide some history on the property.

Some years after our confrontation I had the pleasure of meeting with two members of the Weckquaesgeek Indians, Elder Chieftain Alo and his grandson Nahele. The Weckquaesgeek had occupied what is now Sleepy Hollow for half a millennium before they were forced from their home. It was a chance meeting and one that shed light on our previous conflict with the demon. It was Chief

Alo who provided the necessary information. The following is an abridged version of his story.

Chief Alo referred to the teachings of his ancestors who spoke about a place in the woods where the trees refused to grow. A clearing in the woods that at first had seemed like a miracle. A place where crops could be harvested in abundance. They immediately began tilling the ground, preparing the soil to make a good seed bed. However, it was during this time that they discovered the cave in the center of the clearing. Chief Alo reported that a cavern had opened in the earth, a result of the consistent tillage, revealing a cave that led to the darkest pit of pitch black they had ever seen.

The tribe members of the time had described an awful stench that came from the cave. According to Chief Alo, the word used to describe the foul smell would translate to our modern English as 'rot.' Putrid and foul and noxious was the stench. The tribal members provided their findings to the elders upon their return home-the Weckquaesgeek had occupied what is now the property where the Old Dutch Church resides-who decided to visit the grounds the next day.

Considering the stank and rot coming from the cave, the elders believed the ground had become sour, although they thought it was best to venture into the woods to confirm their suspicions. But that night, as the tribe slept peacefully, the constant howling from wolves awakened them. They could hear it everywhere, coming from every part of the woods. The elders heard it, as did the entire tribe. They had also discovered one of their own was missing, the same tribal member who first discovered the cave. They referred to the young man as Jasa Mucad.

He was never seen again.

At daybreak on the following morning, the elders and tribal members ventured into the western woods to the clearing. The elders confirmed that the moment they crossed the property's threshold they could feel the evil that ventured from that cave. They referred to it as Xibalba, a portal to the underworld where the Wendigo roamed. I was informed that the word Wendigo is the natives' term for demon or malevolent spirit and that Xibalba is their word for Hades or Hell. The elders wasted no time, believing the area in the woods was compromised by evil spirits and forbade all tribal members from entering its confines.

The next day is when the sickness arrived. A noxious sickness that found its way through the tribe and it was during that night that the wolves surrounded them.

Chief Alo told the story of the Wendigo Wolves that brought death to their tribe. In the night, they stole tribal members from their slumber. More than a dozen were taken before anyone noticed. They found them with their hearts torn from their chests. A battle then ensued between man and beast. The elders told of the wolves' red beaming eyes and how they moved unlike any wolf the tribe had ever known. It was as if they were plotting and strategizing, as if they were in tune with each other while they attacked. If it weren't for the large numbers of the tribe, the elders were certain everyone would have vanished that night. However, the Weckquaesgeek were triumphant, and the very next day they placed deterrents around the property to ward off all forest creatures from venturing into the clearing. They also marked trees with the Wendigo symbol as a warning to neighboring tribes.

It was then that the elders forbade all tribal members from entering the grounds, which, over time, had lost its power and within a month the sickness that had befallen the tribe subsided.

I provide this foundation as a warning to future residents of Sleepy Hollow. The ground is sour and houses an evil no man, woman, or child should ever encounter. The mansion in the woods must never be occupied, nor should human hearts or hands touch it. It is best left to rot for I fear that should the cave be opened once again, the Wendigo will grow stronger and with the steady growth of the human population should the sickness be carried across the globe, the evil that persists in the Hollow has the potential to infect every person on earth.

———

Detective Carver sat in silence, staring at the last line on the page. Allowing the meaning to sink into his brain.

Infect every person on earth.

Humanity's end as a new beginning.

After he received the news that he was officially off the case Carver returned to the precinct. He first thought about cleaning out his desk but then thought better of it. He wasn't fired, and he was damn sure he wasn't putting in his resignation, although the thought passed through his angered brain more than a few times during the drive from Hardwood Realty to the precinct. The uniformed officer had little to say to Carver during the drive, reserved to a few apologies and spouting injustices over Captain Flannery's decision to remove Carver from the case.

"What does he expect? Bodies are being dumped daily, and we have no leads. Does he expect the guy to come out of the woods with his hands held high?"

To which Carver gave no response. Never bitch, moan, groan, or confide in a subordinate was Caver's philosophy. Once that line was crossed personal boundaries get all fucked up, and no one knows which way is up or down and eventually someone's got a resentment. It was best to keep it yourself. Like he was now, in his office with all the blinds closed. The last thing he wanted was for his fellow officers to come barging into his office and talking shit. Plus, he wanted to be alone and read the book because what else did he have? He couldn't care less what Flannery wanted. He'll be damned before he let this case go.

The information about Marc Saduj was concerning and put a chink in his theory about Mr. Saduj, but what Carver knew was to trust his instincts. Instincts come from the gut not the head, and his stomach was rumbling when he was in that house with Mr. Saduj and his faithful servant, Wren. Plus, Carver's theory that Jerry was acting at the behest of someone else also feeds the Saduj theory.

Considering he wasn't around when Zoe Hardwood had her heart ripped out took the man out of the mix but not entirely. He was still living in the house Jerry was showing on that fateful day. Owned the house too, but the way he received the house was suspect. All ownership was transferred on the same day Jerry went off the rails.

Something wasn't adding up, and he was dead set on finding out what it was. He may not have all the details on the additional bodies that were dumped around the Hollow throughout the day, but he can always obtain the information if he needs it-through some plotting and planning on his part and using his team to provide the information to him. That wasn't an issue, but now that he's officially off the case he sought the book.

The answers are in the book.

He could hear the priest's voice as if he was in the room with him. Now that he was deeper into the story, he found the similarities striking. He knew the house was at the center of it all and if he could find some relevance that would give him the ability to enter the house-albeit with a SWAT team-he knew this would all end in a heartbeat. Carver wasn't one to believe in the supernatural and he knew the stories in the book had a rational, scientific explanation. However, considering the things he's seen so far, he was taking the supernatural into consideration.

It would be best if you let go of your modern beliefs. In order to fight the demon, you'll need to believe.

The thought struck him as odd, as if it was dropped into his conscious thought from the other side of living. He paused and looked around his office. Listening. It was quiet in the precinct—most every officer was out in the field as either a part of the investigation or patrolling the Hollow in a display of safety for its citizens. After a moment, he dismissed the thought and went back to the book when there was a knock on his door. Carver covered the book with a folder from his desk, telling the knocker it was okay to enter.

The blinds on the door's window shifted when the door opened. Margaret Hatchwater was in the doorway. She worked at the front desk and always went by Mags to anyone who'd known her for any length of time.

"Mags, how are you?" Carver leaned back in his chair and popped a toothpick between his lips.

Of course, the first thing she did was apologize that he was taken off the case, a notion that Carver dismissed with a wave of his hand as if to say, *just get to it, Mags.*

He cleared his throat. "What can I do for you?"

She hesitated a moment before she answered. "Well, it may be nothing, but there's an FBI agent here from Long Island."

Carver's face pinched in confusion. "Why?"

"He said he needed access to our database."

Carver thought about it and shrugged. "Happens. He's probably working a case in the area and needs information on a potential suspect."

Margaret clenched her jaw, the look on her face skeptical. "I'm not so sure about that."

"What do you mean?"

"Well, I was walking to get some coffee and glanced over his shoulder and noticed the name of his potential suspect."

Now Carver perked up, leaning into his desk. He took the toothpick from his lips. "And?"

"Saduj," she said. "The person he's searching for is Marc Saduj."

Now that was a bit too coincidental.

Logan heard the wind howl through the trees. He'd been following the wisp through the woods, fighting through the cold and the darkness. The sky was overcast, and the only light came from the slivered moon that bathed the clouds into a soft silvery glow that draped across the trees.

He stopped briefly to take a breath when a branch snapped on his left and his head snapped to the sound, staring. Quiet. Couldn't see much of anything. He looked around the woods.

"The house is in the west," he said, talking to the wisp as if it could hear him. "But you seem to be taking me east."

He watched as the wisp kept moving away from where he stood. Logan looked around again before following dutifully.

"I hope you're not leading me into hell." He kept moving, stepping over fallen trees, roots and dead leaves frozen from the cold. "Because that would not be cool."

She kept looking at him from across the bar with that same demonic grin, the same black metallic eyes. He could see that his mother's wrists were bleeding as she sat by the bar beside the old man who kept bending the barkeep's ear about forming a militia to go hunting in the western woods.

Marc's hands were shaky. Every time he picked up his glass he had to steady his cracked and bleeding hand. He sipped his drink and felt the burn across his bloodied lips. His scar itched, burning across his skull. He scanned across the bar and all the patrons stuffed into booths, some standing with drinks in their hands while talking to the people in those booths. It seemed as if the bar had become overstuffed with people and was ripping at the seams to hold everyone in its embrace.

And still Marc sat alone. Other than a few shared stares, no one paid him any attention as if he was non-existent in their alcohol-infused reality. Even more, it was as if the entire booth existed on some other plane in a parallel universe and he was rubbing up against their universe like a windshield wiper, glimpsing their alternate reality.

He watched them, all of them, as if they were in slow motion, moving meticulously and mechanically as if they were all following suit in some damnation game where their souls were on the line. Little pieces to the puzzle that were required for the scene to be set just right. Extras on the movie set. That's how Marc saw them with their petty grievances and limiting philosophies. Noticed the barkeep kept eyeballing him from the corner of his eyes. No matter what task the barkeep tended to-serving drinks or cashing people out, wiping down glasses or wiping down the bar-his eyes were always on Marc.

Marc looked across the street through the glass on the front door. Now the chatter that had grown to a fever pitch cut off like the flick of a power switch. All Marc could hear was his own breathing with his neck craned around to the front door and his drink cupped in his hand. He wasn't certain if he was looking for the cop car or to see if Lori was on her way.

He saw neither and when he turned around everyone in the bar had collectively paused. They sat in mid riff, some holding drinks they had yet to press to their lips, some with a freshly lit cigarette, the smoke frozen in midair and others on the verge of tossing out words from their throats. Even the barkeep was paused, his hands frozen with a towel wrapped around the glass in his hand.

Marc saw the man in black whisper in his mother's ear and his heart dropped into his stomach. The man in black turned to him, his cane in his palm and that conniving grin plastered across his lips. Marc's mother whispered in his ear. Marc swallowed his breath.

The man in black nodded, his stare stoic yet accusatory. Now he stood tall. Stood tall then glided over to Marc, his footsteps echoing across the wooden floor the same as his cane with his shadow stretching across Marc, growing larger the closer he came.

"Haven't seen you in a long while," said Marc, so nonchalant, as if this was a chance meeting between old friends.

"Since the cemetery," said the man in black when he gestured to the seat. "May I?"

"Of course." Marc gestured to the seat, gripping his glass tight as the man in black placed his cane on the tabletop then sat across from him, folding one hand over the other on the table.

Now Marc took a good, long look at the man in black and noticed how faded he seemed as if he were projecting himself from far away.

"I do admit, my power fades during the in-between. But I believe this conversation is necessary. Considering where the night is going, I felt it was best to be here."

"Now, what the hell is that supposed to mean?"

196

Carver had introduced himself to FBI Agent Henry Clavell before inviting him to his office. Carver asked a few general questions, attempting to assess where the FBI agent was coming from and mainly how he came across Marc Saduj. Obviously, the timing couldn't be more suspect, and Carver noticed a tremor of trepidation run through Henry's bones with a cringe when Carver asked about his interest in Marc Saduj.

The agent also paused before answering, as if he was struggling with some internal moral dilemma of whether or not to lie.

"Honestly, a good friend is looking for him and asked for my help."

To this Carver paused, eyeballing Henry and rolling his toothpick to the opposite corner of his mouth. "All the way from Long Island just to check our computer? Why not just do that from your home office?"

Henry laughed. "It's never that easy, is it? She came here to find him and her mother asked for my help. Friend of the family type of favor." He paused, waiting for a response but when Carver gave none, he continued. "The mother thought it was best for her to return home, but when she refused, I was brought in to try to talk some sense into her."

"And she got you to come here."

Henry cocked his head and grinned. "That she did. I thought it was best to placate and play nice. Find out what information I can and use it to convince her to come home."

Now Carver paused before asking, "What is your friend's name? If you don't mind sharing the information."

Henry waved him off, shaking his head. "Not at all. Lori Francon is her name."

Francon, thought Carver. Where did I hear that name? He looked at Henry. "What is her interest with Marc Saduj? Old girlfriend, or does he owe her money?"

"Old flame. Seems the relationship ended on a sour note, and she wanted to reconcile."

Carver tilted his head. "Sour note?"

"Correct. They were in a car accident last summer and the relationship broke off soon after. I guess she feels she never had the closure she would have preferred."

Car accident, thought Carver. That would explain the hospital stay when Zoe Hardwood died.

"Something wrong, Detective? I've used other offices before, but this is the first time I was questioned about it. Did I miss something?"

Carver narrowed his eyes, assessing the young agent. "You are aware there's a murder investigation going on, correct? Multiple murders too, so we find it suspect that out of the blue and in the middle of all this carnage an FBI agent comes strolling into our precinct to use our computer."

Now Henry paused again, thinking. "If Marc Saduj is a suspect, then I would find that very strange."

"Indeed." Carver shifted in his seat, draping his arms across his desk and folding his hands in front of him. The two detectives eyeballed each other like a mental standoff.

"Is he?" asked Henry. "Is Marc Saduj a suspect in your investigation?"

Carver thought about his response. He knew never to comment on an ongoing investigation, but Henry was with the FBI and what harm could come from Carver divulging information that he could find out on his own? It would be best to placate the young agent if Carver wants the chance to interview his friend Lori Francon. Although he's officially off the case, unofficially-in Carver's mind at least-he'll be working until it's over. Plus, it's not as if Henry couldn't find the information through other means. Although he does have a personal interest in the case that may cause him to act less cordial and investigative than Carver would like, he was, after all, a fellow officer in law enforcement. And how could Carver not warn him about the potential that Marc Saduj is a mass murdering son of a bitch? If something were to happen to Lori Francon, her blood would be on Carver's hands, and he had enough guilt from the case already. Best to tell the truth. "He was until recently."

"So, he's been cleared of all wrongdoing?"

"I wouldn't say that exactly. He remains a person of interest."

Henry nodded, thinking. "Which means there's a good chance you know where he lives. Could you possibly share that information with me, please? It would help if I can get these two together to hash out whatever is going on between them and get my friend home as soon as possible."

Carver shot his head back. "Did you not hear me? Marc Saduj is still a person of interest. Maybe it's best for your friend to get in her car and drive back to Long Island."

Henry shook his head. "That'll never happen. Not until she sees him…" His face turned a brighter shade of red as if he heard what he'd just said and fit the pieces to the puzzle together with a dawning shock to the system. Allowing his friend to meet with a potential madman was more than likely not a good idea. "Although I'll insist on being there, at least within ear shot in case there's something sinister at play." Then he added, "And I'll make sure they meet in a public place."

Now Carver's thoughts hopped into overdrive. Every single possibility raced through his brain at lightning speed. Was he still investigating the case? Even though he's officially off the case, there's no way he could put it to bed that quickly. He'd love to interview Henry's friend, but what would happen if he did? If Flannery catches wind of him poking his nose where it doesn't belong, he'll be thrown off the force and could lose everything he's worked an entire career for. But now he had a link to Marc Saduj staring right in front of him. He glanced down at the book hiding beneath the folder on his desk.

The answers are in the book.

Conflicted, possibly for the first time in his life, Carver concluded what he couldn't do was allow an innocent person to walk into the line of fire. He'll have to solve the case through other means.

"I apologize, but I do not feel comfortable providing that information."

Henry pressed his lips together and gave a nod. "Understood. You really believe it's him, don't you?"

"Well, it's more than that. I don't feel comfortable sending a sheep into the wolf's den. If it is him, and I allow such a meeting to take place, what does that say about me? That's not who I am, nor who I intend to be."

Henry sat back, gripping the armrests in both hands. "I get it. Trust me, I do. It seems you got him in your sights and you're not letting go."

Carver cocked his head. "I have seen no information to the contrary. Not yet at least."

"But will you be able to see it if the contrary arrives?"

To this Carver's eyes narrowed. He felt insulted. "Not sure what you mean?"

"Well, my experience is that sometimes we catch something in our sights and that's all we see. As if we're looking at the world through a tunnel and any evidence to the contrary is deleted or generalized to match our belief. All indications from Lori are that Marc has always been a gentle soul. She never indicated that he was violent. So, the question is Detective, if you discover that Marc Saduj is certainly not your man will you be able to dust off your belief and begin looking in another direction?"

Now Carver smiled. Nothing like a standoff between officers. "I believe I'll do just fine in that regard." He cocked his head, sitting tall in his chair. "But thank you for the psychology lesson."

"It's a field of study called Neuro Linguistic Programming. When we hold a belief, all information we receive pertaining to the contrary is either deleted because we refuse to see it because it negates the belief, or we distort or generalize the information to validate our belief. It's why two people can have the same experience but see it differently. Also how the federal government keeps the masses under control. Solidify a belief in their minds and even if they're shown proof to the contrary, they'll never accept it because it doesn't validate their belief system."

"Mind control," Carver whispered as if to himself, thinking about the demon from the book and current circumstance.

"Exactly," said Henry. "They've been doing it since the forties. Maybe even longer."

Carver asked himself, *Who the hell is this person?*

Henry took the silence as an opportunity to leave. "Well, thank you, Detective." He stood up and offered his hand that Carver shook.

Carver eyeballed Henry. "But if you find anything pertaining to the investigation, you'll share that information, correct?"

"Of course. Once an officer, always an officer. You have my word."

"Thank you," Carver said when he took a business card from his desk drawer along with a pen then scribbled his phone number on the back before offering it to Henry. "My home number is on the back. I'll be there in a few hours." He paused while Henry took the card. "If she's willing to talk, I'd welcome the chance to speak to her." Carver paused, watching Henry looking over his card that he stuffed into his pocket.

"I'll talk to her about it. If she's ok with it, I'll call you."

"Thank you," said Carver when there was a knock on his door and good old Mags opened it up. "Hey, what can I do for you?"

She looked at Henry before speaking.

"It's okay, Mags, he's not a problem."

Mags swallowed her breath. "Captain Flannery wishes to speak with you in his office."

"He's here?" Mags nodded. Carver thought it was strange. Since Flannery took Carver off the case, if he's here, then who the hell is coordinating the investigation? Carver turned away, his stare lost. "Okay, I'll be there in a minute." He looked at Mags, standing in his office, not moving but scanning his office. Carver shrugged. "Everything okay?"

He noticed she glanced at the folder hiding the book. "Yes," she said, all nervous like. "Everything is fine."

197

"The wolves are coming tonight," said the man in black. "Some are already here, donning the clothes of the sheep… and they are quite hungry."

His eyes reflected the satisfaction he felt in his revelation. Those red-beaming eyes stared stoic but held a depth of determination equal to the fires of hell devouring its latest victim. He looked at Marc like a disappointed father.

"And you're telling me this information because?"

"Because it's not safe to be in the Hollow tonight." He cocked his head to the right as if attempting to lift Marc's downtrodden eyes. "I thought it would be best for you to return home before the Hollow turns into a bloodbath."

Marc laughed. "Like it's not already," he said, gesturing to the frozen television with the image of Sleepy Hollow Cemetery and the pentagram and inscription sitting center stage on the screen. "No, I don't believe a word you say." He paused, gritting his teeth while shaking his head and looking away. "All you know how to do is manipulate." He turned to the man in black. "My mother. My father. Now Lori. You're telling me you didn't write that letter?"

"I did no such thing."

"Probably manipulated Lori's mother to do it. You get your minions to do your leg work so you can come up clean.

Manipulating the scene so the truth is always on your side. Tell me, what's this all about? What is it all really about because I've grown tired of your antics and self-serving manipulations?"

The man in black raised his arms as if in triumph. "Humanity's end as a new beginning."

Marc shook his head, then shrugged. "And what the hell is that supposed to mean? Do you really believe you have the power to take over humanity? Seems rather ambitious, if you ask me." He sat back in the booth, scowling at the man in black as a devilish grin crept across his lips.

"It all just starts with a thought, whispered on the heels of the wind. A thought forgotten and lost in time that uses time to take root in the mind of humanity. Like a flower in the darkness, it blooms and releases its noxious poison, although not in one powerful gust, but a little at a time. Like cyanide, it takes time to poison the well of the mind, but once it takes hold there is nothing that can stop its progression."

"So, it seems you've got a long while to go."

"The seed was planted centuries ago."

Marc gestured around the bar. "So, this is it, then? Is that what you're telling me?"

"Indeed. And you, you have been my most prized possession. My ticket to destruction."

Marc shook his head vehemently. "I don't believe that either."

"How could you not? Look at your life, Marc. It was you who cut your mother's wrists. It was you who waved your finger across your father's neck that caused his heart attack, and it was you who sought *me* to help Lori. Everything you've wished for I have provided and everything I asked you to do in return you have obliged." He gestured to the green rope around Marc's wrist. "We are the same, Marc. We always have been. Locked together across time. Two distinct pieces to the same puzzle. It has always been you and I, and *I* am always with you. Always Marc. You think when you left this morning I wasn't with you, helping to hoist your body through the window?" He laughed, covering his mouth with his hand. "Oh Marc. What was the point? Why do you believe you can do whatever you wish without my knowledge? You granted me access. You called me in and then you convince yourself it never happened. Tsk. Tsk. Tsk." He clucked his tongue while moving his head left to right.

Marc ground his teeth, glowering at the man in black. "If we're so connected then I should know everything you're thinking too, but I don't. So, it looks like our bargain won't hold up in a court of law. I want my money back."

"We all make choices on the subconscious level. All the information is right at our fingertips. All we need to do is flip through the pages and read." He cocked his head again, sitting upright in the booth. "You choose not to know. You choose not to remember, to not engage in these deeds we deem are necessary. You find comfort in that godforsaken cemetery like a lost child who found refuge with the delusions in his head. You want to be kept in the dark, Marc. It offers you the excuse of a denial. But I am afraid our little ruse is coming full swing and the time for your ignorance must also end. It is time for you to *see* and to take your rightful place by my side."

"I've given you enough. Once I find Lori we're leaving and you'll never find us, nor will we ever return to the Hollow."

The man in black glared at Marc as Marc looked away, then returned his gaze to the man in black like an abused child turns to his father, filled with regret and shame.

"As you wish, Marc. As you wish." He gripped his cane then glided out of the booth, standing over Marc, tall and gripping his cane tight in his palm. "But I came here with a single purpose..."

"Yeah, how's the cemetery treating you today?" He downed his drink then rolled the glass across the table before turning to the man in black.

"Do not allow Lori to come here tonight. The wolves will not be kind. You should leave this place. Leave and return home. Lori will find you, Marc. This, I know, is true. At the hour of three in the afternoon tomorrow Lori will be sitting on a bench overlooking the Hudson. Waiting for you. Do you know what bench I am referring to?"

Marc saw the bench in his mind's eye. The bench was located outside the tennis courts by the river. He and Lori used to play there during the summer months. Marc had carved their names into the wooden bench on one of those many days.

"It is then that you will have your reunion, although I implore you to steer the conversation in the right direction. Bring her into our union, Marc. She will make a most dutiful bride."

"I'm not bringing her anywhere near you." His voice raised and the man in black smiled, smug and uncaring.

"As you wish, Marc. But I suggest you return home." He looked around the bar. "Wouldn't want you to witness the carnage that'll occur in this very room." He returned his stare to Marc.

"I'll take it under consideration." Marc refused to look at him, knowing the man in black would have enjoyed one last stare. Instead, the bar hopped back on the train of time as the chatter, television, and laughter returned, although Marc could still smell the man in black. That earthy scent from the cemetery he remembered all too well. It stunk like rot and death.

Three o'clock tomorrow afternoon. How the hell does he know that?

He was staring at the green rope around his wrist. He'd attempted many times to take it off but with no success. The damn rope wouldn't budge, and the pain that rippled up his arm every time he tried was unbearable. Like his veins were on fire and filled with venom.

He knew the man in black was lying, but Marc had to admit that some of what he said seemed like the truth. That's how manipulation worked best, mixed in with truth. Marc knew the man in black required Lori, but for what he wasn't certain. Some secrets he never revealed.

Marc turned to the newscast that continued to report the murders. A reporter was in front of Hardwood Realty, but Marc couldn't hear a word she said over the chatter in the bar.

He knew those people were dead because of him. Because he was too weak to accept the inevitable. Because he feared death and even more, he feared being alone. Feared losing the love he found with Lori.

3 PM tomorrow.

It's another manipulation, I know it.

Of course it was, but what else was he going to do? It seemed that all his efforts had gone into the void. Perhaps feeding the manipulation was the only way out.

The man in black was holding all the cards and playing him like a fiddle.

"Are you staying with us?" asked the barkeep. Marc hadn't noticed he was standing over him until he talked.

Marc looked up when a red sliver sliced through the barkeep's pupils.

"It would be nice if you did. Tonight's entertainment is to die for."

Logan arrived at the edge of the woods and scanned across the parking lot below the hill he stood on. He turned to the wisp.

"The police precinct," he muttered. "You're better than a personal guide. Not bad at all."

He turned back to the precinct. From where he was standing, he could see the roof and the lights that were on in the offices on the second floor. He'd seen a picture of the lead detective on the television. It was the same person he was staring at on the second floor, walking out of an office with whom Logan assumed was another officer. Logan looked down the hill that led to the parking lot then turned to the wisp as it floated away, back into the woods.

"Well, good luck… whoever you are. Or whatever you are and thank you for your help."

He stood watching while the wisp disappeared before beginning his descent to the precinct. Logan remembered the name of the officer. John had mentioned it, and the television had his name plastered across every news headline concerning the investigation.

Carver, he thought. The officer's name is Carver.

Wren's footsteps echoed across the dungeon. His stare fixed on the light beaming through the fissures as if it were alive. Alive, hungry and angry, with a heart filled with hate. He could hear the growl rumbling beneath his feet. A consistent rickety snarl born from the depths of hell. His patrons slept around him. They may be dead already, he knew, or simply between one life and the next.

Wren gritted his teeth, his eyes rolling beneath fluttering eyelids. The energy pumping from the fissures was magnificent, saturating his cells with the venom of hate.

Over his shoulder, he could hear the muffled whimper conjured from pure fear. The child, John, was in hell already, and that knowledge brought a smile to Wren's face. Now a scream from the young one when Wren heard the cell shift under his weight. The demons are with him, tearing apart his heart and soul. A righteous punishment for the centuries of injustice handed down by the boy's ancestors. Moans from the young one, followed by huffing breaths forced through restricted lungs.

Wren closed his eyes, basking in the astral plane's glory. His arms outstretched, holding his palms up as if he could embrace the energy flowing from the fissures into the Hollow. He could feel it flowing through every part of his body like a hurricane gale that tore through trees and foliage, bathing in the glory of pure evil. Everything he'd ever wanted.

To see the earth drenched in darkness. To see humanity bathed in blood.

Everything the master said would happen has come to fruition. The Hollow was being infected by a dark energy as evil as it was determined. Determined to expose every human to its malicious embrace. They were all being infected, and they had no understanding that the infection even existed. So subtle it was, like a master fiddler playing a tune with mesmerizing effect, capturing the mind until all it knows is the tune being played.

Tomorrow begins the final descent. At midnight, the stars will align with Xibalba. Wren raised his head, gazing at the ceiling. Looking past the ceiling to the stars as he closed his eyes with a gentle calm. He could feel the dark gravity pulling the constellation closer. Saw the alignment to Xibalba above the earth with its pitch-black darkness screaming for throats to be cut and for hearts to be swallowed.

Now panting, huffing breaths from the cage above him. The huffing a pretense to the bloodcurdling scream that erupted a moment after. Wren regarded the cage through the corner of his eyes as a grin crept across his lips while John's scream filled the dungeon and then some. Wren was certain his screams were heard across the globe. He noticed his precious Ian awakened from that scream.

In the morning, the real work begins. The master was in the ether, regenerating for the day to come. The host, Marc, continued to be kept in the dark, unknowing how the master used his body to manifest in this world. He is only aware of the master's ability to read his mind without understanding that the master is a part of that mind. Wren couldn't help but grin over the manipulation.

But it is time for him to see!

Another scream erupted from the cage and Wren turned to the cell. The boy was lying down, one hand holding the bars. Huffing his breath in a fever. Now another scream from the young one. An endless barrage of scream after scream. Wren looked around and located his knife on the slab. He picked it up.

"Come Ian. Let's see if we can give young John a scream to rival his own."

He stepped over to Ian, who did nothing in response. Wren was certain he'd gotten used to the torture, welcoming it like an old friend. Wren raised the knife to his eye.

"And then, I have a letter to write."

"Who was that person?" asked Flannery the moment Carver walked into his office.

Carver stopped in the doorway. He didn't appreciate the condescending tone nor the deep-seated anger he could see in Flannery's eyes. He looked like a man teetering between hate and suffering. Plus, there was a smell in the room that curled Carver's nose. Smelled like rot and death. Carver attributed it to the fact that Flannery had been around dead bodies all day.

Carver looked through the office windows, watching Henry walk out of the investigating unit after Carver introduced the two officers, although offering no more than a brief introduction before Henry took leave. "As I said when I introduced you, he's an agent with the FBI." He turned to Flannery, the two men standing and staring at each other like some western gun slinging standoff. "Henry Clavell is his name."

"Yes, I heard you then, but who is he to you and why is he here?" Flannery's voice was curt and agitated.

"He's helping a friend locate an old flame." Carver left out the fact that the old flame was Marc Saduj.

Flannery looked out the window, then returned his gaze to Carver. "And you don't find it odd that in the middle of all these murders an FBI agent just happens to come strolling into our precinct to use our computer? And it's all just to help a friend."

"It's odd but it happens all the time."

"Well, I find that very strange." He raised his chin and stretched his back, standing tall. "And I find the timing even more suspect."

"You think he had something to do with the murders?"

"At this moment, every single person in the Hollow is a suspect."

"Except Marc Saduj." Carver mostly whispered the name, but the mere mention of Marc Saduj brought Flannery's anger into the fold. It was written all over his contorted face.

"Your boy wasn't even in the Hollow the night Zoe Hardwood was murdered. You've wasted valuable manpower, resources, and most importantly *time*, investigating someone who wasn't even here when this all started."

Carver shook his head. "That may be so, but all that means is there's another way Marc Saduj is involved. It may not be him pulling the strings, but I know he has a part in it. Call it a hunch if you want, but *damnit, you need to open your eyes*." He paused, waiting for a response, but Flannery just stood there eyeballing Carver like he could strangle him and judging by the look in his eyes, Carver wouldn't be surprised if he launched himself over the desk and did just that. "Taking me off the case was not only wrong but foolish too. The body count keeps rising and now you've got to start all over. It makes no sense."

"You were looking in the wrong direction and before you went too far, I needed the investigation to take a complete U-turn." Carver could see Flannery grinding his teeth and the stare plastered across his face revealed a growing despise for Carver. "I should have had my head checked when I allowed you to take the case. You're too involved, and it affected your judgment."

"That's a complete lie."

Now Carver watched as his team entered the precinct, most of them carrying a box of evidence. They looked faded, as if the last few hours drained them of every ounce of energy they had. They passed Flannery's office, stealing glances as they walked by.

"I'll be honest with you Stephen, you lost your ability a long time ago and this latest fuck up is just the straw that broke the camel's back."

Carver's eyes narrowed. "What is that supposed to mean?"

Flannery pointed his thick finger at Carver. "I want you out of the Hollow."

"What?" Carver huffed, his disappointment spiraling.

"That's right. You're headed back to talk to Jerry. Officially this time. And Reilly is going with you so there's a witness to everything Jerry says and does."

Reilly was promoted to detective a few years ago. He wasn't that good of a detective, but his family history in law enforcement nabbed him the promotion. Couple that with the fact that he was Flannery's lackey, Carver braced himself for what could be the longest day of his life.

"I got everything I need from Jerry. Another trip upstate will take all day. This is a waste of time. The murderer is here, not in upstate New York."

"And when your interview is done, I want your report on my desk and then you're on leave."

Carver gritted his teeth.

"One month with pay. Now get the hell out of my face."

Now Carver wanted to leap across the desk and strangle Flannery.

"And before you leave, I want every piece of evidence you have in your possession. Everything. On my desk A-Sap."

Carver was about to speak when there was a knock on the door. Flannery called for them to enter, and Mag's opened the door, standing in the doorway with the door half open.

"What is it, Mags?" Flannery huffed.

She swallowed her breath before speaking.

"There's a boy here to see Detective Carver."

Flannery shot his stare over to Carver. The two men locked eyes when Flannery said through gritted teeth, "I'll meet with him. *Personally.*"

201

When Henry returned to the hotel he was immediately stopped by the girl at the front desk and provided an envelope from Elena. The message was simple. She wrote down the name of the motel she went to along with her room number, phone number to the motel and instructions to call her later this evening with a full report.

He stuffed the envelope into his inside breast pocket then went to Lori's room. He hoped she would heed the warning that her beloved was the prime suspect in all the murders and choose to return home. Perhaps he could convince her that despite who Marc had been he was not the same person she fell in love with. That he changed since the accident, and it was best to leave the relationship as it was and not pursue alternative realities.

His conversation with Carver was enough to convince him that there was something rotten with Lori's old flame. Even if he wasn't directly responsible, he had a hand in it. At some level, Henry was certain. Sometimes people just take a dive off the ledge into insanity. Henry knew he was skating a fine line, sneaking around the Hollow on a foolhardy recognizance mission and in doing so he was inserting himself into a situation that should he go too far may come crashing down with catastrophic consequences.

But that million dollars in cash was biting at his conscience, tearing holes the size of the Milky Way Galaxy. The fact that he could help keep an acquaintance out of harm's way was a fringe benefit. He respected Lori. Respected her for her heart, sincerity and integrity, and wished her no harm. She was in love and, as Henry knew all too well, love was blind.

Perhaps Lori refused to see the inevitable, deleting information from her conscious mind to hold onto her belief that Marc was gentle and would never hurt another human being. Henry understood he had to skate that fine line with Lori. A push too hard in either direction and she may discard him completely from her search and that was something he could not allow to happen. The implications could be severe. He agreed with Elena in that regard. Lori needs to get out of the Hollow. With all that's going on, she's better off anywhere than Sleepy Hollow.

He came to the door and rapped against the wood three times, then waited. He looked down the hall in both directions. Empty and quiet greeted him and for the first time he noticed the quiet. The subtle stillness was like the calm before the storm. He waited for the door to open when a cold hand brushed across the nape of his neck as if some phantom mocked his moment of revelation. His bones cringed and the hair on his neck and arms stood erect as his spine tightened.

He rapped against the door again and breathed a sigh of relief when he heard the dead bolt click.

202

"So, tell me what this is about?" asked Flannery.

Logan was seated in the captain's office. After the wisp left he climbed down the hill to the precinct and just about ran into it. He felt safer inside, as if everyone in the Hollow was an enemy and trust had gone out the door. Trust few. Love all. He read somewhere that Shakespeare coined the term as a philosophy for life, but Logan was thinking that he should trust no one and maybe a little hate wasn't so bad either. It kept one sharp and on point. Nonetheless, now that he was seated in the captain's office, he could feel a sliver of trepidation in his bones.

He'd asked to speak with Detective Stephen Carver, but he was taken to Flannery's office instead. His trust no one philosophy was being tested right in front of his eyes. John had talked about Carver when they were in the woods yesterday. Talked about him enough to offer Logan the peace of mind that the detective was trustworthy and considering John's whereabouts are currently unknown-well, unknown to most but Logan knew John was somewhere in that damn house-Logan believed the only person he could trust was Carver.

"Is Stephen Carver here?" he asked, looking around the precinct like his head was on a swivel before fixing his gaze on

Flannery. "I want to speak to Detective Carver and only Detective Carver."

He felt a little shameful, making demands to an adult who was also a cop, but not just any cop, the captain of the police force. Logan swallowed his breath with a gulp.

Flannery cocked his head to the right, assessing Logan. "Carver's not here, but whatever it is, son, you can tell me." He paused, allowing Logan a moment to collect his thoughts. But unknown to Flannery was that Logan knew that was a lie. He'd seen Carver in the window before he walked into the precinct, adding to the ever-growing lack of trust he currently held towards his fellow humans. "Now, what is this about?"

There was a knock on the door and Logan watched as Flannery's eyes turned hateful, as if the intrusion should be met with extreme prejudice.

Saw a flicker race across his eyes too. A blood-red flicker and Logan's heart skipped a few beats as his mouth opened to the proverbial 'O.' A second later, a woman opened the door and requested to speak with Flannery in private.

"Can't this wait, Cindy?" Flannery raised his voice, but the look that flashed across Cindy's face was both dire and rushed.

She shook her head. "Unfortunately, not. We need you in the war room." She looked at Logan. "It won't take long."

Logan looked at Flannery, and Flannery turned to him. "Stay here, son. This won't take more than a minute." And with that, he stood up and followed Cindy out of the office, around the corner and out of sight.

The moment he disappeared Logan released the breath he'd been holding. His mind went numb. Every thought other than Flannery's red flickering eyes went out the window. He couldn't deny what he saw and what normal human casts a red flicker across his eyes like that? None. Which means the police are compromised, or, at the very least, Flannery was compromised and he was running the show, which means the police are compromised. Logan wondered if Carver was compromised, too. He felt an overwhelming urge to leave. He had to leave. To get out of Dodge and be gone.

But go where? Home? The mansion in the woods? The very thought cringed his bones. How many more have been compromised? The entire town? Certainly not, but how long will they last until some ghost demon possessed everyone in the Hollow? He was running out of time, and the walls were closing around him and closing fast.

Logan shot up from his chair and paused. Felt frozen, stiff, and it was difficult to move as if his feet weren't receiving signals from his brain.

"Go," he whispered, then swallowed his breath. "Just go."

Then a thought flickered through his brain. *Go where?*

He shook his head. "It doesn't matter. Doesn't matter at all." He looked through the windows. "But you can't stay here. We need to find Carver."

But what if he, too, is compromised?

Remember the wisp, he told himself. The wisp saved you in the woods and brought you here. Brought you here to see Carver and only Carver and, by that logic alone, Carver wasn't compromised. Logan couldn't believe he was making decisions based on some wisp that he may or may not have conjured from the depths of his own mind.

Nonetheless, he knew there was a lot more going on in the Hollow than he could explain.

He gripped the doorknob and opened the door. He could hear people talking about a dead girl and the way she met her death. Something about a lifeforce being drained from the body. The rest of the precinct was like a ghost town. He noticed it when he first arrived and chalked it up to current circumstances, certain that every officer on duty was either part of the investigation or patrolling the Hollow for suspects. He knew Carver was here, but it was obvious Flannery didn't want Logan to talk to him, although Logan refused to allow Flannery to deter him from trying. But what could he do now? Start screaming Carver's name? No, that wouldn't go over too well, and Flannery may detain him based on that behavior alone. What he knew was that Carver was here and if Carver was here, sooner or later he'd have to leave.

He could hole up outside and wait for him.

It was the only solution he could come up with. He walked away from Flannery's office, his feet padding through the precinct. Not fast but not slow either.

Just walk normally, he told himself. Be inconspicuous.

He took the stairs with a hurried step then beelined to the front door, holding his breath the entire time and hoping Flannery doesn't come calling his name. Saw his reflection in the glass door and noticed how disheveled he looked, how pale and frightened. He pushed through the door to the two officers standing outside, talking.

Logan held his collar close to his throat, put his head down and walked away. He scanned across the parking lot.

Looking for a place to hide to wait for Carver.

203

"Do you really want to take a chance with a potential murderer?" Henry was sitting on the chair beside the desk in Lori's room. She was on the bed and the look in her eyes told Henry all he needed to know. There was no way, shape, or form that she would ever believe that Marc had anything to do with the murders in Sleepy Hollow. Henry swallowed his breath, needing to rethink his approach.

Lori was gritting her teeth and shaking her head when she said, "Did you find out anything useful? Like, where he is. Anything at all?"

Now Henry shook his head, defeated. "No, I didn't." He sat back in the chair. "This seems, quite frankly, very dangerous. I think it's best to fold up the tents and head home."

"I am not leaving here until I speak to him."

"Why?" Henry just about hollered, his frustration growing.

"Because I need to look in his eyes. I need to know for myself what happened to him."

"This is futile." He leaned forward, his arms on his knees. "Do you have any idea what is happening in this town? It's heading into a hell storm I don't want to even think about. Everyone's paranoid and that paranoia keeps escalating the longer this case goes on, and your boyfriend is the primary suspect."

"You said he was cleared from all wrongdoing…"

He cut her off. "But he's still a person of interest, Lori, and all that typically means in police lingo is that they're watching him like a hawk." He sat back, head shaking. "Do you really want to be seen with him?"

"I couldn't care less what the police have to say about him… I know who he is, and Marc Saduj could never hurt another human being." She turned away. "The police are wrong. I know it's true."

Henry eased back in the chair, his elbow on the desk when he turned to the window and the dark night outside, thinking, knowing Lori was waiting. "If I can arrange a meeting between you and the lead detective… this Stephen Carver guy, would you agree to it?" He looked at Lori, hoping that perhaps the detective could talk some sense into her.

"What would be the reason for such a meeting?"

"Well, two-fold, actually. According to Carver, Marc moved to a house, but I don't have the address, and I couldn't find anything about it on the computer so maybe he'd be willing to give us the address, plus you can give him your history with Marc which may help ease him off the potential suspect list. Considering he was the primary suspect until recently but remains a person of interest, perhaps what you have to say will put the detectives fears to rest." He waited, then added, "He asked to speak to you when I met with him, so I know he'll be more than accommodating to our request. If not, what else do we have? We can walk around the Hollow all day and night and still never find him."

He studied Lori while she thought, seeing the cogs in her brain working overtime as she considered Henry's plan, waiting with bated breath to hear her decision.

She looked at Henry and nodded. "Okay."

There wasn't much more she could do. Marc Saduj must have seemed like a ghost to Lori Francon.

"Perfect," said Henry, rising from his seat. "I'll call him and set it up. I'm going to my room. I'll call you and let you know what time we're leaving." He went to the door.

"Are you certain he'll take the meeting?"

Henry turned around. "Considering everything that's going on, I'm pretty damn sure he'll be more than willing to meet with you."

204

"It's absolutely ridiculous. There's no reason to take you off the case." Detective Montgomery was standing in Carver's office. Carver was going through his desk, placing pieces of evidence inside a box. The office door was closed, knowing Flannery was within an earshot of their conversation. Montgomery started shaking his head. "There's something more to tell about this. It just doesn't sit right with me. Something's off."

"There's not much I can do about it. If he feels it's best for the case to take me off that's his decision. He's the captain and I am not." Carver paused to look at Montgomery. Carver remembered when he first made detective ten years ago. A well-deserved promotion according to Carver. Montgomery was a rising star. His keen insight and his understanding of the criminal mind-he had a degree in criminal psychology-put him on the fast track to a stellar career and Carver did all he could to be a positive influence in the young detective's career. Took him under his wing and showed him the ropes. He was grateful that Montgomery came to talk to him. His respect for his elders was paramount, but even more, Carver knew he was spot on about Flannery. Something was definitely suspicious about him.

Some part of how he acted that didn't sit right with Carver. Sure, the two officers had their history, and they both knew-along with the entire Sleepy Hollow police force-that there was no love lost between them, but this was different. More manipulative than sincere, as if Flannery was grasping at straws for a reason to take Carver off the case.

"I'll be appealing to internal affairs when the case is over. He can't get away with this."

Now Carver was shaking his head. "It'll never fly. And it won't help matters. Not for me and definitely not for you. It's a bad situation all around. I should have done more research on Saduj before unleashing the dogs on him. Captain's right in that regard."

"You were following a hunch. Doing what you're supposed to do. We have nothing. No leads. Nothing to tell us who might be doing all this. Saduj was our only potential suspect and from what you told me it made perfect sense. Now we're at square one."

Carver could see the frustration across Montgomery's face. "You'll solve the case. I'm certain of it. Just follow the leads and trust your instincts."

Montgomery had no response. The pause between them was thick with tension. There was a knock on the door. The pause lasted another second before Carver called the person in. Detective Reilly opened the door, and Carver shot his head back. He looked different, cockier than the usual dumbfounded expression. He took a moment to scan across Carver's office.

"Am I interrupting something?" he asked.

"Not at all," responded Carver, then redirected the conversation. "I understand the two of us have a long drive tomorrow."

It took Reilly an extra minute to peel his eyes away from Montgomery before training those eyes on Carver. "We do, and I'd like to be on the road before sunrise."

"Same here," said Carver. "Meet here at six?"

Reilly nodded. "Sounds good. I'm looking forward to it."

Carver narrowed his eyes. His comment seemed strange, but then again Reilly had always been strange. Carver noticed he remained in the door for longer than necessary, staring at Montgomery who kept his back to him then scanning across Carver's desk. "Well, I'll see you in the morning." And with that he left. Carver noticed he kept the door open.

A second later Carver said to Montgomery, "Keep looking through the evidence. The answers are in the evidence." No response from Montgomery. "Detective?"

Montgomery raised his eyes to Carver. He nodded. "Go through the evidence," he repeated.

Carver had a fleeting thought to give him the book, but that thought was quickly dismissed. He didn't feel safe leaving it with anyone other than himself.

"Good luck," said Carver, offering his hand that Montgomery shook before walking through the door when he stopped and paused.

He looked at Carver. "Be careful with Reilly. I don't trust him at all." And with that he closed the door and walked away, leaving Carver alone.

Carver looked down at his desk and the file covering the book. He put his hand on top of it and felt a ripple of gooseflesh surge up his arm. Carver knew the book was one piece of evidence he would not be sharing with Flannery.

He was thinking about the best way to sneak the book out of the precinct when his phone rang, and he snatched it off the cradle. Carver was surprised that Henry Clavell had called him so quickly.

205

The barkeep howled like a wolf and every single patron looked at him. His howl echoed into the night. The noise and chatter in the bar were cut off at the seams with his spot on depiction of the wolf's howl. Even the jukebox that had been pumping Bush's *Glycerine* from its speakers cut off as if it was afraid it couldn't compete with the howl.

Marc could see the television was still playing, although mute with captions scrolling across the screen. Tension then rose inside the bar. Marc sensed how everyone's bones cringed and their blood curdled from that howl.

"What's gotten into you?" shouted the old man sitting at the bar, although it wasn't the same old man. His face looked like rot as if all the alcohol he'd ever drank sent a sudden shock to his system, his skin deteriorating in front of Marc's eyes. His mother was no longer sitting next to this rotting old man, but Marc could hear her laugh. That high-pitched cackle rang through the bar like an echo toppling over on itself that pierced Marc's ears.

Marc's heart stammered in his chest, restricting the airflow to his lungs. He grunted to bring air into his throat, his jaw trembling. Every part of him was trembling as he closed his eyes hard and shook his head, his lips pressed tight, attempting to make sense of what he'd seen.

It is time for you to begin to see Marc...

He could hear the record spinning in the jukebox. Constant static streamed from the speakers.

"Calling my brethren," he heard the barkeep say.

... and to take your rightful place by my side.

The man in black's words drifted from his mind as he opened his eyes. Thought he was floating through darkness until the scene came into focus. His jaw dropped when he saw it. The existential consequence of his heart looked back.

And the barkeep said with a grin, "*They* are on the way."

206

Henry hung up the phone and leaned back in the chair he was sitting on in front of the desk in his room. Carver was coming to the hotel to meet with him and Lori. The detective was all too eager for the opportunity to question the girlfriend of his primary suspect-until recently, of course, but Henry knew how that went. Marc will remain in the detective's crosshairs until some other evidence proves he's wrong.

Personally speaking, Henry couldn't fathom Lori's position. He understood she was in love with Marc Saduj, but considering the circumstances how many red flags did the woman need to pack up and head back home? Plus, there was something about Lori that didn't sit right with him, as if she knows Marc has a hand in the Sleepy Hollow murders, at least on some level. She almost seems like her plan is to convince him to stop the bloodshed. Maybe she knows why he went on a murdering rampage and believes she can put an end to his tirade. Love conquers all type of philosophy.

"What the fuck?" he said out loud, throwing his hands up and shaking his head. "This is frigin insane."

It was difficult to fathom that he was even in this current position. No wonder Elena was willing to cough up a million dollars. He'd do the same if it was his daughter and he had the money to spare. He sympathized with Elena's position, attempting to save her daughter from a potentially catastrophic life-changing decision to seek out her murdering ex-fiancé. That was enough to drive anyone to the brink of insanity.

He pulled the letter Elena had left for him from his coat pocket, unfolded the paper on the desk then picked up the phone and dialed. He received the receptionist and asked for a transfer to Elena's room. She picked up on the first ring.

"When are we leaving?" Elena immediately asked. Henry wondered how she knew it was him, but who else would call her? It's not like anyone knew where she was.

He provided her with the latest update, offering a bit of hope that whatever Carver had to say may just be what is needed to convince Lori to take Elena's offer.

"He's the one murdering all these people," said Elena, referring to Marc. Henry kept what Carver had said about Marc being a potential suspect to himself, but why Elena was so convinced it was Marc threw him off. As if she had information she wasn't sharing.

"Even more reason to convince her to leave the Hollow." He paused as his thoughts drifted. He cleared his throat. "I'll call with an update after our conversation with Carver."

He hung up after Elena provided her agreement. Henry Clavell stood up, listening to the silence in his room. The same silence that greeted him in the hall before he knocked on Lori's door. The silence was thick with tension as if something was stirring beneath Sleepy Hollow, ready to boil over and spill its venom across the city. He could feel it, like the beginning of an illness that was infecting every atom in his body with a fearful trepidation.

A vibration he could feel in his bones, weighing him down and turning his instincts on high alert.

207

Logan was hiding behind a dumpster with a clear view of the precinct's entrance. He was waiting for Carver to leave. After what he saw with Flannery, the number of people he knew he could trust were dwindling and dwindling fast. He hoped Carver wasn't compromised. Considering Flannery refused Logan's desire to speak to him Logan was certain Carver was still among the trustworthy. Nonetheless, he will need to be on point and ready to bolt the moment Carver showed any sign of being compromised.

He hoped Carver would show himself soon. The temperature was dropping rapidly. Logan pushed his hands into his coat pockets, wishing he'd remembered to bring his gloves. A hat would have been good too. His ears were freezing, and his jaw was chattering. He didn't know how long he could hold out but he thought about John every time his instinct told him to run and go home. Thought about everything he'd learned over the past twenty-four hours. The dark web was a host of information on the occult and what he'd discovered was troubling, even for the dark web.

However, troubling wasn't the best word to describe it. While Logan was reading through the website he kept having a sense of déjà vu. It was as if he'd read through the information before. As if he'd lived through it and what he was reading broke open memories from a past life. Memories that existed somewhere deep inside his subconscious. He read about wolves and ghost demons and cult rituals with the purpose of bringing about the end of the world through mind control, manipulation, debauchery, and brutality. Infecting the consciousness of humanity by infecting their atoms with the venom of sin, changing the internal vibrational frequency of the species with a direction towards hatred and fear. Power and control.

Logan shook the cobwebs from his brain. He lost time. The memories were thick when he went into them, capturing his consciousness in a spiderweb of distraction. His slow, shallow breath plumed off his lips like vapor. He hugged himself tight, his hands in the crook of his arms and looked at the precinct's entrance. Saw nothing but the light from the reception area. He scanned across the precinct to the second floor and saw Carver's office light was off. His cue that Carver should stroll through the front door at any moment.

"As soon as he walks out that door, start walking and ask to speak to him."

He braced himself for the coming meeting. From what John had said Carver knew his family and no matter what the detective believed about Logan's story, the fact that Grandpa Claude was lying dead by his front door would begin an investigation and Logan's story would take hold. Maybe he'll leave off the dark web information and just confess that he and John entered the property unlawfully. He was certain the information would receive no more than a slap on the wrist considering a murder had taken place. And then Carver will go to the house and that's where this story will end.

Inside the house.

He heard a car approaching from the back of the precinct. The headlights trolled across the dumpster before the car stopped at a stop sign to make a right-hand turn. Logan investigated the car.

"Wait? Is that?"

Carver was driving the car. He must have come through the back. Logan darted from behind the dumpster, his hands held high and hollered, "Detective," as loud as he could but the car was already turning. Carver must have been in a rush because the car sped away like he was racing in the Indy 500.

"Fuuuucckkkk!" Logan muttered, watching the car drift away. He was standing on the sidewalk, daunted and unnerved. Felt stupid for not keeping his eyes on the back. Felt like his heart dropped into his stomach, watching that car disappear, devoid of all hope.

"Now what?" He shook his head and looked at the precinct. He could see Flannery through a window on the second floor.

And Flannery was staring back.

208

The scene was drenched in a red film as if the world was suddenly thrust into a bonfire. A buzz existed beneath the surface. A vibration of constricted atoms packed together like wolves huddled in masses for an epic feast. Marc felt that buzz in his bones. It weighed him down, turning his stomach into a cesspool of noxious fumes that churned acid in the back of his throat.

The barkeep laughed. A hearty laugh accompanied by a sickly grin. Marc gnashed his teeth, forcing his stare from the barkeep then scanning across the bar. He saw ghosts from days long gone, hovering over shoulders and whispering in patron's ears sinister thoughts filled with nefarious intent. So many of them, as if the gates of hell had opened and all of hell's demons sought refuge in the tavern. They came to the bar like moths to the flame. Some ghosts were in full form as if they died yesterday, their skin littered with blotches on the brink of rotting. Others were already rotten, and the rot squeezed an inky black from their pores. They seemed as if they were in pain, as if the rot and ink were venom, poisoning their blood with hate. And yet there were others. Dark wisps floated around patron heads while snapping their billowy jaws.

The barkeep howled once again. Marc's mother's high-pitched cackle echoed across the bar. His scar itched, burning with a fever. His cracked lips stung with a pulsing throb and those cracked hands itched and bled. His breath hitched in his throat. He fought to swallow it down with a gasp.

Now he could see the patron's faces. They contorted and shifted, revealing animal features reflective of the soul. A boar, a horse. One a goat, the other a snake, its tongue wiggling across its lips. One face of stone. Another of worn leather that strangled the head as if that leather mask was pulled too tight around the head. Marc's eyes flitted from one person to the other, his heart pounding against his chest bone.

Heard a ripping tear and saw the knife he held slicing across human flesh, followed by a scream. In some dungeon with fires crackling, the air burning his skin.

He felt giddy with a laugh in his throat.

Now to the bar and the boar who was staring at him from the nearest booth. He forced his eyes away. Saw the drink in his hand, a thick black liquid that stunk like sewage he could now taste on his tongue. The stank was everywhere.

A screaming holler born from the depths of pain and suffering sliced through his brain. He could see his hand cut into skin like a hunter fileting a deer. He tore the skin off the bone.

His innards twisted. Felt like a knife was tearing apart his insides. He could sense the boar's eyes on him, willing him to return the gaze. The ghosts all spoke at once, sending shuddering waves of terror to Marc's ears. So many whispers he couldn't make out any of them with clarity. He felt sick. Pressure bearing down on his stomach as noxious fumes rifled up to his chest and throat. Beads of sweat, as thick as bullets, dripped from his brow as he raised his weary eyes to the boar. Felt weary, as if his lifeforce were being tapped, drained into an abyss and never to return.

Marc could feel her heart. He could see it beating in her chest. He licked his salivating lips, wanting nothing more than to taste that heart on his tongue. Couldn't take his eyes off her heart as he ground his teeth, his nose curled, and his nostrils flared.

The barkeep howled, but Marc couldn't remove his eyes from her heart. Somewhere inside that beating raging organ, he could feel her essence. It was dubious and nefarious and sexy and drove his mind mad with fever. He wanted to devour every part of it.

It is time for you to begin to see Marc...

He snapped his eyes shut when the vision came again. In the dungeon. A memory, he knew. Well aware the truth was here. He tore the skin off a skull and his chest blossomed with elation.

Peeled his eyes open to the scene in the bar and the vibration rifling off every heart in the room. His head was spinning. Felt pressure across his skull, his scar pulsating, throbbing with a thick pressure, and Marc vomited all over the table. His breath huffed through his lungs. Threw up again, sick and nauseous. Felt the rising heat across his skin, his eyes watery and weary. He looked up and saw that no one noticed, as if he were invisible. The scene had returned to normal. Marc noticed the thin fog slithering from the crack beneath the back door. He looked over his shoulder at the front door where the same dense fog streamed into the bar.

"Ah, tonight's entertainment," said the barkeep and the old man at the bar looked at him with confusion. The barkeep laughed and kept laughing.

"I feel sick," was all the old man said.

So do I, Marc thought when he pushed himself to his feet, using the booth to help himself up. The fog thickened around his feet. Marc felt like he weighed a thousand pounds. His legs like concrete as he forced his feet forward. Making it into the bathroom took more effort than he would ever believe was possible. The small bathroom with a urinal, single stall and sink. He leaned against the door. The walls were yellowed from decades of cigarette smoke. The light flickered on and off.

On, then off. On, then off.

He shuffled to the sink, twisting the knob for the cold water that he doused across his face. The light continued to flick. He gazed into the mirror, assessing the blood racing from his scar down the side of his face when the light went off and the man in black was staring at him in the mirror.

Sudden silence gripped the moment. The light returned, and Marc saw his reflection. Off the light went and the man in black was there.

"You're beginning to see. The memories will continue until our deed is complete." His words were heard not from his lips, but from the center of Marc's mind.

The light returned, and Marc snapped his head to the lightbulb in the ceiling. When he returned his gaze to the mirror, the man in black remained.

"We are one Marc. I need for you to see how much that is true."

Marc gripped the sink. He could tear it off the wall if he wanted to.

"Go Marc," said the man in black. "Be with your brethren. They wish to show you the extent of their loyalty." He stretched his arm, pointing towards the door. "Go, indulge yourself and allow them to lead you back to me."

The rope around his wrist burned with a searing heat that rifled up Marc's arm. He attempted to yank it from his wrist with no such luck.

"Why can't I take it off?" he groaned, pulling and tugging. "Come off," he hollered. "Fuckin come off!" His fingers burned, welting as the man in black laughed.

"You made the choice, Marc. And you chose me."

Now he could hear screams coming from the bar mixed in with the howls from the barkeep and thick thuds as if bodies were falling to the floor. He licked his lips and the blood from his scar that nipped in the corner of his mouth.

"Go Marc. They wait for you. This is a part of the seeing. You must know the extent of what you've done. And the consequence of a dying heart filled with the passion of true love."

His breath was thick yet shallow. He gripped the doorknob.

"Oh my… Marc, I envy you for the things you are about to witness."

209

Logan didn't know what to do other than to get away from the precinct.

After he saw Flannery in the window he bolted. Ran as fast and as hard and as far as his legs could manage. Ran until his blood pumped battery acid into his heart, breathing ragged and hoarse like there was dry ice in his lungs. Fear the driving force behind his ability to keep going. To keep running until he collapsed.

Or found a place to hide.

He thought twice about entering the sewer system. The stank coming from beneath the grate was putrid and foul, insulting his nostrils and invading his throat. He wasn't even certain if he could travel through the tunnels beneath the Hollow. Didn't know if he'd be able to make it home but what he did know, judging by the police cruiser that passed by him as he hid, crouched down and praying the officer never saw him, was that Flannery would be searching for him. He was certain the cruiser was looking for him.

The officer had gotten out of the car and beamed the strobe light attached to his vehicle into the woods, unaware that Logan wasn't more than a few feet from where he stood, hiding behind a truck parked on the street. Logan saw the grate then; on the sidewalk, waiting for him. He wondered if the officer would take a few steps into the woods because if he does, he'll see Logan hiding.

He was that close, but the officer strolled back to his car. A second later, he pulled away from the curb then drove down the street where Logan saw him park once again and get out. Strobe light on, beaming into the woods.

Logan took the opportunity. What he knew above everything was that there was no way in hell's damnation he was going to allow himself to be brought under their thumb. If they catch him, he knew he was fucked beyond all recognition. He'd turn into one of them. Carver was his only saving grace, and he watched that grace pass him by like a summer breeze disappears into autumn. He lifted the grate then eased himself into the storm drain that will take him down into the sewer system, replacing the grate as best as he could, pulling it back into place.

He wondered if the cop was still out there, scanning the woods looking for him. Logan's hands were burning cold. He stuffed them into his pockets. His heart was thundering, he could feel it hammering against his chest as he breathed deeply. Quite obvious to the young Logan that he couldn't stay where he was. He'd be dead by morning and freezing to death wasn't in the cards.

But where do I go?

Home?

He wished he had searched for Carver's home address before he made the trek out of his home earlier.

Home!

He thought about his dad. *Will they drive by the house to see if I'm there?* He didn't remember giving Flannery his name, but that didn't mean he didn't give him his name, and more than likely he did. What officer wouldn't ask for a name? And if Flannery had his name, Logan was certain he'd send a cruiser to his house.

This was bad. He wasn't too concerned about the police going to the house. His father will know how to deal with them. He always knew how to deal with cops. It was a part of his job-if being a hitman for the mob was something you could call employment-and he wouldn't take kindly to the police showing up at his door.

But they aren't the police, he reminded himself. Not real police, at least. His dad would send them packing, unless they get to him too, and that thought was enough to send the shivers racing down his spine into overdrive. A possessed hitman wasn't someone he wanted to come face to face with. Not in this life, or any life for that matter.

Footsteps on the sidewalk above him. Logan investigated both sides of the sewer. Nothing but blackness looked back.

Coming closer now, those footsteps sounded hurried. *Fuucckkk*, he thought and stepped into the darkness, not understanding where he was headed.

Nonetheless, he knew he wasn't alone.

He could feel a presence the moment he stepped in.

Something was down here with him.

210

Excerpt from *The Demon and Sleepy Hollow* by the Original Knickerbocker Dated 1856.

The Fog and The Sickness

On the eve of the fifth day after the first body was discovered, the Hollow was drenched in a thick fog. It is also wise for me to explain the circumstances that led to the coming of the fog. I shall do that now.

Additional bodies were discovered every morning, scattered across the Hollow with random precision. I use the word *precision* here as a foreshadowing of a later discovery that revealed how the demon could walk among us in the shadows, unseen by our hawk-like eyes. If only we had heeded the warning of our dear Olga, perhaps we could have saved some of the deceased. I often wonder if they remain in the cemetery, waiting for the precise moment when they may have their revenge on the Hollow. But I digress. Allow me to come back to our purpose here.

A new death was reported every morning, sometimes three or four, and a curfew was placed on the townsfolk the night the fog arrived. Constables were selected to watch over the Hollow as its citizens slept, strategically placed across town in the most densely populated areas. It would be a decision we would later regret. As Chief Alo had so delicately reported, the wolves arrived that night, but these were not actual wolves, but the very constables poisoned by evil and possessed by demons.

On the morn of the sixth day, we awakened to screams and horrors we were certain were heard around the world. Grown men, women, and children had been torn apart in the very beds they slept sound and peacefully in. Eaten with their hearts torn from their bodies. Those who were spared death's wrath spoke of a waking dream-a nightmare of sorts-where they watched their loved one being torn apart, witnessing the carnage as if they were in a trance, mesmerized by whatever specter sought to twist their minds. And from their weary states, they all confirmed one sneaking suspicion: it was the constables who had murdered their loved ones. They recounted the visions, seeing the constables in their rooms, devouring the flesh of their loved ones, devouring their hearts, with blood across their mouths and chins, and blood in their eyes.

It was the stare, they said. The stare from the constables that they could not relinquish from their minds. Those blood-red eyes staring through the haze of a blue-gray fog that hung inside their rooms like phantoms as the constables sat eating flesh raw.

Why some were spared we have not yet come to understand. Not even Olga could provide us with an explanation, suggesting the possibility that there was something about the spared that drove the decision to keep them alive. We have yet to come to terms with the reason why.

The constables were nowhere to be found the next morning. As I previously indicated, we awakened to bloodcurdling screams from multiple houses in the Hollow. It was a very dire morning. One that was accompanied by a sickness that left us in a state of weakness, as if our lives were being drained. Pale and frail we had all turned within a very short period of time.

This sickness drove irritability, confusion, and irrational thinking.

———

Carver closed the book when Henry Clavell, along with who he assumed was Lori Francon, walked into the hotel bar and restaurant. He placed the book on the table, front side down to cover the title while he scanned over Lori, assessing body language and the dire stare she projected towards Carver. He did all he could to not look at the abrasions and apparent bite marks across her jaw.

He rolled his toothpick from one side of his mouth to the other. The restaurant was barren, his table the only one occupied. Officially closed, Carver had to pull rank with his detective's badge to earn his entrance, although he was glad the locals were obeying the curfew. He stood up when they arrived, offered his hand and exchanged pleasantries.

After they sat, Carver addressed Lori directly. "Officially, we are off the record. I want to make that clear. What we say in this meeting will not leave this table." He leaned back in his seat. "I'm sure you have questions. Maybe we can start there?"

There was a pause before Lori spoke. A subtle stillness that drifted across the table in solemn contemplation. Lori eyeballed Carver, assessing him and his intentions. Obviously, she didn't trust him and was second guessing her decision to meet with him. She seemed innocent to Carver, more naïve than she let on to. Carver noticed Henry looked at her. The pause lasted longer than expected.

Lori cleared her throat and Carver noticed she glanced at his book. "The only real question I have is, where is Marc?" She looked at Henry, then turned to Carver. "I'm told he moved from his apartment, but I haven't been able to locate his new residence. Can you provide me with the address?"

Now it was Carver's turn to pause. He eased back in his chair, gnawing on the toothpick pinched between his teeth. A million thoughts raced through Carver's brain, but they all led to the same conclusion: he wasn't comfortable sending an innocent person into a situation that has the potential to cause mass catastrophe. He shook his head. "Honestly, I don't feel comfortable providing that information."

Lori shook her head and looked at Henry. "This is a waste of time." She stood up, ready to leave when Carver stood up.

"Don't go," he said. "Let me explain my reasoning." He looked at her dead in the eyes and gestured to the seat. "Please…"

Lori chewed on her bottom lip. Carver could see the cogs in her brain working overtime. She looked tired and stressed, and Carver was certain he looked the same.

"Okay, Detective," said Lori as she retook her seat. "Convince me why I should stay."

Carver glanced at Henry, then turned to Lori. "You do understand that Marc is the prime suspect in our investigation?"

"I was told so, yes…" She looked at Henry. "Until recently, correct?"

"Yes, but he remains a person of interest and honestly, if I am right, sending you to his home would be like rolling up a snowball and throwing it into hell."

Lori's eyes narrowed. Carver wasn't certain if his use of the word hell brought the reaction or referring to her as a snowball. Or maybe it was because of his strong belief in Marc's guilt. Either way, he preferred providing the dire warning.

"However, you seem very convinced of his innocence."

"I am."

"Then perhaps you can shed some light on Marc Saduj. Please… tell me about him and why you believe he is innocent. What you have to say might be exactly what we need to officially take him off the list of suspects." Of course he lied. Carver was certain Marc Saduj had a hand in the murders and no matter what Lori said about him wouldn't change that fact, other than shedding some light on how he came to be a part of it.

Lori was biting her lip while staring at Carver. He wasn't certain why-maybe Lori saw this as her chance to prove Marc's innocence-but she started talking, recounting how they met in the tearoom off Broadway and how she was immediately smitten with him. He wrote romance novels-now that was a part of Marc Saduj that Carver did not expect-and had a calm disposition that was uncanny.

"You don't understand what he went through as a child," Lori said, and to this statement Carver perked up. Knowing the killer's history was vital to understanding the motive. "He was tortured by his mother. Psychologically. And his father travelled for work, which means he was alone with her most of the time." She shook her head; her arms wrapped tight around her waist. "He's so gentle. I can't even think about what he went through when he found her." Lori seemed lost in the thought as if rehashing Marc's memories were personal to her own.

Carver cocked his head. "What do you mean? Found her?"

"She slit her wrists while he was sleeping." She cleared her throat. "Marc found her the next morning, but she was already gone... there was nothing he could do." She wiped the tears from her eyes and sat forward. "Marc Saduj has been through hell already. He can't be the one murdering all these people. His heart is too gentle to hurt another human being. It's a result of his mother's death."

211

Marc opened the door to a thick fog that overtook the bar, illuminated in dark orange and red from the lamps, neon beer signs, and light bulbs scattered across the ceiling and walls. His stare pierced through the fog. He could see shapes moving within-people, he thought-as his eyes flitted from one corner of the bar to the other.

Now the sounds of choking, convulsing, and gnawing. He noticed the old man was no longer sitting at the bar and the barkeep was nowhere to be seen. Heard a grunt followed by a howl and his bones tensed, shivering down his spine. More gnawing now, as if someone were indulging in a fantastic feast, squishing bits of flesh between their jaws then slurping the remnants down their gullet. The fog drifted closer like a thousand wisps in front of his eyes.

He saw eyes in the fog. Eyes like electric sparks that fizzled with a hiss. Heard a patron fall and hit the ground with a thud when Marc stepped closer, further into the thicket as the fog drifted over him only to dissipate and reveal what was lying at his feet.

Her blonde hair was thick and curly. Marc couldn't see her face, only the mop of blonde curls, as she dipped her hands into the body lying dead on the floor. Marc had no idea who this dead person was, but his eyes were wide open as if he'd been caught off guard and his last moment on earth was filled with anguish. There was a gaping hole in his chest and the blonde woman's hands were burrowing into that hole.

She pulled out his heart then handed it to the man standing beside her. He took a bite then passed it down the line that Marc now noticed. His heart stammered as his stomach roiled from the sight of blood when the blonde raised her eyes to him.

Those blood-red eyes beamed from the depths of damnation. Her mouth, lips, and chin smeared with blood and tiny tendrils of flesh.

"My master," she said with blood across her teeth. "We bend to your will."

212

The darkness greeted him like a conniving friend. Logan had no idea where he was going, traveling through the sewer beneath the Hollow, his feet sloshing through the thin stream coating the ground. He stopped a few times to catch his breath, looking both ways into the dark envelope that seemed to wrap around him as if suffocating the life from his lungs. The cold bit into his hands and nipped at his face and the smell emitting from the sewer was enough to send his tastebuds into a nauseous fit.

He thought about where he must be, noting the location of the precinct, how far he ran from it and where he entered the storm drains, but his thoughts hit a wall, unable to recollect any memory from after he climbed down. Logan couldn't remember if he first went right or left, which meant he was either close to Patriots Park or on the other side of town.

Freezing, hungry, angry, lonely, and scared to death, Logan wanted to cry. Faced with a darkness he was certain he'd remember for all his days, he felt trapped. The police are compromised and going home could either be the best decision he's ever made or the worst. If they got to his dad, he was fucked and losing his life to the very man who brought him into it was not a fate he wished to see come true.

Logan looked right then left, wishing the wisp was here to help him. Wishing he never left his house, because where was he going now? He was fucked and he knew it, and sleeping in the sewer was not in his best interest. More than likely, he'd freeze to death by morning and that thought was enough to keep him moving.

Now he heard a thud followed by a splash as if something fell into the well and hit the shallow water. Logan's heart skipped a few beats. The sound came from his right, down the tunnel about fifty yards from where he stood. He went to call out, but his voice died in his throat when the ground beneath him rumbled.

213

"So, tell me, Detective," Lori said to Carver. "Why do you believe Marc is the one killing these people?"

Henry looked from Lori to Carver. The detective sat back in his chair, rolling the toothpick pinched between his fingers in the corner of his mouth. Henry had sat and listened while Lori told her story. A story he wasn't expecting and if Lori was telling the truth, he couldn't see any angle that would tell him Carver was right about Mr. Saduj. Maybe Carver was thinking the same, although Henry couldn't tell from his body language. He seemed to be assessing Lori's story while fitting her narrative into the puzzle he's worked out in his brain. His stare pierced through Lori as if he was wrestling with an internal struggle forged between what he heard and what he'd seen with his own eyes.

Carver looked away-either to break his concentration on Lori or to wipe his thoughts clear-then sat closer to the table, elbows on the top, hands folded across the wood. His eyes on Lori. Perhaps, Henry thought, he was selecting his words carefully. "Understand that the person you are describing is the complete opposite of the man I met." He paused, but only briefly. "You describe him as young and energetic… kind and compassionate, with the boyish charm of an innocent child." He shook his head. "The Marc Saduj I met seemed old, like a broken old man with a taste for rage. You say he wrote romance novels?" Carver's eyes narrowed, skeptical. "If I had to guess, the Marc I met would write extreme horror, but he wasn't writing anything… all I saw were paintings."

"Paintings?" Now Lori shook her head, her eyes narrowed, confused.

"Yes, paintings," Carver repeated. "Paintings of hearts."

Lori's jaw dropped. Her body cringed. Henry could tell the word was unsettling. She seemed to drift away.

Carver must have caught the change too. His voice turned soft, and his body relaxed, but his eyes remained stern, assessing Lori. "Which I find strange considering every victim's heart is missing."

Now Henry understood. He hadn't been following the case that closely to know about the missing hearts, but now he understood where Carver was coming from. A potential suspect is painting pictures of hearts when, at the same time, bodies are piling up and the one thing they have in common is the hearts are missing.

Carver pressed further. "Has Marc had any experience with the occult or demonology?"

Lori shot her gaze at Carver. "What? No." She shook her head, and Henry could tell the question was jarring. She seemed startled, as if the question held a deeper meaning. "Not at all." Her stare drifted inward, as if keeping a secret.

"Has he ever mentioned witches or spells or Satanism?"

Lori floated back in her chair. Quite obvious she was thinking, her thoughts tumbling over one on top of the other as if she had a revelation. Her eyes were lost, staring at the table as if recounting some part of her story or her time with Marc.

She shook her head and provided a resounding although unconvincing, "No."

"What about the pentagram?" asked Carver. "Or the inscription Initium Novum?"

"What does that mean?" asked Henry. He thought it was best to stall the conversation considering he could tell Lori was wrestling with an internal catastrophe, staring at Carver while grinding her teeth as if she just took a punch to the gut.

Carver turned to him. "The killer leaves a calling card. An inverted pentagram with the inscription *Initium Novum* beneath it." He turned to Lori. "It's Latin. Translates to *a new beginning. Humanity's end as a new beginning.*"

Lori's stare cut through Carver. Apparently, she was not pleased. She shook her head, slowly to the left than right. "Not at all."

214

The howls started in low, growing like a kettle conjuring steam. The wolves-as the man in black referred to them-all stood tall, raising their chins to the ceiling as they howled into the night.

Marc had stood by, watching with bated breath as the bar patrons were consumed by the fog. It slithered into their noses and mouths. Some of them rose to their feet, swallowing the fog like a fine wine, while others dropped with a thud, their bodies twisting and jerking across the floor. Marc watched as the people who rose to their feet attacked the people on the floor. Torsos were ripped open and hearts were passed around like sharing a bottle of century old scotch. The patrons dined on flesh and swallowed blood. The fog hovered inside the bar like a b-rated creature feature from the sixties, casting a dull glow across the patrons, their eyes gleaming inside the fog when the howling began, reaching a fever pitch as those howls took on a life of their own, drifting into the Hollow as a warning.

He could feel the energy beating furiously from their hearts. The scene in front of him was like electrical energy he could see in real time. Buzzing, vibrating energy that enveloped the bar, connecting every wolf to the other. This buzzing energy flitted with pale light like energetic wisps, the sparks born from opaque geometric shapes that Marc could see ran from one heart to the other.

Marc hadn't noticed his scar was bleeding across his cheek, or how his heart was racing in his chest and how that racing strangled the breath from his throat. His cracked and bleeding hands trembled by his sides. He couldn't take his eyes off the energetic wisps. Like watching ghosts in real time, leaving him paralyzed with the fear that he was helpless against them. The wolves stood at attention as if waiting for further instruction. Marc noticed they trained their eyes on him.

My army, said the man in black. His voice, smooth like silk, howled from the center of Marc's brain. *Such sweet sounds they make. Like the booming laughter from a child. My wolves have returned, donning the skin of the Hollow citizens. How sweet their endeavor is. They will secure the hearts required to assist our portal, offering souls to Xibalba to be devoured for eternity.*

The barkeep slithered through the crowd like a snake around its prey, his red eyes fixed on Marc. His steps, heavy on the wooden floor, echoed in Marc's ears. And the breathing. The thick, heavy breathing from those who had eaten accompanied the echoes to his ears. Marc stood, conflicted between wanting to puke, run and hide, and pure satisfaction while his heart hammered in his chest.

He felt like an outsider, like watching the scene unfold on a television screen, both a voyeur and an actor. A phantom among the dead. Images flitted through his brain. Images of the cemetery. He saw a crypt in his mind's eye. He stepped closer to it while listening to the raspy wretched voice-a witch's voice he was certain-talking in tongues.

The crypt is closer now, in the dark, coming closer.

The witch's voice grumbled, *Initium Novum,* then followed it with a laugh.

Marc could see the name inscribed on the black marble that looked like glass. Worn from years of rain, sleet, snow, and heat, the inscription was difficult to see but Marc stretched his arm to it, wiping off the soot with his palm to reveal the name beneath.

Selena Vonder Dutch

Now that witch's laugh reached a fever pitch. Marc could feel it echoing in his bones. The echo followed him to the bar where the barkeep took center stage, addressing the wolves.

"Our hunt has begun," he declared. "Return to your homes and to your friends and families." He scanned across the wolves, his stare stoic as he gritted his teeth. "Bring their hearts to the master. Tomorrow, we usher hell into Sleepy Hollow and a new phase for humanity. By the bite of our jaws a new world will be born."

Marc attempted to turn. He wanted to run, but his feet refused to follow his command.

I told you Marc, it is time for you to see. Complete transparency is required. No more running, Marc. No more hiding.

The barkeep stood tall, staring at Marc, scanning him, assessing, when a smile crept across his lips. He stood with his shoulders back, apparently proud of his desperate pack. Marc clenched his jaw and swallowed his breath, his eyes fixed on the wolves, scanning across them with wide fearful eyes. Although, beneath the fear there existed a subtle thread filled with admiration, pride, and connection. The wolves stood, sweat oozing from their pores, soaked in blood and carnage with bits of flesh and hearts dripping off their chins.

The man in black's voice boomed in the center of Marc's brain. *Look at them, my children. They will bring humanity to its knees in honor of Baphomet. They will bathe in the blood of humanity's future.*

One of the wolves-the old man from the bar-howled thick and forceful into the night.

They represent the beginning. The grunts of our little ruse. Once the fog arrives at the break of tomorrow's dusk our ghost demons will unleash hell. One wolf for every ancestor in the Hollow.

Marc felt pain in his chest, as if his heart was suddenly squeezed by a hand made from iron.

Provide permission, my dear Marc. Allow them to invade the night.

Now his head moved without a thought to do so. Marc bowed to the wolves, the man in black's ghost demons, before he stretched his arm and pointed to the door.

The barkeep bowed. "Thank you, my master," he muttered before turning to the wolves. "Go, and paint the night red."

The wolves shared glances filled with delight. Marc watched them go, relieved and yet utterly dismayed. They looked like wraiths as they exited. Like flitting balls of dark light coursing through the fog-drenched bar. One by one, they filed through the door, one ghostly light after the other. When he turned, the barkeep was in front of him. His red eyes beaming at Marc.

"The time has come. Allow me to be your escort home." He gestured to the back of the tavern to the basement door.

"Come," he said. "Follow me."

215

The ground beneath him continued to shake with a rumbling he could feel in his bones. A coming storm rooted in the core foundation of the Hollow. Logan was schlepping through the storm drains, his heart hammering in his chest.

After he heard the splash, the rumble arrived and he took off running in the opposite direction, refusing to look back. Either someone was after him or his imagination had gotten the better of him, but Logan couldn't care less. He needed to move and find a way to crawl out. His stomach was twisted into a knot. He felt sick, wanting to puke but unable to do so. Logan wasn't certain, but he believed the rumble was the cause of his sudden sickness. The rumble seemed to vibrate his internal organs, infecting his cells with what he assumed was a virus determined to turn his heart into a black stone filled with anguish.

The nausea crawled into the back of his throat. He slowed his run, his feet slapping through puddles as he halted. Breathing heavy, he swallowed his breath with a gulp. Felt sweat across his brow and temples. He felt sick, pale and drawn, wiping down his forehead with his sleeve. He bent over, hands on his knees, his back against the tunnel wall, catching his breath and feeling the rumble beneath his feet. Logan closed his eyes, inhaling thick and slow and deep through his nose. When he caught his breath, he leaned his head against the cold wall, looking left and right. An icy wind howled through the tunnel.

Logan looked up to the storm drain forty feet to his left. Saw a ladder leading up to the street.

Where does it lead?

He looked back down into the tunnel where darkness greeted him. His hands were freezing. He put them in his coat pockets and stepped towards the grate, his feet sloshing through the water. A light beamed from the street above, dull but enough to help him see.

Logan stood beneath the grate, looking up.

Looks like…

Moved his head left and right, assessing, eyes narrowed.

I do believe those are the streetlights outside the school across from Patriot's Park.

He looked down, thinking. Looked back up, assessing.

What else am I going to do? Might as well take a look.

Logan pulled his long sleeve shirt over his hands then gripped the ladder, taking the steps up to the grate where he assessed the street, confirming he was across from Patriot's Park, which also meant he was a long way from home.

What now? Sleep in Patriot's Park? He shook his head. *No way. Frigin body was in Patriot's Park, and I'll freeze to death. They'll find me dead in the morning.*

What to do? What?

He was assessing possible places to go when the thought hit him.

The church.

If they keep their doors unlocked, I can go inside. It'll be warm and aren't demons not allowed in churches?

Another splash on his right. Logan's heart jumped in his chest, panicked. The splash sounded more like a footstep from someone running in his direction. He gripped the grate and pushed with every ounce of strength he could garner. He could feel something approaching from the tunnel. Logan's breath hitched in his throat, forcing the grate to the side then climbed up to the street and scurried away while watching the drain. He had an inclination that something supernatural would come crawling out to claim his soul. The rumble grew louder, and the darkness seemed to transform into a monster of energy as if the very night had come alive.

It was enough to scare Logan. He scuttled to his feet then ran across the street with the church in his sights. The street was barren; the wind swept across the ground like death's final breath. Logan raced to the church and hurried up the steps to the door, hoping, praying it was unlocked.

Please be open. He hobbled to the door. *Jesus Christ, please be open.*

He gripped the doorknob, twisted, and the door opened.

My God Thank You!

Before he stepped inside, he looked over his shoulder to the storm drain he crawled from. Thought his eyes were playing tricks on him. It seemed like the night itself was staring at him. And it had eyes. Blood-red eyes.

216

Carver kept talking, speaking with Henry more than he was with Lori. He kept talking, but Lori heard nothing. His lips just kept moving. Lori wasn't having it. Everything Carver said about Marc made no sense. It seemed like they were talking about different people, and she couldn't wrap her head around Carver's assumptions.

Although she had to admit that once the detective mentioned the pentagram and inscription the conversation was officially over. At least to Lori. The inscription on the back of Marc's book burned in her thoughts while Carver continued his unstoppable question-and-answer session. Marc's participation in the murders was clear to Lori. The fact that he had written a book containing similar circumstances could not be ignored or scoffed at like some damnable coincidence.

However, what Lori knew all too well-knew it because she could feel it, in her heart Marc was not at the helm of this debacle-was that something was missing. Some part of the story that had yet to be revealed that would shed light on Marc's participation, or lack thereof. Lori felt an overwhelming need to protect him, no matter what the cost. Even if that cost was her very soul. She knew Marc would never inflict pain on another human being. There was someone else pulling the strings.

The demon.

Images flitted through her consciousness. The demon in the hallway outside her mother's bedroom. The demon in Gerard's eyes when he hid in the closet. The same demon who had been following her all her life, inside her nightmares or sitting center stage in one of her many night terrors. He has always been there, in the darkness and beneath the folds of time, waiting. So patiently waiting.

Her mother's words rang through her mind. *There're forces we're dealing with. Nefarious forces and they've got their eyes on you.*

Eyes on me?

Why?

Now she realized Carver had asked her a question. Both he and Henry were staring at her, waiting for an answer. She cleared her throat, said, "I'm sorry, what was the question?"

Carver's face pinched in confusion. "Wren," he said. "Have you ever met his servant? Some guy that goes by the name Wren."

Lori shook her head. "No. I've never met anyone named Wren before."

Carver gave no response other than a quick shake of his head.

"Listen," Lori said, moving closer to the table. "You're mentioning things that never existed when I was with Marc. He lived in that small apartment all his life and never talked about distant relatives or any house in the woods." She paused to collect her thoughts. "You mention servants and mansions and paintings and an old rickety man who needs a cane to move around." She shook her head. "It's like we're talking about two completely different people and I'll be honest; the situation is a bit daunting. It's difficult to wrap my head around, but what I would really like to do is speak to him directly. You say he lives in a house in the western woods?" She stared at Carver, dead in his eyes. "Then I'll just have to take a walk through the woods until I find it, since you won't give me the address."

She let her statement hang in the air for a while, but when no one responded, she continued. "Which means our little conversation is over." She stood up, and both Carver and Henry followed suit. "I understand you have a job to do, and I hope you find the person committing these murders, but what I know is that it's not Marc who's hurting these people and I highly suggest you look into alternative theories."

Carver gave no response other than thanking Lori for meeting with him before she excused herself. Henry said he'd come to her room after walking Carver to his vehicle, after which Lori went back to her room.

Went back to her room to find an envelope on the floor when she opened the door. Her name was spelled in cursive across the front. She paused for no more than a few seconds before she closed the door and locked it. Her hands trembled when she picked up the envelope.

217

His footsteps echoed down the staircase. Marc watched the barkeep take the stairs into the basement as he followed. He gave no pause, following like a dutiful son. Felt like he no longer had control of his limbs, his thoughts refusing to connect to the brain synapses controlling his legs as an insatiable thirst and hunger swelled in the empty spaces between his organs, ballooning into the back of his brain and across his salivating tongue.

The scent drifting up the staircase from the basement was overwhelming, sending the hunger and thirst into overdrive. So sweet was the scent. It thundered in his veins, culminating in a racing heart as he took the stairs down. Feeling unsteady, his hands shaking, holding the banister and noticing the air grew hotter the further down he stepped. Sweat across his forehead, the salty chemistry burning into his bleeding scar. The heat came in waves that brushed across his skin, raising Marc's internal temperature. The staircase was long and winding. Marc thought he was descending into hell.

What some refer to as hell, others take comfort in calling home.

The man in black's voice echoed in Marc's mind.

You've come home, Marc. I've waited so long to find you. To meet with you once again and return you to our embrace.

He took the last step down and was immediately greeted by a thick blackness that clung to the basement. He could see shapes in the darkness. Heard whimpers and squelched screeches filled with terror.

But you must see, Marc. You must take responsibility for your actions.

Thoughts flitted through his mind's eye with scenes he understood were memories. Images of torture. Of blood and bone and hearts roasting over hot coals accompanied by echoes that screamed across stone walls, reverberating in his bones like ecstasy. He saw himself, with blood all over him, grinning with blood-red eyes.

That's not me. The thought died quickly. *That's the man in black. That's… me?*

His hands shook over his mouth as the memory faded, revealing a door at the end of the basement, fifty feet from where he stood. The door was old and made from thick wood. It was round and large with three thick straps stretching from one end to the other. Marc wasn't certain, but he thought he saw the door swell like a balloon into the basement. There was light behind the door, a thick dark emerald that seemed to breathe through the lining around the door from the other side. Marc stood, mesmerized by the light that turned a darker shade of crimson, then a plum color that radiated fumes filled with the stank of death and decay. Now the color churned into a blue hue under the veil of a dark night. The light called to him as if it meant to swallow him whole. Marc stood frozen in the basement, staring at the light seeping through the cracks in the door. The light that now turned bright white only to be followed by a smoky gray. White, then gray. White, then gray, casting shadows across Marc's eyes.

He could hear whispers in the light like a million demons waiting, watching with bated breath while calling him into their embrace. Now he saw the barkeep step to the door, a shadowy silhouette with no face or identifiable features. The light pumped through the door in waves that were brought to Marc's ears with a fluttering hum, capturing his heart in a vise grip. The barkeep opened the door. The color washed across the basement.

All he could see was light.

"You must enter," said the barkeep. "Wren waits for you on the other side."

Marc bent his head, staring, attempting to see what lived beyond the light that flitted like an old television screen that lost its connection. He didn't notice it at first, but he was moving towards the door. Into the dark light that now swirled like a vortex, pulling him towards its embrace. He could see nothing beyond the first layer of light. Like standing on an event horizon and staring into a black hole.

Allow me to welcome you home, Mr. Saduj.

His feet were moving. The door was coming closer. Marc looked around the basement, numb to his core. He saw cages on both sides of the basement. Saw children in those cages with wide, fearful eyes staring.

Now a rickety groan erupted from within the light.

They are waiting for you, Marc, welcoming your return.

He saw fires inside the light and death at its core. Felt the destruction of innocence at his fingertips and the welcoming of fear. Fear like a vibration he could feel in his bones like ecstasy.

What you are about to learn will consume every fiber of your being. To understand what you've unleashed, you must see it with your own eyes.

He stood at the edge of the door with the light batting across his skin. Felt like he was a part of the dark light, his cells merging with it. The light fluttered into the basement with a loud, obnoxious thump. He stretched his hand to the light and a rickety groan growled from his touch.

Hell is nothing more than a home for those with dark hearts.

It is time for you to see.

He looked at the barkeep, dazzled with light dancing across him.

Truth is nothing more than perspective. We make our own to meet our desires.

Marc stepped into the light. The man in black's voice followed.

Welcome home!

218

A fierce wind tore through Father McKenzie's rectory, flitting the pages of his sermon and extinguishing the flames from the candles on his desk.

"My God," he breathed, his hands covering the pages to keep them from ripping and tearing, looking through the window where the slivered moon hung like a curved dagger ready to strike down on the Hollow. Clouds raced across the moon shining in the sky with a silvery glow as a thin fog drifted past his window.

He sat unmoving, staring, thinking.

Has it begun?

He stood up in the darkness, never removing his attention from the window. He needed to see if the constellation had taken form. McKenzie walked to his door, opening it to the bitter cold. Quiet and darkness greeted him, the stars blinking in the night sky. He looked up and around when a subtle groan graced his ears. So low it was difficult to hear.

He forced his attention back to the stars.

Wrong location, he thought and closed the door, flicking the light switch by the door that bathed the rectory in light. He walked into the church, his steps echoing with a wooden clomp while clenching the rosary in his pocket as he opened the door, his stare fixed on the stars. The moon was on his right. He scanned across the trees past Patriot's Park where the library stood above the park and there, he could see it. The Perseus Constellation with the demon star Algol hovered over the Hollow. The star's light wavered, garnering the strength to come full bloom.

He understood what this meant. Hell was coming to the Hollow and that hell will be here soon. It was time for him to prepare. To bring as many people to the church as he could. The ground the church was built on was sacred and could not be penetrated by the forces of darkness.

Now that groan again. A rumble beneath the street, he was certain of it. Father McKenzie gazed at the street, listening, feeling for the rumble that seemed to grow stronger, louder, stretching into Patriot's Park. He scanned across the park to the cavern where they found that boy. The groan was louder there. He knew it was true. His eyes squinted to the fog that billowed from the cavern into the park like specters communing in sacred blasphemy.

Father McKenzie stepped back, maintaining his stare on the park where he was certain an army of devils and ghosts were forming like…

Like a fog, he thought, swallowing his breath as he stepped inside then closed and locked the door.

"They can't get in here, right, Father?"

McKenzie jumped then twisted around, startled and unnerved. He held his hand over his chest, staring at the young boy in front of him. "My lord, you scared the bejesus out of me."

The boy stepped closer. "I'm sorry, Father. I didn't mean to scare you, but I had no other place to go."

McKenzie shook his head. "Who are you and why are you here so late at night?"

The boy-McKenzie put him between thirteen and fifteen-had this stare across his face that convinced him the boy was frightened out of his mind.

"Logan Reeves," he said. "My name is Logan Reeves and the reason I'm here is because of what is happening outside, Father." He paused briefly as if to gather his thoughts. "I saw them too. When you opened the door, I saw them the same as you." He shook his head. "They can't, right, Father? Devils aren't allowed in church, are they?"

A million thoughts raced through McKenzie's mind at that moment. His first instinct was to lie to the young child to keep him calm and safe, but it was obvious to McKenzie that the boy knew more than any child should and lying to him wasn't the Catholic thing to do. That whole Thou Shall Not command rang through his brain.

Obviously, Logan had seen a thing or two that prompted his retreat to the church, and lying to the boy was not in his best interest. Plus, McKenzie needed to call Carver, for that he was certain. He needed to force the need for immediate action. They had little time. Maybe a little more than twenty-four hours. Maybe less, but McKenzie knew Logan arriving on his doorstep was no coincidence. He was here for a reason McKenzie had yet to discover.

"Father?" Logan swallowed his breath, anticipating his answer.

"Devils come with the skin of humanity," he said. "It is impossible to keep them out. Darkness is always attracted to the light it seeks to destroy." He shook his head. "If you were the devil, where would you go? Our institutions are ripe for the devil to enter. It's how he casts a shadow over God by turning his children against him. But our church and the ground it sits on were cast in a protective prayer. We are safe here as long as the prayer holds."

"And if it doesn't? Or if they find a way past the prayer?"

It took McKenzie a long while to answer, his thoughts flitting through his brain with catastrophic conclusions. He looked at Logan dead in his eyes. "Then I'm afraid we are all doomed."

Logan stepped closer. "Do you know what's happening out there, Father? I can see in your eyes that you do. Please don't lie to me. I've seen enough already to understand what we're dealing with."

Father McKenzie nodded. "I do, yes." He paused, looking over the young man in front of him.

"Then how do we fight it? What do we need to do?"

McKenzie thought and thought. "We need to call Detective Carver, then I'll tell you everything. It may be the only thing that can save you."

219

Carver arrived home the moment his answering machine clicked off with a new message. He was carrying a box with some personal items; the book wedged under his jacket.

He had so much to do and even more to think about. So much had happened and he needed to wrap his head around it if he's going to be able to fit the pieces to the puzzle together and create a plausible plan to stop the carnage taking place in the Hollow. Flannery, Lori, Marc Saduj, and the Demon and Sleepy Hollow all competed for center stage in his brain. He needed to think, to sit quietly and allow his thoughts to unfold. He needed to step away from everything to see it in a new light. Most of all, he needed a drink to put his mind at ease.

Carver fixed himself two fingers of scotch from the bottle on his kitchen table then downed those fingers in one large gulp before pulling the book from beneath his jacket and laying it on the table when a loud groan erupted outside his house. Carver snapped his head to it, staring through the bay window in his living room. Fog raced past his window like a million wisps racing to the Hollow as his stomach rumbled with anxious intent. He couldn't see anything beyond the fog.

Carver poured himself another then sat down, staring at the book. He believed that time was coming to a crashing halt and he was powerless against it. He could feel it in his bones, a foreboding he couldn't shake. His window to stop the evil infecting the Hollow was about to close. He had to come up with a solution and come up with one fast.

The answers are in the book.

Father McKenzie's voice rang through his mind. He sipped his scotch, his lips burning from the sting. Carver was a man of action and what he wanted to do was go to the house to confront Marc. Find a way into the basement he knew was there, hidden somewhere in the walls of the home. But what would he do then? Arrest Marc? Flannery would have his badge for breakfast. And what about Wren? Carver was certain Wren wouldn't allow Marc out of his sight without a fight. And then there was the context he was still having difficulty committing to. The supernatural and all the magic he'd always believed were tricks played on the mind through subliminal suggestion. The book talked about demons and witches and ghosts and rituals and sacrifice and the coming of a new humanity. Considering all he's seen recently he'd be a fool not to believe in it.

But how do we kill something supernatural? How does a demon die?

The answers are in the book.

Carver understood that knowing the enemy is the key to victory. He'll need to know how to battle the demon and know all the ins and outs surrounding the enemy. Understanding he'll need to confront Marc soon, Carver poured another drink and opened the book.

220

"This is insane," Henry said, throwing his hands up in defeat. "Did you not hear what he said? Is it me or did we both not have the same conversation? Your boy's got some serious issues. That's what it sounds like to me." He pointed at Lori sitting on the bed, staring at him. "And there's something you're not telling me about him. I know it's true."

"Like what?" Lori ran her hand through her hair, brushing it away from her eyes. "You're just acting paranoid?"

Henry was shaking his head. "The look on your face when Carver mentioned that damn pentagram was too telling, Lori. It was obvious there's a connection between Marc and the pentagram that you're aware of. Any officer worth his badge could see that."

Now Lori looked away, head shaking. A certain part of Marc's book kept ringing through her head. It was towards the end of what he'd written, a reference to how to destroy the demon. In the story, Marc's fictional female protagonist was the essential component in the demon's game and the only means to put an end to the carnage.

Only love can kill the demon!

To Lori, it seemed like a calling card. If Marc went off the deep end then somewhere in his subconscious he wanted her to put an end to it. To end all the pain and suffering, both external and internal. To find peace before dying, which made sense to Lori. She needed to speak to him, believing that in doing so whatever role he had to play in the murders would end.

"Lori?" Henry called, snapping her out of her trance. She turned to him and his shoulders dropped, defeated. "Tell me what you know? It's the only way I can help you."

Lori thought about it, but she knew she wouldn't say a word. Henry may be a good guy, but he was still an officer and if she tells him about the book, he'll more than likely share it with Carver, and she knew she did not want that to happen. The fact that Marc wrote a book detailing current murders would throw up some red flags and offer proof of his intent. No, Lori knew she was in this alone and would need to face Marc the same. Just the two of them.

And she knew she'd have her chance. The letter she found was written in Marc's hand, requesting to meet with him tomorrow afternoon at three. She didn't tell Henry about the letter either.

"Lori, listen, just so you know, if you have information you're not sharing, and Marc *is* the one committing these murders you can be implicated in it too. Interfering in a police investigation is a crime, Lori." He looked out the window, shaking his head before training his eyes on her. "I don't want to see that happen to you."

"Then you can't cash in, right?" She knew it was wrong, but she said it anyway.

"C'mon Lori. You know it's more than that. I don't want to see anyone hurt or killed or dragged through the mud. I hope you know me better than that."

She knew it was true. Henry's heart was pure and who the hell wouldn't accept a million dollars to help a friend if it was offered? She stood up. "I know and I'm sorry. You didn't deserve that comment. It's been a long day and I'm exhausted. Can we continue this conversation in the morning?"

Henry paused, staring at her as if he was assessing potential lies and manipulations. He nodded. "Okay. But I'll be here in the morning and honestly, I think we should leave at that point." He looked through the window. "I don't know what it is, but I've got a really bad feeling about tomorrow."

221

Excerpt from *The Demon and Sleepy Hollow* by the Original Knickerbocker Dated 1856.

The Ground Is Sacred

Now we come to a detail that, should the demon return to Sleepy Hollow, must be noted as a place to provide safety should such a resurgence occur. It is up to you, the reader of this book, to know all its details. Proper preparation is paramount to success, and I write this chapter to save lives and provide refuge for the weary.

In 1853, we erected a statue commemorating the 1780 capture of Major John Andre-an homage to John Paulding and his militiamen for the historic capture. Although we had debated for years over the most appropriate location to erect the statue, in the end it was decided that the location should serve the best interests of our future lineage. Hence, the statue now serves as a starting point for the sacred ground.

The area directly north of the monument at one time had been the home to Olga's coven. It is also the area where the people of Sleepy Hollow congregated on the night we confronted the demon. The ground is sacred, and no demon or wretch may walk across its threshold without permission. We sought refuge in the area while we plotted and planned. Olga's coven was more than accommodating to our needs and strengthened the ground with a protective spell.

I often find myself strolling across the same ground on Sunday afternoons, following the marsh I had written about in my novel. I've always found it ironic how this very marsh where the Headless Horseman begins to pursue Ichabod is the same where we erected the statue, as if the Horseman delivered the information through my dreams as a foreboding for what I would later endure.

Many believe I do so to recount my own story, and I allow such rumors to take place for the benefit of those who have forgotten and for those who remember what we endured. Nevertheless, I return to the ground to feel safe and to commune with a good friend. There's a piece of Olga in the spaces between the air and the trees. The marsh and the brook. A presence that puts my fears to rest.

Should the demon return, know this, the ground is sacred and should be used as a place for safety. I only hope the ground never becomes tainted, nor for the protective spell to fade. Should this happen, I fear the demon's ability to claim victory would rise substantially, as it was largely because of the sacredness of these grounds that we could thwart the demon by entering the underground tunnels that brought us to Sam J. Curad.

———

Carver stared at the name Sam J. Curad with a profound sense of confusion and mystery. The name was nagging at his instincts.

"What was the name of the first Indian?" he whispered beneath his breath. He put the book down and took up the pad he'd been taking notes on. Flipped back a few pages and scanned across the page, finding the name he was looking for.

Jasa Mucad

He was the tribal member who first discovered the cave then disappeared. Noting the spelling, he flipped to a blank page and wrote the names in order:

Jasa Mucad

Sam J. Curad

Marc Saduj.

He sat and stared at the names, looking for similarities when the thought crossed his mind and he took his pencil and crossed off each individual letter that was consistent between Sam and Jasa to Marc Saduj. One letter after the other, he crossed them all off until there were no more letters to cross off and no more letters in Marc's name. All three names contained the same letters in a different order like a foreboding anagram.

"Well, I'll be damned."

Carver looked up from the book, thinking, and leaned back in his chair. Now that was too much of a coincidence. The fact that all three names associated with the demon all contain the same letters like some cosmic enigma playing games with the dimension of time could not be a coincidence. His mind was reeling, although a certain clarity had come through with the revelation. Carver's suspicion of Marc Saduj was spot on. He definitely has a hand in the Sleepy Hollow murders, although another revelation also stood profound and prominent. Like Sam and Jasa, Marc represented the victim in Carver's story. Possessed by the demon and not a part of the murders.

Although there's always a reason such a person is chosen and Carver now wondered what that reason was. Had Marc called on the demon for some reason Carver was unaware of? Had he been manipulated by the demonic presence with the promise of riches and fame? And most importantly, did he partake in the murders or turn the other cheek when the torture began?

I can't believe I'm considering these stories as viable reasons and theories.

Nonetheless, he couldn't deny what he'd already seen with his own eyes and there were so many nuances to current circumstance that could only be explained by something otherworldly. He'd be a fool if he didn't consider the possibility. Still, it was difficult to give in and let go when everything he always believed was called into question. Having to consider demonic influence was never a part of the detective's protocol.

Carver yawned and closed his eyes, then shook his head and stretched his eyelids. Looked at the clock on the wall and noticed the second hand ticking close to midnight when the lights flickered through the house. He looked at the light above the table, watching it flicker. On, then off. Off then on. On, then off. Heard his refrigerator hum before it clicked off. He sat in the darkness, listening, waiting for the light to return. In the quiet he could hear the subtle thread of a rumble like constant distant thunder existing beneath the ground accompanied by a whispered groan underneath the breath of bitter wind outside his window. As if the wind carried the desires from ghosts and specters from the netherworld to our own.

The lights did not return. Carver shuffled out of his seat to a kitchen drawer where he retrieved a flashlight then clicked it on, the beam slicing through the darkness. He went through his home, checking every room and closet. Carver didn't know why, but he had a feeling someone was in the house. That nagging instinct remained even after he discovered the house was clear.

The thought flitted through his mind that perhaps he'd forgotten to pay his electric bill. It happened sometimes, and considering his mind had been occupied by the murders it was a large possibility. Now he stood by his bay window, his house on top of a hill that overlooked the Hollow. Noticed the entire town was bathed in darkness. No streetlights, no house lights, no store lights. Just the cold dead of night and the thin fog that hovered over the Hollow like a dark veil ready to strike down and swallow the Hollow whole.

222

Father McKenzie and Logan both looked up at the ceiling when the lights went out. They were sitting in the rectory, talking and hoping Detective Carver would call them back.

Logan noticed how on-edge the priest was. Like a man watching his own destruction with no means to stop it. McKenzie told Logan about the book that was currently in Detective Carver's possession, divulging everything he could remember while Logan pieced together his own dark web research. It was all beginning to make sense.

The book Father McKenzie talked about seemed strangely similar to Logan's own research. But Logan's research also revealed that the house in the western woods was reopened in the 1920s and used for cult and satanic rituals until John's great grandfather along with a group of people who referred to themselves as the authority moved in to put an end to their tirade. Although there was no mention of the demon during that time, now that Logan had Father McKenzie's story to fill in the gaps it made sense that there was no mention of the demon. Nonetheless, the demon's influence on the people in the house was evident. Somehow, he was able to manipulate them from the ether he'd been cast into.

Now they were staring at the ceiling, waiting, hoping and praying the lights would return. After a few minutes Logan returned his gaze to the priest. The whites of his eyes glowed in the darkness. Logan could make out his clothes and little else, but he could see Father McKenzie was still looking up.

"Is it them?" asked Logan.

McKenzie kept his gaze on the ceiling. "Is it a coincidence that the lights would go out on this night? What is so different about this night from all the others?" He clucked his tongue and looked at Logan.

"I'm beginning to believe there are no coincidences, Father." He stood up and walked to the window where thin streams of gray fog flitted past. "And what's different about this night is that there is evil in the air. I can feel it in my bones, rumbling from below."

He turned to Father McKenzie, who was turned in his direction. McKenzie opened his desk drawer and rifled through it. A second later, he lit the candles on his desk then offered one to Logan.

"We must secure the church grounds with prayer and fortify all entrances and exits."

Logan noticed how calm the priest had grown in the last few minutes, as if complete acceptance fell upon his shoulders and he had one task to complete: protect the flock at all costs.

"Our task tomorrow is to bring as many people as possible to the church before sunset. After nightfall, the true battle begins."

Logan looked at the flame dancing above the white candle in his hand. His thoughts went to John. He was enduring hell at this very moment. Logan knew this was true. And why? Because John was the key, the fly in their ointment.

And knowing, more than anything, that it was up to him to find that key.

He could feel it in his bones.

223

John jolted in his cage, his legs stretched as his pelvis jumped when pain tore up his chest, squeezing his heart. Felt sweat across his burning skin, his eyes wide open but he saw nothing concerning his cage or the dungeon the cage was in. Nor did he see the fleshless Jennifer hanging from the rafters. To John, he was in hell, and everything he witnessed was born from that same hell.

Torture and truth are what he saw. The dark hearts of humanity and their willful actions wrought with hate. He watched as his father squeezed the life from his assistant then gutted his lifelong friend Lyndsay. Tasted her heart on his tongue as his father bit into that heart and then he was with his mother the moment she shot herself, reliving the moment as if it had happened in front of him.

My son. Bang!

My son.

Relived the torture of every victim who had lost their lives in this very dungeon. Saw himself cutting and tearing and carving and holding beating hearts that he offered to the fire. Replaying every event as if his memories were in a constant demonic loop. He saw wolves devouring children and mothers tearing their babies apart. Tasted their blood on his tongue.

Where does it end?

It's got to end.

Has to.

Now pain gripped his solar plexus as if his liver swelled, swollen, bruised and battered. The pain rifled through his brain as his body cringed. Blood on his tongue now, dripping from his nose as his eyelids fluttered. His brain twisted in his skull like an aneurism about to explode.

He rolled over on his side the moment blood jettisoned from his throat like a floodgate had been opened. It kept coming, projectile vomiting like he did in kindergarten when he had the stomach flu. John tried to push himself up, but his sweating hands slipped, and his head rapped against the bottom of the cage. John laid in a pool of his own bloody vomit, his thoughts flitting between where he had been and where he recognized he was now, the dungeon where his vampire had brought him.

His eyes were lazy. They drifted in his skull as his shallow breath huffed over his lips. His thoughts spiraled as his eyes closed. Spiraling into darkness only to be forgotten.

When he opened his eyes again, he was back in hell.

224

Marc was walking through a dark fog drenched tunnel as if he had emerged out of thin air. The tunnel was drenched in a thick black, but it didn't matter. He was well aware of where he was.

Silence walked with him, although he could feel the hum beneath the Hollow like a rumbled foreboding of things to come. The cold bit into his skin from the icy wind howling through the tunnel. His mind was numb, his thoughts removed as if his memory had been wiped clean. He knew only instinct and the driving force behind his intentions.

Wren was waiting for him. Marc could see his silhouette standing in the distance, holding a tray with the bottle of absinthe and the shot glass ready. The sugar cube on the feuille spoon fizzled from the flame dancing across it, turning those fairies into golden fiery hues plummeting to the bottom of the glass.

Marc wondered how Wren came to be in the tunnel. The bartender had said Wren would meet him on the other side of the door, although how the barkeep knew this Marc did not know. When Marc first laid eyes on Wren a sudden sense of relief washed over him, although his spine kept tightening the closer to Wren he came.

Marc's hands and arms were trembling. His whole body was shaking, terror rippling through his bones. He felt tapped, drained of all energy, life, and fervor. He wrapped his arms around himself, hoping to provide some warmth from the freezing cold and comfort to the nagging pain in his stomach. His jaw clenched as he stared straight ahead, seeing Wren and the tray with the shot glass and the empty bottle of absinthe.

Marc gazed at the shot glass and the faeries dancing in the green liquid. Dancing just for him. He stopped in front of Wren as he blew out the flame then twisted the spoon, allowing the remnants of sugar to drop into the glass before offering it to Marc.

Wren's beady eyes roamed over Marc. "To aid you in your endeavor. The master waits for you." He craned his head over his shoulder then gestured to a staircase on Marc's left, tucked away in a dark alcove in the tunnel. "In there, he waits." Wren returned his gaze to Marc. "It is time for you to see."

Marc looked from the staircase to Wren, his jaw trembling. His brow knitted in confusion, staring at Wren with his ghostly vampire features and the anticipatory stare in his eyes. "You too, Wren? The man in black got to you too?"

Wren said nothing in response, gazing at Marc over the shot glass pinched between his fingers.

Marc noted the empty absinthe bottle. "It seems he's run out of time." He paused, gazing into Wren's eyes and swallowed his breath. "How will he find me now?" He wasn't certain if he was asking Wren or himself.

"When you hear the gong shuddering through your heart… that is where you will find him. In your bleeding heart." He raised the glass. "One final drink. One last swallow and the transformation will be complete. It would be best for you to finish the game."

Marc looked up the stairs and his heart fluttered in his chest. Looked back at Wren and the shot glass when he pinched the glass between his fingers. "Am I to become Judas then? Cast off for my sins for all eternity."

"All in time, my dear Marc. All answers come in time. The drink will help you see. The master will carry you forward. He waits for you… up the stairs."

Marc's hand had the slightest tremble. He looked at the glass, mesmerized by the fairies that danced and laughed and welcomed him in. They brought a profound sensation of loss coupled with the solution to heartache. Marc downed the drink.

"Good," said Wren. "So very good." He took the glass from Marc, then stepped to the side, waving his arm in front of him like an usher in a theatre. "You may enter."

Marc looked at the stairs and his stomach rumbled, twisting his innards. "What's waiting for me up there, Wren?" He locked eyes with his servant.

Wren shook his head. "Only what you take with you. All the choices that have led to this moment." He took a step back into the darkness, his pale complexion faded in the black pitch. "Best to not keep the master waiting," said Wren. His stare cut through Marc as if he could carve his heart out with his eyes. "He wants his body back and won't wait too long."

A red glow washed over the staircase, catching Marc's attention. He stepped closer then paused, sensing the rumble beneath the earth while listening to the screams coming from the top of the stairs. Quiet screams, as if he was listening to the hollers from hell rising to the surface to greet his ears. He lost sight of Wren when he went to the stairs and looked up. The steps continued around a corner and Marc walked up to the landing then turned.

His jaw tightened, his spine cringed, staring into the room above the stairs. He could feel the energy pumping from that room. It was overwhelming, racing across him with the intent to destroy. Subtle moans, groans, and screams drifted from that room like specters calling from the netherworld. Marc looked back down the stairs to the darkness that enveloped the staircase, turning it into a black hole of anguish. He could feel that anguish erupt in his heart with a hollow suffering that stabbed every inch of his body.

It is time for you to see. The man in black whispered in his ear. Marc took the steps up.

He stepped into a dungeon. The man in black's dungeon, and the moment he stepped in his heart stopped. His jaw hung open and his eyes widened. There were people chained to the wall, obviously waiting for their turn for torture. They stared at him as if he were the devil himself. A fire raged inside a firepit-its flames licking the hot air that buzzed around the room-next to a slab that he understood had seen an ocean of blood. Memories then flashed through his mind.

Memories of the torture and brutality that had taken place in this very room.

Tearing flesh off the bone. Slicing across skin. Decapitation and disembowelment. Chunks of flesh fed to the fire. Marc's head shuddered across his shoulders when another image twisted in his brain. He saw himself, not the man in black, delivering that torture, and then he knew. He understood it was he who inflicted each torture. The man in black wasn't in some far away ethereal dungeon. He was here all the time, using Marc's body, forcing him to take part in his game of absolute power. And Marc was the pawn who allowed it to happen.

A rattle raged above him. He snapped his head to the cage hanging from the rafters where a young man was breathing heavy while struggling through a nightmare.

"Jennifer?" The name drifted off his lips while staring at the skinless skeleton hanging dead from the rafters beside the cage.

The hand of evil exists in the human heart. The depths of which can never be equaled.

He didn't see Wren until he heard him speak. "Initium Novum," clucked off his tongue while standing in front of a pedestal with a crystal bowl sitting on top of it. Wren rapped against the bowl with a wooden mallet and the vibration that erupted from it snatched Marc's heart in a vise grip. He gripped his chest and dropped to his knees.

The dungeon shook around him when a rickety growl escaped from beyond the doors with the fissures where a purple, beaming light washed into the dungeon.

Wren rapped against the bowl again, and again the vibration squeezed Marc's heart.

It is you who brought hell to the Hollow. And it is you who has blood on your hands.

His breath was stolen from his lungs, gasping for air that refused his request. His eyes locked on the fissures when the revelation struck.

It's all my fault. I allowed him in. And then the ultimate insult: *Provided the body for him to breathe in my world. I opened the door and invited the devil in. Through my desperation I gave birth to a monster. Everything and everyone have been a manipulation. Wren. The accident. My parents. Everything in my life was a part of his manipulation and I fell right into his game. It was my hand that delivered death to these people. I have doomed us all, a pawn in the devil's game.*

Fear gripped every atom in his body. The fear that he could do nothing about what had happened more profound than any fear he'd ever experienced.

You lost this round, Mr. Saduj.

Another rap against the bowl. Another strangle squeezing his heart.

Time for you to go away now, Marc.

Every bone in his body cracked and snapped, stretched and contorted. His veins swelled from his neck to his face, rippling with white-hot heat that crawled across his eyes. He could feel the veins burning across his eye sockets then washing into his eyes with an inky-black poison, casting the dungeon in a black veil. His skull cracked in two spots on opposite sides of his forehead as blood raced from the wounds where he could feel horns tearing out of his skull and he howled something awful. Anguish burning in his veins.

I cast you into the ether. A slave to our macabre. Your purpose is best served from the cemetery where you can cause no more trouble.

Wren thwacked that bowl again and Marc screamed from the top of his lungs when the three doors with the fissures cracked and splintered, then tore apart. Sucked into the black void beyond the dungeon when a fierce wind tore through the open doorways like a specter from hell.

Beyond those doors existed a hollowed-out cave with a black-marble sphere two meters in diameter spinning and churning deep inside the cave with profound evil infecting Marc's cell.

A final rap against the bowl, and Marc felt himself plummeting.

Plummeting into the cemetery.

The battle for Sleepy Hollow is no longer about survival. It is about salvation — or surrendering the world to eternal night.

The final descent into hell has begun.

Grab your copy of Book Four today at www.pdalleva.com!

Also by PD Alleva
<u>Horror</u>

Golem: A haunting tale of suspense, loss, isolation, contempt, and fear. The Devil is in the details!

Jigglyspot and the Zero Intellect: A satirical cosmic horror fantasy thriller novel. Jigglyspot is a half-human, half-warlock, travelling carnival clown moonlighting as a drug dealing pimp and lackey for a demonic army from Xibalba.

<u>Sci-Fi/Fantasy</u>

The Dark Veil: The Rose Vol 1 & 2: A masterful, dystopian science fiction thriller of telepathic evil greys, mysterious rebellion, martial arts, and Alien Vampires.

<u>Dark Fantasy</u>

Presenting the Marriage of Kelli Anne & Gerri Denemer: One known terrorist. A protest about to erupt. A family on the brink of collapse. Is the bond between husband and wife strong enough to defeat evil?

Purchase these and other fine books of horror, scifi, and psychological thrillers from Chamber Door Publishing today.

www.pdalleva.com

About the Author

PD writes books. Horror, scifi, psychological thrillers, fantasy, and sometimes a literary gem. Good ones, crazy ones, fun books, entertaining books, terrifying books that are absolutely insane, and books with depth and thrills that rip out the heart of humanity then tosses it on a slab to be feasted on. Yeah, that's what he does, he writes books. Any questions?

To learn more or join PD's newsletter visit www.pdalleva.com.